Jim Powell was born in London in 1949 and was educated at Cambridge. His first career was in advertising, becoming Managing Director of a major London agency. He then co-founded a pottery that produced hand-painted tableware for leading stores. He was previously active in politics, contesting the 1987 Election. He lives in Northamptonshire.

THE BREAKING OF EGGS

Feliks Zhukovski is a Pole in Paris — a hangover from another age. Estranged from his family by the Second World War, Feliks has given his life to Communism. As a travel guide to the old eastern bloc, his personal life is a resounding failure. Unfortunately for Feliks, it's 1991. Europe pulls back the Iron Curtain, taking away the certainties of his life. Potentially unemployed, Feliks is surprised to be selling his guide to an American firm, setting in motion life-changing events. Reunited with a brother he hasn't seen for fifty years, Feliks has hope of finding his mother and a long-lost love . . . after he finds a way through the smoke and mirrors of Europe's past. And the convictions on which he based his adult life.

JIM POWELL

THE BREAKING OF EGGS

Complete and Unabridged

CHARNWOOD
Leicester

First published in Great Britain in 2010 by
Weidenfeld & Nicolson
An imprint of the
Orion Publishing Group Ltd., London

First Charnwood Edition
published 2011
by arrangement with the
Orion Publishing Group Ltd.
An Hachette UK Company, London

Artificer by Czeslaw Milosz, translated from the
Polish by Czeslaw Milosc and Robert Hass, is here
reproduced with the kind permission of
HarperCollins USA

British Library CIP Data

Powell, Jim, *1949 –*
    The breaking of eggs.
    1. Travel writers- -Fiction. 2. Older men- -Fiction.
    3. Polish people- -France- -Paris- -Fiction.
    4. Families- -Fiction. 5. Europe, Eastern- -Fiction.
    6. Large type books.
    I. Title
    823.9′2–dc22

    ISBN 978–1–4448–0755–4

For my great-aunt 'Thos'
Dorothy Letitia Powell
(1884–1977)

1

I suppose that Madame Lefèvre was the catalyst for most of what happened next. This is surprising, since I doubt that Madame Lefèvre has otherwise been the catalyst for anything in her entire life. Even now I look at the words 'catalyst' and 'Madame Lefèvre' and wonder how they came to cohabit the same sentence.

'It's always good to be at home when you're ill, Monsieur Zhukovski.'

That was the first of two remarks which set in motion a chain of events that transformed my life in a way I would have found unimaginable at the time. It is hard to think of a more commonplace remark, a more unremarkable remark, yet it had such profound consequences.

'If you don't mind my saying so, Monsieur Zhukovski, you're getting a bit too old for all this running around. You should slow down, if you ask me.'

That was the second remark. At the time, I did mind her saying so, especially as I had not asked her, but it is hard to take offence when you are laid up in bed with a raging temperature and your self-appointed nurse chooses to offer unsought advice. So I probably said 'I expect you are right, Madame Lefèvre' and left it at that before receiving the sacrament of the latest parcel of medicines that she had procured at inordinate expense at the pharmacy across the street.

Both remarks were made on the same day: 1st January 1991. That made no impression on me at the time. I am not one to attach significance to such coincidences, or to any other superstitions or hocus-pocus, but now even I must admit that the date was appropriate. I had started to feel unwell on Christmas Eve and had thought nothing of it. Apart from the occasional cold, my health has always been good. I do not make a fuss about it. I do not announce the arrival of the flu the first time I blow my nose. As far as I can remember, I had never previously suffered the flu. Nor can I recall being ill in bed before.

To start with, I thought I was run down. 1990 had been a demanding year with a great deal of travel. I had needed to work harder and more rapidly than for a long time and I am sure it took a lot out of me. October and November had been especially difficult months. So when I started to feel unwell, in a way I was glad for the respite. Christmas is not my favourite time of year. I abhor the absurdities of religion. I have no family on whom to bestow unwanted presents. The handful of acquaintances who can normally be relied upon to help me prop up a bar in the evening all go to stay with relatives they detest. Paris closes down for a fortnight. There is nothing to do. Even without being ill, home is the best place to be; in fact the only place to be.

But I had never considered my apartment to be home, which is why Madame Lefèvre's remark made such a strong impression on me. It was not that I considered anywhere else to be home. I simply had no concept of home. I am not sure I had considered the question. There I was, a settled and comfortably-off man approaching his 61st birthday, who had lived in the same apartment for 36 years, and who was yet homeless. And the more I thought about that simple word 'home', the more complicated it became for me. I realised it was not a word I used. When I returned from my travels each autumn, I did not think to myself 'I am going home'. When I put on my coat in some bar at the end of an evening, I did not say to my companions 'time to go home'. No. I would think 'I am going to Paris now', or say 'back to the apartment for me'. Home was not a word I used.

Perhaps this would have remained idle speculation but for Madame Lefèvre's second remark about being too old for all the running around. For the previous 36 years I had lived a life that others would perhaps call unusual and interesting, but which for me had long since become routine. In 1955 I started a small travel guide to the countries of eastern Europe. Like many things that turn out to be important in one's life, it began almost by accident. I found myself out of work and needing to do something quickly. I was interested in travel. Particularly, I was interested in eastern Europe. At the time I was a member of the French Communist Party and the idea of explaining communist societies objectively to others appealed to me. It is true that there were relatively few tourists to eastern Europe at that time, but there were some and no French travel guides were catering for them.

So I started the *Guide Jaune*. It was a modest

3

publication initially. There was a section on every country within the Soviet bloc, each containing a brief commentary on the country, a description of principal cities and places of interest, and a list of hotels and restaurants. It had expanded over the years so that by 1991 it had become a sizeable volume. It sold steadily in independent bookshops in France. Later, German and English editions followed. Sales were never huge, but they were reliable and I managed to acquire a life that many people would envy: independent, varied and, if not exactly prosperous, then at least comfortable.

There were no staff. I was able to update the *Guide* quite easily myself, aided of course by helpful information from the tourist bureaux and government agencies in the various countries. My old friend Benoît Picard had printing works in Paris and he looked after the sales and distribution for me. Everything worked smoothly.

For all that time, I spent more than seven months each year travelling, setting out metronomically on 1st March and returning in early October, living out of a suitcase in the meantime. I made sure I visited each country and each major city at least once every two years. Some places — Moscow, Leningrad, Berlin, Warsaw, Prague, Budapest — I would visit annually. Another pattern followed my return to Paris each autumn. October was always a feverish month, in which I made the corrections and additions to the publication. The *Guide* was printed in the second half of November, so that the new edition could be in bookshops before

Christmas, in time for people to plan their holidays for the following year. And this was how things continued for 36 years.

I must have known that at some point it would have to end, but I do not remember spending much time thinking about how or when it would happen, or what I would do with my life afterwards. But, even before Madame Lefèvre's remark, I had the sense that events were pressing in on me. It had started in 1989, of course. I still find the events of that year utterly bewildering. It would be fair to say that my own attachment to communism was already weaker by then. I had ceased to be a Party member in 1968. But I remained, in principle, a supporter of what the Soviet system sought to achieve and I had no doubt about the permanence of that system in eastern Europe, even if I no longer anticipated its triumph elsewhere. So, when the Soviet bloc collapsed like a pack of cards within a few months, I was astounded. I could not believe it was happening. It felt as if the entire edifice of my life was being torn down in front of me.

It was ironic, but the immediate effect of this on the *Guide* was most beneficial. Suddenly there was this new interest in tourism to eastern Europe and mine was one of the few guides available. But I did not need to be a clairvoyant to know there would be many other consequential changes that would be less comfortable for me.

This became apparent during my travels in 1990. Everywhere I went, I encountered vast change. In less than a year, the situation had been transformed. All the old familiarities were evaporating. I found myself wondering whether more had not changed in a single year than in all the previous 35 put together. Naturally I cannot pretend that I thought most of this change had been for the better. I found the effect altogether unwholesome. It had also created severe pressure in my working life. Whereas previously it had been easy for me to update the *Guide* single-handedly, I could now see this was becoming impossible.

It was also becoming expensive. Perhaps I was stupid not to anticipate the personal greed that would follow such events. In March 1990 I had gone first to Prague, where I stayed in the same hotel as for many years. When I left, I was surprised to be presented with a bill. I assumed that the new manager could not have been informed of the arrangements but, when I summoned him, I was told bluntly that there no longer were any arrangements. I encountered the same situation elsewhere, to the extent that upon arrival anywhere I now needed first to check the financial status of my visit. I did not find this approach sympathetic. In fact it represented everything I loathed about the opening of eastern Europe to capitalism.

So the entire summer of 1990 had been problematical in one way or another. Everything took longer than it had before. Everything cost more. I found myself in Warsaw at the end of September, torn between the imperative of visiting Berlin on my way back to Paris and the equal imperative of beginning the amendments

6

to the 1991 edition immediately, as there were so many to make and so little time available. In the end I did not go to Berlin, although that may have owed something to my reluctance to be in the city on 3rd October, when East and West Germany were reunited. In any event, it was a major omission in the circumstances. I would be producing a guide for people to use in 1991 that had no first-hand account of the effects of the demolition of the Wall two years earlier. It was not good enough.

In spite of all this, I had no immediate intention of stopping the *Guide*. When, in October, I had received a letter from an American publisher asking if I might be interested in selling the title, I did not even bother to reply. I was in no mood to sell the *Guide* to anyone, and certainly not to some avaricious American firm. It was a temporary upheaval, I told myself: a lot of hard work for the time being and then everything would settle down again. Besides which, perhaps the eastern Europeans — once they had sampled the unfairness of their new system — would decide they had not been so badly off after all.

The illness changed my attitude; the illness and Madame Lefèvre's remarks. Perhaps she was right. Perhaps I was getting too old for all this running around. Perhaps I had taken more out of myself in 1990 than I had realised. Perhaps it was time to think of retirement. But what would happen to the *Guide?* And to where would I retire? Where did people retire? They retired to home. And where was home?

I came to this apartment at the same time as I started the *Guide*. October 1955: the last time there were major changes in my life. I had been staying with the Picards previously, above the printing works in St Germain. That was where the idea for the *Guide* first came about as a matter of fact, in discussions with Benoît Picard in those rooms. I think the Picards were rather afraid I would stay for ever. When a few orders for the first edition started to come in, old man Picard gently suggested I might like to look for a place of my own and offered to advance me the money for the rent deposit.

I saw several apartments that I liked but was not offered. Maybe they did not want a foreigner. Maybe they did not like what I was doing. They all asked what my line of work was, of course, and when I told them I could see the disapproval in their faces. One or two asked me if I was a communist and they liked the answer to that question even less.

At first Madame Lefèvre promised to be no different. She owned 22 Avenue Secrétan in the 19th *arrondissement*, a scruffy district of Paris, but a house and a street that have a certain shabby nobility. Her own apartment is on one half of the second floor and she was looking for a tenant for the neighbouring apartment. The rest of the building was already let. She asked the usual questions. I gave the usual answers and expected the usual rebuff. In this case I did not get it. I was certain that Madame Lefèvre had no more sympathy for my politics than the other prospective landladies. When she offered me the rooms, I concluded it was only because it suited her to have a tenant next door who was both single and absent for a large part of the year.

The apartment comprised a large sitting room at the front, overlooking the street, and a smaller bedroom at the back, with a separate kitchen and bathroom. The furnishings were hardly smart or contemporary, but at the time they did not seem dated. The rooms were full of heavy *bourgeois* furniture, with slightly threadbare carpets, nondescript coverings and the odd mirror on the wall. It was perfectly comfortable. Madame Lefèvre was not someone to spend money unnecessarily and, since I had demanded no alterations subsequently, she had made none. I suppose a visitor would have said the apartment was now hopelessly old-fashioned, some relic of a 1950s time warp. They might have said the same of me. I do not know. I do not think I had ever had a visitor. For myself, I liked it the way it was and had become used to its little eccentricities. I had never seen a particular need to make changes myself. It was not as if it were my home.

If the apartment had changed little over the years, neither had Madame Lefèvre. She had struck me as middle-aged when I first saw her and she has struck me as middle-aged ever since. As I was young when I moved in and am now getting on for being old, how she has managed to be consistently middle-aged for 36 years I could not say. I suppose she must have been about 40 in 1955 and, at that time, it was easy to be middle-aged at 40 if one wanted to be. I do not know why she wanted to be. She could have been very pretty when she was younger. The striking thing about her has always been her abnormally long hair. Most of the time it is worn like a ball of string on the back of her head, held in place by a minor ironmongery. But at times I have seen it unsecured, and it is extraordinarily long and actually very beautiful.

Madame Lefèvre's clothes belonged to the same ordered world as the rest of her. After a while I noticed that she had a different dress for each day of the week: seven dresses for seven days. The best dress was of course for Sundays. If I forgot what day it was, I merely needed to see which dress she was wearing. At first I thought that these dresses never changed, that she had discovered some magical fabric that never wore out or discoloured. Then I noticed subtle changes to the cut and realised that the truth was even more peculiar: that every few years she replaced an old dress with one made from an identical fabric, cut slightly differently to make a token, barely perceptible nod towards fashion. Where did she get them from? Was there some *costumier* in Paris with an inexhaustible supply of timeless fabrics? But I suppose she might have looked at me and thought the same.

I never saw a visitor come to her door either. I think we established at some early point that neither of us had any family. I do not know what she did with her time. One might have thought the two of us would use some of it talking to each other, but we never did. It would have been easy enough. Although I was away so much and always working hard in October and November, I still had my three rest months of the year — December, January and February. You would think we would have talked then. But we did not. Right up until January 1991, until the time I am writing about, I did not even know her first name. She would have known mine, but never used it.

Why was this? Well, I cannot speak for Madame Lefèvre of course, but for my part I think it was a number of things. I am a reserved person, on the whole. I keep myself to myself and do not go much out of my way to make new friends. Then, Madame Lefèvre represented a class that I despised. I had nothing against her personally; she seemed a reasonable enough woman; but I do not have much time for the *bourgeoisie* in general, and for *les petites rentières* less still. And what would we have talked about? We could not discuss politics. She knew mine from the beginning and I had no difficulty guessing hers. Every so often she would find a subtle way of making her opinions plain. If there had been some big election in France while I was away, she would be sure to leave a little parcel of literature for me from conspicuously right-wing candidates, together with a helpful note saying she hoped I would find it interesting. So we could not talk about politics. We could not talk about my work, although there was plenty to talk about, because that involved politics too, certainly as far as she was concerned and also for me. In fact, as I had always said, everything involved politics in the end. Life was political.

We could have talked about the weather, and needless to say we did, and about small uncontroversial changes in the neighbourhood. Those conversations filled the odd few minutes on the second-floor landing, but hardly constituted a friendship. To me this was neither surprising nor unwelcome. The surprise was that after 36 years, by which time I was by far the longest-standing tenant in the building, things suddenly changed. The surprise was that it was Madame Lefèvre who became the catalyst for all the other changes in my life. The surprise was also, I suppose, that I chose to respond.

When I was first ill I wanted to eat nothing. After a couple of days, with womanly concern, Madame Lefèvre appeared in my apartment with a bowl of soup and some bread. She had the key to my apartment, of course, and for all I know had frequently inspected its contents while I was away. Indeed she could have been reletting the rooms for six months of every year. I would not have known. I had no reciprocal knowledge of her apartment; in fact I had never been inside it. But I had always imagined this cauldron of soup simmering on her hob, constantly replenished, never entirely depleted, bubbling away over the decades. I had speculated what would be revealed if this soup was subjected to carbon dating. I suspected it would show trace elements of every year since Madame Lefèvre had acquired the building, whenever that had been.

Now she was knocking at my bedroom door and offering me a real bowl of this imagined soup, a bowl that perhaps contained minute

12

particles of a cabbage harvested at the Liberation, a bowl that offered me the opportunity to eat our shared history. As the days went by and I became stronger, other offerings emerged from across the landing: omelettes, cheeses, a *fricassée* of chicken. Few words were exchanged, apart from those two significant remarks, but I must admit that a certain pressure built up to commence a conversation, to express something more than polite appreciation for her care. Perhaps that was why she did it. Maybe she was lonely. Maybe I was.

It still took me well into January to summon the nerve and to find the words to say. In the end I think I said: 'Madame Lefèvre, we have known each other for a long time. I think it would be appropriate for you to call me Feliks.'

'Thank you Monsieur Zhukovski, I mean Feliks,' she said. There was a pause while she summoned equal nerve. 'And do please call me Sandrine, if you would care to.'

'Thank you, Sandrine,' I said. And then neither of us knew what to say, so we smiled at each other and no doubt both thought how ridiculous it was not to have said those few words many years before.

Madame Lefèvre was the first to recover from our mutual embarrassment and she did it by plunging into the previously taboo subject of politics.

'Have you heard what's happening in Lithuania?' she demanded.

I had heard. It had been on the radio that

morning. Soviet troops were storming Vilnius in an attempt to prevent Lithuanian independence.

'It won't do them any good,' she said. 'It's far too late for that sort of thing now.'

'I dare say you are right,' I replied. Then, feeling that this sounded like a terminal remark to a conversation that had barely started, I wondered what else I could say. 'For me it is a funny thing to think of Lithuanian independence,' I said. 'I was not brought up to think of Lithuania as an independent country.'

'Really?' she said. 'Well that's communism for you.'

'It was not communism actually, Sandrine. I grew up in Poland before the war, before communism.'

'I always wondered if you might be Polish.'

'Yes I am. By birth anyway. And of course for many centuries Lithuania was part of Poland, as I am sure you know.' Madame Lefèvre did not know. She seemed to have little intrinsic interest in the history of Lithuania. I did not have much myself, as a matter of fact. I think she felt the conversation had strayed from its original starting point, namely her great satisfaction at the collapse of communism.

'I'm surprised at you being a communist, Feliks, especially with you being Polish.'

'Not so much a communist,' I said. 'I have always described myself as a leftist.'

The distinction did not impress Madame Lefèvre. 'Same difference,' she said.

I did not know myself why I insisted on the distinction. I used to tell myself it was to do with

14

accuracy and precision, but of course 'leftist' is a less precise term. It could describe anyone from a hard-line Marxist to a moderate Social Democrat. So was I trying to conceal something? No, I do not think so. I never hid my opinions from anyone. Perhaps I had an abhorrence of labels, of being put in a box neatly labelled 'communist'. Perhaps it was a simple declaration of independence. As time went by, the qualification came closer to the truth. By 1991, I did not know whether I was any longer a communist or not, and it was ceasing to matter. But I did know I was still very much a leftist.

'When did you leave Poland?' By now it was clear that neither the history of Poland nor the precise ideological distinctions of the left would deter Madame Lefèvre from finding out more about me after 36 years.

'In 1939,' I said. 'My brother and I were sent to stay with an aunt in Switzerland.'

'The war again.'

'I do not think so. I believe it was something else.'

'What else could it have been?'

'Oh, personal things,' I said.

'Were there problems at home?'

Well, really! Not a word for 36 years, and then this sudden inquisition into the most private family matters.

'It was a long time ago,' I said. 'A great deal has changed since then.'

'And a great deal is changing now,' she said, accepting my return of the conversation to less personal matters. 'It must be disappointing for you.' The last remark may have suggested sympathy, but did not convey it.

'Yes, it is disappointing for me,' I said. 'It is not what I hoped would happen. I do not like a lot of the changes that are taking place in eastern Europe. I do not expect they will prove to be changes for the better. I preferred things as they were before, when everything was settled and everyone knew where they were.'

'If I may say so, Feliks, I find it strange that someone who wanted to change everything should find himself regretting change.'

'And if I may say so, Sandrine, I find it strange that someone who wanted to change nothing should find herself welcoming it.'

She had no answer to that. Indeed, there was no answer. It depended on what sort of change one was looking for, if any. It was in fact a long time since I had sought change of any kind, in the world or in my own life. As a young man, in the years after the war, I was fearless for change. I wanted everything to change and believed that it would. But at some point, and I cannot now remember when it was, I came to accept things the way they were, to accept my own life the way it was. After that, I no longer looked for change. An ideological split divided Europe. I accepted that. I worked on one side of the divide, where my heart was or where I thought it was, and the rest of the time I lived behind enemy lines. I accepted that too.

I found myself telling Madame Lefèvre about my travels the previous summer and what I had discovered. I did not know if it interested her. I doubted she had set foot outside France. Perhaps she had never set foot outside Paris. Certainly, everywhere else was foreign and where I went was communist foreign, or had been, which was worse still.

'How much longer will you do it for?'

'I do not know,' I said. For the previous week, restless in a slowly improving illness, I had thought of little else. I had reached no conclusions.

'Is there someone who could take it over?'

'I do not think so,' I said. 'I mean, the only other person involved is the printer and I do not think he could do it or would want to.'

'Could you sell it?'

'I do not know. Perhaps.' I remembered the approach I had received three months earlier from the American firm. 'Actually, someone did contact me recently about it.'

'What did you say?'

'Nothing. I did not reply. I was not interested.'

'Why not?'

That was an easy question, but I was reluctant to admit to the honest answer. There were of course any number of reasons why the enquiry might have led to nothing, but only one reason why I did not even want to discuss it. In the end, I did give the honest answer.

'It was from an American company.'

'So?'

'Sandrine, it is probably hard for you to understand, but I do not want to sell my *Guide* to the Americans. It goes against everything I have believed my entire life, everything I have

17

done. It would be a complete betrayal.'

Madame Lefèvre shrugged her shoulders. 'Well, I don't know,' she said. 'It's your business. But I can't see what harm it would do to talk to them. Still, if you want to cut your nose off to spite your face, that's up to you.'

'It is important to me.'

'Still?'

'Yes. I do not know how to explain it to you. It is not just a question of what I believe. It is also . . . well, I suppose that for a great deal of my life the Communist Party was my family. And you do not turn your back on family.'

'Perhaps not,' said Madame Lefèvre. 'But sometimes family turns its back on you.' And I still recall the sourness with which she spoke those words.

That concluded our belated foray into the art of conversation. I did not doubt that others would follow assuming I remained in Paris, in that apartment. Would I? I spent the rest of the day thinking about the *Guide* and its future, my future. I still did not want to sell to the Americans, but no one else had expressed an interest. What was I saying? That I refused to sell the *Guide* to a capitalist company? That was tantamount to saying I refused to sell it to anybody. Would it be a better epitaph for the *Guide* if it subsided to nothing, accompanying me sickly through my declining years? I was forced to admit that, actually, it would be rather appropriate, but it was not what I wanted.

Then there was the question of money. It had never been my first priority, nor needed to be, but it could not be ignored. I was not rich. I had some savings, but they were not huge. Pension provisions in France were generous, but they would not enable me to stay in this apartment indefinitely, assuming that I wanted to. There was no one to look after me if I became ill, apart from Madame Lefèvre, and she was a good deal older than I was. Conscience was all very well, but if I did not assume responsibility for my own life, who would? If I were living in a different society, maybe things would be different, but I was not.

Sandrine Lefèvre was right. There was no harm in having the conversation. I hauled myself out of bed and rummaged in my desk for the discarded letter. Eventually I found it. It was from a Mike Martins, who styled himself the European Vice-President of a New York firm called Bergelson & King. I decided that, as soon as I was well enough, I would telephone Mike Martins and see if he was still interested.

2

I did my best to dislike Mike Martins, but by the time we met my heart was no longer in it.

I had telephoned him in late January, as soon as I felt better. He said he was still interested in the *Guide* and invited me to lunch the following week. As it happens, it was my 61st birthday. At about the same time I received a call from Benoît Picard, who said he had matters he needed to discuss with me. Since Benoît's printing works were only a short distance from where Martins was taking me to lunch, I arranged to go there first.

The Picard Printworks were located in a backstreet of St Germain, near the church of St Sulpice, in an area that had once housed dozens of small printers. Now there were few left, most of them driven out by the exorbitant rents that accompanied Left Bank chic. Despite being a stalwart of the Paris Communist Party, old man Picard had possessed the foresight to acquire the freehold in the 1930s, so this particular problem did not affect him. He turned down all offers for the site, and most requests for commercial printing, and concentrated on producing political literature of impeccable ideological purity. The windows of his works were decorated with the most provocative posters he could find, to the increasing discomfort of the smart boutiques that were taking over the rest of the street, not to

20

mention the fascist louts of the neighbourhood. His bill for replacement glass must have been enormous.

I met old man Picard in 1949, the year I first came to Paris. He printed a number of communist newspapers and periodicals, amongst which was *La Vague de la Gauche* — the paper on which I was working at the time. I came to know him well. Not least, I was most grateful to him for giving me a roof when my job disappeared and for making it possible for the *Guide* to be published in the first place. I owed him a great deal and it was a real blow when he died suddenly in 1961.

His son Benoît took over the business and I had known him for as long. In fact, I would have to say that he is my oldest friend, despite the fact I have never been sure how much I like him. I find this strange: that one can have a close friendship with someone about whom one has deep reservations, whilst other people, whom one likes unreservedly, are not nearly such close friends. I do not know whether it is force of habit, or force of circumstance, or the particular time in one's life that one happens to meet certain people, or what it is.

When old man Picard died, Benoît started to make changes immediately. The first things to go were the posters in the windows. Instead of clarion calls to direct action, they now advertised the company's services. Old man Picard would have been appalled. Benoît also resigned his membership of the Communist Party. I suppose I should not complain as I did the same thing myself a few years later, but I had a reason for it, or thought I did, whereas for Benoît I think it was opportunism. That sort of baggage became inconvenient for him. He started taking on different work. In fact you would say that he became a small mainstream commercial printer. He was always busy.

Some things did not change. The printing works remained resolutely old-fashioned, chaotic in fact. This was surprising as Benoît had always been a modernist. Although we were more or less the same age — I think he is two years younger than me — it was almost as if we belonged to different generations. I felt I had far more in common with his father. So one would have expected there to have been technological changes. By now, for example, one would have thought Benoît would have embraced computers and digital printing and goodness knows what else. But he had not. At first I had found that comforting, as I also did the continuing occupation of the building near St Sulpice, but then I found myself starting to wonder about both those things.

The Picards had always lived above the printing works. In the early '70s Benoît moved his family out to the suburbs, refurbished the apartment and let it out at an astronomical rent. I taunted him and said he had become another *petit rentier* and he smiled and said no, he would be a *grand rentier*. I came to realise that for Benoît it was all to do with money. The freehold was capital, an investment that could be realised at any time and in a number of ways. Retaining it

22

was a question of expediency. There was no point in him investing a small fortune in printing technology. He could continue with the old equipment until the time came to sell up and take an early and no doubt comfortable retirement. It was an entirely capitalist calculation; it had nothing to do with principle or with people. Apart from Benoît and his family, of course.

If this was depressing, the fact remained that we had known each other for a long time. I also owed much to him. Benoît had been as instrumental as his father in the birth of the *Guide*: in fact, it may even have been his idea. I cannot remember now. The Picard family represented such a large part of my life, stretching back to when I was 19, that its absence from it would feel like the loss of a limb. We saw each other less often than previously. In the '50s we would drink late into the night several times a week. Together with others from those times, we must have sung the 'Internationale' in half the bars of Paris, especially the smarter ones, where it would cause most offence. One cannot take away things like that. So, whatever my reservations, Benoît was still a dear old friend and it was always good to see him.

I walked into the printing works, as I had hundreds of times before, and found Benoît, as usual, in the back office, surrounded by empty coffee cups and ashtrays full of half-smoked cigarettes.

'Feliks!' he said, embracing me warmly. 'I haven't seen you for weeks. Where've you been?'

'Ill,' I said. 'In fact I was in bed from Christmas until last week.'

'Ah well, age catches up with us all.'

'It was not age. It was the flu.'

'They usually go together,' said Benoît. 'Anyway, you're looking all right now.'

'Yes, I am much better. What did you want to see me about?'

'Good news and bad news. Which do you want first?'

'Oh, the good,' I said. 'I could do with some good news.'

'Well,' said Benoît. 'The good news is that sales of the new edition are fantastic. We've sold out. I've never known anything like it. I'm reprinting already and I expect I'll need to reprint again.'

'Good,' I said. I could not remember the *Guide* ever needing to be reprinted.

'You might sound a little more pleased about it.'

'Oh, I am pleased,' I said. 'But . . . '

' . . . but you're peeved that far more people want to visit eastern Europe now than they did when it was communist.'

'Yes, I suppose so.'

'Feliks, you're so predictable. Why does every silver lining always have a cloud?'

'Well, you know what I think. I am too old to change now. But I suppose I should say 'well done'.'

'Thank you. In view of the conspicuous success of the good news, I now rather hesitate to give you the bad.'

'Which is?'

'That I am retiring. Later on in the year.'

'You are only 59!'

'It's as good a time as any.'

'But why?'

'There are lots of reasons,' said Benoît. 'First of all, business is not good and I can't see it getting any better.'

'But you have just told me how well it is going. Sales are fantastic, you said.'

'That's your book, Feliks. It may surprise you, but I can't earn a living from that. I do have other clients, you know, and things are not so good there.'

'Why not?'

'Well, to my certain knowledge, at least three of them are planning to transfer their production to Hungary or Czechoslovakia.'

'Why?'

'Why do you think? Because it will be a lot cheaper for them. Because there is already a lot of investment going into those countries to provide new technology. As you know, I have never chosen to invest in new equipment. Now there's no point in trying to catch up. Even with the same equipment I would be twice as expensive as those other places.'

'It is ridiculous,' I said. 'What has this got to do with human life? What has it even got to do with economics? You are losing your livelihood because a few gangsters see easy money to be made by investing in poor countries.'

'You could look at it that way,' agreed Benoît. 'On the other hand, and at the risk of upsetting your delicate sensibilities still further, one could ask why nearly 50 years of communism have left those countries so poor.'

'One could also ask why 50 years of capitalism have left you with such antiquated equipment.'

'That was my choice,' said Benoît. 'I could have done things differently. I chose not to.'

'You have changed,' I said. 'You would not have spoken like this 30 years ago.'

Benoît shrugged his shoulders. 'I didn't have a bald head and a paunch 30 years ago. The world changes. I take it as I find it. There are no medals for consistency.'

'I have not changed.'

'No, Feliks, you haven't. And if they ever create a museum about the Cold War, you will be the prize exhibit. But, if you will allow me to say so, even you will need to change now. And, if you don't, the world will not wait for you. It never does.'

'So what will happen to the business? Are you selling it?'

'I doubt it. I'm not sure it's worth anything as a going concern.'

'But this building must be worth a fortune, Benoît.'

'Oh, the building, yes. But not the business inside it.'

'So you are selling the property?'

'Yes.'

I said nothing.

'I know what you're thinking,' he said. 'I knew exactly what your attitude would be. It's all very well sitting there with your lofty detachment and these fine principles when you have no one to think about but yourself. I have a family. I have a wife and four children, and I can assure you it's not so simple then. The tenant is leaving the flat at the end of June. I have received a huge offer for the building: a mad offer, frankly. We have talked about it. We are all agreed it is the right thing to do at this time.'

'And what about me, Benoît?'

'Feliks, I am sorry to say that this will be the last edition I will be able to produce for you. At least we will be going out with a bang.'

'So who will produce it if you do not?'

'I don't know, Feliks. I will give you all the help I can. You've got the best part of a year to sort it out. I've told you before anyone else. No one outside the family knows about it yet. I can't do more. There are people I know, people I can introduce you to, who are in a position to help you. I will gladly do that. Maybe you should think about going to Hungary or Czechoslovakia yourself. You know those countries as well as anyone.'

'I do not think I would care for that,' I said.

'Well, please yourself. But I wouldn't worry about it either way, if I were you. There are plenty of printers who would be happy to have your business, especially with sales the way they are.'

'It would not be the same, Benoît.'

'No, Feliks; it wouldn't. But I think we've already discussed that point.'

I stood up to go.

'Have a think about it, Feliks, and let me know

if there is anything I can do to help.'

'Thank you. I will.'

'And we must have a drink soon, hey?'

'Yes. That would be nice.'

'I'll give you a call.'

We did not embrace each other on this occasion, but we shook hands, and I left the Picard works for the last time and stepped out into the cold January street. The next time I passed this way the place would no doubt be a boutique or a perfumery or a jeweller's, selling inessential and frivolous things for a thousand times more than some poor bastard earned to make them. Perhaps I would not pass this way again.

The walk from St Sulpice to the restaurant was a short one, but there was time for many thoughts before I arrived. To start with I was angry: angry at Benoît's greed, angry that he could make such a decision without consulting me. It was a selfish reaction, I know, but that is how I felt. The anger wore off quickly. Who knows if I would have made the same choice in the same circumstances, but it was Benoît's decision and not mine. What was unarguable was that my situation had now changed too, whether I liked it or not.

My next thought was that this was the end of the *Guide*. At least it was the end of my *Guide*: the one I had started and had maintained with Benoît's help for all these years. Whatever happened now, things would never be the same. I had no desire to start a search for a new printer. My heart was not in it. It would involve all sorts of grubby conversations about money. I am not good at things like that, nor have any desire to become good at them. With Benoît the money was simple. Twice a year he gave me a large cheque. It was always accompanied by a detailed statement showing exactly how the sum had been calculated, but I never looked at it. I trusted him. Whatever I may have thought of his *bourgeois* susceptibilities, I always trusted him when it came to business. It would be impossible, not to mention naïve, to attempt the same relationship with someone else.

So if everything would change anyway, why continue with it at all? Why not step away from it? I could see that closing down the *Guide* would be self-destructive. In which case, I would need to find a buyer for it. In which case, why not an American? It was true that I detested America. The country represented everything I disliked in the world. But, if whoever bought it would be doing so with no respect for the past and with the sole aim of making money from it, did it matter what nationality they were? Suppose I scrupulously sold the *Guide* to a company in another country, and then that company was bought by the Americans? They were buying everything else. The fact was that I had no control over the matter.

By the time I reached the restaurant I was certain what I wanted to do, and that was to be shot of the whole thing as quickly as possible and with the minimum of fuss. When I had left the apartment that morning I had been a detached sceptic, allowing himself the luxury of listening to the blandishments of a suitor before grandly rejecting his advances. Now I was going to meet the prospective purchaser of my business.

Martins had booked a table at the Brasserie du Temps Perdu on the Boulevard St Germain. I was early and arrived before him. Asked if I would like a drink, I surprised myself by ordering a glass of champagne.

The choice of restaurant was predictable. It was precisely what an American would take to be an authentic Parisian restaurant. The irony was that it once had been an authentic Parisian restaurant, before the likes of Mike Martins had turned it into something else. I had eaten there only once before and that had been years earlier, soon after my arrival in Paris.

The Brasserie du Temps Perdu had changed little in the meantime. It was still furnished with red plush banquettes and chairs, with mirrored walls behind. It was still staffed by antique male waiters in black attire and large white aprons, an ancient tiding of magpies. It still featured the menu of traditional France — *pieds de pacquet, quenelles de brochet, boudin blanc* and so on — that was now only to be found in remote provincial towns, and perhaps not even there. I would not know. The menu itself was set in a typeface not used since the 1950s, at least until its recent resurrection on facsimile gift items manufactured in the Philippines. The clientele seemed to consist almost entirely of tourists. Indeed the restaurant itself seemed to be a pastiche of the era that had given the Left Bank its reputation, when artists and intellectuals had commingled and copulated with each other, with politicians, with socialites, with showgirls and prostitutes, with anyone. Now the Left Bank was a brand name, visited by Americans in much the same manner and for the same purpose as they would put on a Ralph Lauren shirt or Calvin Klein chinos, in the hope that a small residue of style would rub off and deposit itself on confident squared shoulders and toned legs.

And through this time, while the European world had fought its battle of ideas, while the principles of Marxism and democracy had pitted themselves against the class interests of capitalism, only by some unimaginable coition to produce the screaming bastard of consumerism — through all this time, the Brasserie du Temps Perdu had stood sedately on the Boulevard St Germain, changing not at all. And in not changing, it had changed. And in not compromising its authenticity, it had become a replica. And in remaining itself, it had become something else.

Mike Martins walked into the restaurant about five minutes after the appointed time and there was no mistaking him. A waiter brought him to the table, as Martins followed with what seemed a curious mixture of confidence and the lack of it.

'Hi,' he said, 'Mike Martins.'

'Zhukovski,' I said.

'It's good to meet you, Monsieur Zhukovski. I am so sorry to have kept you waiting.'

He launched into what might have become a lengthy apologia for his lateness, had it not been interrupted by the waiter enquiring after our need for drinks. I permitted myself another glass of champagne. Martins looked apprehensive and I wondered if he was teetering on the edge of his expense allowance. He ordered a mineral water for himself, but perhaps he would have done that anyway.

He had spoken in French so far, or had at least made the attempt. It was the sort of French that did not suggest a conversational fluency. He was taking great pains to achieve grammatical accuracy, correcting himself after every small mistake, so that each sentence took twice as long to deliver as it need have. I was not sure I could bear an hour or two of conversation conducted in this manner, so I asked him if he would rather speak in English.

'Well, that is kind of you,' he said. 'Are you sure you don't mind?'

'Not at all,' I said.

'I've not been long in Paris and, although I learnt French in school, I guess I'm a little rusty. I'm taking evening classes to catch up. I do think it is so rude to live in someone else's country and not be able to speak their language.'

I had no difficulty in pigeonholing Mike Martins by now. Most Americans I had met in Europe over the years addressed you in English as a matter of course and with no apology, and seemed insusceptible to the thought that this might be considered impolite or insensitive. It was a part of the American cultural imperialism that I detested especially. The few exceptions, like Martins, went to the opposite extreme and were fawningly deferential, not to say obsequious. Their respect for old Europe and its assorted cultural arcana amounted almost to a religious devotion. They were mortified by unintended solecisms and venerated each and every absurd and antiquated social custom as if it were the bone of a medieval saint. Mike Martins was a perfect example of the species. He was an eager, preppy East Coaster, probably in his early 30s. It would have been hard not to patronise him and I had no intention of trying. I was starting to be irked by his sensitive use of my surname. I naturally expected Americans to use my first name instantly and without permission. That irked me too. I dare say this sounds irrational, but what is the point in having prejudices if one cannot indulge them?

'You speak several languages I expect, Mr Zhukovski?' Now he was flattering me.

'Naturally,' I said. 'I speak French of course, even though I am not French . . . ' (This statement was technically incorrect, but I wanted Martins to know that it was not unusual in Europe for non-Frenchmen to speak French.) ' . . . I speak English, as you can hear. I speak German. I have some Russian. I also speak Polish, which is my native tongue.'

'Wow,' he said, which I thought an inadequate response, although no doubt the best of which he was capable.

The waiter came to take our order and Martins judged this a good moment to move the conversation towards the matter in hand.

'I was so pleased to hear from you, Mr

Zhukovski,' he said. 'I thought perhaps you were not interested.'

'I was busy when you wrote,' I replied. 'And I have been ill for the past few weeks.'

'I am so sorry. I trust you are now recovered?'

'Completely, thank you. So I thought I would take the opportunity to hear what you wanted to say. You are the European Vice-President of a New York publishing firm, I believe?' I think I said that in a tone that put his profession on a par with prostitution or drug trafficking, but Martins was disappointingly slow to take offence. He laughed.

'Yeah, well that's the title,' he said. 'And you do know how we love titles. To be honest, there's just me and a secretary and a small office. But, yes, I do work for Bergelson & King, the New York publishers.'

'What do you do?'

'Two things really,' said Martins. 'B & K is a large firm. We have a long list. Part of my job is to see which of our US titles might sell in Europe and to arrange translation, distribution and so on. The other part is to find European works that might sell in the US, as well as suitable European acquisition targets for us.'

'So I am an acquisition target, then?'

'Yes, if you put it that way.'

'I think it was you that put it that way, Mr Martins.'

'Yes I did. I'm sorry.' I was flustering him. 'Yes, we have an extensive travel catalogue, but nothing that covers eastern Europe. As I'm sure you know, there is real interest in travel to eastern Europe at this moment in time. It's very much a growth market and we see it expanding hugely in the future. Mr Bergelson asked me to keep an eye open for any suitable guides that we might be able, hmmm, to develop, and I came across yours in a bookshop here. I thought I'd be in touch to see if this would be of any interest to you.'

'I see. Yes, well, that might be something that would interest me.'

'I must confess I know very little about your business operation,' said Martins. 'I am familiar with the *Guide* itself, of course, but I don't know anything about your set-up. I mean, I've no idea whether you publish other titles or anything. Actually, I could not find any contact details for you, so in the end I wrote to your printers, if you recall.'

I did not recall that particular point, as it happens. So Benoît had forwarded the letter. In which case, he had probably read it. I had not mentioned to Benoît that I was meeting Mike Martins. Also, I realised that I was being unnecessarily awkward with Martins, which was not justified by the man himself or by the fact that I was in the position of trying to sell to him. I decided I would try to be more amenable and started to tell him a little more about the *Guide* and how it was produced. I also made sure he was aware how well sales were going. If I was to prostrate myself in front of the dollar, I wanted to make sure I scooped as many of them as possible.

'Fascinating,' said Martins, with reasonable

conviction. 'That's a really lean operation you have.' (I thought that a fatuous comment; it was the only sensible way of doing it. Why were Americans always surprised when Europeans did anything efficiently?) 'So,' he continued, making sure he had understood; 'it's your baby and, if you want to sell, it's up to you and no one else?'

'Yes,' I said.

'And do you want to sell?'

'Well, that depends on several things. The price, of course. And also what you want to do with the *Guide*.'

'How do you mean?'

'Are you planning to continue it the way it is or will you want to change it?'

'I'm sorry, Mr Zhukovski, I don't have the answer to that question. That would be for Mr Bergelson to decide.'

'It is important to me.'

'Yes, I understand that, Mr Zhukovski. But it's not up to me to decide.'

'So you will change it.'

'No, I didn't say that either. I simply don't know.'

'You say you have read the *Guide*, Mr Martins. What did you think of it?'

'I thought it was excellent,' said Martins. 'I wouldn't be here otherwise. Very informative; very thorough. Of course I'm not familiar with these countries in the way you are, but it seemed to me to give a pretty good picture.'

'What about the politics?'

'I'm sorry?'

'Well, you can see that I am not afraid to spell

36

out a few political truths.'

'Yes, I see that. I realise it is written from what one might call a leftist perspective.' I began to warm to Martins. Improbably, he had been able to discern my exact political position. Then again, perhaps he was too nervous to suggest I was a communist.

'Indeed. I am not ashamed to call myself a leftist, Mr Martins. A progressive.'

'Sure. I respect that.'

'You respect it?'

'Yes, I respect it. That is your right. I understand that.'

'So how would Mr Bergelson react to publishing a guide that is sympathetic to what communism has tried to achieve in eastern Europe since the war?'

'I don't know. That would be for him to say. I've not discussed politics with him.'

'Hmmm,' I said.

'Are you saying you would only consider selling the *Guide* if it continued in its present form and with its present political leanings?'

Was I saying that? I suppose it sounded like it, and of course that was what I wanted. But I knew it was absurd even as I was saying it. Of course there would be changes to the *Guide*, whoever owned it. There would need to be; part of the reason I was contemplating selling was to avoid making those changes myself. Of course a New York publisher would not print a Marxist guide to eastern Europe for the American market. I knew that. So did Mike Martins. He was trying not to upset me and risk losing the deal. And much though I wanted to answer 'yes' to his question, that would have been ridiculous. If I took that attitude, I might as well not bother talking to him, or to anyone else for that matter. It was hopeless. I was not engaged in some exercise of intellectual continuity, but in a commercial transaction. I was looking for a way out, not a cul-de-sac. I did not answer his question directly.

'Mr Martins, I have devoted the greater part of my life to the *Guide*. When I started it, Europe was mired in the aftermath of two internecine conflicts. At your age, you can have no idea what it was like. It was not just that things were a little more backward and people a little worse off, that there were fewer gadgets and conveniences. It was fundamentally different. On one side of Europe was a group of people who wanted to change things, who wanted to sweep away the privileges and unfairnesses and aggression that had caused the conflicts in the first place and that had made life unbearable for most people. And on the other side was a group of people who wanted to do exactly the opposite, who wanted to restore the privileges, perpetuate the unfairnesses, let loose the aggression once again. And these were the people who owned the newspapers and radio stations and TV stations. And these were the people, out of their own self-interest, who denied and denigrated what was happening in the East and who prejudiced the populations of the West against it.

'In my own small way, I have offered an alternative to this process. I have explained

38

eastern Europe to the West. I have tried to clear away the lies and misconceptions. I have encouraged people to come and see for themselves and not to rely on the propaganda they were fed at home. In answer to your question, no I do not expect the *Guide* to continue in its present form. In the circumstances that would be unrealistic. But you cannot expect me not to mind about it and you cannot expect me not to ask about it.'

'I don't,' said Martins. He seemed unfazed by my ideological polemic. 'So tell me, Mr Zhukovski, how much does the fact that you are considering selling the *Guide* at the present time have to do with the fact that the communist bloc has collapsed?'

I found myself unwilling to answer the question. Mike Martins waited a few moments before asking a supplementary. 'How do you feel about communism now?'

'I find it hard to say,' I admitted. 'Whatever impression I may give, I am not a hard-line communist and have not been for a considerable time. I have disliked many of the practicalities of communist rule. I do not think that eastern Europe was paradise on earth. But it is nevertheless on that side of the fence that my intellectual beliefs lie, and my emotional attachments as well. And whatever misgivings I may have about the side I chose to support, I am unaltered in my opinion of the side I chose to oppose. I feel that what is happening now is a reactionary step. I regret it immensely and believe that, in time, the people of eastern

Europe will do the same.'

'So the wrong side won?'

'Yes.'

'And now it's trying to buy you out.'

'Yes.'

'I can see that must be difficult.'

Rather improbably, Mike Martins had managed to draw me into a serious conversation. I had imagined he would talk about money, but he had not even mentioned it. I could not expect him to share my opinions, but he seemed to respect them and I detected none of the triumphalism I had feared. In one way this was irritating. I suppose, if I am honest, that I did feel a sense of moral superiority in my politics. Certainly other people would say I did. Martins was depriving me of a natural opportunity to indulge it. Yet, as the conversation went on, I found myself not resenting this fact, but positively enjoying the freedom that flowed from it.

'Tell me,' said Martins. 'How did you first get interested in politics?'

'That is a long story,' I said. 'I am Polish originally. I was born in Łódź in 1930. But in 1939 I was separated from my mother and went to live in Switzerland with my aunt and uncle. So that is where I grew up. In Basle. That is where I was educated.'

'I doubt you were taught communism in Swiss schools.'

I laughed. 'No I was not. That came later. But perhaps you could say that the ground was prepared for me in Switzerland. I did not like

Swiss society. I found it stifling. It was so money orientated in both big and little ways. I think I reacted against it. And of course my entire childhood had been destroyed by fascism.'

'Did you go to university?'

'No. I would have liked to, but there was no money. Actually, that is not true. There was money, but my uncle did not want to spend it on me. I suppose I cannot blame him. I was not his son, not that they had children of their own. But I never got on with him. He was not a sympathetic man.'

'Did you come to France then?'

'Yes. In 1947. I crossed the border and found myself in Montbéliard. It was not difficult to get a work permit. I found a job in the Peugeot factory at Sochaux. That is where I became involved in politics. I joined the union and became an activist. They were heady times. It may be hard for you to believe, in fact I find it hard to believe myself, but the communists were the largest party in France at that time. They were in the government. We thought that France would be the first Western country to have a democratically elected communist government.'

'So how did you get from making cars to starting a travel guide?'

'By accident, I suppose. I always enjoyed writing. I was always good at writing. So, when I first started to get involved politically at Peugeot, I was roped in to help with the propaganda. There were always things to write: pamphlets, posters, press statements. I did that. Anyway, some of my stuff was seen by a man called

Fernand Meurice in Paris. You will not have heard of him. He was quite famous then. He had been one of the legendary figures in the Paris Communist Party in the '30s. After the war he started a communist newspaper called *La Vague de la Gauche*. He invited me to Paris to work on the paper.'

'That was a good break.'

'Yes, I suppose it was, although at the time I nearly turned it down.'

'Why?'

'I was happy at Sochaux. I was spending far more time with the union than I was making cars and what I was doing was, well, if not exactly illegal, then at least subversive. I loved it. And I liked the people around me. It is hard to describe the camaraderie of those times. For the first time since I was nine, I felt that I belonged to a family. I did not want to leave all that behind. But, as you say, *La Vague de la Gauche* was too good an opportunity to ignore in the end.'

'I'm sorry, I'm not familiar with the paper,' said Martins. 'Does it still exist?'

'No, not for a long time. But it had a certain prestige in its time.'

'Did it have a large staff?'

I laughed again. 'Goodness, no. There was just Monsieur Meurice and I. And the cat, of course. The cat was called Lenin.'

'Was the cat on the payroll?'

'Quite probably, I should think. Monsieur Meurice was keen to create the impression of a large staff. It was a competitive world, left-wing newspapers after the war, and very fissiparous. New ones started up every month and old ones closed down. Probably none of them was successful apart from *L'Humanité*, but it was vital to create the impression of success. No one knew there were only the two of us. We each had about six pseudonyms. Anyone reading the paper would have gained the impression of a large journalistic staff. Monsieur Meurice kept the best portfolios for himself. He appeared under his own name as the Editor-in-Chief and under different names as the Political Editor, Foreign Editor, Economics Editor, Social Affairs Editor and so forth.'

'And what were you?'

'I did not get to be an editor, of course. I was the Paris Correspondent. I was the Sports Correspondent, which was ridiculous because I had no interest in sport. Later, I became the Travel Correspondent.'

'You must have been a busy man.'

'Not that busy,' I said. 'I am ashamed to say that much of the material was copied from other sources.'

'And you lived in Paris?'

'Yes, I lived with the Meurices. I did not pay rent. On the other hand, Monsieur Meurice paid me so little for my work that it came to much the same thing. They did not have children, so I suppose I was like a surrogate son to them. That was a funny set-up. Albertine Meurice did not share her husband's political sympathies. I think she came from quite a prosperous family, as did Fernand himself. She insisted on living in one of the smarter Paris suburbs, which did not suit Monsieur Meurice at all. They were constantly at war with each other. She would tell the neighbours that he was the editor of a leading national newspaper. He would tell them that they were running a communist cell from their house. I do not know what was believed. It was very funny.'

'It doesn't sound like the ideal marriage to me.'

'No, but it worked. They had a great deal of affection for each other, expressed mostly in insults. I never once heard them address each other by their first names. She was always *Madame la Bourgeoise* and he was always *Monsieur l'Intellectuel*. I remember when he forgot to bring home a cabbage for supper one evening, Albertine saying 'I'm so sorry to have troubled your towering mind with such a trifle. It must have been an intolerable burden for an intellectual.' They were always saying things like that to each other.'

Martins laughed. 'How long did you do this for?' he asked.

'For about six years. I came to Paris in 1949 and *La Vague de la Gauche* folded in 1955. By that time, in my capacity as Travel Correspondent, I was running a regular feature on tourism to different countries in eastern Europe. I had not actually been to any of the countries. Nor had Monsieur Meurice, as far as I know. We asked the embassies for their official literature and cobbled it together with some photographs. It was a popular feature, though I say it myself.

44

'When the paper folded, I did not know what to do. I was living with the printer and his family at the time, Monsieur Meurice having more or less evicted me. I cannot remember if it was Benoît or myself who came up with the idea of putting these old travel articles together into a guidebook, but that is what happened.'

'And the rest is history,' said Martins.

'It would appear so. At the time I hoped it was the future.' I do not think he understood the joke. Few people understood my jokes, so I had largely given up making them.

'I feel so privileged you have told me all this,' said Martins.

I think he meant it. I think he felt as if he had been granted a favoured insight into the rituals of old Europe. I could imagine him relating my story to a hushed audience in Boston or wherever he came from.

I enjoyed talking about it too. It must have been decades since I had even thought about that part of my life, let alone told anyone about it. And, in the telling, I realised myself that I was describing a vanished world, a world that had in fact vanished a long time ago. The offices of *La Vague de la Gauche* had been round the corner from the Brasserie du Temps Perdu, in a small garret close to the Picard Printworks. The only time I had been to this restaurant was when Monsieur Meurice had marched me here in 1952 to celebrate the downfall of a rival and, in his view, ideologically unsound publication. I had drunk champagne then too.

That seemed to belong to a different life. So it

was not the case that now, suddenly, on my 61st birthday, I was being confronted with change. There had always been change. There had been huge changes. It was just that the seamlessness of my life had disguised them. Living day to day there were so many things one did not notice. Which was the greater reality? The idealistic young communist who had sat in this restaurant toasting the demise of *Le Nouvel Citoyen*, or the slightly more cynical leftist who was sat in the same place allowing himself to be seduced by an American publisher? Neither, I supposed. They were both real. Life had moved on.

'So how would you feel now about selling the *Guide* to us?' It was almost a relief that Martins had brought the conversation back to a place where he could be the person I thought he would be, and I could be the person I thought I was.

'Yes, well, I am interested,' I replied. 'How much were you proposing to pay for it?'

'That would be for Mr Bergelson to decide.' (Why was everything important for Mr Bergelson to decide?) 'I sent him your *Guide* last summer and he liked it very much.' (Most unlikely; more probably he saw it as an opportunity to make money.) 'He knows I am meeting with you today and he has asked me to say that he is most keen that a deal should proceed. But he will wish to negotiate all the terms personally.'

'When does that happen?'

'As soon as you like.'

'So he would come over to Paris to discuss it?'

'No. Mr Bergelson doesn't travel widely himself.' (A publisher of travel guides who does not travel widely!) 'He will wish you to go to New York.'

'New York!'

'Yes. That is where our offices are.'

I had not been prepared for that. Mr Bergelson might not travel widely, but as a matter of fact neither did I. I travelled frequently; I travelled intensely; but these were not the same things. Rather shockingly, since leaving Switzerland in 1947, I did not think I had been to any other country beyond eastern Europe and France. I did not think I had been further west than Paris in my life. That was where the civilised world ended as far as I was concerned.

'Is that strictly necessary?'

'I'm afraid so, yes.'

I thought about it, but not for long. I wanted to sell the *Guide* and I was prepared to sell it to Martins. If I needed to go to New York to do it, that is what I would have to do. Perhaps a part of me was also intrigued to know how it would feel to be inside the lion's den.

'Very well,' I said.

'When would you like to go?'

'The sooner the better, I suppose.'

'Do you have a visa?'

'A what?'

'A visa. You will need a visa to enter the United States.'

'No I do not. What does that involve?'

'Oh, just a visit to the American embassy in

47

Paris and a short interview with a consular official.'

'Is that normal?'

'Entirely. That's the procedure for everyone.'

'Well I suppose that is all right,' I said.

'I know one of the officials there,' said Martins. 'Would you like me to get things going?'

'Thank you,' I said. Now that he had the scent of a deal in his nostrils, Martins had suddenly become businesslike. I do not know if he thought I might change my mind, but he had somehow managed to take control of the situation.

'The process should not take too long,' he said. 'Why don't I check Mr Bergelson's availability in late March, if that is convenient for you?'

'Fine,' I said.

3

It was on a freezing cold morning in mid-February that I walked down to Jaurès and took the Metro to Concorde. Living where I did, I was well served with Metro stations that evoked a more optimistic leftist past: Jean Jaurès, Stalingrad, Colonel Fabien.

I had not been to the Place de la Concorde for many years. It is strange how one can live in a city, know parts of it like the back of one's hand, yet be unfamiliar with the rest of it. The area around Concorde is not to my taste. It reeks of imperial grandeur and old money, with its decadent hotels and swanky shops. The proximity of the American embassy does nothing to increase its appeal. If anyone had told me that one day I would walk voluntarily into the embassy compound, I would not have believed them.

I had an appointment to see John Oberman, some minor functionary, at 11:00. When I was shown into his office, I found a man to whom I took an instant dislike. It emerged that he had taken a dislike to me even earlier. Whatever qualities Mike Martins possessed to compensate him for his nationality, Oberman lacked. About the same age as Martins, he had rimless glasses, short-cut hair and not a gram of sympathy. His office contained the minimum of furniture and no personality. Emblems, flags, portraits of the

President and other nationalistic paraphernalia decorated the walls. I was relieved that this interview was a formality. I had no desire to be there a moment longer than necessary.

Oberman was not the only person in the room. On a chair in the corner that was much too small for him sat a large Frenchman. (At the time I suppose I did not know he was French, although his appearance allowed no other possibility.) He was older, older than myself even. He did not get up. I was not introduced to him and Oberman did not explain why he was there. He sat through the interview, visible out of the corner of my eye, methodically excavating his teeth with a wooden toothpick. It was an odd arrangement.

Oberman gestured me to a chair and we sat facing each other across his sterile desk.

'So, Monsieur Zhukovski, you wish to visit the United States?' At least he was speaking French, quite good French actually, which was something.

'I do, yes.'

'And this would be your first visit, would it?'

'It would.'

'Perhaps you could tell me, Monsieur Zhukovski, what attracts you to America. As a communist.'

'I am not a communist.'

'Not a communist? Oh, I thought you were.'

'No. I am a leftist.'

'A leftist?'

'Yes.'

'And yet you used to be a member of the

Communist Party.' Oberman had a large stack of files on his desk. I could not imagine they could all concern me. He looked at one of them. 'It says here that you joined the Communist Party on 17th May 1949.'

'I may have done.'

'You did.'

'All right, I did.'

'Despite the fact that you say you are not a communist.'

'Yes.'

'Monsieur Zhukovski, perhaps you could explain to me why you, as a non-communist, should join a party dedicated to the advancement of communism?'

'It was a condition of my employment.'

'Ah yes, that would have been when you were working for Comrade Meurice at *La Vague de la Gauche*.'

'Monsieur Meurice, yes.'

'And Comrade Meurice ordered you to join the Communist Party.'

'More or less.'

'So you, a leftist but not a communist, nevertheless chose to work for a communist newspaper and ended up being forced to join the Communist Party. More or less.'

'Yes.'

'I see.'

'I resigned from the Party in 1968.'

'So I understand. Along with many others. It's encouraging that some good came out of the Prague Spring.'

'It had nothing to do with that.'

51

'Well anyway, you resigned from the Party in 1968. That was, what, some 13 years after you had ceased working for Comrade Meurice.'

'About that.'

'Always wise to take one's time over important decisions, I think. No doubt you had more pressing things to do than resign the Party membership so reluctantly forced upon you.'

'It was a legitimate political party.'

'Yes, of course it was. I'm so sorry if I suggested otherwise. It was indeed a legitimate political party. In France. But we are not discussing a visa for you to enter France. You are here already, I see.'

I said nothing to the sarcastic idiot.

'So let us turn now to what happened when you first came to France in 1947.' He riffled through some more papers in the file. 'I believe you worked for the Peugeot company, in Sochaux.'

'I did.'

'Where you were closely involved in industrial disruption of various kinds.'

'I was a member of the union.'

'An active member of the union, it would appear. Which, I hasten to add, was an entirely legitimate organisation.'

'Yes,' I said. 'As in America, I am told.'

'Oh indeed,' said Oberman. 'And your activities within the union were, I am sure, devoted to improving the conditions of you and your fellow workers?'

'Absolutely.'

'And not in any way concerned with destabilising the government of France at that time?'

'Of course not.'

'Hmmm,' said Oberman. 'Well I suppose that is in the past, isn't it?'

'Yes.'

'All a very long time ago.'

'Yes.'

'So then you came to Paris. I believe you live in the Avenue Secrétan.'

'I do.'

'Which must be most convenient for you.'

'I do not know what you mean.'

'Well, it's around the corner from the headquarters of the French Communist Party, is it not?'

'At the time I moved there, the Party was based in the Rue Pelletier, as I would expect you to have known.'

'I'm sorry. I'm afraid my knowledge of the French Communist Party is so inadequate compared with yours. Anyway, you came to Paris. You worked for Comrade Meurice. And then you started this book.' He fingered the copy of the *Guide Jaune* on his desk as if it might be contaminated. 'You started this book which, it might be said, falls over backwards to portray the communist regimes in eastern Europe in a favourable light. I'm sorry; the former communist regimes, I should say.'

'I have always tried to be honest.'

'Such a subjective commodity, the truth, isn't it? It's none of my business, but when I flicked through it, I thought it seemed dated.'

'It needs changes, yes,' I admitted.

'Almost a complete rewrite I would say, wouldn't you?'

'As you say, it is none of your business.'

'Of course not. Now let us consider why it is, Monsieur Zhukovski, that you wish to visit the United States: a country with which you have no obvious affinity, and which may well not have much of an affinity with you.'

'I am thinking of selling my business.'

'Really?'

'Yes.'

'Surely not to an American company?'

'Yes.'

'So — let me get this right. You, a communist — no, I'm so sorry, not a communist — you, a leftist, want to visit America to discuss selling your business to what I can only assume is a capitalist firm.'

'That is correct.'

'Bit of an about-turn, isn't it?'

'I should have thought you would be pleased.'

'Oh, I really don't have an opinion on the subject.'

'I am not sure I see the point of this interview,' I said. 'You seem to know a great deal about me already.'

'It would seem there is a great deal about you to know, Monsieur Zhukovski.' He patted the stack of files.

'There is a great deal to know about everyone if you spend all your time spying on them.'

'Oh, I can assure you that we haven't spent any

of our time spying on you. We have far better things to do.'

'Like bombing Baghdad,' I said. That had happened the previous day. Not content with evicting the Iraqi army from Kuwait, the Americans had decided to terrorise the population of Baghdad. I should not have said it. I had been admirably restrained until then, despite the provocation. But I could not resist it. I heard the Frenchman chuckle.

'Monsieur Zhukovski, in normal circumstances I would be delighted to pass the time of day with you debating the finer points of American foreign policy, but I'm afraid that today I have other appointments. I think we have finished. I will let you know our decision on the visa in due course.'

He stood up and extended his hand, which I took briefly and reluctantly. The Frenchman remained seated. I left Oberman's office and the embassy compound and walked distractedly down the Rue Royale towards the Rue du Faubourg St Honoré. I was not proud of myself. The only reason for submitting myself to this humiliation had been to obtain a visa for the United States. It appeared that the chances of that had been slim to start with and I had only made them worse. What would I tell Mike Martins?

Hearing rapid footsteps behind me, I turned to find myself facing the silent Frenchman. He was out of breath, and I must have looked startled.

'Don't worry,' he said. 'I'm not about to attack

you. Do you fancy a drink?'

'I fancy several,' I said, 'but preferably not around here.'

'I tend not to pick bars by sociology,' he said. 'But if you would like somewhere a little more earthy, there's a perfectly decent bar around the corner in the Rue d'Anjou.' We walked the 200 metres in silence, down a surprisingly nondescript street considering the neighbourhood, and installed ourselves in Le Comptoir du Faubourg. It was a bar I would come to know well. I let him buy us both a beer and waited for him to tell me why he had pursued me.

'Cheers,' he said. 'Here's to your trip to America.'

'Hardly likely,' I said.

'Oh, I wouldn't say that. That's why I wanted to see you. I could tell you were pretty gloomy. Pretty angry too, I would say.'

'Who are you?'

'I'm sorry. My name is René Dufour.' He extended a large warm hand.

'Feliks Zhukovski,' I said. I do not know why I added my first name. It is not something I normally do. His reply had told me his name, but it had not answered my question.

'What do you do?'

'Not much,' said Dufour cheerfully. 'I'm retired.' He knew quite well what I meant, but enjoyed failing to answer the question.

'There are millions of retired people in France,' I said, 'and I dare say few of them are to be found sitting in corners in the American embassy listening to political undesirables being

56

interviewed by a complete imbecile.'

'True,' said Dufour. 'I probably do have one of the more interesting sidelines.'

'What did you do before you retired?'

'I worked for the government.'

'Which one?'

'Oh, the French.' He was plainly not going to tell me more, nor did he need to. It seemed evident that Dufour had been in the police, or perhaps the security services, and was now assisting the Americans in keeping the riff-raff out of their country.

'What do you do for Oberman?'

'I sort of act as his interpreter.'

'His French was perfect,' I said.

Dufour laughed. 'Oh, I don't mean literally,' he said. 'I interpret the real world for him.'

'Into which language?'

'The language of common sense. I like Americans personally, but I find they have a habit of seeing things in rather black-and-white terms. I, on the other hand, have a large palette, composed of every conceivable shade of grey, and I acquaint Oberman with it from time to time.'

'So I am a shade of grey, am I?'

'Almost everyone is a shade of grey. It would be absurd for anyone to think you could pose a threat to the American state. I told Oberman that before you arrived. You'll get your visa.'

'Why did he talk to me like that, then?'

'He enjoys it. It's a pastime to him. Other people read, or keep bees. Oberman likes being rude to people.'

'Strange hobby for a diplomat,' I said.

'Yes. I don't suppose he gets much chance to indulge it these days. Perhaps you were too good an opportunity to miss.'

'I am pleased to have been able to assist.'

'Mind you, you're not much better yourself,' said Dufour. 'I'm not sure I would care to engage in verbal fisticuffs with you.'

'I am not always like that. I get rather prickly with Americans.'

'I should curb the habit before you go there, if I were you.'

'I will try,' I said. 'Do you want another beer?'

'That would be nice.' He took a large gulp of it when it arrived. 'So, Feliks, where else are you planning to go when you get to America?'

I was surprised that he used my first name. It was not what I would have expected from a Frenchman of his age. However, it did not irritate me as it normally would.

'Are you asking that question in an official capacity?'

'Stop being paranoid,' said Dufour.

'Well, do you wonder with that stack of files on Oberman's desk. Yours, I suppose?' Dufour smiled but said nothing. 'Why do you ask?' I said.

'No particular reason. I just wondered.'

'I am not planning to go anywhere else,' I said. 'Go to New York. Sell the business. Come back. That is what I hope, anyway.'

'Rather a waste of an opportunity.'

'What has it got to do with you?'

'Absolutely nothing. I'm not American, Feliks,

so you don't need to be prickly with me. I've never been to America myself, but if I did go I would want to see as much of it as possible.'

'I do not know that I would care to do that.'

'Feliks, the world has changed. You might as well see it as it is.'

'I am not sure that I particularly want to.'

'You're not alone. But where does the emotion go when this sentimental attachment to communism no longer has a focus? I suppose all that is left is to hate America.'

'I do not hate America.'

'You give a good impression of it.'

In fact, there was something else I could have done in America, only it was so difficult — impossible, really — and I was not even sure that I wanted to do it. I thought I had a brother in America: a half-brother, to be precise. That may seem a strange way of putting it, but by now I had got used to the idea of not knowing whether I still had any family, and of not knowing where they might be if I did.

Woodrow was nine years older than me. We grew up together, but were not particularly close, no doubt because of the age difference. When I went to Basle in 1939, Woodrow came with me. In fact, he was in charge of me. In the next two years we did become close, although he was a man by then and I was still a child. I looked up to him, I suppose. Woodrow talked incessantly about the future. He was full of great plans and all those plans revolved around America. He was determined he would go there as soon as the war ended. I had not seen him since 1941. That March, abruptly and in dramatic circumstances, he had left our aunt and uncle's house in Basle in the middle of the night. He woke me as he was leaving, kissed me goodbye and told me he was going across the French border to join the Resistance. That was the last I had heard of him. I had no idea if he was in America although, being Woodrow, I imagined he would have found a way of getting there if he was still alive at the end of the war. But how would I find him? I had no idea where he was. I had no information to go on. And, on top of this, I was not sure that I wanted to see him.

Woodrow promised he would look after me. He promised that, and he let me down. It was not easy in Switzerland. I was in a strange country, far from home. I arrived to meet an aunt and uncle I did not know and who showed no signs of wanting our presence in their house. The war was all around us and, although detailed news was often lacking, I knew enough of what the Nazis were doing in Poland to be afraid of what might be happening to our family and to our friends, and to wonder when I would be able to go home. I missed my mother too. I hated her for shunting us off to Switzerland like some unwanted item of baggage, but I missed her. It was a double misfortune: to be abandoned by my own mother and then to find that the war prevented me from going home. The only point of continuity was Woodrow and then he abandoned me too. He left me in Basle, all alone. Well, I suppose I cannot blame him for wanting to join the Resistance. I like to think that, had I been older, I would have done the same myself. But he could have written. He knew where I was. He could have stayed in touch. When the war was over, he could have visited. He promised he would look after me and he did not.

I thought about this constantly during and immediately after the war. I wondered of course if Woodrow was dead, as that would account for everything. For a while, I convinced myself that he was. It was easier to think that, and easier to hate myself for having thought such unworthy things about him, than to face the other alternative — that he had washed his hands of me. But I did not know he was dead and I did not feel he was dead. After a while, I decided to stop thinking about these things, about Woodrow, about Mama, about Poland. It was too painful and there were no answers. This happened at the time I left Basle and went to France. I told myself that, unlike other people, I had no history, that here I was aged 17 starting life altogether afresh with no home, no family and no past. I banished all thoughts of what had been, what might have been, what might still be, from my head and from my heart.

But something in me still wanted an answer to the questions. And when, after Dufour's prompting, the remembrance of Woodrow came into my mind, along with the sliver of a possibility that he might be in America and that I might be able to find him, the thought would not go away. I wanted to know the truth. I wanted to know if Woodrow was still alive. And, if he was alive, I wanted to know why he had made no attempt to contact me after he had left Switzerland. I also did not want to know the answer to that question. It was confusing.

'You've gone very quiet,' said Dufour.

'I am sorry; I was thinking.'

'It seems to me you spend too much of your time doing that.'

This was an impertinent remark and I ignored it. 'I was thinking about my brother, my half-brother. He may be in America.'

'Do you want to see him?'

'Yes,' I said. I do not know why I made that reply so emphatically. It was not what I thought I felt.

'When did you last see each other?'

'In 1941,' I said. 'I do not know what happened to him after that. But he always said he would go to America.'

'Feliks,' said Dufour, 'I don't want to promise anything. But I still have connections and — if your brother did go to America — it's not impossible that I could find his address for you.'

I said nothing. I think I was a little frightened by the implications. It had been more comfortable to know nothing and to believe that I could know nothing. Dufour was not deterred by my silence.

'Would you like me to try?'

'Yes,' I said.

'What is your brother's name?'

'Woodrow.'

'Woodrow Zhukovski?'

'Yes, unless he has changed it. Woodrow Wilson Zhukovski.'

'Even in America there can't be too many people called Woodrow Wilson Zhukovski,' said Dufour. 'I'll see what I can do.'

I gave Dufour my address and telephone number. Afterwards I reflected that this was a redundant gesture as he would already know them, as he knew so much else about me. I came back to my apartment. It had been a curious morning.

For the next few days I found myself in a state of enormous excitement. I could not account for it. I was unable to remember when I had last felt so animated. I even found myself having trouble sleeping, which had never been a problem for me before.

The following week I received a telephone call from Dufour. He had located a Woodrow Wilson Zhukovski in Columbus, Ohio. He gave me an address and telephone number. I wanted to ring the number that instant. I so much wanted to make the call. But I made myself wait. I did not yet know whether I would be granted a visa and, although Dufour had said there would be no problem and although Dufour had already acquired a certain credibility with me, I did not want to be presumptuous.

Mike Martins also telephoned at around this time to say that Mr Bergelson would be free for an appointment on Monday 25th March, if that would be convenient. I did not tell Martins that the visa was still uncertain and accepted the appointment. And then, early in March, news on the visa came through. Dufour was right. The government of the United States would be pleased to receive me. I picked up the telephone for Ohio that instant and then remembered there would be a time difference. I had no idea what the time difference was; it had been of no concern to me previously. In the end, I had to call the US embassy to ask them. I would have to wait a few hours. They were agony. I walked around the apartment. I went out and paced the streets. I stopped for lunch at a small pavement bistro, but found I could not eat. I paced the streets some more. Finally, in mid-afternoon, I came back to the apartment and dialled the number. A man's voice answered. I did not recognise it.

'Hello,' I said. 'Is that Mr Woodrow Zhuk-ovski?'

'Yes.'

'Formerly of Łódź in Poland and later of Basle?'

'Yes. Who's that?'

'Woodrow,' I said; 'this is Feliks.'

'What did you say?'

'Feliks. Your brother Feliks.'

'Feliks! I don't believe it. Wait. I must tell Wanda.' I heard his voice grow fainter as his hand partially covered the receiver. 'Wanda! It's Feliks on the line. Can you believe it? It's Feliks!'

'Feliks, it is so wonderful to hear you.' He was

back with me now. 'How've you been?'

'Fine,' I said. Somehow that seemed an adequate summary of 50 years of life.

'Where are you?'

'Paris,' I said. 'But I am coming to America soon.'

'I'm in Ohio.'

'I know that,' I said. 'How are you?'

'I'm great. Just great. Wow, Feliks, I can't believe I'm talking to you. When are you coming over?'

'I am coming to New York at the end of the month.'

'That's wonderful. Come up to Columbus. Come and stay. Come for a week. Come for a month.'

'Thank you, Woodrow; I would love to. But it will only be for a couple of days, I am afraid. I have business to attend to in Paris.' That of course was not true, but I did not feel it wise to commit myself to more than a brief visit in the circumstances.

'That's fine. Whatever's good for you. Just come. Hey, what are you doing with yourself, Feliks? No, don't tell me. We'll save that for when we meet. Don't tell me anything. Just say when you're coming. Oh, and you better tell me if you're bringing your wife with you. Wanda will want to know.'

'I do not have a wife,' I said. 'It will just be me.'

So we fixed the date and he told me how I should go about booking a flight from New York to Columbus. And it was settled quickly. And I knew now the answer to the first question. Woodrow had been pleased to hear from me, extravagantly pleased in fact, and that made me wonder even more why he had never tried to contact me. And when I put the receiver down, I cried.

4

I flew into John F. Kennedy airport on the afternoon of Saturday 23rd March and, although I had some idea of what I would encounter, I was not prepared for it. Dufour was right. I did hate America. I hated its culture. I hated its determination to export that culture, to impose it on peoples around the world, the trampling of other cultures: older cultures, better ones. I hated the greed that drove the culture, the materialism that fuelled it. I hated the indifference to social values, the premium placed on success at all costs, the deification of self-interest. I hated the arrogance of America, its insistence on the superiority of its values, the absence of doubt. I hated the fact that it had dedicated itself for half a century to the eradication of another system of values, one based on a social concept of life and not purely on the individual. Most of all I hated the fact that it now seemed to have accomplished that defeat, and to have done so through the force of money.

Yet I was not altogether lying when I told Dufour that I did not hate America. By that I mean I was aware that my loathing was visceral and emotional, but not altogether informed or rational. I had never been to America. I did not expect to like what I found, but — if I am honest, and I find it painfully difficult to say this

67

— I did not like what I saw in eastern Europe through the 1970s and '80s. I would never admit that to anyone else, and barely to myself, but the more I saw of life in those countries as the years went by, the harder I found it to reconcile what I saw with the ideals that had inspired the founding of those societies and that had inspired me as a young man. I could see that the societies were functional, that they worked, but I saw little happiness in people's lives, and too much fear. If anything, these uncomfortable conclusions intensified my dislike of America, and that was irrational too. Perhaps I resented the existence of another standard, a material standard admittedly, by which progress could be judged. Had contemporary Western capitalism not existed, the material progress of communist societies would have been judged against the past alone, and that was a more favourable comparison. Yet part of me recognised that the image I held of America was no more than a cartoon, a crude caricature that suited what I wanted to believe, that might be based on a reality, but did not represent a subtle or balanced representation of it. I would also acknowledge privately that, the more doubts assailed my previous certainties, the more violently I defended them.

I took a cab from the airport. Billboards screamed at me along the route and, as the skyline of Manhattan came into view, I realised that what my mind was thinking mirrored what my eyes were seeing. I was driving into a caricature.

68

Manhattan was so familiar to me. I do not watch much television, but I suppose that with all the newsreels and films and the occasional cop show over the years, a precise image of that skyline had been filtered into my brain by a process of osmosis. Manhattan was as familiar to me as the outlines of the cities of eastern Europe. But those other cities were places I did know — not just the icon of the cities, but the cities themselves, the people who lived in them, what made them breathe. That was what I would now discover about New York. I was driving from image into reality and that was also a strange feeling because in America I would normally assume I would be driving from reality into image. Perhaps I was doing that too.

My journey had been booked on one of those packages that comes with a hotel included. It was a large hotel and, I imagined, quite a grand hotel, although I learned later that this was not the case. It was apparently an average hotel. I do not dare think what a grand hotel would have been like. I was tired when I arrived and not much in the mood for going out. In any case I had the whole of Sunday to explore the city, so I thought I would pass a quiet time in the hotel, and have an early night and a good long sleep.

I do try to be objective. I know some people would laugh at that, but they see things in a different way from me. Honesty is important to me. I will not therefore deny that the standard of the hotel was high, and certainly higher than anything I had been accustomed to in eastern Europe. The service in particular was faultless, and that is something that cannot always be said elsewhere. And the facilities! I could have had an entire vacation in that hotel, with swimming baths and saunas and massage rooms. As for the choice on the television, it was extraordinary. Far too much choice, in my opinion. I tried looking at it but found I did not care for it with those commercials shouting at you all the time.

In the evening, I examined carefully the options for my supper. I was used to hotels with a restaurant, but this hotel seemed to have four restaurants of varying formality and ethnicity. I decided to try the European Bistro, and I am afraid this is where my prejudices resurfaced. I am not an extravagant man but, by virtue of my work, I have naturally eaten out much of the time. I did not eat at expensive restaurants, but I ate at good ones, restaurants I had come to know well over a period of many years. I was familiar with all the main cuisines of Europe and I have to say that this monstrosity bore no relationship to any of them. Everything was a bastardised version of something else. There was nothing technically wrong with it, I suppose, other than that it was anodyne and pretended to an authenticity it did not possess. On top of that, the portions were so large they were positively obscene. I could not possibly eat it all, yet felt guilty about leaving it.

It was even worse at breakfast the next day. I took severe umbrage at something that called itself a Continental Breakfast. An altercation with the restaurant manager ensued. What did they mean by describing an orange juice, croissant and coffee as a Continental breakfast? Which continent were they talking about? Not my continent, certainly. I have eaten breakfast throughout Europe and the first thing I would say is that it differs widely from country to country. You would not think of offering a Continental Lunch or a Continental Dinner, so why offer a Continental Breakfast? This is what I mean about the Americans. There is no respect for accuracy, for history, for tradition. Everything has to change; everything has to become their version of whatever it was to start with; everything has to conform to some image, no matter how tenuous the connection with reality.

After this so-called breakfast, I walked out to the street and prepared myself for a day in the city. I had spent much of my life walking the streets of different cities, absorbing the atmosphere, observing the life. So I was happy to spend the day doing the same thing in New York. I say 'New York', but I mean Manhattan. I never left Manhattan and I have to say that, if the variety of life there is matched by the other boroughs, it is a remarkably diverse city.

I was astonished at the vitality of the city, the sheer energy of it. I suppose I am not a particularly energetic person myself. I am not lazy, but I do things at my own pace, which is a measured pace. No one did anything at a measured pace in New York. It was at double time, like one of those speeded-up old films. It seemed so frenetic. I found myself exhausted just watching it. I could see no way I could live life that way myself, or would want to. If that was what it was like on a Sunday, I asked myself, what on earth would it be like during the week? Surely people could not physically live this way seven days a week, but apparently they did.

I found myself examining the people I passed, looking into their eyes, and I did not like what I saw. I noticed a great deal of tension, of desperation almost, a lack of relaxation, a lack of what I would describe as normality. I was not surprised. You cannot live that sort of life and be relaxed: it is not possible. There was such a wide variety of people too, from every conceivable race under the sun, far more than I had seen together in one place before. Of course, much of this had to do with America's history of enslavement and imperialism. I was aware of that. But I also had to accept the fact that millions of people had positively chosen to live in America. My own brother, for a start. However mistaken I thought they might have been, however selfish their motives, they had made the choice to go there and to stay there.

They had come from all over the world, but many of them had come from Europe. Where was their homeland? From which particular European disaster or oppression did they flee? Did they feel at home here? Did they feel American? If so, why did I not feel French? Why had I not subsumed myself in France as they had appeared to enter into the spirit of America? I wondered whether this said something about America, or about France, or about me. Yet again, I was forced to consider the question of home. Why would I feel at home in Paris if I did not feel French? But, if I was not French, what was I? Nothing, really. I was a leftist, but that was a state of mind, not of domicile. Where did I belong? Everywhere and nowhere. If I were forced to anchor myself to geography, I could only say that I was a European. And I did not any longer know what that meant, other than that it was different from what it had meant for the previous half-century and doubtless different from what it would mean in the next half-century, whatever that might be.

I found it an exhausting day, a perplexing day. I could not exactly say what I felt at the end of it, except confusion. If I wanted evidence for my prejudices, and of course I did, then I found it. I found it most in those tired, tense, pressurised eyes. But when I compared those eyes with the dull, sullen, downcast eyes I so often encountered in eastern Europe, I found the comparison disconcerting. I had always attributed those eyes to the nature of the people themselves, but maybe I was wrong. Perhaps they stemmed from the ordered, predictable and — I do not like to say this — in some ways controlling aspects of the society, just as the tense eyes of New York perhaps stemmed from the energy and vibrancy of that society.

I ate early when I returned to the hotel and did not make the mistake of revisiting the Bistro. I chose instead something called a Diner, where I had a very acceptable steak. Whatever else, it felt American.

At 10:30 the following morning I presented myself at the offices of Bergelson & King on 5th

Avenue. I was trying hard to remind myself that this was my publication, that I did not need to sell it if I did not want to, and that I was therefore in charge of the situation, not this large American company. But I was feeling diffident and somewhat overawed. Life had not previously required me to engage with the snapping jaws of the corporate world and I found the prospect intimidating.

The first thing I saw when I entered the building was a large sign in the reception area saying 'Today Bergelson & King welcomes — ' and there at the top of the board was nearly my name: 'Felix Zhukovski of *Guide Jeune*', the last word sadly being inaccurate as well as misspelt. For a moment I was proud to see my visit so honoured, but then I became suspicious of the motives and felt it was part of some psychological ploy to flatter me into conceding more than I should. My name was familiar to the receptionist, as well it might have been since it was blazoned on the board next to her. I was ushered unctuously into an armchair, presented with a cup of coffee which I had not requested and assured that Mr Bergelson would be with me shortly. After a few minutes, a brisk businesslike woman emerged who announced that she was Mr Bergelson's PA and she escorted me in a noiseless lift to the sixth floor. There, she smiled me through the open door of a large office and I found myself in the presence of Mark Bergelson.

'Mark Bergelson,' he said to confirm the fact, extending an eager hand and a large smile towards me.

'Zhukovski,' I said.

'Good to meet you, Mr Zhukovski,' he said. That was an encouraging start. Bergelson showed every sign of being the sort of person who would call me Feliks immediately. Perhaps Mike Martins had briefed him on my sensibilities. Martins would be sympathetic enough to do that.

Bergelson was a small, dapper, balding man of perhaps 50. He was dressed in an expensive suit and smelt of aftershave, which I do not use myself. I felt shabby by comparison. I was also wearing a suit, the only one I possessed, which I had bought hurriedly in Warsaw about 15 years earlier when unexpectedly faced with a meeting with some government officials. I felt I was at a disadvantage already and Bergelson's self-confidence made me feel even more awkward. He was a bouncy little man, exuding energy. I was probably one of many meetings he had lined up for the day.

His office was large and light and expensively decorated. It had probably received more investment in the last six months than my apartment had in 36 years. It was not devoid of personality. There were several photographs of Bergelson with someone whom I supposed was Mrs Bergelson, along with assorted junior Bergelsons. There were a great many books, not all of them neatly arranged. It was rather a nice office. I expected to be shown to the chair on the opposite side of his desk, but instead Bergelson indicated a pair of comfortable armchairs. Another coffee arrived, again unrequested, but welcome as I had not had time to drink the first.

I was not sure what I was feeling by then. I was being accorded the respect that was my due, but did not know whether this was standard civility or an attempt at ingratiation. I felt like the head of some small country summoned to the White House to meet the President of the United States. It was flattering, suspicious and intimidating at the same time. After a few opening pleasantries, we turned to the matter in hand.

'So,' said Bergelson. 'I know you've met with Mike Martins and he tells me you are willing to discuss the sale of your guide.' He patted my book on the table next to him, presumably to establish that we were both discussing the same thing. 'I guess the first thing is for me to make you an offer.'

'Yes,' I said.

'Let me get straight to the point. We would like to pay you $300,000 to acquire the rights to your guide.'

$300,000! I had of course spent some time considering what price I might be offered and what price I might accept. The task was made harder by the fact that I had no means of making such an evaluation. I had thought that perhaps I might be offered about 500,000 francs, which would equate to $75,000. Bergelson was offering me four times as much. I could not see that the *Guide* could conceivably be worth that much and part of me instantly assumed that Bergelson had got his figures wrong. But another part of me distrusted American businessmen and felt they did not often make that kind of mistake and that, if I was being offered $300,000, perhaps it was worth a great deal more (although I could not see how) and I was being cheated. I decided not to give a direct answer for the time being.

'Yes I see,' I said. 'Perhaps, Mr Bergelson, you could tell me how you are sure this is the correct amount.'

'The correct amount?' Bergelson looked nonplussed. 'I'm not sure there is any such thing as the correct amount.'

'Surely there must be,' I said.

'All I can say,' said Bergelson, 'is that there is the price we are prepared to pay and the price you are prepared to accept, and hopefully they are about the same, in which case that is the correct amount.'

I found this a strange thing to say. I know I am not a businessman, but surely the world could not conduct itself in this imprecise way. 'But it must have a value,' I said. 'Everything has a value.'

'That is the value,' said Bergelson. 'What I just said.' He was showing signs of exasperation, but I did not see why I should appease it.

'Perhaps you could tell me,' I said, 'how you managed to arrive at such a valuation.'

'Well,' said Bergelson with a suppressed irritation, 'as you know, we are keen to have a travel guide to eastern Europe on our list. We've costed what it would take in terms of ground-work and research to start a new one from scratch. We've taken into account the sales base of your guide, and the goodwill in the business, and the fact we would be quicker into the market if we did it that way. We've estimated how many copies we can sell: here in the States, in Europe and elsewhere. We're planning to wholesale it at $3. It will cost about 80 cents to produce. So we can estimate how much we'll make from it if we amortise the purchase price over, say, five years. And when we put that information together, $300,000 seemed like a fair price. Does that satisfy you?'

No it did not. I was bewildered by this. I did not understand half of it. I seized on the one thing I did understand although, in retrospect, it was not a sensible point to make in such a negotiation.

'You cannot possibly produce it for 80 cents.'

'On the contrary,' said Bergelson. 'You cannot possibly produce it for 80 cents. We can.'

'But how?' I asked. 'I mean, costs may be lower here than in Paris, but how can you possibly do that?'

'In China,' he said.

So that was what would happen. My guide would now be printed in China. Goodbye Benoît Picard, hello Lao Tseu. I thought about old man Picard. What would he have had to say about it? About our guide to communist Europe being printed in China? He would probably have said that the Chinese had always been deviationists. Now eastern Europe was deviationist as well. There was a certain symmetry to it.

'Oh,' I said.

'I appreciate this is a lot of change for you to grasp,' said Bergelson, 'but that is the way things

78

will be. I think it's a fair price. Do you accept it?'

'Yes,' I said.

'Do we have a deal?'

'Yes,' I said again, and he extended the eager hand once more and shook mine.

'I was wondering,' I said, 'whether there might be a continuing role for me in the future, in some advisory capacity?' A friend in Paris had assured me that this arrangement was normal when a business changed hands and I felt it might give me an easier transition into retirement.

'No,' said Bergelson; 'no, I don't think that will be possible. I'm sorry.'

'So you are planning to make major changes?'

'Yes we are. As you will appreciate, events are moving rapidly in eastern Europe. The guide must reflect these changes. It's already out of date, as I'm sure you must be aware. And some parts of the commentary just won't do.'

'Which parts?'

Bergelson picked up the guide next to him and opened it at a marked page. He had clearly been prepared for the question. 'The German Democratic Republic,' he read, 'has experienced a continuing economic miracle since 1945 and is now universally recognised as one of the most advanced states in the world.'

I waited. 'Do you see anything wrong with that statement?' he asked.

'It is not from the current edition,' I said.

'Yeah, well do you see anything wrong with it otherwise?'

79

'Well obviously I do. The GDR does not exist any more.'

'Apart from that?'

'Not really. What do you find wrong with it?'

'It's complete crap.'

'That may be your opinion, but it is not mine.'

'I don't think you'll find it's a question of opinion,' said Bergelson.

I should have been furious, but I was not. I could have thought that Bergelson had waited until he had secured the deal and had chosen that moment to insult me, but I did not. There was an honesty and a directness to Bergelson that I found appealing. I had still not signed any agreement. I could still change my mind. Yet that had not deterred him from stating his opinion. Besides which, when I had heard my own words read back to me like that, I was no longer sure I agreed with them myself, not that I would tell him so. Had I believed that? If I was truthful, I had been aware for many years of a certain contradiction in what I had written, what I had been expected to write. On the one hand, I was claiming that the communist system had proved at least the economic equal of capitalism. On the other hand, I was asserting that capitalism put too much of a premium on economic achievement and that the true measure of communism's success was in social progress. Technically it was possible for both those claims to be true, but arguing both of them with equal vigour did suggest a fundamental doubt as to which of the two statements was true and an indecisive hope that, if both were asserted, one of them might

80

eventually prove to be true. I was no longer certain that either had turned out to be true.

'You have to face it, Feliks — may I call you Feliks?' Bergelson did not wait for an answer. 'That world is over. It's not coming back.'

'Maybe it will not change as much as you think.' I was not confident in that statement; on the whole it seemed likely to change even more.

'When dams burst,' said Bergelson, 'they burst. Now, shall we have some lunch?'

I allowed him to take me out to lunch. We went to a smart, and no doubt very expensive, restaurant nearby. The food was surprisingly good; very good indeed. I was touched by the gesture. Bergelson did not need to do that. I expected him to show me the door as soon as an agreement had been reached. I expressed my gratitude.

'Oh well,' he said, 'I could hardly drag you all the way across the Atlantic just for that meeting. The least I can do is give you a good lunch. Besides, I really do appreciate that you are selling us the *Guide*. I should have said it before, but I recognise this is your life's work and that it must take a lot for you to part with it to anyone, let alone to some shark in New York.' He smiled as he said this.

'You manage to disguise your shark tendencies quite well,' I said.

'I don't see why business should not be civilised. There do not need to be winners and losers. Sometimes both sides are winners; sometimes they are both losers. In this case, I think we are both winners. I doubt that anyone else would have offered you nearly as much, and I don't deny that, if we do our job properly, we will make good profits out of it for a long time to come. That's the sort of deal I like.'

'I will drink to that.' It was champagne again. I had nothing but disdain for champagne socialists, and this was becoming a habit. 'Tell me,' I said: 'you are Jewish, I suppose. How long have your family been over here? Why did they come here?' It was unusual for me to ask questions like this. Normally I did not enquire too much into people's lives. I preferred to discuss ideas.

'Yes,' he said, 'I am Jewish. My grandparents left Russia in the 1930s to escape Stalin's purges. My parents came with them. I was born in New York City myself.'

'And do you feel American?'

'Yes of course.' Bergelson seemed surprised to be asked. 'I feel absolutely American. So did my parents. So did my grandparents, come to that. They never spoke English too well, but they were so grateful to America for taking them in. Why do you ask the question?'

'Because, although I have lived in Paris for over 40 years, I find I do not feel French. Paris does not seem like home to me, the way that New York does to you.'

'Home is where the heart is,' said Bergelson. 'My heart is right here in this city. Where's yours?'

I was taken aback. I never cease to be astonished by the power of clichés. First Sandrine Lefèvre and now Mark Bergelson. Where was my heart? I did not think it was a question I had ever been asked, or had asked myself. If I had been forced to answer, I would probably have said that it was in the same place as my head, but I was no longer sure where my head was.

'I do not know,' I said.

'With a name like Zhukovski, I imagine you were not French originally. Where's your family from?'

'Poland. I was born in Łódź. My family was Jewish too. Or partly Jewish. I am a quarter Jewish, to be precise.'

'So you were a Zhuravski once?'

'Yes. Or rather, my grandfather was.'

'Your father's father?'

'No, my mother's. I never knew my father.'

'Were you raised Jewish?'

'I was not raised anything. My grandfather abandoned Judaism when he married my grandmother, but the Church still did not like the fact she had married a Jew. My grandmother was bitter about that, and my mother too.'

'Did your family suffer in the war?'

'I do not know. I was sent away to Switzerland with my brother in 1939, although in my opinion that had nothing to do with the war. I never saw my mother again, nor any of my family. I do not know what happened to them.'

'I'm sorry,' said Bergelson, 'I did not mean to intrude. It's always such a difficult subject.'

'No, it is all right,' I said. 'I can discuss it. It is not something I am emotional about.'

'Of course, if your family were fully Jewish, it would be possible to find out what happened to many of them. There has been extensive research into victims of the Shoah, as I'm sure you know.'

'Thank you, but I am not sure it would help in my case. I find it such a strange subject, this question of race, when we are most of us a mixture of all sorts of things anyway. Take my family, for example. My mother did not look Jewish. She looked Polish. Yet she had a twin sister, Aunt Lilia, who looked entirely Jewish. How can that happen? They both had the same parents. They were twins, for goodness' sake. And the curious thing was that, although the two of them were extremely close, my mother identified herself as a Pole, whereas Aunt Lilia identified herself as a Jew. She married a Jew. She converted to Judaism. I have often wondered if she did that because of the way she looked.'

'When the Nazis invaded Poland,' said Bergelson, 'they had great trouble knowing who was Jewish and who was not. I mean, in many cases it was obvious, but in many it was not. And it was so important for them to know, so they could be sure that the *Lebensraum* would be ethnically pure. In the end, they measured the size of people's heads and the size of their noses and that was it. Race reduced to a series of measurements. A millimetre one side of the line and you were Jewish; a millimetre the other side and you weren't.'

'I do not know where that would have left my family,' I said. 'One twin sister on one side of the line and the other on the other, I expect. Complete lunacy.'

'I think that always happens with truly evil

regimes,' said Bergelson. 'They always have some system of belief that justifies what they do, that has some superficial plausibility, that makes you say 'yes, all right, I don't go along with it myself, but I can see why you might be doing it'. But then they go and do something absolutely insane, something that is literally mad. Hitler was like that and personally I don't feel Stalin was any different.'

This was a delicate subject for me and I did not feel we had reached it by accident. I felt that Bergelson had steered the conversation towards that comparison to put me on the spot. I felt uncomfortable, as I always did when the subject of Stalin was mentioned. The fact is that, when I first became politically conscious in the late '40s, I greatly admired Stalin. That was not unusual. Almost all of my generation who were on the left did the same. When Stalin died, we felt an immense sense of loss. The turning point came when Khrushchev denounced Stalin's so-called crimes at the 20th Party Congress in 1956. That speech tore us apart. The hardliners thought it was treachery; the revisionists accepted that Stalin had made grave errors that needed to be corrected. Families were divided. Communism, certainly in the West, was never the same again.

I was not sure what I thought. I agreed with the revisionists that mistakes had been made, but that was inevitable with the scale and ambition of the enterprise. I was forced to acknowledge that there had been a grievous loss of life and liberty under Stalin, but I always said that you could not expect to make an omelette without breaking eggs. I also felt that dirty linen should not be washed in public; it only gave comfort to our enemies. I never did have a decided view on the matter. I suppose that, on the whole, I must have sided with the revisionists. After 1956, when everyone changed whom they saw, changed whom they drank with, I saw less of my old Stalinist friends and spent more time in the company of other leftists. But, even now in 1991, I retained a residue of respect for Stalin and was not prepared to put him on a par with Hitler.

'There are still millions of people in Russia who would vote for him,' I said.

'I dare say there are still millions of people in Germany who would vote for Hitler,' said Bergelson. 'That's beside the point.'

We continued the debate while Bergelson settled the bill and then we were standing outside on the pavement, preparing to say goodbye. He would not let the subject drop.

'We have a lot in common,' he said, 'but our experiences are not the same. Your family's world was destroyed by Hitler; mine was destroyed by Stalin. I guess that gives us each a different perspective. But, as far as I'm concerned, they were both monsters, both psychopaths. Morally it would have made as much sense for the Allies to have joined up with Hitler against Stalin. Not strategically, maybe, but morally. There was nothing to choose between them.'

'I know which one I would have chosen to live under.'

'Yes, Feliks. But you didn't, though, did you?'

5

On the plane from New York to Columbus the next day, I reflected on Bergelson's parting remark. As a series of words, it sounded harsh, unsympathetic, critical, yet it had not felt like that at the time. Bergelson had spoken gently and kindly. Like Dufour earlier, he had hinted that he understood me better than I understood myself. In one sense this was intensely irritating. How could anyone know me better than I knew myself? But the simplicity and relevance of his question would not go away. Why had I not chosen to live under communism? Or, as Bergelson had implied, why had I chosen not to live under communism?

I was not sure I had asked myself that question, which seemed a peculiar omission. Now that I did ask it, I found it hard to explain in particular why I had not gone back to Poland after the war. It would have been the natural thing to do. I was Polish. I had been separated involuntarily and unhappily from my home and family and friends throughout my adolescence. Surely, at the first available opportunity, I would have returned home. By then, of course, Poland was coming under communist control, but that should have been an added attraction for me, not a deterrent.

My adult life had always made sense to me. I had left Basle and crossed into France in 1947 because I needed work and I disliked Switzerland and my aunt and uncle wanted me to leave. I had come to Paris because Fernand Meurice had asked me to. I had started the *Guide* because *La Vague de la Gauche* had collapsed and because it made best use of my interests and experience. I had remained in Paris because it was convenient. I was now selling the *Guide* because it had become impossible, both practically and emotionally, to continue with it. Yes, this was all quite logical. Yet, in another sense, it was purely a retrospective rationale for what had actually happened. It explained how I got to B from A. It did not explain why, when I was at A, I did not choose C or D. Every life has its own continuity. Every stage of life foreshadows its next stage, otherwise it would not reach it. But perhaps the choices that are not made, the options that are not taken, are as revealing as the ones that are.

I remembered conversations with Aunt Maria in Basle at the end of the war. When hostilities ended in Europe, the first thing my aunt did — under severe pressure from her husband, no doubt — was to write to my mother to make arrangements for my return. There was no reply. There had been some letters from Mama during the war: I never saw them, which, in retrospect, seems strange, but Aunt Maria told me they had come and that Mama sent her love. Now there was nothing. Aunt Maria wrote several times more. She sent photographs of me. On one occasion, I was asked to write myself, begging to be allowed to come home. When there was still no reply, she wrote to her other sister, Mama's twin Lilia. Again there was no reply. We did not have a telephone in Poland, but Aunt Maria contacted all sorts of authorities there asking for news of Teresa Zhukovska. She received no information. This went on for months and months. I could still remember what I had overheard one evening when I was crouched outside the sitting room door in Basle.

'He can't stay here,' Uncle Ernst had said in his aggressive way.

'What are we to do then?' Aunt Maria simpered to her husband.

'Send him back to Poland.'

'Ernst, dear, you cannot send a 15-year-old child back to Poland at this moment. Not unless we can find someone to take care of him.'

'Don't be so weak, Maria. He can fend for himself. Millions of poor Germans are having to. He's only Polish, for God's sake.'

'Yes I know, dear, but he is my nephew.'

This angered me: not what my aunt said, but what she failed to say. She was Polish too. How dare she let him speak to her like that? I suppose, though, that I should give her credit for standing up for me. I do not know what followed that exchange, but Aunt Maria must have won her point because I was not repatriated. I was allowed to stay on sufferance. Shortly afterwards, Uncle Ernst made it plain that I would leave their house as soon as my education was completed and that I need not entertain the idea of attending college or university unless I earned the money to pay for it myself. I had no means of doing that.

I could clearly remember, as I overheard that conversation, silently begging 'don't send me back; don't send me back'. And it was not because I was happy in Basle, because I was not. And I do not think it was because of the uncertainty of what awaited me in Poland. Throughout this whole period, I had known that my aunt would receive no reply to her letters to my mother. It was not that I believed that Mama was dead, or that something had happened to her. No, I was firmly convinced that our mother had not wanted us, that she had packed Woodrow and me off to Switzerland to get us out of the way. In that case, why would she want us to return? It seemed perfectly logical to me. I imagined that Mama was at home in Łódź, deliberately choosing not to respond to Aunt Maria's letters. It did not occur to me that she might not have received them. I am not sure I even understood at that age that letters were sometimes not received. Someone sent you a letter; you received it; it was simple.

The more I considered the matter on the flight to Columbus, the more I became convinced that the reason I had not returned to Poland had little to do with communism, little intrinsically to do with Poland, but a great deal to do with Mama. It was my conviction that Mama had abandoned me in 1939 and that Woodrow had abandoned me in 1941. My subsequent life had been constructed on those assumptions. I had tried to obliterate everything that reminded me of my family. I had made no attempt to discover whether I still had a family. Yet — and this was curious, to say the least — on the two occasions in my life when the possibility of seeing Mama or Woodrow had presented itself, I had jumped at the opportunities. When Dufour offered to locate Woodrow, I said yes, and I was now on my way to see him. Once a long time ago, back in 1968, the opportunity had appeared to arise to find Mama. And again I seized it, although in the event it came to nothing.

So why should I take these opportunities when they were offered to me, yet make no effort to initiate them myself? One would almost think I had a mental block on the subject. What in my life had I ever initiated? As I now saw it, from the moment I had left the platform of Warsaw Central station in 1939, I had seldom made a positive, significant choice. Things had happened to me. I had gone along with them. I suppose it had been some sort of positive choice to move to France in 1947 and again, in 1955, to start the *Guide*. But both these choices had been directed by circumstance and by the opinions and urgings of others. It had been made easy for me. At no point had I said to myself: 'this is my life; this is what I want to do with it; this is what I will make happen'.

Looked at in this way, I had never decided not to return to Poland. I had an emotional reluctance to do so because of my feelings for Mama and my conviction that she had not wanted me. I had a practical reluctance to do so because other, easier alternatives had presented themselves. But I had never decided not to; I had made no sort of decision, merely neglected to make one. In one sense, I felt relieved by this. However gently it had been expressed, Bergelson's remark had stung me. Why indeed had I never chosen to live in a communist country, more especially since one of them was the country of my birth? Now I could see the answer to that question. But the answer disconcerted me as much as the question. For my whole adult life I had subscribed to an ideology that advocated change, radical change, as the solution to society's problems. Yet I did not welcome change in my own life. I resisted it. Put that way, I was as much of a conservative as those on the right I had always despised. The major changes in my life had been forced on me, and there had been no changes at all for 36 years. I did not like change. I did not like the changes that were being forced on me now.

I wondered whether I would be able to discuss these things with Woodrow. I thought not. Woodrow and I were different. Perhaps having different fathers had something to do with it. Back in Łódź, he was always outdoors, playing in the street with his friends, going on adventures. He could not wait to leave school. He wanted to work. He was apprenticed to a furniture maker at the time we had to leave. I, on the other hand, was usually indoors. Even at that age, I was reading, studying. I liked school. I did not have many friends there, but neither did I have enemies. I was self-contained. If I wanted company I saw my cousin Mordechaj, Aunt Lilia's son, who lived down the street. That was someone else I had not seen for decades. I wondered what had happened to him.

When I first heard we were going to Switzerland, I was so excited. There was no time for contemplation. One day I heard we were going and the next day we went. At the time I did not understand that Mama wanted rid of us; that realisation came later, and the hurt that went with it. That is when it stopped being an adventure. For Woodrow, I think it was always an adventure. I do not remember him being unhappy in Basle, although he disliked our uncle as much as I did. He was much older, of course. He went to work as soon as we arrived, making furniture. During the day I never saw him, but in the evenings it was different. We were not encouraged to share the company of our aunt and uncle, except at mealtimes. Sometimes we were summoned to hear the radio news, after which Uncle Ernst would remark with satisfaction on German progress and remind us how lucky we were that the Germans were providing the organisation and strength for our country that it had so woefully failed to provide for itself.

Uncle Ernst was one of the few overt Nazi sympathisers I encountered in Switzerland. He was German by birth and had come to Basle to work, so perhaps that was not surprising. More surprising was the fact that Aunt Maria had married him. Woodrow told me they had met in Łódź towards the end of the First World War, when Uncle Ernst was serving in the German army. That was still more surprising and would account for why Aunt Maria should have no desire to return to Poland. She would have been about 20 at the time, and Uncle Ernst several years older. Now I would say that Aunt Maria was a frightened, neurotic woman who had married an older bully for security and got what she deserved. At the time, I could not think things like this. But I did see a highly strung, nervous woman, always sad, always doing what her husband told her to do and thinking what he told her to think. Uncle Ernst, who worked in a bank although not in any exalted capacity, was cold, precise and meticulous, utterly inaccessible. He had a slavish addiction to order and control. Their house was gloomy and forbidding, full of dark, heavy furniture and containing no joy whatsoever. It was not the happiest of households in which to spend one's teenage years.

School came as something of a relief. There were a few children who were on the German side, or whose parents were, but most were firm supporters of the Allies. As a Pole, I attracted a certain sympathy; I think I had some sort of cachet even. Most of the time I was left alone to pursue my studies. When the school day finished, I came back to my aunt's house to do my homework. When Woodrow returned from his work, we all had supper together and then Woodrow and I would be on our own. Sometimes we talked. Sometimes we would read. Woodrow had never been one for reading, but now he had discovered a library to fuel his dreams of America and was devouring it at every opportunity. Sometimes he would take me out into the city. It must have been boring for him; I am sure he would have wanted to go drinking with his friends and not be encumbered by a 10-year-old brother. But he was good to me like that. He looked after me, which made his subsequent neglect all the more surprising and painful.

The thing I remember most about Basle is the bells, all those bells. I must have been able to hear five different bells from the house, tolling each quarter hour through the day and night, all at precisely the same time. On one sleepless night I calculated how many strokes of a bell I would hear if I stayed in Switzerland for ten years. I cannot remember the exact answer, but I think it was about one and a half million. There had been bells in Łódź, of course, and there were to be bells in Paris and perhaps as many of them. But they did not sound the same. They were more individualistic, less well co-ordinated, more melodic. For five different bells to toll the same quarter hour would take as long as ten minutes. Only in Switzerland did they clang at the same time; only there was life so rigidly divided into segments. I came to hate the bells of Basle.

But Woodrow left in 1941 and everything was different after that. I am never likely to forget the manner of his leaving, the drama of it. It had been a perfectly ordinary day in March, a Thursday I think. We were seated around the heavy oak table, eating our evening meal with Aunt Maria and Uncle Ernst. There was little conversation; there seldom was. Uncle Ernst would hold forth with his opinions and the rest of us were expected to sit there and agree with them. On this occasion, he was expounding with typical vigour on the deficiencies of the Jewish race and on Herr Hitler's admirable plans for addressing them, when Woodrow suddenly slammed his glass down and said 'shut up you fucking bastard'. Well, you can imagine the atmosphere in that room. Uncle Ernst was speechless with rage, the only time I did find him speechless. Aunt Maria did not say anything. Woodrow was not in the least perturbed. He looked directly at my uncle and said, slowly and calmly: 'not only are your views poisonous, but the fact you have chosen to utter them in front of three people who are all partly Jewish themselves makes them doubly offensive'.

Uncle Ernst's face had been red with fury. Now, his jaw dropped in amazement. His head turned slowly to look at his petrified wife. Then it turned back to regard the two of us.

'What did you say?'

'You heard me,' said Woodrow.

Uncle Ernst turned back to look at his wife. 'Tell me, my dear,' he said, 'that this outrageous allegation is not true.'

Aunt Maria had turned as white as snow and was biting her lip in anxiety. 'Not true,' she murmured. 'Certainly not true. Quite untrue. Not true at all.'

'Thank you, my dear. I knew you'd be able to reassure me.' If I had been Uncle Ernst, I would not have felt remotely reassured, but fortunately I was not Uncle Ernst.

My uncle then addressed Woodrow. 'Herr Zhukovski, I have welcomed you into my house as a refugee, as a member of our family in his hour of need. We have fed you and sheltered you, and you have repaid us by uttering the most filthy and repugnant calumny against my dear wife that it is possible for a decent person to imagine. You will leave my house forthwith. I do not expect to find you here in the morning. And perhaps you will care to reflect on the distress you have caused with your revolting lie.'

Woodrow did not reply. He rose from the table and walked out of the house. I was left alone with my aunt and uncle, which was the last place I wanted to be. I was terrified they would ask me to leave too. Or that Uncle Ernst would ask me to deny Woodrow's statement. I mumbled my apologies and left the room. I was asleep when Woodrow came back. He woke me and put a finger to my lips.

'I'm leaving, Feliks,' he said.

'Where are you going?'

'To France. I'm going to join the Resistance.'

'Can I come with you?'

'No, Feliks; I'm sorry, but you can't. It will be dangerous. You're better off here. You'll be all right. I'll come when I can. I'll write. Don't worry. I'll still look after you.' And he was gone.

Now I was about to see him again for the first time since that promise.

The plane had begun its descent to Columbus Airport. Soon I would see Woodrow again. Once I knew where he was, I had thought of him as the one who had taken the easy route, who had chosen the soft option of America and had fallen upon the bosom of the consumer society, whereas I had made the harder choice and had remained true to my beliefs and principles. Now I thought that I had made no choice at all; he was the one who had done that. And remembering that last night in Basle, and what Woodrow must have done afterwards, I wondered if he had not shown more courage in a single moment than I had in my life.

I had not thought how Woodrow and I would meet at the airport. We would be most unlikely to recognise each other. Fortunately he had been more practical and, as I left the baggage area and went into the concourse, I saw a large handwritten sign that read 'Zhukovski', as if I were a minor dignitary awaiting a courtesy car. When he saw me making towards him, he dropped the sign, rushed up to me and gave me the biggest hug you could imagine.

It nearly knocked me off my feet. There had always been a great physical difference between us and age had accentuated it. Woodrow was a bear of a man now, nearly bald and with a big, round, beaming face. He was warm, assured and expressive — all the things that I am not. Next to him I seemed small and inconsequential, with my slim build, neat appearance and glasses. I was very much the younger brother, but at least I still had my hair.

'Feliks!' He pushed me back so he could look at me, but still kept his hands on my shoulders. I was beginning to feel embarrassed. I did not know what other people would be thinking. 'Jeez,

Feliks, it's good to see you.'

He was speaking to me in English, with some trace of a European accent. When I had telephoned him, we had spoken in Polish, as we always had. Now, on home territory, he had resumed his new identity so thoroughly that it did not appear to have occurred to him that I might not speak English. My accent was even more pronounced.

'It is good to see you too, Woodrow.'

'Hey, forget the Woodrow. It's Woody now. Has been for years. Everyone calls me Woody.'

'I am still Feliks,' I said.

'Yeah, I can tell you're still Feliks. Wouldn't want you any other way. Here, let me take your bag. The car's a little way off.'

I do not know why I let him take my bag, but I did. I felt strange. Somehow none of this seemed the slightest bit real. We walked to the car exchanging pleasantries about the journey and the weather, neither wanting to broach the more serious subjects so soon. It was a large car, a sort of glorified military vehicle with every conceivable gadget. I had never seen a car like that before. I had never owned a car myself. In fact, I did not know how to drive. I had never needed to learn. I could not imagine driving a behemoth of a vehicle like this. Woodrow put my bag in the back. We climbed up into soft luxurious seats and he eased the car out of the car park.

'Let me tell you what I thought,' he said. 'There's so much we've got to catch up on, Feliks, but I thought we might leave that for tomorrow. It would be kinda hard to jump into that stuff straight away. Is that all right with you?'

'Fine,' I said.

'Good. Well, let me take you to my home. It's about half an hour away, on the other side of town. Wanda is there. She's dying to meet you. You'll like Wanda, Feliks. I know you'll like her.'

'I am sure I will,' I said.

'Good. Then we'll have a light lunch at home. In the afternoon, we need to take care of two of the grandchildren. We thought we'd go to a theme park nearby and we thought you might like that too, Feliks. It would be the chance for you to see a bit of real America. But there's no need to if you don't want to. Wanda can take the kids herself and we can do something else.'

'No, that would be fine,' I said. 'I would like to do that.'

'Good. This evening, we've got the family coming over. Wanda's cooking a huge meal for everyone. I hope it won't embarrass you, Feliks, but they wanted to meet you. We're all so psyched about seeing you.'

'That is kind of you, Woody. I would love to meet them.'

'Good. Good.'

After a lapse of 50 years, we had fallen back easily into the familiar routine: the elder brother full of plans, proposing action, and the younger brother acquiescing. I was finding it hard to take in what he was saying. I was overwhelmed by seeing him again. I was remembering our last goodbye in a small bedroom in wartime

Switzerland, and looking out of the car window at suburban America drifting past on the freeway, and trying to reconcile those two images and to remind myself that we were the same two people.

'Do you have a large family?' I asked.

'Large enough. Three kids and seven grandchildren. Marvin's our eldest boy. He's in real estate, like I was. He's married to Alaina and they have three kids. Then there's Kellie. She's married to Elliot and they've got two. They're both teachers. Kellie and Elliot, that is, not the kids. Then there's Bradley. He's in IT and married to Larissa. They've got two as well. That's the pair we're taking to the theme park this afternoon.'

'I wonder you can remember them all,' I said. 'Do they live nearby?'

'Oh yeah,' said Woody. 'All on the same side of the city. We're real close.'

'That must be nice.'

'Yeah, it's good.'

'And you say you were in real estate, Woody?'

'That's right. I'm retired. Been retired six years now. I had my own real estate business. Marvin runs it now. Nothing big — wouldn't want you to get the wrong idea, Feliks — just a good solid little business. We've done all right out of it.'

'I am glad,' I said.

'You retired yet, Feliks? How old are you now? Sixty-one, I reckon. Must be coming up to it.'

'Yes, I am expecting to retire soon. As a matter of fact, I have been in New York to discuss the

101

sale of my business.'

'You have your own business? Never thought you'd be an entrepreneur, Feliks, but that's great. I want to hear all about it.'

So I told him about the *Guide*. I did not mention anything about the political side. There did not seem any point in risking an argument so soon. Nor did I quibble at the use of the word 'entrepreneur', although it was not a term I would think of using to describe myself. Those debates could wait until the next day. For now it was wiser to emphasise the similarities, spurious though they might be, because there were few enough of them.

'So soon I will have a lot of time on my hands,' I said.

'I wouldn't bet on it,' said Woody. 'I've never been so busy in my life as the last six years.'

'Really? What do you find to do?'

'What don't I find to do? The family take up a lot of time. We've usually got one or more of the grandchildren round our place, or we're picking them up and taking them somewhere. Then there's the golf club. I play golf several times a week. Do you play golf, Feliks?'

'No; I do not.'

'Pity. We could have had a game tomorrow. Anyway, what else is there? There's the shopping of course; plenty of that. Wanda enjoys her shopping and often I go with her. We've got some terrific malls near here, Feliks. Maybe we'll take one in tomorrow. What else? Well, there's the church, of course. That's more

Wanda's thing than mine, but we're both pretty involved in that.'

'That doesn't sound like you, Woody. You always hated church.'

'Yeah, well it's not the same thing here.'

'Are you Catholic?'

'No. Shit, no. We didn't exactly grow up with any great love of the Catholic Church, did we? No. Wanda is Baptist, so when we married, I sort of became one too.'

'You have been married a long time?'

'Forty-four years and I don't regret a day of it.'

'You met over here?'

'Yeah. I came over right after the war. Went to Cleveland originally, for a year or so. Then I found a job in real estate down here and met Wanda the moment I arrived. We were married six months later. Haven't looked back since.'

So, at about the same time as I was gaining my first experience of political activism in the Peugeot works at Sochaux, Woody was starting a career in real estate in Ohio and marrying Wanda. It was not that our lives had slightly diverged and had then grown apart. The difference was already radical in 1947. Our lives had split completely from the moment Woody had kissed me goodbye in 1941.

'You make it sound like the American dream,' I said.

'That's exactly what it's been,' said Woody. 'Of course there've been a few ups and downs. You expect that. I've skipped those bits. But, yep, it's been exactly like I knew it would be. Best thing I

103

ever did, coming here.'

We had turned off the freeway and were driving down a series of roads of diminishing width. The area was a collection of housing estates, some grand and imposing with their own security gates, others more modest, but all new, all recently carved out of virgin territory. We drove two kilometres without passing a single shop and then Woody turned into a small cul-de-sac and stopped outside a house that looked like a mansion to me, but was about in the middle of the scale for the neighbourhood. It was one of those neo-Georgian affairs, with colonnades and a portico and a double garage, that I had seen subliminally on American soap operas on TVs propped in the corner of so many European bars. I knew he would live in a house like that.

'Honey, we're here.' Woody led me in through the front door and Wanda emerged from the sitting room to greet me. I did not know what I was supposed to do. Should I kiss her or something? Wanda solved the problem by putting out her hand and clasping mine.

'Feliks,' she said, 'it's so good to meet you. I've heard so much about you.'

She could not have heard much, I thought, and nothing at all since the age of 11. Still, I supposed one had to say something and I had not managed to think of anything.

'I am pleased to be here,' I said.

Wanda reminded me of a marginally younger version of Nancy Reagan. Everything about her was perfectly in place from her coiffed hair, to her immaculate make-up, to her manicured hands, to her elegant clothes, yet she did not seem real. I felt as if I was talking to an elaborate life-sized doll, whose manufacturers had used the latest technology to mimic the most minute detail of human physiognomy and had so nearly got it right. She complemented her setting exactly. I was beginning to feel as if the whole of American society was an almost successful attempt to replicate life.

Everything in the house was sumptuous to my eyes. It was lavish beyond anything I had encountered before, yet — on the evidence of the other housing estates we had passed — there was nothing special, nothing exceptional about it. It was also anaemic. Despite the fact that every room was filled with family photographs and with trophies of the lives the family had led, it seemed curiously impersonal. Everything had been arranged for effect. Nothing was a millimetre out of place. In the en suite bathroom of my perfect bedroom was a set of towels with the initial 'F' embroidered on them. Since, as far as I knew, none of the family's names had that initial, I could only assume that these towels had been procured especially for my visit. Or perhaps Wanda had found a job lot of towels monogrammed with every letter from A to Z in one of her shopping malls. I suppose I should have felt honoured by the gesture, but instead it struck me as a pointless extravagance.

Suddenly, and for the first time, my Paris apartment began to feel like home, or something close to home. All its eccentricities and untidiness, its frugality and its imperfections, began now to seem desirable. I wondered whether, for me, home could only be defined by eliminating what was not home, as this was not. I think, more than anything, it was the striving for an illusory perfection that repelled me. And, as I thought that, I could not help thinking that I had devoted my life to another credo that had sought perfection and one that had also proved illusory, so far at least.

We ate a simple lunch which, Wanda assured me, was a precaution against the feast planned for the evening and not a deficiency of hospitality on her part. Wanda asked Woody about my life, which was strange as I was sitting there and could perfectly well have told her myself. Instead I sat in silence and heard myself described as a business tycoon. I was not sure when would be the right moment to correct this misimpression. After lunch, the three of us got into the behemoth and drove through a further labyrinth of nearby housing estates before collecting a couple of children from a house similar to the one we had left. Ethan and Sierra, I think they were called, although this was the moment at which I started to get confused by the family names.

We drove for another half an hour until we arrived at a gaudy apparition called The Wild West Extravaganza. The children became agitated at this point and wanted to go on all the rides. Woody and Wanda were consumed with their excitement and went on most of the rides themselves. I had no desire to do that, so I wandered around and formed my own impressions.

The theme park purported to recreate the world of America's frontiersmen and women, of cowboys and Indians, of wide open spaces. It would give me the chance, Woody had said, to see a bit of real America. I could not see anything real about it. Many words could be used to describe the experience, few of them flattering, but real would not be one of them.

For most of my trip to America, I had found comparisons hard to make. It was such an alien world, with so few points of reference to my own experience. It stood separate, side by side with what I knew, but distinct, so that to compare the two seemed to have no validity. But the theme park was different. This was something that I did know about. I had spent much of my life visiting the tourist attractions of eastern Europe and commenting on them for my readers. There, history was not reinvented. There, history was what had happened, not what someone imagined had happened, or hoped had happened, or thought would be more commercially appealing if it had happened.

I did not know exactly what the Wild West had been like, of course, except that it had not been like this. Many people had died. Acres of land had been despoiled. Cultures and communities had been destroyed. That had been the reality. I noticed that the proprietors were generously donating one cent out of every dollar to a foundation that ran rehabilitation programmes for native Americans. I presumed this meant that

99 cents were going into the pockets of the descendants of those who had made the rehabilitation necessary in the first place. There were rides and sideshows and spectacles that could only have been a grotesque parody of the actual historical events, located in an area where — as far as I knew — they had never taken place anyway.

I had read once what had happened to the great vineyards of France. Centuries ago, cuttings from the French vines had been taken to America and had created the vineyards of California. Later, when phylloxera destroyed the French vineyards, cuttings from the American vines had been shipped back to France to replenish them. This seemed an apt metaphor for everything else in life. Vigorous European cuttings of so many things had been sent to America, where they had been grafted on to new stock, repackaged and given brand names, before being re-exported to Europe.

Would historical truth be the next casualty of this process? What would happen to Auschwitz, for example, if it fell into the hands of capitalist entrepreneurs? Would they turn it into a theme park? Would it be taken down, piece by piece, and reconstructed as a facsimile of itself, cleverly redesigned to improve traffic flow and maximise takings? Would they add a few extra features to make it more child friendly? Who could even use the term 'child friendly' in relation to Auschwitz?

The previous winter, during my quiet months, bored with endless cafés and political discussions, I had made a visit to Verdun for the weekend. The catacombs under the fortress of Verdun, which had been the impregnable headquarters of the French army as it resisted the German siege, had now been transformed into a visitor attraction. A small railway transported tourists round the hollowed-out cliffs. Vignettes of life in 1916 appeared under spotlights. Holograms of generals made rousing speeches, had arguments. I did not find it satisfactory.

And I wondered where it was that reality stopped and illusion took over. Auschwitz was real. There was no doubt about that. The Wild West Extravaganza was illusion. There was no doubt about that either. Verdun hovered somewhere between the two: not a travesty of reality, as this was, but hardly an authentic representation of it either. Time had something to do with it, of course. But the truth should not gradually become variable, or amenable to slander, the further back in time it lay. Yet it did. As the years went by, the slide into illusion began: the start of the process whereby commercial considerations compromised historical accuracy.

It seemed fundamental, this issue, because it had so much to do with what I disliked about America. This habit of seeing the world precisely as you wanted to see it, of bending the facts until they suited a particular explanation. The malleability of the truth. The contempt that greeted any opposing view. It was all dedicated to the same end: to seeing things in one way, the way the Americans saw them and wanted us to see them.

Woody and Wanda wanted to know how I had enjoyed The Wild West Extravaganza, and I replied that I had found it interesting, which was true. We piled back into the behemoth, drove around more freeways, deposited the grandchildren at their home and returned to the mansion. Wanda excused herself to deal with preparations for the evening. Woody kindly suggested that I might like a rest and a bath, which I certainly did. I was finding it hard to cope with all this energy.

The party started at 6. I imagined that we would drink for a few hours and then have something to eat, but the food arrived almost immediately and no one drank much, except me. I did not know whether this was because there were young children present, or because it was what they normally did. Personally I was not used to eating before 9 o'clock and found it rather strange. There was so much food too: it was a gargantuan feast. I had never seen anything like it.

When bigots make remarks such as that all Chinese people, or all black people, look alike to them and they cannot tell them apart, I am offended. Yet, I must confess, I could not tell these Americans apart. They all had perfect teeth. They all had neatly arranged hair. They all had matching casual clothes. They all had exactly the same conversation. After a while, I could not remember who they were. I became confused between the daughter and the daughters-in-law. I could not remember which was the teacher and which the IT man. I did not know whether

Amber and Dexter belonged to Marvin and Kellie or to Elliot and Alaina, or whether those two couples belonged to each other, or whether Amber and Dexter were brother and sister anyway. I expect I made any number of faux pas. No one appeared to mind.

'No, I'm Larissa. That's Bradley. He's my husband. You met Ethan and Sierra this afternoon. You all went to the theme park. You all had a real good time.'

'Does it snow in Europe, Great-Uncle Feliks?'

'So, of course I said to him 'well you stick to plastics, buddy, if you think there's money in it, but I'm getting the hell out'.'

'Why don't you look like Grandpa, Great-Uncle Feliks?'

'I do so much want to go to Paris. We went to Florida last year.'

'This is your first trip to the USA, I understand, Uncle Feliks. It's a great country, isn't it? You must love it here.'

'Have you never married?'

I was the centre of attention, of course. They had all come to see me, to meet this strange relic of old Europe who had crawled out of the family woodwork. I cannot say that I did not enjoy it. Maybe it helped that I had drunk more than the others. Certainly by the end of the evening I was quite merry. I seem to remember telling one of the children that there were bears in the woods outside Paris. I dare say he would have been told so many lies already that one more could do no harm. No one spoke to me of politics. The subject never arose. I do not know if this was because they had no interest in politics, or because it did not occur to them that I might have views that differed in any way from their own, or that anyone did. At any rate I was grateful for the omission.

I expect this sounds condescending. But I had to admit that these people, my family as I now had to think of them, were genuinely pleased to see me. They were friendly, generous with their suggestions that I must visit them on my next trip, and I did not sense that any of it was insincere. They were plain, uncomplicated people — if there are such things — who were glad to meet a long-lost relative. It seemed so simple for them, yet a great deal more complicated for me.

At 9 o'clock precisely everyone left, as if a klaxon had sounded, audible to everyone except me. In Paris the evening would just be starting. I was excused the clearing up and was installed in Woody's study with a large bourbon, a drink I had never sampled previously and of which I could become fond. I tried to sort out in my mind who these people were, and who was related to whom. Well, of course they were all related to each other. And to me, apparently. I wondered how I found it so easy to distinguish between intellectual concepts and could isolate all their nuances, yet found it so hard to differentiate people. After a while, Woody came into the room and perched on the edge of a chair.

'There's so much we've got to talk about, Feliks.'

'I know.'

'Well, that can wait until tomorrow.'

'I think it better.'

'I guess it's been a bit much for you.'

'Yes, it has rather.'

'Glad you came?'

I allowed rather too long a pause. 'Yes,' I said.

6

'How did you manage to track me down?' asked Woody.

It was the following morning and we were seated in the conservatory of the Glenvale Country Club, warmed by the pale sunshine of early spring. Outside, garishly dressed men of a certain age practised their putting on an immaculate green. I was glad I did not play golf. A silent waiter replenished our drinks: strong coffee for me and mineral water for Woody. His was the only black face I saw at the club all day. This was the private leisure world of moneyed, male America, the place where prosperous businessmen and retired businessmen retreated for the reaffirmation of an American dream that could exclude the uncomfortable elements of everyday life. Much as I did when I went drinking with old comrades in some grubby *zinc* in the 19th, I suppose. They were all white too. And male. I did not think myself a racist or a sexist and I doubt that Woody did either. That was not really the point. The process was a primeval bonding of old clans. It was depressing nevertheless.

'It is a strange story,' I replied. I recounted the tale of the visa application, the vituperative interview with Oberman and the mysterious Frenchman who had followed me and taken me for a drink. I did not go into the political details of the questioning, but I expect I dropped a few hints. I still did not want to tell Woody about my politics, but perhaps I hoped he would ask me.

'Hmmm,' he said. 'And what made you get in touch after all this time?'

That, of course, was a question I could not answer, or perhaps did not want to answer. There were two possible replies. One was the personal reply and had to do with needing to know why Woody had abandoned me, why he had made no attempt to keep in touch. The other was the political reply and had to do with how the collapse of communism was prompting radical changes in my working life and, in some way I did not comprehend, was engendering radical changes in other areas of life too. I did not give either answer. I fudged some general reply that purported to answer the question without actually doing so. It was not satisfactory. When your brother asks you a question like that after 50 years, you cannot say 'oh, I thought I would look you up' or some such. Woody was not satisfied with my answer either and said 'hmmm' again. I could see this becoming a most embarrassing day. There was silence. I could sense Woody wrestling with a decision. Then he made it.

'Feliks,' he said; 'let me put it like this. I had lost you. You were my lost brother. I had no idea where you were, what country you were in even. I had no means of finding you, no place to make a start. I figured I would never see you again. Then, miraculously, you rang. And here you are! But you're not talking to me. There are things you're not telling me. I don't know what things, or why you won't tell me, but there are. And I want you to know you can tell me anything. Anything at all. Jeez, Feliks, I'm your brother. Talk to me. Because, until you do, you're as lost to me as you were for all those years. Only now it's worse, because you're here and yet you're not here.'

He was right, of course. And I made the reciprocal decision.

I told Woody the story of my life. I had never done that to anyone before. I had told parts of it to different people at different times, but never the whole of it to one person and at one time. I told him about life in Basle after he had left. I told him about the move to France in 1947 and about my union activities in Sochaux. I told him how I came to move to Paris, about Fernand Meurice and *La Vague de la Gauche*. That made him laugh. That story makes everyone laugh. I told him about the Picards and the start of the *Guide* and how I had spent the long years since. I told him what was happening now. Woody said nothing until I had finished. He was a good listener. He did not even react when I was talking about the politics.

'But no wife then, Feliks?' I found it strange that, after I had explained my intellectual convictions and preoccupations so carefully, his first question should be about something so trivial.

'No,' I said.

'Girlfriends?'

'A few. I do not know if I would call them

116

girlfriends. They were mainly people I met on my travels and came to know briefly. Casual encounters, I suppose they were. One-night stands, if you want to be crude about it.'

'No one serious, then?'

'Not really. Well one, perhaps. She was important to me, I think. I do not know if I was important to her. We only saw each other a few times.'

'What happened?'

'She lived in Berlin. In East Berlin. The last time I saw her was in the spring of 1961. Then the Wall went up. Pffff. Just like that. I never saw her again.'

'You couldn't find her?'

'No. I tried. I tried several times, in fact. You see, I never knew where she lived. She worked in a bar. We met there. And in my hotel room. But when I next went back to Berlin she had left the bar and no one knew where she was.'

'Weren't you upset?'

'Well, I was a little upset, of course. But there we are.'

'And since then?'

'No one much since then. No one at all for many years, in fact.'

'Feliks, I hope this won't upset you. I'm trying to understand you, that's all. I don't care about your politics. It won't surprise you to hear I'm not a communist myself. In fact, I don't know that I've met a communist since I left Europe. But that's your business and I've no quarrel with that. What I can't understand is how you could watch the frigging Soviets put up a wall that separated you from the woman you loved and still call yourself a communist.'

'A leftist,' I corrected.

'Whatever.'

'I would not say that I loved her.'

'You sound as though you did.'

'What on earth makes you say that, Woody?'

'Feliks, dear Feliks, you haven't changed. When you say you tried several times to find her, that's the same as someone else saying he turned the world upside down. And when you say you were a little upset when you couldn't find her, that's the same as someone else saying they bawled their heart out for a year. Is that fair?'

'Possibly,' I said.

'You know it is.'

'Anyway, this has nothing to do with the Berlin Wall, nothing to do with politics. It would have been exactly the same without the Wall. I was not denied access to East Berlin. I could go there. I did go there. It must just be that she had moved. It could have happened at any time. Probably she was not that keen on me to start with.'

'You don't know that. And you don't know the rest of it either.'

'It is a reasonable supposition.'

I did not know whether it was a reasonable supposition or not. Probably it was. I did not care to debate the Berlin Wall with Woody anyhow. That was another difficult topic. Stalin, the Berlin Wall, the Hungarian Uprising, the Prague Spring, Solidarity, Afghanistan: all difficult topics. I did my best to avoid them. I had found over the years that the enemy would ignore the larger issues and focus on these small details. Small details are always harder to defend. I confess to my own doubts about the Wall. But I could understand that a communist society took a long time to build, and involved many sacrifices, so it seemed reasonable that the GDR should want to keep its most able people and deter them from enjoying the superficial promise of easy material gain. If this had created, possibly and unprovably, a small personal difficulty for myself, that was a minor issue.

'Would it be fair to say, Feliks, that perhaps ideas have mattered to you more than people?'

'Not at all,' I replied. 'I do not see any distinction. My ideas are entirely concerned with people.'

'Yes, people in general. But not people in particular.'

'All political ideas are to do with people in general. That is what makes them political.'

I knew what he was getting at, of course. He was not the first person to level that accusation at me. I had learned how to defend it in principle. But no one had previously connected the general charge with the specific issue of Kristin and Berlin. Admittedly, I had never previously spoken of Kristin and Berlin. Woody had somehow managed to make me do that too. I should have expected it. I had forgotten his unnerving talent (if you can call it a talent) for making me talk about things I did not wish to discuss. He had been exactly the same when we were children. If I had not changed in 50 years, neither had he.

'Same old Feliks,' he said. 'Why are you always so goddarned defensive?'

'I am defensive when people attack me. It is natural.'

'I'm not attacking you. I'm trying to find out what makes you tick. Forget it. Let's talk about something else. What do you make of America? Have you been here before?'

'No, never. Well, I have found it most interesting.'

'Interesting?'

'Yes. Interesting.'

'Which means, I suppose, that you don't approve of it.'

'Well of course I do not entirely approve of it. You could not expect me to.'

'OK, so what don't you like about it?'

That was another difficult question to answer. Normally, if I was given carte blanche to say what I disliked about America, no one could stop me for an hour. But that would have been unkind to Woody. Besides which, I had to admit that my experience of America had modified the views I had previously formed in ignorance. I would still make the same criticisms, and indeed they had been reinforced. If I had been looking for ammunition for my prejudices, I had found plenty of it. But I had to admit there was another side to the coin. I had been overwhelmed by the simple human warmth and friendliness I had found. I was struck by the straightforwardness of attitudes, by the uncomplicated approach to life.

It was, in my estimation, a false approach: the reality was that life was indeed complicated. However, I could not help but envy the naïvety that saw only simplicity, especially as I was not sure that my preoccupation with every nuance of complexity had done me much good. Or made me happy. That was it, I suppose. The people I had met had been happy. They could not be happy the whole time, of course. No one could. I was not disgruntled the whole time. But I was for much of it.

'You don't like the people?' Woody wanted his answer.

'The people have been very nice,' I said. 'And you and your family have been most kind to me, Woody.'

'You don't like the life we lead?'

'I can see that it is a comfortable life. It is not a life that I would choose for myself, of course, but I can see that it suits you.'

'So what's not to like?'

'There are things about American society I do not like. I find it very materialistic, very acquisitive. Also, of course, I find it exploitative. I mean, you may have a comfortable life yourself, Woody, but there are millions who do not.'

'No different than any other place. Better than most.'

'Other places care more about changing that situation. Then, of course, there is the racism here. I notice that your club does not appear to welcome black people. Except as servants.'

'We do have black members actually, Feliks.

121

Not many, but some. Black folk have their own places to go. I'm not sure they want us around.'

'In South Africa that is called apartheid. Here it can be justified as normal social practice.'

'I don't think there is any comparison with South Africa.'

'I seem to remember, only a few weeks ago, seeing a film of one of your police officers in Los Angeles beating up a black suspect. Perhaps they did not show that on your television.'

'You're wrong there, Feliks. We see everything on our television. Rather more than you do in France, I expect, and certainly more than your friends have been used to elsewhere. I agree with you. That was truly awful. But I don't think it's fair to judge a whole society by isolated incidents like that.'

'Sometimes,' I said, 'it is the small details that are the most revealing.'

'So you don't like it here?'

'I would not say that. I have mixed feelings about it. That is natural for someone in my position. I do not want to sound ungrateful, Woody. I am moved by the kindness you have shown me. But you cannot expect me to change my opinions in two days.'

Woody laughed. 'Feliks, I wouldn't expect you to change your opinions in a lifetime. Nor would I expect you to say anything you didn't believe. But at least you're saying something now.'

'I am sorry. I find it rather difficult after so long. And I do not want to offend you.'

'Nothing much offends me, Feliks. And it has been a long time. Fifty years this month. Now that's a real anniversary. We better have some champagne later.'

'I have drunk champagne twice this year already,' I said. 'I do not think it is good for my image. Perhaps I will have a bourbon.'

'Oh you liked that, did you?'

'Very much.'

'The funny thing is, Feliks, that you and I see things in a pretty similar way; it's just that we draw different conclusions. You see a country with regular, friendly people and you're suspicious of it. I say, what's wrong with that? You see a country where people have the chance to make money for themselves and get on in life and you think it's unfair. I say, why the hell not? You see a country where people see things in a simple, uncomplicated way and you think they must be stupid. I say, that sounds like a pretty good attitude to life.

'That's why I wanted to come here. That's exactly why I came. I hadn't seen much of life by then, I know, but I'd seen enough. I could see this tangled, incestuous past in Europe, the whole weight of it, the burden of it. There had never been an end to it; there never looked like being an end to it. And there was no refuge from the weight of that history, not for a Pole anyway. Turn to one side and you were screwed by Russia. Turn to the other and you were screwed by Germany. Lie flat on your back and you were screwed by everyone.

'All that history. All those little packages of history. A little bit of it shovelled into a duffel bag. Another bit in an old biscuit tin. Whole

123

great wodges of the stuff in unopened trunks and suitcases in dusty untended attics. Other bits of it wrapped up in paper and string and fastened with cracked sealing wax. All that darned history. And always the certainty that every few years some crazy guy would fetch out a bit of it, or someone would trip over the biscuit tin and spill the contents and the whole goddam thing would start over again and create yet more bits of history, that would have to be parcelled up into new containers, new hatboxes, new Tupperware, new God knows what.

'I'd had enough of that. At 21, I'd had enough of it already. I didn't want any of that baggage. I came here with all my belongings in one sack. I wanted to make my own future. I wanted to live a simple, uncomplicated life with simple, uncomplicated people. And no history. Or not that history, anyway. No more dead, clinging hands from the past. No more eyeing people in the street and saying 'oh, they're German really; they're not proper Poles' or 'they're Lithuanians' or 'they're Jews', or one-sixteenth Jewish or whatever. All that crap. That's why we're so happy to be Americans. It puts us all on an even footing; it makes us the same. The past took our childhood, Feliks. It took our home. It took our mother. It took God knows what other members of our family. I wanted a wife. I wanted kids. And there was no way on earth I would let that be clawed away by the clammy hands of history in the way we were clawed away. Does that make sense to you, Feliks? Can you understand that?'

'Yes,' I said. And it did make sense. It made

perfect sense, in fact, although not a sense I could have acted upon.

'I'm sorry,' he said. 'That was a long speech.'

I laughed. 'I am usually the one who is accused of making long political speeches.'

'Oh, it wasn't political. Come to think of it, perhaps it was. I see what you mean. If it was, that's the kind of politics I understand. Not your sort, Feliks. Sorry.'

'That is all right,' I said. 'I am used to it.'

'Tell me,' said Woody. 'What exactly happened on the night I left Basle? I've always wanted to know.'

'You mean you have forgotten?'

'Yeah, most of it. I was so pumped up. I mean, I know I had a blazing row with Uncle Ernst, but I can't remember what it was about.'

So I started to tell him. Woody interrupted.

'I swore at him like that?'

'You did.'

'I used those words?'

'Yes.'

'Jeez. I'm glad Wanda wasn't around to hear it. She disapproves of language like that.'

I related the rest of the story.

'I told Uncle Ernst that Aunt Maria was part Jewish? And that we were?'

'Yes.'

'I don't remember doing that. I guess I didn't care any more. Thing is, my departure was not as sudden as it looked. I was going that night anyway. I'd fallen in love with a French girl in Basle. Her name was Yvette. That day she'd told me she was going over to France during the

125

night. I wanted to go with her.'

'And I thought my elder brother was a hero, going off to join the Resistance.'

'Oh, I did. We both did. That's why she was going.'

'What happened to her?'

Woody gulped. 'She was killed. Just before the end of the war. Our cell was betrayed. Not many of us survived.'

'I am sorry.'

'That's OK.' Woody did not look OK. 'As a matter of fact,' he said, 'Yvette was a communist. So you can't all be bad.' He forced a smile. 'I think perhaps that was why I said what I did that night. That and the fact I no longer cared what I said to Uncle Ernst. It was the first time I had been in love, properly in love. I think I wanted to know what sort of things couples told each other. And what they didn't tell. I must have wondered whether Aunt Maria had told Uncle Ernst she was Jewish, or part Jewish. I guess I wanted to know what happened when an anti-Semite fell in love with a Jew. Perhaps I also wanted to know what would happen if an anti-communist fell in love with a Red, married a Red. I never got to discover that bit.'

While Woody was talking, I remembered something else about that last evening in Basle: something I had forgotten until then. In the stunned silence that had followed Woody's revelation of our origins, I had made a connection. On the heavy oak sideboard of the dining room in Basle stood a framed photograph of Aunt Maria and our mother as children. I had

126

looked at that photograph many times, and there was something familiar about it, and also something wrong with it, but I did not know what. At that moment I understood. It was the same photograph — exactly the same photograph, not just similar — as one that had stood on the mantelpiece at home in Łódź. Only in the photograph at home, there were three sisters: Aunt Maria in the centre, Mama to one side and Aunt Lilia to the other. In the photograph in Basle, there were only two sisters. Aunt Lilia, with her unmistakably Jewish looks, had been excised. I suddenly understood why. Seated across the table from me, already seized with terror, Aunt Maria saw me looking at the photograph, saw me making the connection. There was a desperate look in her eyes as they silently beseeched me not to reveal what I had understood. Now I told this to Woody.

'It's dreadful,' he said. 'Just dreadful. Why on earth did she put the photograph there in the first place? Every time she looked at it, it must have reminded her of the lie she was living. Now do you understand the things I had to leave behind?'

'Woody, can I ask you something?'

'Sure.'

'When you left, you promised you would look after me. You promised you would write. You promised you would visit. Why did you not?'

'You never got my letters?'

'I never received a single one.'

Woody sighed. 'I did wonder,' he said, 'but I didn't know. I wrote you lots of times. I couldn't tell you where I was or what I was doing, so the letters were pretty sketchy. But I did write. I couldn't give you a return address, so you could never write back. But at the time I think I assumed that at least my letters were reaching you.'

'No,' I said.

'I'm sorry.'

'It was not your fault, Woody.'

'No, but I'm still sorry.'

'And the visits?'

'That was impossible. I should never have promised that. I don't think I knew what I was getting into with the Resistance. Not surprising, really. It would have been far too dangerous to come back to Basle during the war. For me and for others.'

'And at the end of the war?'

'The end of the war,' said Woody. 'Jeez, that was a difficult period. I was real messed up. I had such a mixture of feelings. I was exhausted. I was angry. So many people I cared about had been killed. I was furious with everything to do with Europe. I was impatient to go to America and to get on with my life. There was all that on the one side. And then I was desperate to see you and Mama again. But it was still 1944. The war may have been over in France, but it certainly wasn't over in Poland. There was no way I could go there. And even if there had been, I wouldn't have gone. I knew that Poles who fought for the Allies were already being denounced as traitors by the communists, although God knows who or what we were meant to have betrayed. I knew

128

that people like me were being sent off to Soviet labour camps. And there was no way I would risk that happening to me. Not even for Mama's sake. Not even for your sake. Not for anyone.

'It's what I was saying earlier about not getting clawed back by that darned history. So I couldn't and wouldn't go back to Poland. I was planning to go to Basle. I didn't know if I'd find you, but I thought — if I timed my arrival right — I might see Aunt Maria without running into Uncle Ernst and could discover where you were. But before I could do that, I was offered a cheap berth on this boat to New York. Take it or leave it; make your mind up now. So I went. I didn't have any doubts about it. I just went. I guess I figured it wouldn't make any difference in the end. I thought I'd find out eventually what had happened to you, that I'd be back in touch with you again.'

'And did you write from America?'

'Sure. I wrote to Aunt Maria in Basle again. I wrote to Mama in Łódź. I never got a reply from Mama. I don't think I was much confident I would. But I did think I'd hear from Aunt Maria sooner or later.'

'And did you?'

Woody sighed again. 'Yes. Or rather, I heard from Uncle Ernst. He wrote me a curt note, with no information about you and the family, saying that my letters were distressing and unwelcome, that I was not to write them and that, if I persisted, they would not be answered.'

'What a charming man he was.'

'A complete bastard. I'm glad I said that to

129

him, actually: what you told me I said. Although, if I hadn't, perhaps things would have been different later. Anyhow, once I'd got that reply, there was not much I could do. I could carry on writing to Łódź and hope that one day I might get an answer. Otherwise, it was a case of hoping that you or Mama would track me down, which didn't seem very likely.'

'But I did.'

'Yes, Feliks, you did. Thank you very much. Mind you, you took your time about it.' But he was smiling and so was I.

'I wish you had talked to me about your plans for going to France,' I said. 'I wish you had trusted me.'

'I wanted to,' said Woody, 'but I couldn't. You were so young, Feliks. It wasn't that I didn't trust you, but I didn't know how much you understood about what was going on, how much you could understand. I was afraid you might tell Aunt Maria what I was planning, not deliberately, but that it might just come out. And if she told Uncle Ernst, God knows what would have happened.'

'Yes, I can see that.'

'You're upset with me, aren't you, Feliks?'

'No, not any more. I admit that I have been. I have felt badly about your behaviour. But not now.'

'I'm sorry,' said Woody. 'I didn't feel too good about things either.'

'There is no need to apologise.'

'Well, I wasn't actually apologising, Feliks. I'm just sorry that you should have felt the way you did. But I don't know what I could have done more, or done different.'

'Neither do I,' I said. 'You did everything you could, Woody. I think I understand things better now. I had not previously considered the matter in this light. It is forgotten.'

'Good.'

So I had my explanation and it satisfied me. I suppose I had not tried to look at things from Woody's perspective before, or to ask myself what situation he might have been in, or to consider what might have prevented him from fulfilling his promise. Now that he had explained it, the matter seemed simple, predictable even. I was not sure why I had believed so adamantly for 50 years that I had been let down by Woody. Perhaps I had wanted to believe it. Now an emotional weight had been lifted from my shoulders. It had not been a difficult conversation to have and I wondered why I had dreaded it so much. I thought this was now the moment to address the other emotional weight and have the other difficult conversation.

'I was wondering, Woody,' I said; 'did you manage to find out what happened to Mama?'

'No, Feliks, I didn't. And I assume from the question that you didn't either.'

'No.'

'I'd sort of been hoping you had. The longer that's gone by without you mentioning it, the more I reckoned it had to be no news or bad news. You were the last chance, I suppose. I feel bad about it. There's hardly a day goes by when I don't think about Mama. I did everything I

131

could think of. I went on writing to Łódź, even when I never got a reply. It was ridiculous, really. They were only lodgings after all, a rented apartment, not a proper family home. Even if nothing had happened to Mama during the war, she might not still be there anyhow. But I went on writing. Every year I sent her a birthday card and a Christmas card, for years and years and years. I knew she wasn't getting them, but I still sent them. I suppose I hoped that maybe one time the card would be seen by someone who knew the name, knew who she was, but I never heard.

'I talked to people over here. There are loads of Poles in Ohio, lots of Polish societies and clubs. I posted my name with them all in case either of you came looking for me in the States. Of course there were quite a few people who came from Łódź, or who had friends or family there. I even met someone who knew of our family and that raised my hopes for a bit. Several of them were in touch with people in Łódź, once things had settled down after the war, and they kindly wrote on my behalf and asked for information. From that, I learned that our house did not exist any more, the street did not exist, the immediate neighbourhood did not exist. It had been flattened after the war. I still went on sending my cards just the same. No one ever had any news of Mama. I never heard anything.

'I even contacted people over here who were compiling records of the Holocaust. It was a long shot. I don't know about you, Feliks, but I've never felt particularly Jewish. I don't think

Mama did either. But it seemed possible that the Nazis could have decided she was, so I thought I'd ask. But there was no news there either.

'Eventually, about 20 years ago, in 1972 I think, I went back to Poland myself. Things had calmed down a bit by then. I didn't think it would be dangerous.' He smiled at me, in deference to our differences. 'And it wasn't. But I didn't discover anything. I went back to where we'd lived. I don't know why. I knew it wasn't there any more. I suppose I wanted to see the area for old time's sake. Probably I thought that if I made enough enquiries, I would succeed where the others had failed. But I didn't. I must have talked to a hundred people or more, but they were the wrong hundred. Someone would have known. I bet there was at least one person in Łódź who knew something about Mama and what had happened to her. That was the most tantalising thing about it. Somewhere there was someone who knew, but I could not find them. So I came back with nothing and after that I stopped sending the cards. There didn't seem to be a point any more. I'm sorry. I'm sorry for you and I'm sorry for me, but I have no news.'

Was I sorry to hear that? I was not sure. I knew I had to ask the question, even though I had seldom thought about Mama for years. I was still angry with her, furious with her in fact, for abandoning me. I had told myself for a long time that I did not care what had happened to her and did not want to know. When I had thought about this meeting in advance, when I had known that the issue would inevitably be raised,

I had fervently hoped that Woody would have no news about Mama either. But, to my surprise, as we sat and talked about her, I found myself wishing the opposite. Now I wanted to know. I could not understand why I should suddenly feel this.

'So,' said Woody; 'that's my side of it. What's yours? Did you discover anything?'

'No,' I said, 'and I must admit that I never tried.'

As a matter of fact, that statement was a lie. I had tried: only the once, but I had. It had not been something that had happened on my own initiative. It was something that had befallen me, an opportunity that had arisen. The problem was that I was so ashamed of it, and angry about it, that I could not possibly admit it to Woody or to anyone else, now or ever.

What happened was this. I had been aware for some time that, believing what I did and travelling constantly within eastern Europe and between there and France, I might become a target for some form of espionage activity. I did not know from which side an approach might come: whether the French might ask me to discover some information for them in the East, or whether the Soviets might ask me to run an errand for them to the West. There was of course no way that I would agree to collaborate with the West, but actually I had decided that I would not collaborate with the East either. I understood why the Soviet Union needed to protect itself in this way. I could see that the insidious disinformation and clandestine operations perpetrated by the Americans above all prompted the need for a defence. But the world of espionage was not one I liked, or felt I had the stomach for, and I was determined not to be implicated. I would say no if I were ever asked.

Then in 1968, I was asked. I was dining alone in my hotel in Warsaw when a man came uninvited to sit at my table. He did not tell me his name, but said that he worked for the Polish government. He had some trivial favour that needed performing: a package that had to be delivered to France that he would rather not entrust to the diplomatic bag. He said that I had been recommended to him as a reliable communist, and as a Pole with ready access to France, and he wondered if I might be able to assist him. I understood of course that I was being invited to act as a courier and I politely declined. He expressed surprise that I should be unwilling to perform such a trifling service to the Party. I replied that I was flattered to be asked, and that indeed I much admired the Party, but that this was not an area with which I wished to involve myself. He said this was a pity since, in addition to a handsome financial reward, he had hoped to give me my mother's current address.

'She is alive?' I had asked.

'Yes.'

'Is she in Poland?'

'Yes.'

'Where?'

'Sadly, I am not now able to give you that information.'

I do not know if you could exactly call this blackmail, but it was not far off. I was being offered the inducement of seeing my mother again, but the man had made it plain that — if I refused — the information would be withheld. I thought this was a contemptible way to behave. If he had that information, the decent thing would be to give it to me. If he had, I might have been more inclined to co-operate. But I suppose that is a ridiculous thing to say, because in the end I co-operated anyway. I do not know why I did. I should have maintained my refusal. It would have been the logical thing for me to do. When I say I was angry with Mama, I suppose what I really mean is that I hated her. Of all the people to whom this inducement might be offered, I was the least likely to respond to it.

So why did I succumb? I do not know, but I did. I found myself accepting the invitation. It was early October and I was due to return directly to Paris from Warsaw. The package was anonymously placed in my hotel room, labelled with an address in Montbéliard. I boarded my train in Warsaw to commence the journey to Paris. I do not think I have been so terrified in my life. But my baggage was not searched; it seldom was. I arrived back in my apartment without incident. The next day I took the train to Montbéliard. It was a town I had known well. In fact, I had lived in lodgings there while I was working at Sochaux. In the evening I delivered the package. I had been asked to hand it over in person, not to push it through the letter box, and I was surprised to find myself face to face with an old comrade from my days in the union at Peugeot. We were delighted to see each other. He invited me in for a drink, for several drinks in fact, and I ended up spending the night on his sofa. He trusted me, of course, and opened the package in my presence. We were both most intrigued to see what it contained. We never did discover, because inside was another package with a letter to my friend instructing him to ensure that it reached the head of the Party organisation in the Franche Comté unopened and without delay.

The next day I took the train back to Paris. I had already been given the money in Warsaw and now I awaited the rest of my reward. But nothing happened. No message arrived with Mama's address. I heard nothing at all. I did not know what to do. I did not know the name of the Pole who had approached me in Warsaw. I considered contacting the Polish embassy in Paris, or even the Soviet embassy, but that seemed far too great a risk. I had no idea of the situation in which I might have become embroiled and had no desire to be further implicated. So I could do nothing. But I was furious. I was furious for having been duped, for having been forced to do something against my will by the trick of a promise that was broken. I was furious that the Party to which I had belonged for nearly 20 years, that I had served faithfully and unquestioningly, should use me of all people in such a cynical and dishonest way. I was also irrationally upset that I would now not be seeing Mama.

That was when I resigned from the Communist Party. It had nothing to do with the Prague Spring, as Oberman had suggested. I did not change my opinions. I did not cease to believe that the ideals of communism offered the best hope for the future of the world. But I was no longer willing to belong to a party that treated me in such a way. I saw the world a little differently after that, a little more sceptically perhaps. Now I come to think of it, this was the moment when I changed the friends I saw, the friends I drank with. I think this was the moment that I started to describe myself as a leftist. When I said earlier that it had started with Khrushchev's speech, I was mistaken. No, I continued to see my old hard-line friends after that. It was only in 1968 that things changed.

I could not say any of this to Woody, of course. He did not speak for a while. We were both sunk in thought. Then he looked at me and asked the really difficult question.

'Feliks, I don't want to pry. Don't tell me if you don't want to. But why did you not try to find out about Mama?'

I decided to answer the question directly. 'Because she abandoned us, Woody. She packed us off to Switzerland because it was more convenient to have us out of the way. I am sorry, but I was angry about that. Very angry, very hurt, very bitter.'

'That's not what happened,' said Woody. 'Is that what you think happened?'

'It is what I have always thought happened.' I burst into tears. I was shocked at myself. I could

138

not think why I had become so emotional. 'I am so sorry, Woody,' I said. 'I do not know why I should suddenly cry.'

'Forget it. I cry all the time.'

'You do?'

'Sure. I'm an emotional guy.'

'Well I am not,' I said. 'In fact I cannot remember the last time I cried.'

'You cried at Christmas 1939.'

'Did I?'

'Absolutely. And the next year too. You were missing Mama.'

'Was I?'

'Sure.'

'I had forgotten that.' I still did not remember, but I did now recall that I had also cried in 1961, when I could not find Kristin. And in 1968, when I was denied Mama's address. And earlier this year, when I had made contact with Woody.

'Feliks, how much do you remember about Mama?'

'Not much,' I said. 'I was only nine when we left. I know there are people who can remember every part of their childhood in microscopic detail, or who claim they can, but I am not one of them. I remember certain things, certain incidents. I have a clear recollection of Mama herself, what she looked like, how she was.'

'Then what makes you think she abandoned us?'

'Well it would be understandable that it should be more convenient for her if we were not around.'

'Why?'

'Oh, for goodness' sake, Woody. You must know.'

'Know what?'

'What Mama did.'

'I haven't the first idea what you're talking about.'

'How can you not have known?'

'Known what?'

'That Mama was a prostitute.'

'What?'

'Well, she was.'

'She was a dancer.'

'Yes, she was a dancer. Then she brought them home afterwards. And they paid.'

'How do you know that?'

'I saw her. One night I could not sleep. I heard voices on the landing, so I opened the bedroom door and peeped through the crack. I saw a man come out of Mama's bedroom doing up his trousers. He handed Mama a wad of notes. And Mama saw me peeping and she looked guilty.'

'And how old were you when this happened?'

'Nine. It was only a little while before we left. I had discovered her secret. She thought I would tell you. She wanted us out of the way.'

'But you didn't tell me.'

'No I did not. I was ashamed.'

'Well I don't know,' said Woody. 'If that's what you saw, that's what you saw. It certainly sounds like you say it was. But even if that did happen, I don't think it happened on any regular basis.'

'Why was Mama never married? Why do we both have different fathers?'

'I don't know that either,' said Woody. 'But I don't think Mama was a prostitute. I mean, I would have known. I don't intend to be patronising, Feliks, but I was a lot older than you and I knew a lot more about life. It was a small community, that quarter of Łódź. Everyone knew what everyone else was up to. Someone would have said something. We'd have been called names in the street. You'd have had things said to you at school. Did you ever?'

'No,' I said.

'Neither did I. One of us would have heard something. I know I don't want to believe it's true, but I don't think it is true. OK, maybe it happened once or twice. Goodness knows, she must have needed the money. But do I think that Mama was a prostitute? No I don't. No way.'

'Well, that is what I have always thought.'

'And you think she sent us to Switzerland because you had found out and because having kids at home was getting in the way of business?'

'Yes.'

'Feliks, I'll put this to you as delicately as I can. By your own admission you've not known many women. I don't know if any of them were mothers, but if they were, I don't think you'd be talking like this. As a general rule, mothers love their children. In fact, they often love them far too much. If a mother has children, loves them, raises them, she doesn't suddenly stop loving them and start wishing them out of her life. Whatever happens, whatever the circumstances. No way. No how. It doesn't happen. And if you had a family, Feliks, you'd know that.'

'If you say so.'

'I do say so. How much do you actually remember about us leaving?'

'Not much, I suppose. I know that some time in the summer of 1939 we were abruptly told we would be going to stay with Aunt Maria for a while. The next day we were bundled off on a train. Then a bit later the war started and we were not able to return.'

'Feliks, it was not just the summer of 1939 that this happened. It was August 1939. Does that mean anything to you?'

'Obviously,' I said.

'In fact, to be precise, we left Poland exactly one week before the Nazis invaded. I don't know if you remember much about what was going on then, but I do. The invasion had been expected for weeks. People talked of nothing else. Everyone was real tense. It was not a question of if, but of when. I've always thought it was perfectly simple. Mama knew what would happen. Everyone did. She had a sister in Switzerland. She took the opportunity to get us some place safe. That's not abandonment, Feliks. That's love.'

'Why then? Why that precise moment?'

'I don't know, other than it was getting more dangerous day by day. But I also think it had something to do with Aunt Lilia. Let me tell you what I remember. You know how close we were to Aunt Lilia and Uncle Szmul? And you were always playing with Mordechaj. Remember?'

'Yes. I remember.'

'They were a couple of doors down the street.

Well, a few days before we left, something happened to them. I don't know what. Mama wouldn't tell me. But we were meant to be seeing them that day and suddenly we couldn't. Mama was real upset about it. The next day she went down to the post office and sent a telegram to Switzerland. I know, because I went with her. When she got the reply the next day, she went straight to the pawnbroker's and hocked her fur coat. I went with her there too. Then we went to the railroad station and she bought two tickets for Basle.

'She told me what she was doing. She said something terrible was going to happen, but we would be safe in Switzerland. I asked her to come with us, so she would be safe too. She said she didn't have enough money for three tickets. I said I had some money. She wouldn't take it. I begged her, Feliks. I begged her to come too, but she wouldn't. She said she was a Pole and her place was in Poland. I said I was a Pole too for Chrissake. She said I was young enough to start my life over if the worst came to the worst. She said she could no longer do that. I said of course she could. But there was no persuading her. She wouldn't come.'

Woody was shaking with emotion. His shoulders were heaving and he was extraordinarily upset. It seemed so strange to be having this conversation, about a railway station in Łódź in 1939, amongst the potted palms and rattan chairs of a country club in Ohio in 1991. 'I begged her to come,' he sobbed. 'I begged her. Why couldn't I make her do that?'

143

Well, of course, 20 minutes earlier I could have given him an answer to that question, the answer I had always given myself, but now I was no longer confident it was the correct answer. Woody had said too much that now made sense to me, albeit a different sense from the one I had always believed.

'Anyhow.' Woody pulled himself together with great effort. 'The next day we left. The two of us. Mama came with us on the train to Warsaw, if you remember, and she put us on the train for Switzerland. And that was the last either of us have seen or heard of her.' He was weeping violently again. 'I remember being put on that train. I remember you too, Feliks. You were so excited. You were going on a great adventure. It's strange. I was always the one for adventures, not you. Your eyes were darting all over the place. But mine were on Mama on the platform. She was crying uncontrollably.'

As he was now. As I was.

I do not know what else we might have talked about. Perhaps there was nothing that could have been said after that. But, as we recovered ourselves, Wanda arrived. Woody and I had talked all morning and now Wanda had come to join us for lunch. It came as something of a relief, I must admit. I am not sure how much more of this I could have taken. Conversation turned to other things. We no longer talked about our family. Woody and Wanda talked more about their family and I listened. As I had to keep reminding myself, this was also my family. When they talked of Marvin and Kellie and

Brad, they were talking of my nephews and niece. They were also talking of Mama's grandchildren. I found that disconcerting.

After lunch, it was time for me to leave. I was catching a late-afternoon flight back to New York and then an evening flight to Paris. I said goodbye to Wanda at the club. We kissed each other this time, on both cheeks in the French way, and it felt like kissing a china doll. At least I imagine it did. I have never kissed a china doll. Wanda said she had enjoyed meeting me and hoped we would meet again soon. I said that I hoped so too. Woody and I drove to the airport in silence. I did not know what to say. We arrived early and I was expecting that he would say goodbye and leave me, but he suggested that we should have a cup of coffee together, so we did that.

'I guess it was always going to be difficult,' said Woody.

'I am not good with emotion,' I said. 'I have always had difficulties with that. I suppose that I do not usually have this type of conversation with people.'

'What sort of conversations do you have?'

'About ideas, I suppose. I am interested in people's minds, what they think, what they believe.'

'Not how they feel?'

'No, not really. I do not look at people like that.'

'How do you look at them then, Feliks?'

'I look at them in relationship to their ideas. I am interested in their backgrounds and in what they do with their lives. The things that make them what they are, that make them believe what they believe.'

'It is people's emotions that make them what they are, that determine what they think,' said Woody. 'I believe that of you too, Feliks. Only I don't think you want to acknowledge your feelings. I think you are ashamed of them. I think you feel them unworthy. I don't know why you should feel that way, but you do. I don't have that problem. I am comfortable with my emotions. I am comfortable with what I feel about Mama. It upsets me, but that's natural. I know why I'm crying. You don't. Mama was an emotional person herself, as I recall: very open, very spontaneous. I liked that. And it's what I hated about Basle and being in that house with its feelings of repression, of everything being closed off, of things that could never be discussed openly. I loathed it. It was like a breath of fresh air when I got to France.'

'Where were you?'

'We moved about. Most of the time I was on the plateau of the Vercors, above Grenoble. Do you know it?'

'I have heard of it. I have not been there.'

'It is a beautiful place. Just being there was enough to make me feel emotional. And then there was the romance of what we were doing. I know I shouldn't speak like this. It's probably what you think of Americans: that they believe all wars are romantic. I don't think that. But, if you ask me whether there was a romance in fighting that particular war from inside the

146

French Resistance, then yes there was. I don't deny it. And it gave me a different perspective on life. I was fighting with all sorts. Communists amongst them, as I told you. So it was ridiculous to judge anybody by their opinions, or by what orthodoxy they adhered to. I was not a communist, but communists were my friends. I was not a Catholic, but Catholics were my friends. You only judged anyone by the sort of person they were. That was all you could do. I've not done any different since.'

'Have you ever been back?'

'No.'

'Do you want to?'

'Yes I do.'

'Would you and Wanda like to visit me in Paris?'

'We would love to. Is that an invitation?'

'Yes.'

'Thank you.'

'Would you like to go anywhere else? To the Vercors, perhaps?'

Woody swallowed hard. 'Yes,' he said. 'I would very much like to go back to the Vercors. And I want to visit the village of Treffort. And I want to lay flowers on Yvette's grave. I was never able to do that.'

'Then we shall do so,' I said. 'Is there anything else you would like to do?'

'See some old friends, if I can. Some of them are dead now, but I know several who are alive. People I lived and fought with for years. People I know like my own skin. People who, even though I haven't seen them in years, I still think of all

147

the time. Men like Pierre Guidry and Armand Joubert and René Dufour.'

'I am sorry,' I said. 'Did you say René Dufour?' I thought I must have misheard him.

'Yes,' he said. 'René Dufour. Do you know him?'

'That is the name of the man I was telling you about, Woody; the one who was in the American embassy and followed me afterwards, the one who discovered your address for me.'

'Well, he wouldn't have had much trouble doing that,' said Woody.

'You are in touch with him?'

'Sure. I haven't seen him since the war, but we still send each other Christmas cards.'

I was astounded. 'Why on earth did he not say so? Pretending he had never heard of you. Pretending to have to research your address.'

'I've no idea,' said Woody. 'But, knowing René, he'll have had a reason. Why don't you ask him?'

'I most certainly will.'

'Be gentle with him. His wife died last year. They had retired to the Gers. They were very close.'

'He is living in Paris now,' I said.

'I know. I expect he found it lonely in the country without Dominique. He worked in Paris most of his life. That's where his friends are. I wasn't surprised to hear he'd gone back. That's probably why he's doing stuff for our embassy there: helps to take his mind off things.'

'What did he used to do?'

'What you guessed. He was in the police after the war and got transferred to the security service. Needless to say, I don't know too much about what he actually did. He clammed up on me when he joined that lot. What did you think of him?'

'I liked him, as a matter of fact,' I said. 'I cannot think why.'

The time had sped by and now my flight was being called. This time we both gave each other a big hug and promised to meet in Paris before the end of the year.

'You take care now,' said Woody as we parted, 'baby brother.'

7

The flight to New York was easy enough, but I did not enjoy the flight to Paris. I had never flown long distance before this trip. Most of my journeys in Europe had been made by train. I did not much like flying. I wanted to sleep, but found it impossible. I kept thinking about something Mark Bergelson had said: 'when dams burst, they burst'. Had that only been two days earlier? It seemed incredible. Well, my dam had well and truly burst. All those walls and fortifications, all those parapets, ledges and machicolations, had given way suddenly and at once. Everything I had so carefully constructed, that had kept the waters in their proper place for all this time, had crumbled and the water had now spread everywhere, seeping beneath the carapace into the furthest recesses of my life. No thought or feeling was spared the flood.

Whatever its faults, the vast monolith that had been the Eastern Bloc had governed my life, had given meaning to it, given comfort to it and given me a livelihood. Now it had gone. Almost overnight, it seemed. Along with it, the Cold War had almost vanished too. For my entire adult life, I had been told — and found it only too easy to believe — that the Cold War was the most significant political fact of the world in which I lived, that it represented the most imminent threat to our lives. How could something like that disappear overnight? It was surreal. And how could people go about their lives as if nothing had changed?

Then there was my own life. That had also changed with bewildering rapidity. I had agreed to sell my business. But it was not just a business, it was my way of life. Every year, for the past 36 years, the exigencies of the *Guide* and its publishing schedule had mapped out my days as rigidly as the bells of Basle. What would I do now? Kick my heels in Paris? I would be bored within weeks. So it was not only that I had to deconstruct and then reconstruct my intellectual viewpoint, my attitudes to the exterior world in which I lived. I needed to do exactly the same with the pattern of my life, with the practical matters of everyday living. And, as if this were not enough, I had to do the selfsame thing with my most deeply held emotions, my most private thoughts. The intellectual, the practical, the emotional: all areas of life were under tumultuous siege.

I now allowed myself to dwell on my conversation with Woody, reflection that had been made impossible at the time by the sudden arrival of Wanda. From more or less the same set of information, Woody and I had reached diametrically opposite conclusions about Mama. My viewpoint depended on Mama having been a prostitute. Without that belief, my opinion was unsustainable. Woody had produced enough evidence about our physical departure from Łódź, and enough evidence as to why Mama might not have been able to contact us after the war or to respond to letters, to make me doubt any thought of premeditated abandonment. But it still left open the question of what had prompted our despatch in the first place. And that question rested on whether Mama had been a prostitute. If she had been, I could understand why we might have been an inconvenience for her, despite Woody's emotional speculation on the nature of motherhood. But if she had not, I could not think of any reason other than Woody's for why we should have gone. I had no prior sense that we were not loved or wanted. On the contrary.

The only evidence I had for my belief was what I had seen through the crack in the door and, the more I thought about it, I realised this was not enough. It seemed indisputable that they had been having sex, but the fact that the man had given Mama money did not necessarily mean it had been for that. Besides which, if Mama had been a prostitute, I am not sure how I could have failed to notice it on other occasions. Admittedly she was absent a great deal in the evenings. Dancing at the club, she said. That could have been a convenient excuse. But she did dance at the club. I had seen the posters with her name in the window. And I had seen her dance. She danced beautifully.

Besides this, Woody was surely right to say that, if Mama had been a prostitute, the neighbourhood would have known about it and so would we. I did not see how that could have failed to happen. So, when I put these different things together, I was obliged to conclude that I had probably been wrong. I do not like being wrong. Who does? But it was a great deal worse than that. If Mama had not abandoned us, she had made an enormous sacrifice for us, as Woody believed. In which case, far from betraying us, I was in fact the one who had betrayed her. If I had not believed what I did, at the very least I would have tried to find her after the war. Maybe I would not have succeeded, but I would have been better placed than Woody, trying to do so from America. Above all, I would not have spent my life believing I had been abandoned by my own mother. Since I now also accepted that I had not been neglected by Woody either, I began to realise that my attitudes towards my closest family rested on false foundations and had done for my whole adult life. It was a most unpleasant and disturbing realisation.

So I started to think about how I could have reached such an erroneous conclusion about Mama, and what had made me cling to it for so long. It was then that I thought of Herr Kastner.

Kastner had been a teacher at my school in Basle. He was the games master, in fact, although I think he taught geography too. The other pupils used to snigger that he took an unhealthy interest in the boys showering after gym. I must admit that he was a somewhat strange man, but he was always kind to me and I liked him. Once or twice, when I had been upset (so it would seem there had been other occasions when I had been upset), he would take me to his classroom and sit me on his knee and massage the back of my thigh as he comforted me. I had not thought there was anything peculiar about this at the time. I was grateful for his concern.

Many years later, in a bar in Paris, I ran into someone who had been at the same school and whom I had known. We were reminiscing about old times, as one does, and I happened to mention Herr Kastner in the conversation.

'Oh Kastner,' he said: 'that old queen.'

I was astonished by this casual revelation that Kastner had been homosexual. But why should I be astonished? The signs were there for all to see and others had pointed them out. So why had I not noticed them? Why, well into my adult life, did this news come to me as a surprise? I concluded it was because, at the time it happened, I had been largely ignorant of homosexuality, possibly entirely ignorant, so that explanation would not naturally occur to me. Later, when of course I was aware of homosexuality and would apply that knowledge to any new situation that arose, I had not applied the knowledge retrospectively. My view of Kastner had remained exactly as it was at the time I had known him, uninformed by later insights.

Now, on the plane back from New York, I wondered if I had not done exactly the same thing with Mama. I had formed the impression at the age of nine, based on partial information, that Mama was a prostitute. I had connected that thought with our abrupt departure for Switzerland and had reached the conclusion that Mama did not want me. Perhaps that was a

154

forgivable conclusion at the time. But why had I never revisited it later? Why had it taken until now for me to use adult eyes to review the evidence? Why had it never occurred to me that there was another, far more likely, reason for two children to be evacuated from Poland in the summer of 1939? At the time, I could perhaps be excused my ignorance. I knew nothing of the political situation, of the preludes and preparations of war. But I had lost that excuse a long time before. I had been aware for years of how the war had started, and what had befallen Poland during the course of it, so why had I never reconsidered previous conclusions in the light of that knowledge? Even if I could not recall the exact date of our exodus, I knew enough not to view the sequence of events with the knowledge and experience of a child. But that was how I always had viewed it. And I had done that, not only with Mama, but with Woody too.

It occurred to me to wonder, if I could do this with my own family, what else in life I might have done it with. What about my attachment to communism, for example? How much attention had I paid to the realities of life in eastern Europe? They had been there, right under my nose, for decades, but had I ever examined them afresh? Had the gradual exposure of the realities of Stalin's regime altered my view of the system that had perpetrated them and justified them? Well, a little maybe, but not much. The Party was family and you did not question or traduce family in public, and very little in private.

These thoughts were thrown into sharper

relief by my experience of America. It was all very well deriding the materialism of American society, but the fact was that most of the people I had met in eastern Europe lived equally materialistic lives, just rather less successful ones. I could not dispute the fact that if people in Russia or in Poland, or anywhere in the Eastern Bloc for that matter, were offered the possibility of an equivalent lifestyle to that of Woody and his family, they would leap at the opportunity. Whether that was wise, or where it would lead, was another matter, but I could not dispute what the choice would be. Indeed, that was the choice now being made by countless families through-out eastern Europe.

These thoughts did not take me to any firm conclusions, but at least I had them and I suppose that was something. It was, as I say, a troubled flight. I had stumbled too far into these changes to be able to extricate myself from them, but not far enough to be able to discern a happy outcome.

8

It felt wonderful to be back in Paris. I had been away for less than a week, but it seemed so much longer. The familiar landmarks looked fresh to me again. The inconsequentialities of everyday life suddenly became appealing. I was not used to Paris in the spring. For the first time it occurred to me that, for many years, I had only experienced the city in autumn and winter. Cities are chameleons; they change and renew their appearances with the seasons. I was looking forward to making the acquaintance of a new Paris. The anxieties of the return flight receded from my mind. Those things could take care of themselves in due course. For the moment, there needed only to be the moment.

I slept for 12 hours on the night of my return and awoke refreshed and optimistic. I telephoned Dufour immediately. He was friendly and we agreed to meet that evening, back in the bar in the Rue d'Anjou. I think I suggested that. I am not sure why. The choice necessitated a journey for both of us. Perhaps I felt that unfinished business should be completed where it had begun, on neutral territory. We did not talk on the telephone, other than to make the arrangement. It was an artificial reticence. We both knew why I had called and Dufour must have been expecting that I would. I had no idea what I was about to hear. Not for the first time in recent weeks, I had the feeling that other people knew a great deal more about my life than I knew myself. I was determined to make sure that this knowledge was now shared.

I arrived early at the bar. That was deliberate. I wanted to be in command of the situation. I wanted to be a beer or two ahead of Dufour. I would not describe myself as an assertive man normally. I am passive most of the time, with occasional displays of cantankerousness when I feel my passivity exploited. I did not intend to be any different this evening, but neither did I intend to be fobbed off with a brief, unsatisfactory story. I could not explain Dufour's behaviour, but I meant to ensure that he did and in full.

I realised that the dynamics between Dufour and myself had already changed before we met. On the first occasion he had been a stranger, an intriguing stranger, with whom I had no relationship, nor expected to have one. Now I would be talking to an old friend and comrade of my brother, someone to whom I owed my reunification with my brother and what had flowed from it. Someone whom, in all probability, I would see again before the end of the year, when Woody came to Paris, when we would presumably be meeting as friends. I suppose I might have felt indebted to Dufour, but I did not. This was because, owing to the withholding of information, I felt that Dufour had some ulterior motive and I wished to suspend my gratitude until I knew what it was. So, psychologically speaking, it was an awkward meeting, with these assorted currents swirling around. That is why I wanted to keep some control over it.

The bar was nearly empty. Most of the shops had been closed for a while and the shoppers would have had their drinks, always assuming that any of the swanks from the Rue du Faubourg St Honoré would have deigned to favour this ordinary establishment. One or two bored men nursed a drink at the bar, killing time before going off to meet their mistresses, or whatever they were about to do. Indeterminate music wafted over the air. I sat on a banquette in the corner with my eye on the door. An apathetic waiter placed a dish of cheap peanuts on my table. At a little after 7, Dufour appeared. We shook hands, formally, and I offered him a drink before he had the chance to offer me one. We sat at the table regarding each other in silence. As far as I was concerned, he was the one who needed to do the talking.

'Did you have a good trip?' he asked eventually.

'I did, thank you. It was most pleasant.'

'And successful? Did you sell your business?'

I had temporarily forgotten about that. 'Oh yes,' I said. 'I have sold the business.'

'So you are now a gentleman of leisure.' Dufour smiled.

I did not allow my hackles to rise at this description. I imagined that my hackles would receive plenty of exercise later in the evening. 'For the time being,' I said.

'I've never been to America,' said Dufour. 'I

159

think I ought to go one of these days.'

I did not answer him directly. I was finding these superficial pleasantries irritating. I thought he was provoking me. He knew why we were there, what we had come to discuss. Although I had planned to force Dufour into raising the issue, I could not be bothered to wait any longer.

'Woody sends his regards.'

'That was kind of him.'

There was a long pause.

'I expect you think I owe you an explanation,' said Dufour.

'Yes,' I said. 'I do.'

'It's rather a long explanation.'

'I am in no hurry. I think you should let me hear all of it.'

'Yes,' said Dufour. 'I think I should.' He took a long gulp from his beer. 'The thing is, Feliks — and I shall call you Feliks, whether you like it or not — the thing is that I feel as if I have known you most of my life, and in a way I have.

'I first met Woody in the spring of 1941, as I expect you know. I was already in the Resistance, on the Vercors. I knew the area well. My family farmed near Die, so I was local. Early one morning, this young man turned up with an astonishingly beautiful girl. Normally we would have been wary. There were a lot of fifth columnists about. We were suspicious of strangers who arrived unannounced. But Yvette was local too. Several of us knew her and her family. She was all right. The fact she vouched for Woody, and the fact he was Polish, made him all right too. We could always trust the Poles.

160

'So I came to know Woody very well. We always got on. We looked at things in the same way. And, I must admit, I fancied Yvette like crazy myself. Not that it did me any good. Nor her, poor girl. Did — ?'

'Yes,' I said. 'Woody told me about that.'

'Anyway, we were pretty much side by side for the rest of the war. I was enormously fond of him. We spoke of many things over those years. Woody talked a lot about his family, about growing up in Poland. So I learned about your mother and Woody's concerns about what had happened to her. And of course I learned about you too, his brother Feliks. He talked about you constantly.'

'What did he say?'

'He thought you were unhappy in Basle. He said he felt responsible for you. He said he felt guilty about leaving you.'

'He said that to me too.'

'And did you feel bad about him leaving?'

'Yes. But not any longer.'

'I'm glad about that. It was not a time for easy decisions. I'm sure you understand. Not for any of us. One evening Woody announced he was slipping back to Basle for the night to see you. He said you always slept with the window open and that he would shin up the drainpipe to surprise you.'

'It certainly would have surprised me.'

'We had to persuade him not to. In the end we had to order him not to. It was a crazy idea. He was far too valuable to us. Anyway, what I am trying to explain is that already, by the end of the war, I knew a lot about you. You were familiar to me. And I felt a great deal of affection for you because of Woody and because of what Woody had told me. So. The end of the war and what happened afterwards. I think we need another drink. Let me get you one.' I allowed him to do so.

'The end of the war,' Dufour resumed, taking a large gulp from his full glass. 'I suppose that I have lived in interesting times, as the Chinese would say, but I think that the end of the war was the most interesting of the lot. I won't pull any punches, Feliks. I know you are sensitive about a lot of this stuff, but I will tell it how it was, or how I saw it at any rate.

'In 1944, France was in turmoil. The country was broke. There were massive food shortages. But worse than that, far worse than that, we were all at each other's throats. There had been the humiliation of the surrender to the Nazis. Then there had been the disgrace of the Vichy government. Democracy had shallow roots in France. The 1930s had been brittle, to put it mildly, and the war made everything worse. It's so difficult to believe that now. Here we are, sitting in a bar in the opulent capital city of a stable, ordered democracy. But in 1944 no one would have put much money on that being the outcome. All possibilities were open. That's what made it so exciting. And dangerous.

'One of the possibilities was a communist takeover. As you know, immediately after the war the communists were the largest single party in France. In elections they got the biggest share of

162

the vote. Just as the Nazis did in Germany in the 1930s, in fact. Another possibility was a military takeover. There were plenty of people longing for de Gaulle to impose a dictatorship, if only to prevent the communists from doing so, as I'm sure you will remember. That's the trouble with times like that. When you have a threat from one extreme, people run to the other extreme to prevent it. It doesn't matter which extreme is the devil and which is the saviour. What matters is that the centre collapses. Everything reasonable goes straight out of the window. Actually, it still seems like a miracle to me that we did manage to avoid both extremes, that the centre did hold and that democracy was gradually able to assert itself. But it was not easy, and it was not achieved without a lot of effort. And I was part of that effort.

'I make no bones about the fact that I loathe communism and always have done. I loathe it for a great many reasons, but above all I loathe it for its dishonesty. Over and over again after the war, in country after country, I saw communism leeching on to frail democracies, imposing its virus on an unsuspecting host, taking advantage of the tolerance of others to impose intolerance, subverting the very institutions it was purporting to uphold. By supposedly democratic means, the communists would gain a toehold in politics. When they had a toehold, they would force a foothold. And when they had a foothold, if no one stopped them, they would acquire a stranglehold. Exactly as the Nazis did, again. And by then it was too late. Because, although the veneer

163

of democracy remained, the interior workings of it had been eroded. It was like an exquisite 18th-century chair of lacquered walnut: perfect on the outside, but honeycombed with wood-worm within, so that if you tried to sit down, it would crumble to dust beneath you.

'It would have been difficult enough anyway, but in France in 1944 it was doubly difficult. That was because the communists claimed to have saved France by mounting the Resistance. The problem with the claim was that, although far from the whole truth, there was sufficient truth in it to make it credible. There were many communists in the Resistance. I know. I fought with them. Yvette was a communist, come to that. Did Woody tell you that?'

'Yes,' I said. 'He did.'

'But there were also many non-communists in the Resistance. Like me, for example. And Woody. And, of course, there were many communists who were not in the Resistance, who sat on their arses and lived quietly under Vichy. The leader of the French Communist Party, Thorez, was not exactly a hero. He spent the war in Moscow, being told what to do when he got back again. But many non-communists didn't distinguish themselves in the war either. The war cut across political lines completely. No one side could claim credit for resisting the Nazis; no side could escape the blame. No single party saved France. To be honest — and I don't like to say this any more than you like to hear it — it was the Americans who saved France. During the war, and after it with their money.

But that's by the by.

'As soon as the war was over, the communists began to infiltrate the police force. Nothing wrong with that, you may say, and no doubt you would, Feliks. They were a legitimate political party, so why should their members not join the police like supporters of other parties? Except that, in the case of the communists, it was like having a cuckoo in the nest. The same old story. They would gain a foothold. Then, gradually, decent non-communist officers would be denounced as collaborators. There was never any evidence; no one could defend themselves; in that atmosphere, the allegation alone was sufficient for them to be drummed out of the force. And, when they were, they were of course replaced by communists. It was an insidious process and it had to be stopped.

'I joined the police force immediately after the Liberation. I wanted to do it anyway, but I was determined to help prevent a communist takeover. Many of us saw what was happening, saw what would happen if it wasn't stopped, and did the same. I supported the socialists at the time, and I can assure you that no one understood communist methods better than the socialists. In fact it was the post-war socialist governments that put an end to this cancer, that started to purge the police force of these anti-democratic elements, and I did all I could to help them.

'In 1947, I transferred to the security services. My first assignment was in the Franche Comté, based in Besançon. My job was to monitor industrial subversion. Well, the Franche Comté is not exactly a heavily industrialised region and by far the biggest plant was the Peugeot works in Sochaux, which was already the scene of substantial communist activity. And that is where I come across you again. I am thumbing through a list I have been given of communist agitators, and there is your name: Feliks Zhukovski. I must admit that I was surprised.'

'I bet you were.'

'Surprised and disappointed, to be honest. It was a difficult moment for me. Not the first in those times, and not the last. I knew Woody had gone to America. I also knew he'd failed to find you before he went, and was searching for you from America. I now had the means to put you in touch with each other. Woody would not have been pleased to hear what you were up to, but at least he would have known where you were and that you were alive and well. Rather too well, if you ask me.'

'Why did you not tell him?'

'It was too risky. It was classified information, of course, and to have passed it on would have been a serious breach of duty. In normal times, I expect I would have turned a blind eye to that, but they were not normal times. It was quite possible that my communist colleagues were intercepting my personal mail and tapping my phone. In fact, I should think they very likely were. If they could produce evidence that I had passed on confidential information, I would have been flung out on my ear. In fact, I could have been charged with treason. I couldn't possibly take that chance. If you want to know why I have now gone out of my way to reunite you with Woody, that is part of the answer. I am more than aware that it was I who took a decision to prevent the reunion many years ago. I want to make amends. I want you both to know what I did, or didn't do, and why. If you feel an apology is required, I am offering it. I will not say I had no alternative. I did have an alternative. But I nevertheless insist that I was right not to take it.'

I did not indicate whether I felt that an apology was required. I was aware that there might be much more to come and I wanted to suspend judgement until I had heard it all. Instead, I bought Dufour another beer.

'So that was Sochaux,' he said. 'In the early '50s I was promoted to a job in Paris. Amongst other things, I had to keep an eye on communist publications, newspapers and periodicals and so on. So of course I came across you again. I was already familiar with *La Vague de la Gauche* and, as for Comrade Meurice, there were files on him bigger even than the ones on you on Oberman's desk.'

'What possible threat was there in *La Vague de la Gauche?*'

'Oh, none at all, I should think. But we liked to keep a watch on it. By the way, I'm intrigued to know how you felt about receiving your weekly pay packet from Uncle Joe?'

'What?'

'Come on, Feliks, don't tell me you didn't know. That rag was funded from Moscow.'

'I had no idea,' I said.

167

'Well, how else do you suppose it kept going? You didn't accept any advertising on principle.'

'We did actually. It was part of my job to get it.'

'Well you didn't do it very well. I don't remember ever seeing an advertisement.'

'It was not easy.'

'I should think not, if you were trying to persuade businessmen to advertise on one page while denouncing them as profiteers on the next.'

'We did have the personals.'

'Oh yes, the *petites annonces*. I remember those. In fact, I used to make a collection of them. I think my favourite was: 'Good home wanted for communist cat'. That was in *La Vague de la Gauche*, wasn't it?'

'It may have been. I do not remember.'

'I think it was. I have made an extensive study of cats over the years and I can assure you there is no such thing as a communist cat. They are all avid free marketeers. Anyway, you didn't have much advertising and you didn't sell many copies.'

'We printed thousands.'

'I wasn't talking about the print run. How many did you actually sell? Most of them were given away to the comrades to boost the circulation, as far as I could tell. The fact is you had next to no income. So where do you think the money came from?'

'I never thought about it.'

'Well, that's the answer. And that is also why it folded so rapidly in 1955. After Stalin's death, his successors were more cautious about their investments. In fact, if you come to think of it, your own business venture owes its existence to Stalin's death, which you may find ironic. Though God knows how it's been so successful if that's your grasp of economics.'

I must have looked hurt, because he leaned forward and patted my forearm. 'It's only a joke, Feliks; don't be upset by it.'

'Is that all you have to tell me?'

'No,' said Dufour; 'it is not.' I had feared it would not be since he had mentioned his assignment in the Franche Comté. 'We now move forward to 1968. I am still in Paris and one day I am approached by a colleague in Besançon. He tells me there is a large and active communist network in the Franche Comté, but they cannot penetrate it or identify its leading members. They know one of the main activists, but he is a long way down the chain. He works at Sochaux. They know he is receiving instructions, probably emanating from Moscow, and always synchronised with major political events. Of course they have attempted to find out where the chain leads. They have followed the man, but he appears to meet no one significant. His mail has been intercepted, but to no effect. The telephone tap has proved more productive and certain coded messages have been passed on. But the calls cannot be traced. They are always made from isolated call boxes in remote areas, and by the time the police have got there, no one is to be found. What is more, there is no single identifiable human voice. Instead, three or four people are speaking the message in unison on a cheap distorted tape recorder. He played one of the tapes to me. It sounded like being subverted by a barber's shop quartet.'

'Was this legal?'

'My dear Feliks, in France anything is legal if it needs to be. You ought to know that by now.'

'It sounds most irregular to me.'

Dufour ignored the remark. 'My colleague wanted to know if I had any ideas. I had not been in the Franche Comté for nearly 20 years, but he thought I might remember someone or something that would help. I think he must have been getting desperate. I was unable to help him directly. I knew no more than he did, probably a great deal less. But I did have an idea. I had always found that, when you were confronted with a large sewerage system, and you didn't have a plan of it, and you didn't know where the pipes led, it was sometimes helpful to drop a little dye into the system and see where the coloured shit emerged.

'I suggested that, if they could not trace messages coming down the chain, why did they not arrange for messages to be passed up the chain? Why not arrange for documents to be delivered to the activist with instructions to see they got safely to the top, and then follow the documents? My colleague mulled this over and said he thought it was a good idea in principle, but did not see how it could credibly be achieved. For it to work, he said, the document would have to be delivered by someone the activist knew, by someone he would trust implicitly, and by someone who could have indisputable access to a document delivered from the Eastern Bloc and be a believable courier for it. He couldn't think of any such person. I could.'

This was becoming unbearable. I did not know if Dufour was dragging it out deliberately, but that is how it felt. It was already clear that my great secret, my only secret, was not only known to someone, but to someone who was a friend of my brother. Furthermore, it was becoming clear that my secret was not what I thought it was; it was beginning to sound as though, far from betraying the West, I had in fact been tricked into betraying my own side. I did not know where the story would end, but the longer it went on, the worse it seemed to get. I was horrified by it. But I was also mesmerised. Who would not be? The tension was palpable. Most of all, I was aware that I needed to piss. The beer had got to me. There were two fresh glasses of it on the table when I returned. I said nothing, but let Dufour continue.

'I suggested you as the courier, Feliks. You had impeccable Party credentials. You had known the activist from your time in Sochaux. In fact both your names were on the list I had then. You were publishing a pro-communist guide to the Soviet bloc. You were constantly travelling in eastern Europe. What could be more natural than that you should be acting as a courier? In fact, to tell the truth, I suspected you might be doing so already. I never found any evidence.'

171

'There was none. It was not something I did.'

'Only the once then,' said Dufour. 'Anyway, the plan was put in place. That end of it was down to me. We were running a double agent in the Polish security services, Mateusz Kowalski his name was, and I arranged for him to approach you in Warsaw and put the offer to you. To your credit, you were reluctant to accept it. So I'm afraid we had to offer your mother's address as an extra inducement.'

'You shit,' I said.

'As you know, of course, you accepted the offer. And you performed the assignment very competently. As a matter of fact I was there when you made the drop, and a hell of a long time you kept me waiting, I must say. It was pouring with rain and I was squashed into a small car with three overweight policemen with bad breath in some back street in Montbéliard. Anyhow, it all worked. It was a successful operation and I'm pleased to say that several important arrests followed. It was quite a feather in my cap, actually. It got me a big promotion.'

'Good for you.'

'It's all right. I don't expect you to be pleased.'

'And did you know where Mama lived, or was that another lie?'

'No, we knew. That was true.'

I stood up violently. My chair crashed to the floor and our beers splashed over the table. I was furious with the man. I wanted to strike him, but that would have been absurd. I wanted to walk out, but I had not yet heard the end of the story.

'But you never delivered your side of the

172

bargain, you fucking little bastard,' I said. Gradually my temper subsided. I picked up my chair and sat down again. Other conversations in the bar resumed. Dufour sat impassively, watching my performance.

'No one has called me little for years,' he said eventually. 'Fucking bastard often, of course, but not little. I shall take that bit as a compliment. Unfortunately things weren't that simple, Feliks. They seldom were in my line of work. Although we didn't know this at the time, Kowalski was already under suspicion in Poland. His efforts, his successful efforts, to trace your mother through the official channels aroused more suspicion. It was the final straw. He was arrested soon after you saw him, and then he disappeared.'

'So what you are saying is that, after he was arrested, you had no access to his information?'

'Well I could say that, Feliks, and it would be perfectly plausible and I am sure you would believe it. But I've made up my mind to tell you the entire truth and that is what I will do. What you suggest is not true. We did have the information. I had it myself.'

'Why are you telling me this?'

'For many reasons, one of which is out of respect for the memory of a brave and honourable man, who had given both you and me his word that he would get your mother's address. A man who may well have known he was under suspicion, but who still ran that risk to honour his promise. A man who was determined to pass his information on to me

173

even if it killed him, which it very likely did. A man who, despite God knows what torture and threats by the communists to force him to disclose his contacts, refused to give your name when he was interrogated because, believe me, you would have known all about it if he had. A man quite unlike that little bastard in Montbéliard, who was only too pleased to give us your name the moment we arrested him.'

'You still have not explained why you did not give me Mama's address,' I said.

'Because I was angry with you. I was bloody livid, in fact. Can't you understand that? I was extremely upset that a decent, courageous man like Kowalski had given his life for a toerag of a fellow-traveller who was prepared to sell the country that had sheltered him down the river. I'm sorry to put it like that, Feliks, but that is precisely how I felt.'

'But that is not what I did.'

'It's what you thought you were doing.'

'And was Kowalski killed?'

'I don't know. I expect so. These are some of the things we are now starting to find out.'

'I cannot see how you could conceivably hold me responsible for what happened to Kowalski. In the end, I was as much a victim of the enterprise as he was.'

'Is that right, Feliks? When have you gone out on a limb? When have you risked your life for what you believe?'

'I am not having this,' I said. 'It was your operation and what happened was your responsibility and not mine. I am not taking the blame

174

for it to make your conscience feel better.'

'If you'd accepted the money in the first place, the rest might not have happened.'

'That is a pathetic argument,' I said. 'You sit here insulting me and now you tell me that, if only I had been entirely venal, it would have made everything all right. What sort of moral world do you inhabit? I am not surprised that you use sewage as an analogy; it seems to be your natural milieu.'

'You asked me to explain why I didn't give you your mother's address,' said Dufour, 'and that's what I'm trying to do. I am not justifying anything. I am simply telling you how I felt at the time. I dare say it was not rational, or defensible even. I felt very emotional about the whole thing, as I am trying to explain. We cannot always behave rationally.'

'I can,' I said.

'I doubt it,' said Dufour.

We could not resolve this argument. I was not interested in Dufour's emotions. All I cared about was that he had reneged on his promise to give me Mama's address. I was angry with Dufour, but I had to admit he had been honest. He had no need to say what he had. He had not taken the get-out clause with which I had presented him. I had the feeling he was even less impressed with his own behaviour than I was, and was now trying to make amends. I had a grudging respect for the man. At least you knew where you were with him. Less creditably, it was also occurring to me that he might have further uses. I did not feel too badly about this: he had

175

used me, so I would use him. Mama would now be 90. It was unlikely she was still alive, but not impossible. It was unlikely that Dufour still had access to her address, but not impossible. It might be the wrong address by now, but a 1968 address was nevertheless a great deal more promising than a 1939 address.

In retrospect, this was the moment when I made a decision about Dufour. I could have made an enemy of him, and there was good reason to do so. I could have walked out and left him as a virtual stranger. But I chose to make a friend of him. And I did it partly out of self-interest, and partly because at root I liked and respected him, but also — I think — for another reason. I was becoming aware of a void in my life. To some extent it was a physical void: the sudden absence of the activity that had consumed my life. But physical voids can be filled with other activities. What alarmed me was that the arrival of the physical void had exposed a much larger emotional void, and one that I was beginning to suspect had been there for a long time. This frenetic activity, all this running around from country to country, had disguised a gaping hollow at the centre of my life. I had no idea how I would fill it, but I felt that I needed to try. I felt also that I needed the company of men who understood the world of emotion and could interpret it for me. Woody had been the start of the process and, in the course of one morning with him, I had learned things about my life and about myself that I had not thought about before. Dufour seemed to be cut from the same

176

cloth: a man prepared to justify an irrational and, to me, dishonest action on the grounds of a superior emotion.

A long silence followed Dufour's last remark. He was making no attempt to leave. Rather, he seemed to be waiting for me to decide what I wanted to do. In the end, I stood up, took our empty glasses to the bar and came back with two full ones. I raised mine to his.

'I still think you were a bastard, René,' I said, 'but you are an honest bastard.'

'A big bastard or a little bastard?'

'I think we had better stick with the little.'

'Thank you.'

'Anything else about my life you would like to tell me? Any more revelations?'

'No, nothing. That is it. You left my life in 1968.'

'Until you turned up at the American embassy.'

'Yes. Until then.'

'So I suppose I can now guess what you were doing there.'

'Yes. It should not surprise you to know that the Americans routinely ask the French security services to check the names of people who apply for visas. I liaise with them often on the subject. It is one of my little retirement jobs. Since I had been so concerned with your case and since it was somewhat complicated, shall we say, I was directly involved in your application. Normally I wouldn't be at the actual interview, but I asked if I could be. I wanted to see how time had treated you. As I said, I have always felt I've known you, always felt I had a connection with you, albeit a somewhat unusual one. And I also felt I would like to be in a position to have this conversation with you one day.'

'If the Americans knew what I had done, why did they give me a visa?'

'Well, the Americans don't know exactly what you did. We're under no obligation to tell them everything. It's a purely voluntary procedure. I omitted to give them certain files. I told them that you had helped us on an important operation. Which was true. As far as it went. I suggested this could outweigh any youthful indiscretions or previous involvement you might have had with the Communist Party. I am pleased to say they agreed.'

I ignored the dismissal of my life as a youthful indiscretion. 'Why did you do it?' I asked.

'Well, for goodness' sake, one has to exercise some judgement. I know I've spent most of my life rooting out communists, but I'm not exactly a fanatic. One always has to use common sense. What possible threat could you be to America? Trouble is, the Americans have a habit of seeing things differently. As I told you last time, I interpret the real world for them. In your case, I assisted them in coming to a sensible decision. Which, after all, is what I was supposed to do.'

'It is a strange world,' I said. 'I spend all those years as a harmless member of the French Communist Party, a legitimate political party in a Western democracy, and find it would have disqualified me from entering the so-called bastion of freedom. I betray the West once, or think I do, and find that it now makes me *persona grata*.'

'That's about the size of it. Funny business, politics, isn't it?'

'And you think you have the superior morality, René?'

'Dear Feliks, if your beloved Communist Party had tried to recruit you, they would not have offered you the promise of seeing your mother, but the threat of something happening to her.'

'So that was the difference, was it? That was what it was about? One lot threaten to kill your mother and the other lot threaten to stop you seeing her?'

'We had the better class of threat, yes.'

'I do not find that particularly funny.'

'It was not meant to be funny. It was dirty work.'

'But somebody had to do it.'

'Yes. Somebody did. I'm sorry, but that goes back to what was happening in France after the war. And for a long time afterwards.'

'So it was a simple choice for you, was it, René?'

He reflected for a moment. 'I suppose you could say that the original choice was simple, yes. But the things that flowed from the choice were anything but simple. Like your situation, for example. My emotions were mixed, to put it mildly. No, of course I don't hold you responsible for Kowalski's death, if he did die. I don't think I even did that at the time, not rationally anyway. If you want to know, I felt guilty as hell. Guilty for what probably happened to Kowalski. As you say, that was my responsibility. I gave him the mission. Guilty for not giving you your mother's address. And guilty for not giving that address to Woody either. I knew how much you wanted it. It was the only thing that persuaded you to deliver the packet. I admired you for that. But I knew how much Woody wanted it too. It was agony to withhold that information.'

'So why did you?'

'In your case because I was angry with you, as I told you. I may have admired your motives, but I didn't admire your behaviour. How do you think I felt to know that Woody's brother was prepared to act as a courier for the communists? I was disgusted by it. And that was before things worked out the way they did with Kowalski.'

'So what would you have done, René, if it had been the only way of finding your mother after 30 years? Would you have run errands for your side?'

'I don't know.'

'Nonsense. You know very well you would.'

'Possibly.'

'So what in fact disgusted you was not my behaviour, but the fact I was a communist.'

'Perhaps.'

'Which is why you never gave me the address.'

'Possibly.'

'So why did you not give it to Woody? Were you still paranoid about communists tapping your phone?'

'Well, not communists, I suppose. Not by then. But someone. In my line of work, you

180

could never assume anything was secure. There was another reason too. By 1968, I had no idea whether you were in touch with Woody or not. And even if you weren't, you could have been soon after. He might have had trouble finding you, but you could have found him quite easily if you'd tried. Given what I've told you, do you think I could possibly risk Woody telling you that he had obtained your mother's address from the French security services?

'This was a huge issue for me. And it went far deeper and wider than Woody. I've told you what I felt about communism in France after the war. I've told you what my work was. You don't have to like it or agree with it, Feliks, but I hope you can accept that these were my convictions. I have also told you that I fought alongside communists in the Resistance. Well, sometimes — not often, but sometimes — I came across these former comrades in my work. Occasionally, I arrested one of them. Actually, I never did that myself. But a few were arrested on my orders. Arrested, interrogated, charged and mostly convicted. One of the men arrested after the operation in which you were involved, the head of the entire network in the Franche Comté as a matter of fact, was someone I'd known very well indeed in the war. How do you think I felt about that?

'For four years, we had shared a life. We had supported each other, protected each other, fought for the same cause. We had laughed together, eaten together, slept side by side. We had mourned dead friends together. And now I was having him arrested. How do you think I felt? How was it possible for me to do it? All I could tell myself was that life had changed. All I could say was that circumstances had once united us, and now they divided us. I didn't tell myself I was only doing my duty, although I was. I had heard that line used to justify too many shitty things during the war. I accepted that I had chosen that duty. It hadn't been forced upon me. I had believed in it and I still did. But neither did I forget all that had gone before. That was still a part of me too. I did not pretend that this man, or any of the others, was a different person to the one I had known during the war. He had believed then what he believed now. He was the same man and so was I. But life had changed and it had created new circumstances.

'The only way I could cope with these conflicting emotions was rigidly to separate my working life from the rest of it. It worked both ways. I didn't use professional knowledge to assist my private life. But neither did I use private knowledge to assist my professional life. I can remember one occasion when I knew a piece of damaging personal information about a man who was under suspicion, something that didn't reflect well on him. But I only possessed that information because of the war, because of something that had happened in the war. So I did not use it. I kept it to myself. And that was what I learned to do: to build an iron curtain between my two lives, you might say. It was the only way I could handle everything. It wasn't easy, I can tell you. And it was certainly not simple. In fact, it was as complicated as hell. Another beer?'

'I do not envy you,' I said when he returned. 'But I suppose that was the choice you made.'

'Yes it was, but it was also the circumstances. Choice determined that I took sides, and which side I took. But it was circumstances that created the moral dilemmas. It was the change in circumstances. As for you now, Feliks. Cheers.'

'It is not easy, I must admit.'

'No it's not. And I think it's tougher for you because you are having to confront these issues late in life, when you have never needed to before. At least I had to do that a long time ago. Conflicts between patriotism and personal loyalty, between the past and the present, between opposing concepts of duty, between heart and head. I've been wrestling with these things all my life. You are only just beginning.'

'Woody is coming over later in the year,' I said.

'Is he?' said René. 'That is wonderful. That is so good. And, you know, I think we will pick up exactly where we left off in 1944. There are some people you can do that with. I'm sure Woody will be one of them.'

'Yes,' I said; 'he is.'

'Is Wanda coming with him?'

'Yes. I have invited them both to stay.'

'I don't know that much about Wanda,' said René. 'I am longing to meet her. What did you think of her?'

'I find it difficult to say, René. She was very friendly to me. I am sure she is very pleasant.

But I would not say I formed any particular impression of her.'

'I think I will find it strange. I still think of Woody with Yvette. They were engaged, you know.'

'No; he did not tell me that.'

'Yes. They'd decided they would marry on the day that France was liberated. They'd spoken to the *curé* and it was agreed. There would be an instant wedding in the church in Corrençon. I teased Yvette about it. I asked her why a communist had decided to get married in church. She said Woody wanted it. Woody said Yvette insisted on it. Perhaps she felt that even a priest was better than a Vichy official. Anyway, it never happened. Yvette was killed early in 1944.'

'Woody wants to visit her grave.'

'I'm not sure that is wise,' said René. 'It's what we were talking about: the sudden flooding of emotions. I have dealt with it myself. I've gone back often. To Die, to the Vercors. To see my family. To visit the graves and memorials. It's been a long process, but I have made my peace with all that now. Woody has never been back. I don't know how he will feel. I don't expect he does. It could be everything, or it could be nothing. And I don't know which would be worse.'

'I do not think there will be any stopping him.'

'I'm sure there won't, Feliks. But I think maybe I should come too.'

'I am sure you would be welcome.'

'Thank you.'

'Woody told me that you had lost your wife recently.'

'Yes. Dominique died last year.'

'I am sorry. Was she in the Resistance too?'

'No. We met after the war.'

René said nothing further. I could tell that this was not a subject he wished to discuss. 'I was wondering,' I said, 'whether you still had my mother's address?'

'Not personally, but I expect I can get it. I should think it is in the file I was looking at recently. The one I didn't show to the Americans.'

'Could you get it for me?'

'Of course I will.'

'There were a great many files on Oberman's desk,' I said, 'not to mention the one that was not there. Were they all about me, René?'

'I expect so.'

'There were so many of them. Surely I have never been that important.'

'They were not all ours.'

'Whose were the others?'

'Feliks, the fact is that every country in the Eastern Bloc would have had a file on you, given your sympathies and what you have done with your life.'

'Are you saying they are all now sitting in the American embassy in Paris?'

'I don't know about all of them, but I should think some of them are. New circumstances, Feliks. Changed circumstances. Several of those countries are now most eager to oblige the Americans. I should think the Stasi files from

185

East Germany are there for a start.'

'Why?'

'When the GDR collapsed and Germany was reunited, the Stasi files on former GDR subjects were opened for public viewing in Germany. The files on other nationalities were retained privately by the German government. I shouldn't be surprised if they are now being shared with other Western countries.'

We were the last people in the bar and it was closing time. The proprietor had cleaned the tables and closed most of the shutters. He was loitering by our table, waiting for us to go. However, there was one more thing I needed to ask René.

'I once knew someone in East Germany,' I said; 'in East Berlin, in fact. I would quite like to know what became of them. Are you saying that their file is now on public view in Germany?'

'If there was one, yes. And there probably was. Not many people escaped having a Stasi file.'

'Could you find out for me?'

'Feliks, I am not a one-man missing persons bureau.'

'I thought that was exactly what you were.'

He laughed. 'You could find out that piece of information perfectly well yourself.'

'But you could find it out quicker.'

'Very well. I will do what I can. But this is the last one.'

'Unless circumstances change, of course,' I said.

'Feliks, you could easily become irritating. Come on. What's her name?'

'How do you know it's a 'she'?'

He looked at me. 'What's her name?'

'Kristin Bauer.'

'Age?'

I tried to remember. 'I do not know exactly. Early to mid 50s, I would think.'

'And she lives in what was East Berlin?'

'Yes. Or at least she did. I should think she lived in the Lichtenberg district. She certainly used to work in a bar there in the early '60s.'

'It's not much to go on, but I will see what I can find out.'

'Thank you.'

We were standing outside on the pavement now, preparing to walk to different Metro stations.

'Goodbye, Feliks. I hope I haven't shocked you too much.'

'I am getting used to it,' I replied. 'Every day seems to bring a shock of one sort or another.'

'It's good for you.'

'That is highly doubtful,' I replied. 'But I appreciate what you have told me. Or, to be precise, I appreciate that you have told me.'

'I always intended to,' said René. 'I'll be in touch. And perhaps we could meet up for another drink soon.'

'That would be nice,' I said.

I decided to walk home. It was a long way and it was late and it was raining and I was not entirely sober, but I wanted to walk. What René had told me had shaken me. It had shaken me more than any of the other things I had learned recently, which was saying something. As we had talked, I had tried to absorb the implications, but I could not do so. I could not assimilate the information. It had completely disorientated me.

It had not been a great surprise that it was in fact the French who had recruited me as a courier. René did not need to tell me that his was a dirty, duplicitous world. I knew that already. Admittedly, I do not believe it had occurred to me to doubt the authenticity of the man who had approached me in Warsaw, but perhaps it should have done, and it did not amaze me to discover the truth now. The impossible thing to absorb was the consequence: namely, that I had resigned from the Party as a direct result of what I saw as the Party's betrayal of me. Now it transpired that, far from the Party betraying me, I had in fact betrayed the Party. I had resigned from the Party because of a misunderstanding. I had allowed my mind to distance itself from Stalin because of a misunderstanding. I had changed my friends because of a misunderstanding. It was an unbearable thought.

The effect of this misunderstanding had been to loosen my bonds with communism, or at least with the practical experience of communism. Since 1968, I had looked at events in a different light. It was not a conversion, or anything like it, but it was a modification. I still saw the world as a leftist. I still identified with the ideals of communism. I still opposed the enemies of communism. I would maintain the Party line when I talked to strangers. But inside, something had changed. After 1968, it was never the same.

So what was I now to do? Was I to dismiss all

heretical thoughts of the last 23 years because they had been occasioned by a falsity? Was I to rejoin the Party, just as it was disintegrating? Was I to telephone my old friends and tell them I had dropped them owing to a misunderstanding? Was I to resume the attitudes of an unreformed Stalinist? Merely to ask myself the questions was to reveal how absurd these things would be. And yet, if that episode had not taken place, would I have modified my views in any way? If nothing that had happened between 1945 and 1968 had altered my opinions, why otherwise should anything that had happened since 1968? Moreover, if I had known the truth of the matter at the time, it would of course have driven me in precisely the opposite direction. I would have become an even more fanatical Party member. I would have excoriated the treachery of France, of the West, still further.

When René had been talking about his early life, I had not liked to interrupt or to contradict him, although of course I found a great deal of fault in what he was saying. Above all, I found his attitude simplistic. He seemed yet another naïve patriot, blind to the idiocies of nationalism, and I had met plenty of those in my life. In contrast, I liked to think that I was sophisticated, that I had a broader and more perceptive view of the world. The latter parts of the conversation had annihilated my assumption. René was not simplistic; in fact he had a highly subtle view of life. Admittedly, he simplified things in order to deal with them, and I could see why he had needed to do that, but it did not mean that he

189

regarded the world as being simple. Plainly he did not.

Perhaps I was the one who did that. Or had done. But I would not be able to do so any longer. I was now in a position so subtle it was impossible fully to grasp. It was not my fault that I had failed to appreciate the subtleties until now, but it would be my fault if I failed to deal with them. There were two undeniable facets of that position. The first was that my attitudes for the past 23 years had been shaped by a lie. The second was that they nevertheless remained my attitudes. I hated it.

The rain had stopped before I reached home and there was a large moon, very nearly full, hanging over Avenue Secrétan as I took the key from my pocket and prepared to unlock another door in my life.

9

A few days later I was riding on the train from Paris to Warsaw, returning to Poland. René Dufour had delivered his second promise. He had telephoned me with the 1968 address, an address in Warsaw. So Mama had not returned to Łódź.

It was a route I had travelled many times before, but it was a different journey. Those had been journeys to do with the present and the near future. This was a journey back to the past. I spent the time looking out of the window and thinking of the longer voyage that had brought me to this point. When had I last made a journey of this nature? Back in 1939, when I had travelled from Warsaw to Switzerland with Woody, when I last saw Mama. I was hoping that, if all went as I expected, I would be making a fresh journey afterwards, starting on tracks that did not lead to Basle, as if the detour to Basle had never happened, as if the intervening half-century had never taken place.

I was convinced that Mama was alive. So what if she was 90? People lived well beyond that. I had this overwhelming sense that this was intended to happen, that somehow there had been a reason for it all. This feeling seemed like an elemental force of nature, something in harmony with the flow of life itself.

I thought about Mama, and how I would find

her and whether she would be well. I imagined that she might have married. I still wondered why she had not got married previously, to our fathers. I wondered again who my father was. I imagined that Mama might have had other children. From what Woody had said, Mama would have missed us desperately, would have wanted a new family. Would she have been too old for that? Not necessarily. So perhaps there would be a new half-brother or half-sister to discover. And perhaps they would have families of their own.

I looked out of the train window at the fields of Germany. It was mid-April and it had been a wet spring. There was water everywhere. Rivers and streams had burst their banks and were flooding the low-lying pastures of central Europe. I thought again about Mark Bergelson and the bursting of dams. But the water no longer seemed a threat; its pervasiveness did not frighten me. Rather, it seemed like a balm that would cool the fevers of my life. Now, and for the first time ever, I was going home. I felt as though I was going home.

Suddenly I noticed the landscape change. Somewhere in the middle of Germany, the neat and well-ordered farmland metamorphosed into ancient bucolic fields. There were no signs, but I knew instantly that I had crossed what, until two years previously, had been the border between East and West Germany. That hedgerow had been the Iron Curtain. I wondered why I had never consciously noticed the change in the landscape before.

And, now that I did notice, what did I make of it? Easy, one side would have said: the change reflected the distinction between ordered human progress on the one hand and a lazy inefficiency on the other. Easy, the other side would have said: it reflected the distinction between impersonal money-driven imperatives on the one hand and the affirmation of human and social values on the other. Which did I believe? I did not know. I was not sure that the question made sense any longer. What did I feel? I felt at home in the old semi-tended fields of eastern Germany. They reminded me of home, of a pre-war, pre-industrialised Poland. They reminded me of trips out into the countryside when I was a boy, with Mama and Woody, with Aunt Lilia and Uncle Szmul and Mordechaj. There were fields like that outside Łódź: one place in particular, by a lake, where Mordechaj and I would splash in the water and dangle string from birch twigs and hope to catch a fish. We went there often, piling on to Uncle Szmul's cart and riding out into the country on those blissful days of high summer. So now I felt an instant affinity with these fields. But was that altogether a healthy thing? Why was a progressive leftist wallowing in nostalgia like some complacent *bourgeois?*

I arrived in Warsaw in the evening and went straight to the MDM hotel. It was a place that I knew well. In fact, it was the place where I had been propositioned by Kowalski, which gave my return a certain piquancy. I made no attempt to go to Mama's address. It would be too late for her and I would have to wait until the next day. But I did not go on the next day either. For some reason, I took it into my head to go to Łódź. I did not know what I expected to find. Or rather, I did know, because Woody had told me, and it would not be what I wanted to find. Which made it even more peculiar that I would choose to go. I think I wanted to make the transition backwards gradually. I wanted to reacquaint myself with home, with what had been home, to imagine myself back as I was, as things were. Perhaps I also wanted to make the journey back to Mama the same as that last journey, to travel by train from Łódź to Warsaw, only this time not to lose her, but to find her.

At any rate, I rose early in the morning and without hesitation went to the railway station and bought a return ticket to Łódź. Strangely, I had never been back before. There had been some good reasons for that. Łódź had not been an important tourist destination. But it was still a large city — the second largest in Poland, in fact. It still rated a significant listing in the *Guide*. Over the years, I had been to every other city in eastern Europe of comparable size and importance, but I had never returned to Łódź. Instead, I had relied on handouts from the Polish tourist people for the information I had published. A pattern seemed to be emerging of things I had shut out of my life.

The train pulled into Fabryczna station, the end of the line from Warsaw. For ten minutes I stood on the platform, a nine-year-old child again, transported back to the day when the

194

three of us had stood on the same platform, boarding a train that went in the opposite direction. At first I thought that nothing had changed. But it had. A new façade had been added at the end of the tracks. And even the main station building, apparently unaltered, had in fact been completely rebuilt after a fire in the 1950s. Yet another place had become a facsimile of itself.

It was a mistake to have gone back. Perhaps it always is. Places are never how you remember them. Maybe they have changed, or maybe one has changed oneself, or maybe it is a trick of memory. One's image of any place is a freak convergence of how it was at a particular moment and the particular eyes through which one viewed it, modified by time and never to be repeated. So it was with me and Łódź. It was shocking how little I knew about what had happened to the city — my home town — since 1939. In the same way that I had obliterated all thoughts of Mama, I had expunged all thoughts of the city from my mind, not even thought it fit to revisit for the *Guide*. Naturally, I had met people from Łódź throughout my life. Some of them must have asked where I came from, and I would have told them. But I do not think I asked for information and, although I must have received some unsolicited, it had made no impression on me and I had forgotten it. All I could recall knowing about Łódź since 1939 was what Woody had told me in Columbus.

That turned out to be misleading: not inaccurate, but misleading. When I heard that our house did not exist, I assumed that this was part of a wider devastation of the city, that Łódź had been another casualty of the ravages and munitions of the war. But it had not. In fact, the war had left it relatively unscathed. The Nazis had walked in on 8th September 1939, two weeks after our flight to Basle, and had taken the city almost unopposed. They incorporated Łódź into Germany and called it Litzmannstadt, as if it had never been Polish, always a German city. And when they left in January 1945, as the Red Army advanced towards them, they left in such a hurry that they did not have time to torch the city in their usual considerate fashion. Of course there had been changes since 1945, as there had been anywhere else in the world, but the skeleton of the city was intact and unchanged, and most of its major buildings with it. At lunchtime I strolled the entire length of Piotrkowska Street, all four kilometres of it, and imagined I could almost be treading in the footprints of my childhood self.

I suppose that children do not consider why they live where they live. That is where they are. That is what nature has ordained. Choices made by parents, exigencies of the adult world, are unknown and incalculable. We lived in this apartment, in this street, because we lived in this apartment, in this street. That is how it was. Later, of course, I would have become more aware of the neighbourhood and how it related to other neighbourhoods, but not at the age of nine and, in my case, not subsequently either because I had never thought about it. Until now.

In retrospect, I realised that we had lived in a predominantly Jewish quarter. This was not surprising. Łódź had a huge Jewish population before the war. At a guess, I should say that about a third of the people in the city were Jewish. There was a large textile industry in Łódź and many of the Jews worked in that, as my Uncle Szmul did in the Poznanski factory. As I remembered it, I did not believe that our neighbourhood had been entirely Jewish. But there had probably not been many Gentiles there like us.

The area had been close to the city centre. When Woody told me it had been badly damaged during the war, I assumed that it had been bombed or bombarded or something, but this was not what happened. During the war, the Nazis established a ghetto in Łódź, into which they corralled the area's Jewish population, some 200,000 of them. In August 1944, the ghetto had been emptied and its inhabitants sent to the death camps. Only 900 people survived. I wondered if Aunt Lilia and Uncle Szmul and Mordechaj had been among them, and feared not. Our apartment had been on the edge of what became the Łódź ghetto, at the top of Wschodnia Street by the synagogue. When Woody was sending birthday cards and Christmas cards to Mama at a lovingly remembered home, he was unknowingly sending them also to the site of mass murder.

Much of the ghetto improbably survived intact. I was able to visit streets and buildings that I recalled from my early childhood. Indeed,

Wschodnia Street still existed, but only the southern section of it. Our part, the part that had been in the ghetto, was now a park. Where our house had stood was now the edge of an ornamental lake. The synagogue had been obliterated by the Nazis and all the streets immediately around it had been rebuilt.

As I wandered the new park on the old ground, with the landmarks erased and nothing but a map and a distant memory to tell me that this was the same earth on which I had played with Mordechaj, I felt dismally unhappy. My head was full of the pain that had been inflicted here, a pain that would have been mine but for Mama's love and intuition. I wondered how much of that pain she had suffered herself. The optimism with which I had returned to Poland was dissipating by the minute. It no longer felt like home. This ridiculous notion I had entertained that I could somehow return to 1939 and begin life again from there, as if the intervening half-century had never occurred, now began to look like the delusion it was. Of course the intervening half-century had occurred and I was now standing on the ruins of part of it. What else had happened during the course of those years that might affect my new foundations? Was it any longer possible for there to be new foundations? I walked back to Fabryczna station, feeling utterly wretched, and waited for the next train to Warsaw.

All my life, I had considered myself unlucky: unlucky to have been deprived of a home, of love, unlucky to have had the rigidity and frigidity of Basle foisted on me throughout my adolescence. I was the hero of my story. I had risen above this loveless, luckless upbringing to make something of myself, of my life. As I stood on the platform of Łódź station, another delusion manifested itself and crumbled. Who could have been more lucky? Would Mordechaj be saying I was the unlucky one? Would Mordechaj be saying anything? Yet luck seemed to be the wrong word. It implied something random, haphazard. My luck had been the product of a loving will. And I had so far failed to discern it that I had denied it, misinterpreted it, made it a travesty of itself and then flung it back in Mama's absent face. For the first time in my life I started to loathe myself.

The journey back was unhappy. The previous day's approach to Warsaw had been filled with bright, optimistic thoughts. I was going home. I was going to see Mama. Now I knew that this would not happen. I would not see Mama because she was dead. She had died at some point between the time when it had taken the deviousness of René Dufour to prompt the thought that I might want to see her, and now, when I really did want to see her. I would deservedly be denied the opportunity. Fate would not make things easy for me. There would be no tearful reunion. No apologies for misunderstandings. No reconciliation. No redemption. I had not earned redemption. Instead, every last nuance of my failures of love, of humanity, of understanding, would be hurled back at me to haunt me for eternity. The only product of this journey would be guilt. It was this scenario that was the elemental force of nature, that was in harmony with the flow of life, not the Hollywood ending I had supplied the previous day.

I returned to Warsaw, to the MDM hotel, and viewed it with distaste. It had always seemed all right before: not grand, but a perfectly acceptable hotel. Now it seemed shabby and down-at-heel. The room was spartan, the fittings antiquated, the appearance dilapidated. Less than a month earlier, I had been in a hotel in New York, the big cheese negotiating the sale of his business in the Big Apple. I had looked down my nose at the extravagance of that hotel, its artificial choices and vacuous, pampering facilities. I did not know what to think now. I still did not like the idea of any of that on principle. But was this any more what I wanted? Increasingly there seemed to be this unwelcome choice: the hyper-driven superflow of consumerism or an arid nothingness. And nothing in between.

I took my time the following morning. I had taken my time the previous morning too. Then I had told myself that, if Mama had waited 50 years to see me, one more day would not hurt. Now I told myself that, as Mama was dead, any number of days would not hurt. As a matter of fact, they would postpone the hurt. It was nearly midday when I caught the bus from the city centre out towards the address that René Dufour had given me: Bobrowiecka Street, in the Sielce district. It was not a propitious neighbourhood. Drab concrete slabs stretched upwards, many storeys high, separated by depressing walkways and grassless earth. I was looking at it objectively now. Not with the rosy lens of a social engineer. Not with the loving heart of a returning son. But as a neutral observer, forensic and dispassionate. I hated it. Mama would have hated it. It represented everything she detested. I wondered why she had moved there. I wondered when. It could not have been after the war; the block would not have been built. Some time in the '60s, perhaps.

I located the correct piece of concrete. The number I wanted was on the sixth floor. There was a lift, but it was not working. I trudged up the staircase and knocked on the door. It was opened by a young woman with peroxide hair, children squabbling in the background. I explained that I was looking for Teresa Zhukovska. She looked blankly back at me. She suggested that I try the man on the next floor down. He had lived there a long time and might know more than she did. I walked down a flight and knocked on another door. There was no answer.

I imagined that he might be at work and would return in a few hours. If he was of working age, which I did not know. If there was work to be found locally, which it looked as if there might not be. I had no desire to return to the city centre and come back later. I decided to walk around the area, killing time, scuffling my soles, kicking my heels. It was a depressing experience. The place was a void, definable only by what was not there. There was no life, for a start. No hope. The feeling it gave was an absence of feeling. There it was, squatting: a collection of minerals from distant quarries deposited on a patch of Warsaw and self-assembled.

I tried to imagine Mama living here and found it impossible. I contrasted life in this place with my own life in metropolitan Paris, with the thriving street life and the jiving cafés. I contrasted it with Woody's life in suburban Columbus, with neo-Georgian porticos and irrigated lawns. They were pointless comparisons, I knew. A few miles away, in the centre of Warsaw, life was also different. There were slums in France and America. If I had been standing in some equivalent place in Marseilles or Detroit, what would I be feeling? There had been half a century of my solution here, and half a century of the other solution there, and what precisely had been solved in either case? But I was not sure that I would be feeling exactly the same in Marseilles or Detroit. I had not been to either, but I wondered whether I would not be feeling other sensations, a greater vibrancy, a greater sense of life, even if it were only the vibrancy of the ghetto and a life of street crime. Here I felt flat. The place was not a slum. It would have been better if it had been. The place was not anything. It was simply dead. Dead, dead, dead.

I looked at my watch. I had been there less than an hour. It already felt too long. I did not know the man was at work. Perhaps he had gone out for a while, or had been asleep. I returned to the fifth floor of the slab and knocked again. This time the door was opened and I found myself

202

talking to a man of about my own age. I explained why I had come.

'Come in,' the man said. 'Please won't you come in.' I wondered whether that would have happened in Marseilles or Detroit. Or in Paris or Columbus. It was a drab apartment. The man moved newspapers off a solitary armchair and beckoned me to occupy it.

'So,' he said, 'you are Teresa Zhukovska's son.'

'Yes,' I said. 'Is she alive?'

'I do not think so. I'm not certain, but I do not think so. She used to live upstairs, you say?'

'Yes. Did you know her?'

'Not myself. I came here in 1981, ten years ago, and she was not here then. But I'm sure I have heard of her. There was another woman who used to live here. Zofia Wisniewska. She lived on this floor: in the flat opposite. We used to talk. I am sure I used to hear her speak of Teresa Zhukovska.'

'Do you know where she is? Zofia Wisniewska?'

'Yes I do. She lives not far from here. In a smaller place. The stairs became too much for her. I see her occasionally. I can tell you where she lives.'

'But you do not think my mother is alive?' This was agony. I was almost sure of the answer, but not absolutely sure.

'I do not think so. I'm sorry. I appreciate that you need to know. But the way that Zofia used to talk of her makes me think she was not alive. Ask Zofia. She will know. She will know for sure.'

So, furnished with a third address, I set off

again. I did not have far to go. About half a kilometre away I found a cluster of small bungalows. It was the same neighbourhood, but somehow this part was less depressing. I knocked on the door and heard slow, difficult footsteps approach from the other side. Zofia Wisniewska was not as old as I had expected. Frail, and with painfully swollen legs, she was probably still in her 60s, but age had not treated her well. She looked at me kindly but suspiciously, the question unasked on her lips.

'Zofia Wisniewska?'

'I am.'

'Excuse me,' I said; 'I am sorry to disturb you. My name is Feliks Zhukovski.'

The words had a profound effect on her. She gave a little gasp, burst into tears and flung her arms around my neck. I thought I had my answer, but I asked all the same.

'No,' she sobbed. 'I am so sorry, Feliks, but no. She died a long time ago. In 1979. On 9th December. On her 79th birthday.' Now we were both in tears.

She led me into the room. It was small and neat, with many photographs and religious paraphernalia. I looked to see if there was a photograph of Mama, but I could not recognise one. She insisted on making me a cup of tea and I could hear her shuffling around in the small kitchen next door. I felt calm now, tearful but calm. The unanswerable question had been answered. I felt that other questions would now be answered too. I had not needed to explain who I was. The mention of my name had been sufficient. At long last I had found the connection that would span these fifty years. Zofia Wisniewska returned to the room precariously carrying a tray with two cups. I should have offered to help her before. I did so now.

'I'm sorry,' she said. 'I do not often have visitors. I ought to be able to manage.' I took one cup and she took the other and we both sat down. She looked at me for a long time.

'So,' she said; 'you are Feliks, young Feliks. I have heard so much about you. I cannot believe that I am talking to you. And in my own house! I am not sure that your mother would have believed it either. Tell me, how old are you now?'

'Sixty-one.'

'Sixty-one!' She shook her head slowly, as if trying to reconcile the middle-aged man in front of her with the nine-year-old child she had heard described. 'Sixty-one. And where are you living? Are you here in Warsaw?'

'No,' I said. 'I live in France. In Paris.'

'In Paris!' She seemed astonished. 'Have you lived there long?'

'Yes,' I said; 'for a very long time. I went there soon after the war.'

'Lucky you,' she said. I smiled. 'And what do you do?' she asked.

'I used to have my own business.' I did not say what it was. 'I have just sold it. So I suppose I am retired now.'

'Well, well. Your mother would have been so proud of you.' I did not feel confident this was true. 'Proud and surprised. She was sure you were going to be a teacher. Now please tell me about Woodrow. How is he?' She was enquiring after us as if we were members of her own family, as if we were as familiar to her as that.

'Woodrow is well,' I said. It had not occurred to her that we might have become separated too — why should it? — and I did not want to tell her. 'He is in the United States. He lives in Columbus, Ohio. He is retired also. He used to have his own real estate business.'

'Well, fancy that. All the way over there, and running real estates too.' I smiled again. (To be honest, I was not entirely sure what it meant either: did it mean there were such things as unreal estates?) 'Your mother would have been so proud of you both. She so much hoped you were still in the West, that you had managed to make a new start for yourselves there. And you, Feliks; you are married?'

'No,' I said.

'Oh. Never been married?'

'No,' I said.

'Oh.'

'But Woodrow is married. He has three children and many grandchildren.' I could not remember exactly how many grandchildren at that moment.

'Good. That is splendid. Your mother always hoped she had grandchildren. It was important to her.'

'Yes.'

'I can't believe I am talking to you, Feliks. After all this time. How did you know about me? How did you manage to find me?'

'It was a big coincidence,' I said. 'I met an old man in Paris recently — another Pole — and, when he heard my name, he said he had once known someone with my name in Warsaw. I said that was not unusual. But we talked about it and I realised that he was speaking of Mama. So he gave me an address — it was an old address; he had known her a long time earlier — and I went to the block of flats and eventually found this man on the fifth floor and he told me about you. So here I am.'

'What an extraordinary thing,' said Zofia, but I had no reason to think she disbelieved me. 'What was his name, this man in Paris?'

'It is ridiculous,' I said, 'but I do not remember now. I am not good with names. It is so strange after all this time. We tried so hard to find Mama. Over so many years.' I hoped that the plural would disguise the difference between Woody's strenuous efforts in this regard and my own singular one. But I started to cry again nonetheless.

'It's all right,' she said. 'You mustn't blame yourselves. It was almost impossible. She knew it was almost impossible, like looking for a needle in a haystack. She tried to find out what happened to you both, of course. If only that coincidence of yours had happened earlier. But there is no use in saying things like that. I should be grateful that you are here now. She would have been.'

'You were a good friend of hers?'

'Yes: a very good friend. When did I move into that apartment? About 1968, I think. Yes, 1968.

207

She was already there. We became friends immediately. So I knew her for 11 years. She told me so much. She was an amazing woman and she had lived an amazing life. She was not alone in that. Many people of her age in Poland had lived amazing lives, and not lives they would have chosen or would care to repeat.'

'Can you tell me about it?'

Zofia Wisniewska paused. 'Feliks, I could tell you about it, but I think it is better if she told you herself.' I must have looked surprised. 'Your mother always hoped she would see you both again. In fact, I think she expected it. It was the hope that kept her going. But in 1979, when she became ill, the hope started to desert her and she realised that she was never going to see you. So she wrote a long letter to you both, explaining everything that had happened to her, telling you everything she wanted to say. She gave it to me. I haven't read it, but I have it here. She asked me that, if either Woodrow or you should appear one day, or if I happened to meet anyone who knew you, I was to give it to them. I will give it to you now.'

She got up unsteadily and walked over to a small bureau beneath a large crucifix. She opened the drawer, took out the letter and gave it to me.

'Feliks,' she said, 'I think this letter will upset you. Don't read it here. Go somewhere safe to read it. If you would like to come back tomorrow to talk about it, please do so. But, if you don't want to, that is all right too and I shall understand.' She gave me a big hug.

Where could I go that was safe? I was not in a safe place. All I could do was take a bus back to the city centre and return to the bare room of the utilitarian hotel. There I sat on the stained bedspread and read Mama's letter.

10

My darling boys, my dearest darling boys,

I think of you so much. I can't tell you how much I long to see you, to hold you, to touch you, to know you're mine again. It's 40 years since I said goodbye to you. Forty years! Yet it seems far, far longer. It seems like a different age. I can't believe I'm the same woman as the mother who gave birth to you, who loved you. Who said goodbye to you.

For all this time, I've had one wish alone, one hope alone, and that is to see you both again. To see you both and to know you're all right, that the world has looked after you, that life has treated you kindly. It matters so much to me that this should be true. Beside it, nothing in the entire world matters.

I've believed in this hope for so long: that, one day, you would walk through my door, and there you'd be, and the years would roll away, all the pain of the years would fade away, and we would be together once more. I have wanted that dream so much. Often, it has been the only thing that's kept me alive. I didn't know how it would happen. I didn't know how it could happen. But I believed in it. I always believed.

But it's hard to believe any longer. I am 78. The doctors tell me I'm not well, but they don't need to tell me that. I know I'm not well. I feel death in my bones. I don't expect to last the year. Now it's not so bad. The trees are green and the birds are singing. I feel a little better at times like these and the pain is easier to bear. But when the summer sun fades away, and the trees lose their leaves, and the life of another year ebbs to its close, my life will ebb away too. And on one grey day quite soon, I'll be gone. I don't expect to see you now, before it happens.

For so long I've lived by hope. I have believed the only thing to give eventual meaning to my life, to give purpose to the suffering, would be to see you again. Now I feel this was another illusion, one of so many that have been stripped away over the years until there are no illusions left. Now I see it wasn't the reunion with you that was the meaning, but the hope itself. Now I see that the meaning of my life has been hope.

And, although the one grand hope has faded, other smaller hopes remain and they're enough for these last few weeks. I know how to eke out small morsels of hope until they become a feast. It's possible to do that, believe me. Really it is.

Last week a Polish Pope came to Warsaw. Can you imagine that! My friend Zofia took me to one of his Masses. I wept. I can see the shock on your faces as you read this: your mama finally swept into the embraces of the Church, a proper Pole at last!

It's all right. I know what I'm doing. It's only an approximation of faith. I was never much good at that sort of faith and things haven't changed. For me, this too is about hope: not the

211

hope I reserve for you, but the hope I still hold for my country. It's a provisional hope, come late at the end of a provisional life. I'm not confident of it. Maybe it will turn out to be another illusion. But maybe not.

One small hope that remains is that one of you will find this letter and will read it. That's such a tiny hope, really, compared with the grand hope that has gone. But maybe you will. And in this last little hope, I'm writing this letter.

I want to tell you everything that's happened to me since the day that changed my life for ever. I've been rehearsing this story for so long — how I'd tell you, the words I'd choose. But I see now I need to go further back than that day. Darling Woodrow, I'm sure I would have told you much about my early life, but perhaps you've forgotten. And darling Feliks, I can't remember how much I told you: you were so young. So I think I should tell it all.

I was born in 1900. When people ask me how old I am, I say I'm as old as the century and, with the 20th century, I'd say this makes me as old as time itself. There were three of us, three girls. Maria was the eldest. She was three years older than me. Then there were Lilia and I, and we were twins. We lived in Piatek, a small town about 30 kilometres from Łódź in Russian Poland. Papa was a Jew. I expect you remember that. He rejected his religion when he married Mama, which was unusual, but it was unusual for a Jew to marry a Pole at all at that time.

I find these things hard to talk about now, after all that's happened. The truth is so difficult to explain. I can't say that being a half-Jew made no difference. There were some Poles who detested Jews, who always did. The priest was one of them. That's why Mama came to hate her Church, as did I. That's why you were never baptised. You can't say the Poles were as guilty as the Germans in this. You really can't say that. But you can't say we were innocent either.

This thing affected the three of us in different ways. Lilia was the only one of us who looked Jewish. It's strange; I don't know why that was, but she was the only one who looked like Papa. Maria and I looked like Poles, like Mama. Lilia bore the brunt of whatever prejudice there was when we were children. For her, it wasn't a possibility to deny her roots, so she became proud of them and flaunted them. We were so close, Lilia and I, but this thing separated us. I don't mean that I minded about it, or that we argued over it. Not at all. I mean it was a difference between us, a difference that was to become important.

It wasn't a surprise to me when she chose to become a Jew or, later, when she met Szmul and married him. I expected those things. She expected them herself.

Maria was the opposite. Lilia and I weren't especially close to Maria. In fact, it's possible you two came to know Maria better than I ever did. There was the age difference, but it wasn't just that. When we were young, I felt Maria was aloof. She seemed to feel herself to be superior. But now I think maybe she was more sensitive about it, about being a half-caste as it were. I feel she lacked confidence, needed to be accepted.

It wasn't altogether easy in Poland to be accepted as a Jew, and not necessarily easy to be accepted as a Pole, but not hard in the right time and place to be accepted as a German. Even before she met Ernst, Maria thought of herself as a German Pole. That wasn't unusual. In our part of the country there were many Poles who felt themselves to be German. We were close to the border, as it was then. It's just that we weren't German in any way, until Maria chose that identity.

So she went one way, and Lilia went the other, and I stayed in the middle. I've always been happy with who I am. I'm a Pole, a Pole who happens to be half-Jewish. I feel comfortable with both parts of that. I'm proud of it. It's who I am.

I've lived most of my life in cities, hemmed in by buildings, crammed by people. I like city life. But I didn't grow up that way. I say Piatek was a small town, but it was no more than a large village. There were no cars. Fields were a few metres away.

Now, as I sit in this horrible concrete block in Warsaw, I can't believe it was I who ran in those fields. Too much has happened. But I did, and Lilia and I would gather flowers in the spring, and pick berries at the summer's end, and run through the winter snow while the boys from the town threw snowballs at us. It does no good to remember these things, but I think of them more and more.

Papa was an agricultural merchant. We weren't

rich. Our town wasn't rich. Poland wasn't rich. But we needed little and wanted for nothing, or nothing we understood. It was a beautiful childhood, for sure. Then in 1914 everything changed for the first time.

The Germans invaded. There was a huge battle with the Russians near Łódź and 200,000 people were killed, Poles amongst them on both sides. That was the first of the great upheavals. Lilia and I were 13 at the time and had left school the year before. We weren't much affected directly. Times got harder, but we managed. We'd been under Russian occupation before the war and now we were under German occupation. At the time, most of us thought that would be an improvement.

In 1917, Lilia and I went to Łódź. It was my idea. There was a boy in Piatek that I liked and, when he said he was going to Łódź, I wanted to go too and I persuaded Lilia to come with me. I was bored with small town life by then and wanted some excitement! So we spent the last two years of the war in Łódź. Stefan — that was the boy — went and lived with his grandparents and I lived there too. I don't mean like that! It was very innocent. We were very young and very innocent. Lilia went to stay with relatives of Papa in the Jewish quarter, but we still saw each other all the time.

Just before the war ended and the Germans left, I saw Maria for the last time. She was strolling down Piotrkowska Street arm in arm with a German soldier.

It shocked me, I can tell you! We didn't much

like the Germans by then. They'd stolen almost everything of value in the city. But I went up to her and we embraced and she introduced me to Ernst and told me they were getting married. She seemed so much more confident than when I'd last seen her, as if Ernst's uniform conferred on her some authority. I didn't like the thought of her parading with the enemy, but love — if it was love — explains things like that, perhaps excuses them.

We spoke for a long time. I think she was embarrassed to see me, but she mellowed as we talked. She planned to go back to Germany with Ernst. I asked if she was also planning to go back to Piatek before she left, to say goodbye to Papa and Mama. She looked at me in panic and changed the subject, which made me wonder what she'd told Ernst of our family. When we parted, I gave her my address in Łódź and asked if she'd get in touch when she reached Germany. She did do that. I never knew why, because she ignored everyone else in the family. But she stayed in touch with me.

Now we come to the best bit! It sounds so happy when I write it, and at the time it was happy. It was only later it came to feel so bitter, but it's the contrast that's bitter, not anything else. Everything was also very difficult, I may say. The Germans might have left, but they'd taken everything of value with them. Łódź — the great industrial city of Poland — was stripped bare of its equipment. Even the German-owned facto-ries were cleaned out.

They were hard times. But they were such

exciting times! And we listened on the radio, and we read in the newspapers, about the talks in Paris and dared to believe Poland would soon be a free country again. We'd waited 150 years for that.

Our hero was the American President, Woodrow Wilson. He was the one who had faith in us. And he was also the man for whom you were named, darling Woodrow. But I expect you've already guessed that. I hope the name hasn't been a burden to you. It was an ostentatious gesture, I know. People thought I was mad. But I felt so grateful to that man and I wanted to express it. I expect you've learned to carry the name. I expect you've lived up to it.

What wonderful years those were; what wonderful, wonderful years. We had our own country back and it was poor and everything was in chaos, but it didn't matter. Really, it didn't matter. And I was young, and I was happy and consumed with life.

I stayed in Łódź. I liked it there. I'd made many friends. There were so many lively people and so much was going on. My friends were doing interesting things. They were writers and artists and actors and political activists. Everything was possible then. All the shackles had been cut. All the taboos had been lifted. All possibilities were open to us and we did what we wanted for the first time.

I wanted to be a writer. I'd always wanted to do that. I wrote poetry. I wrote lots of poems. I don't know if they were any good. Sometimes I would recite them in a club we went to in the city, with jazz musicians improvising behind me.

It was unbelievable life could be this good. But I couldn't make money out of writing poems. So I became a dancer. That was something else I'd always enjoyed. I danced in a club on Przejazd Street. When that closed down, I found another. They were permanently opening and closing, these clubs, but there was always somewhere that would take me.

Let me talk now about love. I've always fallen in love easily, or when I was young anyway. I was impetuous. I did things first and thought about them afterwards. I called it love, but perhaps it wasn't; perhaps I just wanted that first feeling. Certainly I was good at the falling, but less good at what came afterwards. The falling was what I enjoyed: the first exhilaration of a new, unexpected love. And the sex, of course!

I hope I don't shock you. It feels so strange to be writing to my own sons, and yet know so little about you and what you feel. Maybe sons never want to hear their mothers talk about these things, but I shall anyway. I had many lovers. I was always falling head over heels for someone unsuitable. I was a born romantic in a country of romantics. There were so many possibilities.

If you lived in the countryside, or belonged to an older generation, the old rules applied. But they didn't apply to us! Not if you were young and in the city. Older people tut-tutted and told us we were degenerate, as older people do. But I don't think we were degenerate. We were young and in our prime, free Poles in a free Poland, and we were determined to enjoy it. I'm glad we did.

You have to seize the moment. You always have to do that. And we seized it with both hands and with open arms.

Your father, darling Woodrow; he was called Jerzy. I'm sorry, I don't remember his other name. He was a fine young man, a journalist. I was passionately in love with him for several months and you were the result of that love. I don't remember exactly what happened after that. I think he may have moved to Warsaw. I'm not sure he knew I was having his child. Perhaps I didn't know at the time he left. My memory on some things is as clear as a bell; on others it has faded.

I was happy to be pregnant. I wanted a baby and I wanted Jerzy's baby. I was so happy to be a mother. I was young, only 20 when you were born. This happened at the beginning of the period I'm talking about. I had no regrets about it. Only, I suppose, that you should never have known your father, darling Woodrow. I'm sorry about that. But I'm not sorry about anything else.

I had not been living in any fixed place before then, but moving around Łódź, staying with friends, sometimes with lovers. With a baby on the way, that had to change. Lilia came to my rescue. We were so different, Lilia and I: twins, but so different. I don't think she approved of my life, but she was very loyal. We loved each other very much, in all circumstances.

Lilia had found an apartment in the Jewish quarter, at 3 Wschodnia Street. She was teaching at a school nearby. So I moved in with her. This was before she met Szmul. She was still on her own then. I loved my life so much and I didn't want it to change. When the bump got too big I had to stop dancing, but I began again as soon as I could. To start with, I took you with me, darling Woodrow. But that became difficult and before long Lilia was looking after you most evenings. I'm so grateful to her. And I have to say Lilia was nearly as much a mother to you as I was.

So life went on and I was thrilled with every part of it. Thrilled to be in Łódź, thrilled to be a mother, thrilled to be dancing, thrilled to have my wonderful friends and companions, thrilled to be falling in and out of love.

Sometimes I thought about marriage, but I enjoyed my life too much the way it was. I was in no hurry to settle down. I didn't want to be constrained in any way. Money was tight, but it didn't matter. As long as there was food for the day, everything else could take care of itself, and it did.

I don't think I can convey how fantastic those times were, how completely unlike any other times I have known. I don't like sad old people who can talk only about the times of their youth, and now I'm one of them. But it's not only nostalgia that makes me speak like this. It is also the truth.

I always wanted another child. You were growing up into such a delightful boy, darling Woodrow, and I wanted another one of you! In the late '20s I met someone who was special to me. His name was Tadeusz Piotrowski and he was your father, darling Feliks.

He was older than me, by about 10 years I think. He had his own small publishing company. He published poems and short stories, some novels, mainly intellectual books of one sort or another. That's how I met him. I still dreamed of being a poet and I had a large collection of poems from over the years. So I went to see him in case he'd be interested in publishing them. I don't think he thought they were very good! He never did publish them, but he was gentle about it. He arranged for two or three of them to appear in a literary journal, which was kind.

I went around for months with the journals in my bag. I was so proud of them. When I met people, I'd tell them I was a poet. Look, I'd say, here are my poems in this highly respected journal. They were impressed, I could tell. Such a silly thing to do. So vain, but I was full of it.

Tadeusz was lovely; a kind and gentle man. We should have been good for each other. I was a live wire, as I expect you've guessed, and he earthed me. He was quiet and subdued, and I enlivened him. We stimulated each other. But I don't think love made him happy. I'm not sure he even wanted it. We had a strange relationship. He was never properly my boyfriend. I still saw other people. He didn't, I think, but there was no reason he shouldn't have done. There were no commitments.

We saw each other often over many years, but we seldom made love. I don't know why that was — not my choice certainly! Then, when I told him I was pregnant, he melted away. I don't know why; he didn't explain. I said it didn't matter, that he didn't have to marry me, that I'd bring our child up on my own. I said there was no reason it should spoil our friendship. But he melted away.

After you were born, darling Feliks, life started to change. I don't mean you changed it, but circumstances started to alter. I brought you up in the same way as I had Woodrow — rather unorthodox, I admit, but it worked happily. But somehow things weren't the same.

My life, my real life, the life I loved and that I wish still to celebrate with fireworks and circuses, was sandwiched between the births of the two of you. You, darling Woodrow, the harbinger of that glorious decade, born as the '20s dawned, and you, darling Feliks, the memento of it, born a month after it had ended. The advents of you both framed the heart of my life.

The change was to do with politics and what was going on, in Poland and in Europe. I had better tell you something about it. Not that I ever cared much for politics. But there are times and places where you can't help but be involved, and Poland between the wars was one of them.

I grew up in a divided country, ruled by foreigners. Now we were free. But we were poor, we were inexperienced and we had greedy neighbours, so it was a precarious freedom. How we could keep it, and whether we could keep it, were matters of huge importance to us. To all of us, whether we were interested in politics or not.

222

You couldn't be young and care about these things and not have an opinion on the subject.

I spent my time with a creative, intellectual crowd. We were pretty much all on the left, as you'd expect. In the beginning, it was easy to think we all believed in the same things — in freedom, in self-expression, in a more open, fairer society, all those things. A lot of our group were communist. I was never a communist. I called myself a socialist, like my hero Józef Piłsudski, but I'm not sure I was that either, any more than he was. They used to say that Piłsudski rode on a tram called Socialism, but got off at the stop marked Independence. I think I did the same.

I came to hate the communists. They were very arrogant, you know; very contemptuous of anyone else's opinion, which I found a strange attitude for people who said they wanted to make our lives better. They were never interested in our lives, in how our lives actually were, only in their ideas of how they should be.

I remember Tadeusz having an argument with one of them and saying you could never have democracy under communism. Oh, we're demo-crats, you know, said the communist. How can you be democrats, asked Tadeusz, when you have a one-party system? We don't have a one-party system, said the communist, we have two parties: one of them's in power and the other's in jail. You see what I mean? So arrogant. And he thought it was funny.

In the '30s we started getting news of what Stalin was doing — the show trials and the deaths and the disappearances. When people said it was strange to construct the perfect society on a foundation of human bones, all you got was glib self-satisfied answers from the communists. Oh, they said, you can't make an omelette without breaking eggs. They were always saying things like that. How callous. How inhuman. I wonder what they feel about it now: a whole country, half a continent, littered with broken eggs and the shells of broken people.

So it became difficult in the '30s. Everything started to unravel, and when Piłsudski died in 1935, it became worse still. We'd grown up, of course, and people were going their separate ways. The bright young optimists of the '20s were getting married, raising families, trying to make careers, trying to make ends meet. There was still an artistic crowd in the city, but it was smaller.

We argued more and the discussions became edgier, more frantic. We no longer assumed we were on the same side. In fact, we knew that we weren't. The glue that had held us together had dissolved. Everything was fragmenting. We watched the power of Stalin growing in Russia, and we watched the power of Hitler growing in Germany, and we were afraid. Everyone in Europe was afraid, but we Poles had most reason to be afraid.

Everything became nastier. There had always been some anti-Semitism in Poland, but now there was so much more. Piłsudski would never have allowed it. He was very strict about that. Now things changed.

We were still living at 3 Wschodnia Street. Actually we weren't, because when Piłsudski died they renamed the street after him. He had once lived there for a few months in 1900. Can you imagine that? Living in the same street as Piłsudski! Lilia was married by then and Mordechaj was born at about the same time as you, Feliks. They'd moved a few doors down the street, to Szmul's house, and the three of us were left in the old apartment.

Things started to change. Lilia and her family suffered from it far more than me. I don't know whether you two ever did. You went to schools outside the Jewish quarter. I made sure of that. I didn't want to define us in that way, or in any way. But your friends would have known where you lived.

Did it make a difference to you? I wonder. Perhaps not. It was subtle at that point: the things grown-ups notice and that children may not. But I noticed it. Some people I knew would cut me dead in the street. Surprising people. People I'd known for years. People who you didn't think would behave like that. But rats have a keen sense of smell, they say, and they could tell which way the wind was blowing. Everyone was starting to take sides. I didn't want to take sides. I liked life without sides, but that was becoming impossible.

So we all started withdrawing into our own worlds, whatever they were, however we chose to define them. I had two worlds. The first was the world of you two, of where we lived, of Lilia and Szmul and Mordechaj, of schools, of local shops.

The other was the world of dancing. I didn't dance so much. Many of the clubs had closed down. But I could still dance at the big hotels, at the Savoy and the Grand, and I did that two or three nights a week.

I think I danced then better than I ever danced: not with the stupendous abandon of the '20s, but with more feeling. I can't tell you how important it was to me, what it meant to me. I felt bad about it too, because I wasn't with you. But you were a young man by then, my darling Woodrow, and had a life of your own; and you, my darling Feliks, sometimes I could take you with me and there was always Lilia to look after you.

Now I think back, perhaps there was a certain desperation about it. It felt as though, if I could only keep dancing, everything would be all right, the plate would keep spinning on top of the stick, and that if I once stopped . . .

August 1939. What a month. It was strange; August had always been kind to me before. I looked forward to August; it was when good things happened. But not in 1939.

Invasion was imminent. We all knew that. So I made myself think about the future. I didn't want to. I'd been burying my head in the sand until then. Łódź was so close to Germany, an important city on a straight line to Warsaw. We had to get away from it. I thought perhaps if we went somewhere in the south, somewhere deep in the country, we could be safe. But I had no money. I mean, no money at all except what it took to live. I could do nothing without money.

It was already early August, I think.

I don't want to say this, but I will. One of you knows it already — have you remembered, my darling Feliks? — and I'd like to explain. There were always men at the club, men on their own. Of course there were; that's why I had my job; that's who I was dancing for. I suppose I was quite pretty, though I say it myself, so I often had propositions. That was normal. That had been going on for years. I always said no, naturally I did, unless I thought I was in love with them of course, which was different.

Anyway, I began to realise that if I was to have enough money, there was only one way of getting it. It was the last thing I wanted to do except for one other. And that was to be with you in Łódź when the Nazis walked in.

I know what you thought, Feliks. I saw you there, looking at me through the crack in your door, with that anxious grown-up child's face of yours. You saw me see you. I know you did. You saw me coming out of my room with this man and you saw him give me money and I knew exactly what you were thinking. And I'd like to tell you it wasn't true, that he was an old friend, that it was a gift or something. But it was true.

It's an unfair burden to place on you: to tell you that your mother sold herself so we should have the money to escape Łódź. But that's the truth. I did it several times that month, but I was more careful the other times. It wasn't a lot of money. No one had much money for anything, not even that, and I was nearly 40 and my market value had declined! But gradually I was able to scrape together some savings.

Then everything changed. And it changed so suddenly and so appallingly that it altered life for ever. Of all the things I need to tell you, this is the one that causes me the greatest pain. Even now.

It was Sunday 19th August. There was one life for me before that day and another life after it.

This is what happened. It concerned Lilia and Szmul and Mordechaj. I'm sure you remember, both of you, those summer days when we used to go out into the country on Szmul's cart and picnic in the fields. There was one place in particular — the place with that small lake, where you and Mordechaj would pretend you were fishing, darling Feliks. You must remember.

Anyway, the weather was fine that weekend and on the Saturday I went round to Lilia's and she suggested we go out to that place on the Sunday. And I was thrilled, because everything was so tense and so difficult and I thought we'd feel better for it, but I was sad too, because I knew there'd be few days like this left to enjoy, that maybe this was the last even.

On the Sunday morning, Szmul knocked on the door and said he was sorry, but there were things he needed to do and we wouldn't be able to go. He was very calm about it, I remember; not agitated at all. So I was sad, but there was nothing to be done about it and that was that.

This is what I discovered the next day. Szmul did go on the outing. He took Lilia and Mordechaj, all of them dressed in their best clothes, and put them on the cart, and they rode out into the country, to that same place by the lake. And they sat in the field and ate their picnic.

Then he killed them. He shot them. Szmul shot Lilia and Mordechaj. His own wife and child. After he'd done that, he carried their bodies to the lake, weighted them down with stones and put them in. He left the picnic things exactly as they were: pieces of bread, an apple core, a half-drunk bottle of water. Then he got on the cart, rode back to Łódź and went to his house. There he shot himself.

Neighbours heard the shot and the police were called. That's when I heard about it. I went round to their house and there was Szmul, lying on their bed with his brains blown out. I was sick.

I didn't know what had happened to Lilia and Mordechaj. No one did at that moment. Someone had seen them all ride off together in the morning, and someone had seen Szmul come back alone. It was terrible already, but it looked as if it might be worse. I didn't want you to know about it. It was too shocking. I'd have to tell you later, but not then. I went back to our house and you were coming out of the front door, Woodrow. There was a lot of commotion in the street and I expect you wanted to see what it was about. I shooed you back inside. Goodness knows what sort of state I was in. But I managed to pack you both off somewhere for the night, I don't remember where.

The next day, the man who farmed those fields was harvesting. Everyone was harvesting then, I remember; all the farmers wanted to get the crops in before the Germans arrived. He found the remains of the picnic and he found the bodies of Lilia and Mordechaj. The stones had come loose and they'd floated to the surface. That's when I understood what had happened.

Even now, after all these years, after everything else that has occurred, my hands tremble and my whole body shakes as I write these words. But if I am to tell you everything, if I am to explain why things happened the way they did, I have to tell this story. It shocks me in a way I can't describe. I have nightmares about it to this day.

Szmul was a lovely man and a loving man. He adored Lilia and Mordechaj and they adored him. But he was a pessimist, and he was a depressive. Goodness knows, there was enough for an optimist to despair about then.

Everyone knew what the Nazis thought of the Jews, what they'd already started to do to the Jews. The *anschluss* in Austria the year before had affected him badly. Hitler forced the union between Germany and Austria and Jews threw themselves off the tower of St Stephen's Cathedral in Vienna in terror at what would happen. Szmul talked about it a lot. He felt the same thing would happen in Poland; he was convinced of it. He felt we would all be dead before long.

And you can't say he was wrong. When you know about everything that happened afterwards, you can't say he was wrong. Would Lilia and Mordechaj have been any better off if they'd lived to be exterminated at Chelmno or

Auschwitz instead of being executed by a loving hand? Because it was a loving hand, I'm sure of it. I've never doubted that for one moment.

It was an act of love. It was murder as an act of love, and that's what made it so especially shocking.

I couldn't have done it. I suppose it's a question of hope. I can't imagine living life without hope. I've always lived with hope, always always always. And although, almost certainly, they would have died later, they might not have done.

What I found hardest to understand, impossible for a long time, was why Szmul did it the way he did. Why did he not shoot himself right there in the field? What reason was there not to? If his own suicide was an afterthought — which I couldn't believe — what reason would a loving father and husband have to murder his family and to live himself? If not, why should this botched cover-up be of any relevance? Why go to the trouble of returning to Łódź? And, if Szmul wanted what had happened to Lilia and Mordechaj to remain private, to be the subject of speculation but not of certain knowledge, why had he left the picnic things in the field? And did he announce to his family what he was about to do?

You can tell there was a ritualistic element to the story, with the family dressed in their best clothes, not what you'd normally do for a picnic, and then the final meal before death. Rather a Christian symbolism, you might think, but not far from the story of Abraham either. I feel that,

231

after their picnic, Szmul would have spoken to the others. He'd have explained what was about to happen. He'd have declared an act of undying love. He'd have asked them to pray together, as they did.

As to why Szmul returned to Łódź, I think that was because of the horse. The cart belonged to Szmul, but the horse belonged to someone else. He used to borrow it. And I think he felt it irresponsible to leave someone else's horse abandoned in the countryside. He'd have felt the proper thing to do was to return it to its stable in the city.

And if you say this is ridiculous, to be thinking of a borrowed horse in the enormity of a situation like that, I don't agree. From my own experience I can tell you that, in the middle of the most cataclysmic events, it's the mundane, trivial, petty things of life that we do think about. In the middle of chaos, small remembrances of order and propriety are enacted.

I can't know what happened. I've thought about it endlessly, but I can't know. That is what I think must have happened: it's the only explanation that makes sense to me. It is what I now believe. You can't torture yourself about these things for ever.

But that still leaves the question of my darling sister, Lilia. If this is what happened, did Lilia know about it in advance; was it a joint decision? Did Lilia assent to the murder of her son? Lilia was my twin. I knew Lilia better than anyone, better even than Szmul. I don't believe Lilia knew. There are things men do, and things women do, and they both have their reasoning but they're not the same. I don't think Lilia would have done that.

There is another thing too. The police said Mordechaj was shot cleanly in the head, but that Lilia was shot in the stomach, several times at close range. I think she was trying to stop him. I think she was trying to save her son.

I was in such a state after their deaths. If I'd been behaving normally, I don't know if I'd have done what I did do. But I felt I'd been given a sign, an urgent warning. There was no time left. Whatever was done had to be done now. No hesitation whatsoever. Do it.

I thought of Maria. I was thinking of her anyway, because these events made me think about the family, about the innocent time when we were children. I knew Maria was now in Switzerland. We were still in touch. I'd never thought of her before in this connection. Switzerland seemed so distant. The idea of going there had not occurred to me. Now it seemed the obvious choice, the safest place in the world in these circumstances.

I went to the station and found out what it would cost to send you both to Switzerland. I didn't have all the money, but I had most of it, and I still had my old fur coat and thought I could pawn that. So I sent a telegram to Maria, asking if I could send you, and she said yes. I shall always be grateful to her for that. It would have been easy to refuse. I shall never forget that, at the time it most mattered, Maria said yes, and I love her for that.

I didn't think about any of this. There was no time to think. I just did it. I knew what I was doing. I was making you safe. That dreadful picnic was on the Sunday. I found out all that had happened on the Monday. I telegrammed Maria on the Tuesday. The tickets were bought on the Wednesday. You left on the Thursday. Thursday, 24th August 1939.

You were so wonderful during those few days, darling Woodrow; so incredibly caring and supportive. I still didn't tell you what had happened. I couldn't bear to talk about it. But you knew something terrible had occurred and you were wonderful to me. And darling Feliks, I'm sure you'd have been equally wonderful, but you were so much younger and I kept you out of the way of everything as much as possible.

You didn't want to go, Woodrow; do you remember that? In fact, you refused. I think you wanted to take on the whole German army on your own. But I told you it was arranged, and that Feliks was going anyway and had to go, and would you let your nine-year-old brother travel half the way across Europe on his own in those circumstances? So you said you'd go, for my sake, and I was so grateful for that. And then you begged me to come too. You went on and on about it. And that was so hard.

I could have gone. I didn't have enough money, but you did, so I could have gone. There were two reasons why I didn't go: one good, and the other that turned out to be bad.

The first one was to do with Mama. Papa had died a few years before. It had been ridiculous.

The Catholics didn't want him in their cemetery, and the Jews didn't want him in theirs. We had to bury him in a municipal cemetery in another town. And these people think they're better than the rest of us!

So Mama was on her own now. What was I supposed to do? Take the train to Switzerland, and write to Mama from Basle telling her that Maria and I were both there now, oh and by the way, Lilia is dead; Szmul murdered her? I felt at the very least I should go to Piatek myself, and see Mama and tell her everything that had happened. So that was my first reason for staying in Poland.

The second was simple and quite wrong. I had no idea what would happen. I imagined Germany would overrun western Poland again and perhaps Russia would overrun eastern Poland again. In fact, if you can believe it, on the very day I was buying your tickets for Basle, von Ribbentrop was sitting in Moscow, signing a treaty with Molotov, chopping Poland up exactly like that.

I knew things would be worse this time, that the German occupation would be brutal, but I didn't know how much worse. I knew it would be unpleasant to be Jewish and of course I didn't know if I was Jewish, or if the Germans would think I was. But, whatever I imagined, I didn't imagine what would actually happen, or how long it would last, or what would happen afterwards.

If I'd known all that, I'd have been on the train with you like a shot. I was longing to go.

But I felt I shouldn't, and I felt I needn't. A terrible miscalculation, for which I've paid the price ever since. And if, between us, we'd been a few zloty short of the third train ticket, I'd have been flat on my back with my legs open in no time at all! There, I've shocked you again.

So you went and I stayed. I stood on the platform of Warsaw station on that Thursday morning and waved you out of my life for ever. I'm sorry; I'll have a little break now. I'll return to all this tomorrow.

★　★　★

The next day I left Łódź. The apartment was an unhappy place to be. I may not have been thinking straight, but I wasn't stupid. Łódź was no place to be when the Germans attacked, and the Jewish quarter would be the worst place of all. I'd no ties there now, no reason to be there.

I took only a few possessions I could carry, a little food, that was all. And my poems, of course! I made room for some photographs, the one of you two together, the one of Maria and Lilia and me. All gone now. I haven't even had them for company. I don't know what happened to them.

Plenty of people were leaving Łódź, plenty of sensible people. I managed to get lifts easily until I reached Piatek. Mama was pleased to see me. What was happening, what was about to happen, was so unbearable that all anyone wanted to do was to be with family and friends. I told her what I'd done with you two, and she felt I'd done the

236

right thing. I don't think she knew I could be so responsible! And I told her about Lilia, and that was heartbreaking for both of us. It was awful. It slept with us like this huge shared sorrow.

A few days later the Germans invaded. There was a small battle to the west of Piatek, which of course we lost. They set up their own administration. Everyone had to fill in this ridiculous form. I spoke a little German and that was enough for me to be able to tick the third box — the box that kept you out of the dregs. I was ashamed of it, because it meant acknowledging that my home town belonged to Germany, but at least it got me better rations and the chance of work.

I was beyond caring by then. Spent. I was in a state of shock. There had been no time to grieve for Lilia and Szmul and Mordechaj. Nor for you. I was missing you desperately already. I never knew that you'd arrived in Basle. I still don't.

It was a miracle that some of the trains were running when you went. Most of them had been requisitioned for troop movements, for our futile attempt to stop the Nazis. I'd asked Maria to telegram me when you arrived, but I didn't stay long enough in Łódź to receive her message. I wrote to Maria from Mama's of course, but I dare say my letters were not received. I never heard back anyhow.

What followed was a period of recuperation: a few weeks of doing nothing while I tried to come to terms with all this and to help Mama to do the same. I barely went outside the house for days on end. Complete stillness while Europe exploded.

The next few years were quiet for me, if you can believe it. There's not much to tell you. I had no energy. I suspended my feelings. I passed the time gently, in the middle of that maelstrom, waiting for it to end, waiting until you should come back again. It was the existence of a zombie. Life was hard. I did a few odd jobs, but there was no regular work. The Germans took most of the food.

At least they decided I wasn't Jewish. I'm ashamed to say that, selfishly, I was glad Papa wasn't still alive. There had been a thousand Jews in Piatek before the war. Now they had all been forced into a ghetto in the town. Later they were transferred to the Łódź ghetto. Piatek, Łódź and the whole area were incorporated into Germany again.

We had little news, little real news. There was plenty of propaganda and I dare say some of it may have been true, but we didn't know how much or which bits. We knew the war was still being fought in Europe. We knew the Germans were still in Poland. There was no mistaking that. That's probably all we knew for certain. I kept writing to you in Basle and getting no reply. I stopped expecting one. It seemed possible that my letters were arriving, but not your replies, so I continued to write. I sent you birthday cards and Christmas cards every year, which I made myself. No presents, I'm afraid, but I'm sure you'll forgive that!

Mama was becoming more frail. She was in

her early 70s by then, and that was old for the times. She needed more and more care. And so it went on until the autumn of 1943, when Mama died. She went very peacefully. It seemed a contradiction in the middle of a war, but she did. The Catholics kindly agreed to bury her. And that was the end of a chapter and, although it was sad, it was dignified and it was fitting and those were rare things in those days.

Then I needed to decide what to do. I longed to go to Basle, to be with you. But it was completely impossible at that time — not even worth thinking about. I could have stayed in Piatek. It would certainly have been safer. But it felt like time to move on. I like being in the centre of things. It was out of character for me to be sitting in a small town doing nothing. It had been good for me for those years; I'd needed that breathing space for a while. But life had to resume at some point and this felt like the moment.

I could have returned to Łódź, but I didn't want to go. I knew the Nazis had established a ghetto there, incarcerating the Jews in their own quarter, the neighbourhood where we'd lived. They'd not murdered them yet. That came later. I knew many old friends from Piatek were now in the Łódź ghetto. I'd no desire to see any of that. All the happy memories of the city had been erased, and I was left with the painful ones. I had no wish to animate them further.

So I decided to go to Warsaw. It wasn't straightforward. What to me would have been a journey to my capital city was now, according to the Germans, a visit to a foreign country. But I bribed someone to give me the correct papers and it wasn't difficult to find a quiet place to slip over the border. It was only 15 kilometres away.

I didn't know Warsaw well. I'd been there a few times, but that was all. I thought that, if there was any life in Poland, there would be life there. I had the addresses of friends I'd known who had moved to the city. I had no idea whether they were still there, whether they were still alive, but it was a start.

I wasn't prepared for what I'd find. I didn't expect all the damage. I didn't expect so many Germans. It had been peaceful in Piatek; here everything was so tense. The Germans were already losing the war, but I'd not known that before. We had received only their propaganda. I'd heard nothing of the uprising in the Warsaw ghetto. I didn't realise that almost all the Jews in Warsaw had already been exterminated. These were the things I discovered when I arrived.

One of my old friends was still at the address I had for her, in Nowy Swiat, near the city centre. She was a nurse, active in the underground. She introduced me to many friends of hers, also active. I needed to work, if I could, and I also wanted to become involved again. My spirits were rising and I was fed up with being a non-combatant.

So they asked what I could do and I said I wrote poetry, and they said they didn't think that would be much use. And I said I danced, and they looked at me obliquely, and must have wondered if my dancing days might be over. But

I still had my looks and I still had my personality, chutzpah as Papa would have called it, and they suggested I should find a job as a waitress in a café frequented by the German staff. So I did.

One night I did a truly shocking thing. It's the one thing in my life of which I'm utterly ashamed. But one of the reasons for telling you this whole story, if you don't know already, is to impress on you that there are no limits to what any human being may do in certain circumstances.

I don't mean there are few limits. I mean that there are no limits whatsoever. None at all. You have heard what other people were prepared to do, but now I'll tell you what I did.

Like any waitress in any bar in any war, or even not in a war, I was propositioned regularly, mostly by German officers. And every time I said no. I was lucky to have the choice. Plenty of Polish girls were raped in those circumstances. But maybe it was because I was older, or maybe it was because they were officers and not common soldiers, I don't know, but anyhow I wasn't raped and my refusals were always accepted.

Then one night I said yes.

He was a handsome German officer, a little younger than me I should think, and he asked me if I'd like to go with him and I said yes. He knew of a room nearby which was empty and would be safe, so we went there. And I lay there on the bed while a Nazi officer made love to me, looking up into his eyes, kissing his lips. And I enjoyed it.

241

Whatever possessed me to do such a thing? I know I'm impetuous, but why that? In the immediate aftermath of the event, I was terrified. Suppose I'd been observed by someone. I feared that my friends would execute me as a traitor. So I decided to tell them about it immediately.

I made up this story, or twisted the story, about noticing this German officer who'd drunk a lot and seemed to have a loose tongue, and how I'd enticed him into bed in the hope of some valuable pillow talk; how sadly I'd learned nothing — I wasn't going to risk making that bit up — and how I now felt vile and cheap. That part was true by then. I'd no need to play the actress for that bit. Nor when I burst into tears and rushed to the toilet to be sick. And they were so sweet, and so sympathetic and so convinced by it, and that made me feel worse. They said it had been brave of me, but there was no need to do it again, and I said I most certainly wouldn't.

Why did I do it? What can I possibly say to excuse myself? Only that it was a time of intense feeling and acute awareness of the present moment. Only that I was lonely. Only that no one had made love to me for more than four years. Only that he had kind eyes. Maybe he was as sickened by the brutality of his life as I was. I don't know; I stopped him when he tried to talk about it. There were Nazis like that. I'd like to think he was one of them. I felt he was.

I was so ashamed of what I did, but there was no undoing of it. There was an old SS song that used to go: 'And if you don't want my brotherhood, I'll smash your skull and smash it good'. Well, I gave this man my brotherhood, or sisterhood, but for many days afterwards I wished he'd smashed my skull. And, for many years after that, I couldn't help but feel the things that happened to me were the punishment for my wickedness. Sometimes I still do.

In July 1944, the word was that there would be an uprising against the Nazis soon, that we were preparing to evict the invader from our city. At first I couldn't see how we could even think of taking on the military machine that controlled Warsaw. But friends were optimistic and said I was wrong. The Russians were a mile away and would come to our aid once the signal was given. Our government in London had made plans with the British and Americans. Help would come for sure, and I was a silly woman who didn't understand politics.

I don't like to say 'I told you so', but it seemed to me that no one had come to our aid before and I didn't see why they'd come now.

The rising started on 1st August and it lasted for 66 days. It was supposed to be over in a few days, as it always is, when these friends of ours would come to our rescue. But no one came. So we had to do it alone. We withstood the German army for 66 days, entirely on our own, until there were few of us left and nothing whatsoever of our city. And then we had to capitulate.

I can't write properly about these times. I'm a passionate woman. You know that, my darlings! The feelings of those days were so intense, their conclusion so achingly sad, that the only things left at the end were complete numbness, a deadening of sensibility and the departure of the spirit that had made everything possible.

And so it has been ever since. It's not that the emotions aren't there. On the contrary, they are so volatile that, if I dared unleash them, they'd consume me. I can't risk that. So I don't wish to talk much about it. And what I do say will perhaps sound as if it was written by someone else, by a foreign correspondent in a distant war zone, by a reporter commentating on the scarred battle lines of my heart.

I was no hero anyhow. Thousands were, but I wasn't one of them. I risked my life, but we all did. That was a commonplace thing to do.

I wasn't out on the streets, hurling home-made petrol bombs at German tanks, nor firing antiquated rifles with too little ammunition at their positions. For the first and last time in my life, I managed to be a professional writer! I worked on the Home Army's newspaper, writing some things (not poetry!), helping it to be printed, making sure it was distributed. It was a nomadic existence. The Germans were desperate to destroy the presses. We moved often, from the basement of one ruined building to another. We had several presses, in several places, to guard against disaster, but we were always moving.

To begin with, we had glorious victories, unimagined successes. The Nazis were taken by surprise. They had no answer to our guerrilla tactics. It wasn't a type of warfare that appealed to their mentality. If our allies had come to our aid then, we would have been the liberators of our city.

But they didn't. The Russians sat on the opposite bank of the Vistula and watched us die. Occasionally there was an airdrop from British or American planes, but not much, and most of it fell behind German lines. No one had planned for it to continue for so long. There were no preparations for that, just a series of improvisations.

As you'd expect, the Germans were remorseless, pushing us back and back into the heart of the old city. What started boldly on the grand thoroughfares ended in the sewers. We became sewer rats, mired in the filth of the underbelly of humanity. There was hardly anything to eat. We were all scavengers by then, feeding on scraps from the litter heap of history. Thousands of us died, in the anonymous decorum of ruined buildings or publicly on the streets, unburied and unburiable.

Human death was incidental to the process. The objective, for the Nazis, was the death of a city, the death of a country, the death of a culture that had shown the temerity to defy the Third Reich when it was meant to be cowed and defeated. We were never cowed, but now we were defeated. The city was annihilated. By the end, it had been razed almost completely to the ground.

Look at the pictures of the ruins of Warsaw and look at the pictures of the ruins of Hiroshima and see if you can tell which city died a single death, and which died a thousand deaths, strung out over two murderous months.

The picture I retain of those times is the image of a burning horse, set ablaze by an incendiary bomb, galloping in flames through the derelict streets of Warsaw. I still see that horse in my dreams.

There were recriminations, of course. They started immediately. Don't they always, when things go wrong? The leadership, so admired when it began, was ridiculed for incompetence. But what were we supposed to do? We had a chance of making our own destiny. In the process we discovered who our friends were and, as usual, we didn't have any. At least no one can say we didn't try. At least we fought to the very end. History will say we did that.

Or some history will. The communist history says no such thing. Go into any bookshop in Warsaw today and you won't find any book that relates these events. In communist eyes, they didn't happen. They don't want the world to know that in 1944 the victorious Red Army sat a mile away from the centre of Warsaw all through those two months, while the Nazis crushed every breath of life from the city, and lifted not one finger to help us.

So these events didn't happen, as on so many other occasions when the truth was inconvenient. I who, for the only time in my life, helped to write a page of history, now find that — in the place where I live, in the place where it happened — the page has been ripped out. I was a non-person in a time of non-persons, a participant in a non-event.

Well, I've had practice in being a non-person. I spent the next ten years being a non-person.

In October, when we were forced to

capitulate, the Germans emptied the city so they could achieve its total destruction. We were divided into groups — combatants and civilians, men and women — and were marched out of the city. I never considered myself a combatant, not in the way others were. I never held a gun. But I was a member of the Home Army, and to the Germans that made me a combatant. So I was marched out of Warsaw with my women colleagues from the rising — nurses, couriers, other journalists like myself.

We had no idea where we were going. I still don't know what happened to the different groups. One day someone will write a history of this, but it hasn't been written yet, as far as I know. For the moment it remains another chapter in the non-history.

I know something of course, mainly from talking to people in Warsaw many years later, but I don't have the whole picture. I know some of the women's groups from the Home Army went to camps in Germany and became conscripted labour. I know others were sent to Auschwitz and Ravensbruck and were murdered. I don't believe there was any sense to these decisions. No clinical eye discriminated between objective destinations. It was an arbitrary process. Some people the Germans killed. Others they used. Others they forgot about. All I knew at the time was what happened to me. I had no idea if I was lucky or unlucky, or if the same thing happened to all of us.

My group was sent to a camp south of Warsaw and we stayed there from October to January.

There were two or three hundred of us, herded into a compound surrounded by chicken wire, an emaciated clutch of hens on a battery farm. A few uninterested soldiers guarded us. I suppose we might have overpowered them easily, but there no longer seemed a point to that, or to anything. A child with a water pistol could have guarded us then.

We lived in unheated huts, sleeping on the floor. It was one of the coldest winters in memory. We wore the clothes in which we'd left Warsaw. We ate turnip soup. We had no news from the outside. We presumed the Nazis would soon be defeated, but we didn't know that. Nor did it excite us particularly. For years, we'd longed for the day when the Germans would leave, yearned for our liberation, our day of victory. There would be no liberation now. No victory. All that remained was to know which form of defeat would emerge.

We imagined the Russians would come soon. We knew, or most of us did, why they'd waited across the Vistula for two months. It suited Stalin for Polish patriots and Nazis to be killing each other. There would be fewer of each for him to kill later. It suited him for the flower of Polish youth, for the best young people, the ones who would have and should have rebuilt a free country after the war, to die in the ruins of Warsaw.

With each day that passed, the ranks of the future opposition were depleted.

In January 1945, the Russians came. A detachment of the Red Army arrived at the camp on a freezing day. They shot our German guards. We still didn't know what would become of us. We were interviewed, briefly, and assigned our futures. We were told we were traitors. We, who had fought the Nazis for the honour of our country, were told we were traitors. When we asked who or what we had betrayed, we were told we were collaborators. We were called prostitutes by the communists because we'd been raped by the fascists.

It was always so incestuous in Poland. Sleep on one side of the bed and you were raped by the father; sleep on the other and you were raped by the mother. There was no such thing as innocence in Poland.

We were asked what jobs we did, what jobs our husbands did. The wheat was separated from the chaff. One woman said her husband was an engineer. She was wheat. Perhaps I should have said that too. No one would have known. But, with my silly conceit, I said I was a poet, with no husband. I was chaff. She was perplexed and wondered why she was being treated differently from me. I told her it was simple: bridges don't mind who builds them, but poems care very much indeed.

Trucks arrived one morning: grey army trucks. They took us to a station nearby. We were put into carriages, prodded with sticks like cattle. We trundled along the tracks for three days, heading east; that was all we knew. We had no food. I was lucky. I was by the side of the truck. It was colder there, but I could squint between the slats and see something: splinters of Poland, splinters of Russia, splinters of Europe going by.

We arrived where we arrived. I still don't know where it was. Not exactly. It was to be my home for ten years, but I never knew where it was. It was a non-home for a non-person. There was a bleak, unending landscape of frozen fields. There was an encampment. It was empty when we arrived, but others had been there before us. What happened to them, or who they were, I don't know. We were put to work. The encampment grew. The place was a centre for forced work. Or a prison, to put it another way.

I was never told why I was there. I did various jobs. Sometimes I worked in the fields, when they weren't frozen. Sometimes I sewed. Sometimes I helped to build roads. I looked at my legs and remembered they had once danced. I looked at my heart and remembered it had once danced.

We lived in the cabins, sleeping on slatted bunks with thin mattresses and lice. There were blocks for men and blocks for women. We washed under a cold tap when we could. The food was enough to keep us able to work. I never saw a doctor. And that's how I spent ten years of my life.

I expect people would say we were political prisoners, but we weren't. We were prisoners of politics, which is a different thing. A different thing and a safer thing; also a more pointless thing. Had I been a political prisoner, I'd have been interrogated; I'd have been tortured perhaps; I'd have been tried, after a fashion; maybe I'd have been killed. None of these things

250

happened to me. I'm glad of that, but at least it would have meant I existed in someone else's mind. As it was, we existed only in our own minds, and in each other's.

Throughout those ten years, one thing and one thing alone kept me going, and that was the thought that one day I'd see you both again, my darling, darling boys. I thought about you so much. I thought about you all the time. When my back was bent picking cabbages, I thought of you. When it was bent over my sewing, I thought of you. When it was bent shovelling earth, I thought of you. When I lay awake at night, I thought of you. When I wondered how much more of this I could survive, I thought of you.

Whatever else you've done in your lives, my darlings, whatever has become of you, one thing you've both done is to have kept your Mama alive for ten years. And you don't yet know you did this.

I fantasised incessantly about how we would meet. I kept seven different fantasies; one for each day of the week! I had them worked out to the tiniest detail. I envisaged the circumstances, the locations, how we would meet, what we would say to each other, what you'd be doing, the wives you'd married, the children you'd have; everything. I knew each fantasy perfectly by heart. I rehearsed them endlessly. Each one would take several hours to enact in my head. I won't tell you what they were. They were silly. And none of them came true. But for ten years I believed they would, or that one of them would.

It was fantasy, but it was also a form of

subversion, the only form I could manage. Stalin didn't want me to have a family. He wanted the Party to be the only family. No more ties of flesh and blood, only the Party. When children were persuaded to denounce their parents, that was Stalin's triumph. When I thought of you, yearned for you, prayed for you, that was my triumph. I was one egg that wouldn't be broken.

I'm sorry to say, my darling Feliks, that this wasn't true of your father.

I saw Tadeusz again in Russia. We were working on the same road gang one day. He wasn't a young man by then, but he looked so much older than he actually was. I didn't recognise him, but he recognised me. It wasn't easy to talk during work, and the men weren't encouraged to talk to the women anyway, but we snatched a few conversations now and again. They weren't happy.

I'd never seen a man with his spirit so broken. That keen intelligence, all gone. It was like talking to the living dead. I tried to kindle my dream in him. I told him all about you, darling Feliks, everything I could remember. Probably some of it invented! I told him what I'd done with you both. I told him how we would all meet again, how one day we would all be together. I said, look, how proud that should make you, to see your own son as a man, and was that not something worth living for?

But it wasn't. For Tadeusz, nothing was worth living for. He awaited death as a widow awaits her pension. And one day it came to him. One day he wasn't at work and another man told me he'd died. I'm afraid I didn't weep. I'd no tears left to shed for the dead, but tears only for the living.

There would have been no death certificate. There never was, for any of the hundreds that died in that place. If there had been, no doubt there would have been a formal medical explanation. But I don't need a non-existent certificate. I can tell you plainly how your father died, my darling Feliks. He was murdered by Stalin.

One day in 1955 I came home. We all did. It was as sudden as that. One day we were told we would be returning to Poland. We weren't told why, any more than we were told why we'd been taken to Russia in the first place. We were escorted to another train, with seats this time if you were lucky enough to get one, and the train brought me to Warsaw.

I was shown to a cramped apartment that I had to share with many others and was told it was my home. I was given a few zloty. I was provided with work. I was told I was pardoned. I wasn't told for what I'd been pardoned. I was 54. I was exhausted by all those years of toil and hardship. I had not eaten what I'd call a proper meal since before the war. I didn't know whether any of my friends were still alive, or where I could find them if they were.

They say now that 200,000 Poles came home when I did. Stalin had died; the Terror was over; Gomulka was running Poland; some sort of normality resumed. 200,000 people! And that does not include the ones who never came home. We were arrested for no crime, tried on no charge, convicted with no guilt. Then incarcerated for a decade, far from home, in subhuman conditions. And all this by the regime that would usher in a new golden age of human history!

What did it prove? What was the point of it? To show it could be done; to prove who was in control; to demonstrate to the keenest mind and the fiercest spirit that independence was futile, that the individual had been abolished, that the Party now ruled everything: heart, head and soul.

It wasn't even a case of cause and effect, that if you stepped out of line you'd be punished. It was entirely arbitrary. As far as Stalin was concerned, you could still be punished if you didn't step out of line. Laws of cause and effect had been abolished too. And, when they went, all purpose or moral value in the human will went also.

In time, it became fashionable to say that Stalin had gone too far. Gone too far! He'd been to places unimaginable in human history. This was psychological manipulation and control on an epic scale. This was the negation of humanity and the antithesis of life.

I've thought about it a lot and I must say I think Stalin was worse even than Hitler.

This is supposed to be impossible. It is universally accepted that the scale of human evil is calibrated on Hitler. Hitler despised non-Aryans and he exterminated them. But he didn't suddenly turn round one day and say, right, this Wednesday we will now exterminate some

Aryans instead. He wasn't capricious in that way. He wasn't mad in that way, although in plenty of others.

Stalin was. If it pleased him, Stalin could kill his friends and spare his enemies. You could dedicate your life to pleasing Stalin if you were fool enough, and one day he could kill you. People say there are countries where it is illegal to deny that Hitler killed the Jews. I don't know of any country where it is illegal to deny that Stalin killed millions of his own subjects.

Anyway, enough of that, my darlings. I don't have much more to say now. All these pages on the events of a few years, and then nothing. Nothing much to say about the last 24 years at all, really.

The work wasn't much, but it was something. There were no vacancies for poets, you'll be surprised to learn, nor for old dancers with thick, veined legs. I worked as a janitor in a school for some years and then it was time to retire and to receive my pitiful pension with gratitude. At that time I was moved to this new concrete jungle they'd just built. Wherever I'd envisaged ending my days, it wasn't in a place like this.

Sometimes, when the snow falls and it's dangerous to go out, I look out of the window and think of running through the fields of Piatek with Lilia. It does no good to remember that, or her. It does me no good to wonder how life could possibly have turned out this way, or what I might have done differently.

I've found some old friends over the years,

friends from Łódź, friends from the Warsaw rising. It used not to be easy to talk about things, but that's become better now. We talk a lot. And I've made some new friends too, like Zofia Wisniewska, who lives in these flats and to whom I shall entrust this letter. I can't say life has been bad, this last quarter-century. It depends on the point of comparison. Compared with life in Russia, or during the war, it is far, far better. But that's not saying much.

The hardest thing has been learning to accept there is nothing I can now do to find you, my darlings. And yet you, and the seeing of you, had been the reason for all this and was what had made survival possible.

I had no possessions when I returned. None at all. I had no contacts. None at all. When I was first in Russia, I made it one of my little daily tasks to recite Maria's address in Basle. I knew it would be important later. But one day I couldn't remember it, and it never came back to me. So the one thing, the obvious thing, that I might have done wasn't available to me.

No matter, I thought at the time, there will be other ways of finding out. I went to government offices and talked to officials. They were of no help. My case wasn't unusual. I expect they'd spent the last ten years dealing with thousands of similar questions. What could they do? They didn't know what had become of you any more than I did. Well, if I could have found a kind official, perhaps he could have looked in the Basle telephone directory for me, but it would have done no good. I remembered Ernst's surname: Schmidt. Wonderful! Of all names, why did he have to have that one? Please find me the address in Basle for someone called Schmidt.

I considered what you might do to find me. I didn't imagine you'd come looking for me in a concrete block in Warsaw. I thought perhaps you'd write to the old address in Łódź. I knew that would do no good unless I did something.

I managed to save a little money for the train fare to Łódź and one day I went there. It felt strange. I had no desire to return, except as a means of finding you. I knew what had happened in Łódź. It was so peculiar to be back in that city, with so much that was familiar, but with the heart of it — the place where all my memories were — ripped out for ever.

I went to the post office and asked if they ever received letters for the street where we'd lived. The man said they'd received hundreds of thousands for that neighbourhood after the war. They'd been thrown away. What else was there to do with them? I asked if any were still received. He said he didn't know. I asked that, if I gave him the old address, would they forward any letters to me in Warsaw. He looked at me as if this was some insanely impossible request.

And this was a Pole I was talking to, if you can believe it! I think it was too long ago. They were bored with it, I expect. Yet another old woman desperate for news of relatives. They'd seen thousands of those. If it was so important to her, why had she waited more than ten years to ask, I expect they thought. Any emotion had gone by now. All that was left was this vast bureaucratic indifference. I gave him the old address anyway, but no letters were forwarded to Warsaw.

While I was in Łódź, I thought I'd revisit Piatek. It was a painful visit for me, more painful even than Łódź. Piatek was my first home. It was where I'd been born, where I'd lived for 16 years, where I'd returned when the war came. Memories of Łódź may be stronger, more emotional, but — although I call them both home — Piatek is my real home. There was no news of you in Piatek. There was no news of you anywhere.

So I don't wish you to think I didn't try. I did everything I could. But the circumstances made none of it easy. Maybe it would have been easier directly after the war. I don't know. Maybe Stalin took away not only ten years of my life, but my one chance of making contact with you. All I've been able to do since is to wait and to hope. And I've never stopped doing that, at least until recently. It has felt like living permanently under an anaesthetic. The whole of Poland has felt like that.

Perhaps the days of youth are always more vital, old age dull by comparison. Perhaps so much happened to the country in a few short years, with incalculable human consequences, that Poland's nervous system had to shut down for a while. It's getting better now, but only recently.

When I returned, there was no admission of what had happened. I may have been pardoned, but I wasn't acknowledged. There was no official recognition. We were eliminated from the statistics. In those huge filing systems that these people keep, it'll be recorded that Teresa Zhukovska lived in Łódź until 1939 and in Warsaw from 1955. There'll be no record of what happened to her between those years.

Yet my life hasn't been exceptional. There've been many others who have suffered what I've suffered, and many far worse. So many people have comparable stories that they can't bring themselves to talk about.

I suppose that in normal life — whatever that might be — bad luck is the exception. But, if you happened to be living in Poland in the 1930s, bad luck was the rule. It was exceptional to be lucky. Of us all, only Maria was lucky. And perhaps you two, my darlings. Perhaps you two as well.

Yesterday I burnt my frying pan. It was the only pan I had for my cooking. I was concentrating so much on what I was writing that I didn't even smell the burning. So today I had to get a new pan. There's a shop nearby that sells old bits and pieces for very little, so I went there and asked if they'd a pan and the man looked around and produced this brand new pan wrapped up in old newspaper. I tried to pay him for it, but he wouldn't take anything.

When I got home, I looked at the newspaper as I unwrapped the pan, and can you believe it was from May 1935. A newspaper from May 1935! The month Piłsudski died. I saw him once, when he came to Łódź. And there was a picture of him, which I've cut out and put by my bed. It brought back so many memories. Because that,

259

really, was the only good time for so many of us: the years between 1920 and Piłsudski's death in 1935. And what years they were! But haven't we paid for them. Payment. Payment. Payment. And it hasn't stopped yet.

Oh, they said Piłsudski wasn't a proper democrat. They said he wasn't a proper socialist. So what are they saying now, these people? Are they saying that Hitler was a better democrat? Are they saying that Stalin was a better socialist? Are they even alive to say anything?

I don't believe in much any more. Too many things have happened. I don't believe in any politician. I don't believe in any political system. I don't believe what I read in the newspapers. I don't believe in the words that come out of anybody's mouth. They've been twisted and distorted too often, manipulated to say the opposite of what they mean.

I don't believe in the Father, Son and Holy Spirit. I'd like to, but I don't. They weren't there for me when I needed them.

The residue of my non-belief is what I do believe. And that is what I see with my own eyes and what I feel in my own heart. It is nothing and it is everything. The eyes of living, and the heart of feeling, in a shrivelled old body.

I dare to think about anything. I dare to hope, even though I may never see you again, that you'll receive this letter and that it'll mean something to you. I dare to hope you've devoted the same time and anguish to searching for me as I've devoted to searching for you. But I dare to think the opposite too: that you haven't done this, that it hasn't been important to you, that you've made your own lives and let the memory fade of the one who gave you birth.

It's all right. If that is what you've done, you have my permission and my blessing. I know a mother loves her children far more than children can love their mother. Perhaps, if you have wives and children, you'll know that too. So it's all right.

Sometimes I've dared to think what might have happened if I'd not put you on the train to Basle, if we'd stayed to face the future together. Or if I'd chosen to go with you. But these are futile thoughts. They have no merit. I'd be lying if I said I didn't have bitter regrets. There hasn't been a day go by when I haven't wished I'd done things differently, had I known all the things that would happen and all the things that would not. These are selfish regrets.

Well, I'm a selfish person, but on one shining day I made a grand unselfish gesture, and how can I possibly regret that? What meaning would there be to life if I did regret it? Only the meaning Stalin chose to give it.

So I both regret it and I don't regret it. Perhaps it's a question of what happened to you both, my darlings. If you are free and happy, if you've had the chance of a life that's better than mine, then I'm so thrilled I had the courage to make that decision. But if not . . . well, that might be different. And that's the one thing I've never known and now, I think, never will.

When I was in Russia for all those years, I

thought of the poems I'd loved, the poems I'd written, the poems of others I'd read, and tried to hold them in my head and to remember them. That was the other thing I did, the other thing that saved me. Whatever Stalin might do, he couldn't destroy the love of family or the truth of poetry. It was a partial remembrance. I could recall stanzas and fragments from many, but few in completion.

Now I can recall fewer still, and the ones I've lost aren't to be found in bookshops. I think there is only one I remember in its entirety, and it's not one of mine. But oh what a poem! I loved it in the '30s but I didn't know why it had such meaning for me. I do now.

It was written by Czeslaw Milosz, whom I remember from happier times. I didn't meet him personally, as far as I remember, but I read his poems. Someone told me that, about ten years ago, he won the Nobel Prize. What a thing that would be! I don't know if it's true. I didn't read it in the newspaper. This is the poem. I don't remember its title.

Burning, he walks in the stream of flicker-
    ing letters, clarinets, machines throbbing
    quicker than the heart, lopped-off heads,
    silk canvases, and he stops under the sky

and raises toward it his joined clenched
    fists.

Believers fall on their bellies, they suppose
    it's a monstrance that shines,

262

but those are knuckles, sharp knuckles
    shine that way, my friends.

He cuts the glowing, yellow buildings in
    two, breaks the walls into motley halves;
    pensive, he looks at the honey seeping
    from those huge honeycombs: throbs of
    pianos, children's cries, the thud of a
    head banging against the floor.
This is the only landscape able to make
    him feel.

He wonders at his brother's skull shaped
    like an egg, every day he shoves back his
    black hair from his brow, then one day
    he plants a big load of dynamite and is
    surprised that afterward everything
    spouts up in the explosion.
Agape, he observes the clouds and what is
    hanging in them: globes, penal codes,
    dead cats floating on their backs, loco-
    motives.
They turn in the skeins of white clouds
    like trash in a puddle.
While below on the earth a banner, the
    colour of a romantic rose, flutters,
and a long row of military trains crawls on
    the weed-covered tracks.

Now I will go, flying my banner, the colour of
a romantic rose, and leaving the long row of
military trains to do their business. My darling
Woodrow, my darling Feliks, I hope that life has
treated you kindly. If you read these words, now

263

you'll know what happened, everything that happened. Be proud of it. This is your life too. Tell it to your children. Tell it to your grandchildren. Tell them who they are. And know in your hearts the only thing that matters, the only thing that ever matters, that it was all done for love.

Your ever-loving Mama.

11

When I had finished reading Mama's letter I felt sick. Not just a violent physical sickness, but a sickness of emptiness, a sickness of the soul.

I went to the bathroom and threw up in the toilet. I vomited everything: the entire content of my stomach, little though it was, the entire content of myself — everything I thought I was or had been, everything I had ever done or thought or felt or said. My whole life went down the stained toilet bowl of a small hotel room in Warsaw. I pressed the handle and flushed it away. And pressed it again and again and again and again.

I rinsed my mouth and brushed my teeth. I returned to the bedroom and lay on the bed. At first I felt nothing. I was no one. I did not exist. All that had once been me was now eviscerated, flushed away into the sewage system from which I had crawled. All that was left was an empty vessel: alone, innocent, unformed, lying on the bed of a meagre room in Poland, as I had on the day I was born in 1930. Except that then there had been a mother to nurture me, to protect me and to love me, and now there was no one and nothing.

I began to cry. Not the silent tears of an aching sorrow, but the vast exhaled sobs of an unimaginable loss. I wept for Mama. I wept for my country. I wept for humanity. I wept for myself. I grieved for anyone who had ever lived. I grieved in rhythms of utter stillness, in which I seemed not to breathe at all. I grieved in the dissonance of howling anguish, beating impotent fists on the hard unyielding bed.

When I had stopped crying, I felt angry. Volcanoes of fury erupted from the void inside me. Molten lava of hatred flowed incandescent over my body. I wanted to kill. I wanted to maim. I wanted to destroy. I wanted to wreak havoc and destruction on the world. I wanted to feel human bones against the sinews of my fingers and to snap them like dead twigs. I wanted to stamp human skulls with my feet and to splash the brains along my pathway. It did not matter who. Let the innocent die. They would anyway. They had already. Innocent; guilty. Right; wrong. Alive; dead. Absurd antitheses all of them, constructs of tidiness and precision, of the chopping of logic into small pieces. And how small can they get? Not small enough yet. Chop, chop and chop again. Chop until it can be chopped no more. Atomise logic. Annihilate life.

In rage I rose from the bed. In rage I tore the sheets and mattress away. In rage I overturned the bed. In rage I wrenched the TV set from its anchor and hurled it across the room. In rage I took the small metal table and smashed it against the toilet bowl, the bowl that had contained the entirety of my life, and against the cistern above it. I fragmented them into oblivion as they had fragmented me.

Water gushed. It sluiced in spurts from the ruptured system, rivulets of hope, the wellspring of a new day. Water flooded the bathroom. I lay on the floor, soaking myself in it, immersing myself as in a first baptism. I drank it, lapping it from the tiles like manna. The clean, clear water that had replaced me. I am water; the water shall renew me. I am air; the air shall inspire me. I am fire; the fire shall consume me. I am earth; to the earth shall I return.

The hotel manager did not pause to knock on the door. He entered with his pass key. His staff held my arms as the frenzy left me. I envisaged the calling of the police, the arrest, the court case. I had no idea what punishment the Polish penal code might now prescribe for reaction to the crimes of its own history. But, at the moment in my life when I most needed the calm kindness of humanity, when I had most forgotten it existed, it was there.

The manager gestured me to the door and escorted me downstairs to a small room behind the reception desk, his two employees gripping my arms, water dripping on the staircase. Then he asked them to let go of me and to fetch blankets. When they returned, he removed my sodden jacket, wrapped the blankets round me and pointed me to an armchair. He went to the sideboard, poured two large glasses of brandy and gave one to me. He sat down himself. Still he had not addressed a single word to me, but waited until I was ready to explain.

I must have been silent for ten minutes. I sat shivering in my chair, not cold. And he sat there in his, hands cupped round his glass, looking at me and waiting. Then I told him what had happened, what I had discovered. My voice held no emotion. That would return, but for now it was spent. I spoke factually, dispassionately, telling the story of Mama's life. I did not cry. I remember standing outside myself as I was talking, observing this stranger give a meticulous historical account of his mother's life, his own life. Myself, and yet myself no longer.

When I had finished, the manager got up from his chair and squatted in front of me. He took both my hands in his and pressed them firmly. He looked directly into my eyes.

'My name is Tomasz,' he said. 'It will be all right.' They were the first words he had spoken to me.

'I do not see how,' I said.

'You will. It will be all right. Believe me.'

I sighed.

'I am so sorry,' he said.

'You are sorry?'

'Yes, I am sorry. But you are not alone. Everyone has a different story, but everyone has the same story. Are you a religious man?'

'No,' I said.

'I could call a priest for you, if you wanted.'

'No thank you,' I said.

'What will you do now?'

'I want to sleep.'

'And then?'

'I want to go home to Paris.'

'Do you have friends there?'

'Yes.' Did I? Did I have friends in Paris? Was Paris home? I had just called it home.

'Good. It is none of my business, but I hope

you will talk to them about this.'

'I will.'

'Good. Now we must find you another room. I do not think you will be comfortable where you are.' He smiled at me.

'I am sorry,' I said. 'I do not know what I can say about it.'

'There's no need to say anything. We will need to discuss the damage, of course. The owners of the hotel would think I had taken leave of my senses otherwise.'

'Of course,' I said.

'But that can wait until tomorrow. Now let us go and move your things. And make sure that the letter is safe.'

12

The next morning, having paid a large bill and a small price, I went to Warsaw Central station and took the train for Paris. It is hard to describe how I felt. I was calm, numbed even. I imagine I was still in a state of shock. Some reason and feeling had returned to me, but it was a different reasoning and another feeling from ones I had known before.

It was not a question of renunciations and denunciations. Many people had done that and I suspected them, as I suspected all converts. I could not suddenly stop believing everything I had believed for the last 40 years, but I was not able to continue believing it either. All my life there had seemed to be certainties. Now there were none. The letter had destroyed them. All the fixed points of reference in my life had been dynamited up in the air. There they hung suspended: globes, penal codes, dead cats floating on their backs, locomotives. I had no idea how they would rearrange themselves when they fell.

The train sped from Warsaw to Berlin, towards Brussels and Paris, unaffected by borders, largely unmolested by passport controls. Already this was a different world, far away from the one that Mama had described or that I had inherited. I thought of all the armies, over all the centuries, that had traversed this terrain in both directions, all the battles that had been fought, all the lives that had been sacrificed for transitory whims or ideals, defended with an adamantine certainty, all the lost sons and mothers. I thought of all the boundaries that had been redrawn, the nationalities that had been redefined, in the wake of victory and defeat. And to what purpose? So that I could travel unhindered from Warsaw to Paris, untrammelled by their legions? I saw now what Woody meant about Europe and its little parcels of history done up with sealing wax and string, left in the attic to be rediscovered.

I wondered what my political position might now be. I was no longer a communist. I was certain of that. I was a leftist. But that is what I had always claimed to be. There was nothing new in that. Why then had I joined the Communist Party, become active in the Communist Party, agreed to be involved in subversive action on what I thought was its behalf? I clearly had been a communist. Why did I not admit it? Why had I evaded the question for so long, insisted on being described as a leftist? What was that mantra designed to convey? Or to conceal?

Then I thought this was ridiculous. I was dancing around in intellectual circles again, tripping over my own feet. Communist. Marxist. Leninist. Marxist-Leninist. Trotskyist. Socialist. Leftist. What did these words mean? They were mere labels: tags we pinned on ourselves and other people, so we could identify each other if we became strays in the ideological night, or casualties in a philosophical war. They were meaningless. One communist could read

271

Mama's letter and say it was regrettable, but these things needed to happen. Another could read it and weep. Were these the same people? What was more important, the political label they adopted or how they reacted to a human story? And if it did not have to do with labels, all it could have to do with was what kind of person you were and how you behaved in real situations, not in some theoretical exam paper.

I hated Stalin. Mama's letter had achieved what millions of deaths had not. Admittedly, it had been a long time since I had admired Stalin, but a vestigial respect and affection had remained. Now there was none. I thought it had been partly nostalgia: the remembrance of someone who had symbolised communism at its strongest, at its most successful, at its purest, at its best. I could not imagine how I had thought of it as pure, yet in a way purity was what it had been about. It was the impetus to purity that had produced Stalinism in the first place. When it was impure, it needed to be purified further. It had to be filtered through charcoal beds until all organic matter was removed. But what could ever be pure in human life? Only death. That was the only pure thing in life. The striving for purity could only be procured by death. I had supped my fill of death. I wanted life.

And life came back to me in Paris. It burst upon my nostrils when I arrived at the Gare du Nord and filled my lungs as I walked home in the May sunshine. I ran up the stairs, suitcase and all, and flung myself through the door. I took a beer from the fridge and threw open the windows, gazing out at the Avenue Secrétan over a wrought-iron balcony and Sandrine Lefèvre's geraniums. Trees were in fresh green leaf on the pavements. Syncopated footsteps entered cafés and departed them. Young girls sauntered on the boulevard. I sipped my beer from the bottle and felt fantastic. I had signed the contract with Bergelson & King before I left for Warsaw. Now I opened their letter with a cheque for $300,000. Tonight I would celebrate. I would treat myself to some impossibly grand restaurant. I would buy a bottle of the best champagne and drink every glass as a toast to Mama. Then I would come back and put on my Jacques Brel records and listen to 'Les Bourgeois'.

The next morning I decided to confront the difficulty of what I would say to Woody about the events in Warsaw. It was a delicate issue. I could not possibly fail to tell him about the letter. Yet, if I did that, I could not see a way of explaining how I had come to obtain Mama's address without mentioning both René and my own exploits in 1968. And if I did that, how could I conceal the fact that René had withheld Mama's address from his old friend? It may not reflect well on me, but I considered every conceivable lie I might invent to avoid telling the true story. I could not think of a plausible alternative to the truth. So, in the afternoon, I rang Woody and told him everything. To my surprise, he was not remotely perturbed by the fact I had once acted as a communist agent.

'Well, at least you didn't do it just for the money,' he said. 'In fact, by 1968 I might very likely have made the same decision as you did. And I wasn't even a communist.'

I tried to explain René's reasons for not giving Mama's address to either of us. I expect I did it badly, because I remained entirely unimpressed by his behaviour. But even that failed to disconcert Woody unduly.

'I thought you would be angry,' I said.

'I don't think I could be angry with René,' said Woody. 'Not after everything we've been through. Sad, yes. Disappointed, certainly. But not angry. Besides which, there were decisions the two of us needed to make in the war that were not much different. Of course it feels bad when you're on the receiving end, but I can see his point.'

'That is very generous of you, Woody,' I said.

'I trust René. He would have wanted to tell me right away. No question about it. So if he didn't, he must have felt he had a pretty good reason. But I'd still like to talk it over with him. It might be a little uncomfortable for both of us if we met in Paris before the thing had been discussed. Do you have his number?'

So I gave René's telephone number to Woody, and we arranged for him and Wanda to visit me in Paris at Christmas. Then I went to the bureau on the corner, photocopied Mama's letter and posted it to him.

The next day I telephoned Mike Martins and asked if he would care to join me for lunch so I could thank him for instigating the transaction. I think he was surprised to be asked. He was no doubt even more surprised when I called him

Mike all the way through lunch. I did not feel comfortable with it myself, but I wanted to see how it would feel, and it felt all right. We did not go to the Brasserie du Temps Perdu, but around the corner to Aux Charpentiers. I dare say, in reality, that restaurant reflected the same self-conscious retention of authenticity as the other, but it felt more natural. We had a most agreeable lunch and I remembered how much I had liked him when we first met. I offered to give him the printing blocks. I imagined it could be an enormous help in producing the next edition. Mike looked amused at the offer.

'It is most generous of you, Feliks,' he said. 'But the fact is we don't use printing blocks. It's all digital.'

'What does that mean?' I asked.

'It's done on a computer. We've already put it on.' He looked at me and I think he was working out how far he could go without offending me. 'In fact,' he said, 'it's probably being hacked to pieces by some graduate trainee in New York at this very moment.'

I thought that was hilarious. I laughed out loud. I should have been offended, of course. A few weeks earlier, I would have been offended. It was preposterous to think of my life's work, the accumulation of decades of research and experience, being massacred by a spotty graduate who had probably never left America and was being told what to write anyway. In my new surreal environment, however, it seemed appropriate. If I no longer knew what I thought about things, who was I to object? I thought I might see more of Mike Martins.

I was a free man, and free in ways I could not have begun to imagine. I had money in the bank, not that I would have it much longer if I went on spending it like this. But I would not do that; I am frugal by nature. I had the rest of my life to contemplate. More than that, Mama's letter had liberated me. I could not explain to myself how that might have happened, only that it had. I felt guilty about it for a while. I thought there must be something wrong with me for a tale of such misery and confinement to have produced in me feelings of joy and release. Then I realised that I should not feel guilty, because Mama would have wanted me to feel like this. It was entirely what she would have desired. And if the effect of her letter had been that I would go about the world with her burden on my shoulders, that would vitiate everything she had done for us. The only way I could repay Mama, or exculpate myself for the things I had thought about her and had failed to do, was to be free and to be happy and not to feel guilty about it.

I wondered again where I would live. I had been so happy when I had returned to Paris, returned to the apartment, yet, as the days went by, I felt more and more dissatisfied with it. Not with Paris, but with the apartment. Suddenly it seemed to belong to another world. It was in a time warp, preserved like a fly in amber *circa* 1955, like those dreary hotels I had visited in eastern Europe for so many years. When I walked through the door, I expected to find everything in black-and-white. I thought of

Woody's house. It was no prototype for my desires, but somehow it was connected to the present and not to the past. I felt I needed to move, needed to make some statement about my life to myself.

I did not want to leave Paris. If I had learned one thing from my visit to Poland, it was that it was not home. I may have been born there and grown up there; I may have discovered feelings for Poland I did not know I possessed; but nevertheless it was not home. There is a limit to how far the clock may be turned back. Paris might have become home by default, but it was the only home I knew. I did not want to seek another. I liked Paris. I felt comfortable there. But I could always move. I did not need to live in this apartment. I could not afford to buy one, not if I wanted money on which to live, but I could rent another one. Something more modern, perhaps. I spent two days looking around the estate agents, seeing what was available. I inspected minuscule studios in smart *arrondissements*. I surveyed futuristic living spaces on the fringe of the city. I was shown modern loft conversions in run-down areas that I was told would soon be fashionable. I did not like any of them.

Eventually I told myself that this was unnecessary. I did like my apartment. I just did not like many of the things in it. I wanted it to change. To change things, I did not need to change everything, only the things that did not please me, that I had outgrown, that were worn and obsolete, for which I had no future use. I told myself it was not sensible to have spent all those years changing nothing, and now wanting to change everything. There had to be some sort of balance in this. So I looked at my apartment with a new eye and saw that I could make it different. It would cost a certain amount of money, but a great deal less than moving. I would have a new bathroom and kitchen. For the rest, some new furnishings and a coat of paint would transform the appearance. I wondered how I would go about these things and realised I would first need to talk to my landlady.

I had barely seen Sandrine since the end of January. My life had been consumed by the visits to America and Poland and by my preparations for them. We had exchanged the occasional pleasantry on the landing, but — apart from the mutual use of our first names — our relationship was reverting to the arid status of its first 36 years. I did not want that. I felt that, having made the breakthrough, I should seek to sustain it. I had never thanked her properly for her substantial nursing of me during my illness. Nor for her catalytic effect on my life. Now I needed also to discuss the prosaic matter of the redecoration of my apartment, and who would pay for it. I decided to extend an invitation to her to dine with me. We could have gone out to a restaurant, of course, but I was not keen to make a habit of that and, besides, discussing the changes to my apartment *in situ* seemed beneficial, so I invited her there.

I think she was touched to be asked, and certainly astonished, as well she might be. This would be the first time I had entertained in my apartment, a fact of which she — with the acute antennae, not to mention advanced surveillance techniques, that are the property of all Parisian landladies — would have been aware. Cooking is not amongst the skills I have acquired. Spending seven months of each year eating in hotels and restaurants, I had become used to my meals being prepared by others. However, there is a first-class *traîteur* in the Avenue Secrétan and I was able to procure a delicious meal without much preparation on my part. I also invested in two bottles of an excellent wine.

We met on a Saturday evening in mid-May and I naturally expected Sandrine to be wearing her habitual Saturday outfit, a suit of indeterminate cut in charcoal grey. Instead, she paid me the compliment of wearing a pretty floral dress, which I had not seen before and could only assume was reserved for special occasions when reinforcements for the regular wardrobe were required. She had discarded the customary ironmongery on her head, so that her long, thick, luxurious, chestnut hair (natural, so far as I could tell) fell far below her shoulders with only a minor piece of haberdashery to restrain it. She was a remarkably striking woman when she allowed herself to be. She must have been about 15 years older than I was, but I feared that I probably looked the elder. It occurred to me that, if I was to make the effort to redecorate the apartment, perhaps I should also take the trouble to redecorate myself.

'I do not expect you to be here at this time of

year, Monsieur Feliks.' We were facing each other across the small table in the centre of my living room, eating charcuterie.

'I hope it does not inconvenience you,' I said.

'Not in the slightest. It's nice to have you here.'

'Thank you. It is nice to be here. I must confess it had occurred to me that perhaps you relet my rooms to someone else when I am not here each year.' This was a thoroughly mischievous thing to say, but I was feeling in a mischievous mood.

'Well, naturally,' she said. 'What would you expect? As a matter of fact, I had a family of eight Algerians ready to move in a month ago. I have had to cancel them.'

She said this with a straight face so that I had no idea whether she was joking or not. I decided to risk the assumption that she was.

'I am surprised to hear that you would welcome immigrants into your house, Sandrine,' I said.

'As long as they pay the rent, I'll accept anyone,' she said. 'Even a Polish communist.'

'Leftist,' I said.

'I do beg your pardon,' she said. 'No compliment was intended.' She smiled.

'Nor taken,' I replied. I found myself starting to enjoy these skirmishes.

'So why are you here?'

'I have sold my business, Sandrine. And I have to say it is largely thanks to you. If you had not encouraged me to consider the offer from America, it would never have happened.' I raised my glass to her.

'Thank you. It is kind of you to say so.' She raised her glass to me in return. 'So here's to your retirement, assuming you are now retired.'

'Yes,' I said; 'I suppose I am.'

'And a wealthy man too.'

'Well, I would not say that.' Apart from the question of who was to pay for the refurbishment, I did not want to encourage any thought of a rent increase. 'No, I would not say that at all. Of course, as a sum of money it is nice to have, but I now do not have an income, so I shall need to eke it out most carefully.'

'Will you be staying in Paris?' I felt that this was a professional question, anticipating the possible need to recruit a new tenant.

'I will,' I said. 'I like it in Paris. And I should like to stay in this apartment.'

'That would please me too.' The manner was now personal again.

'However' — and, as I said this, I saw the look on Sandrine's face switch back once more from the personal to the professional — 'if I am to be living here all the time, I thought this might be a suitable moment for the apartment to be modernised.'

Her eyes conducted a brief survey of the room and appeared to find nothing amiss. 'What precisely do you have in mind?'

I outlined to her my refurbishment plans.

'Yes, I see,' she said. 'Extensive plans, I would call those. I hope you are not proposing that I should pay for them?'

'That is for discussion,' I said. I am not at my best when discussing matters of this nature and I hoped that my reply suggested both firmness and flexibility.

'I'm afraid it is not for discussion, Monsieur Zhukovski. I couldn't possibly afford the works you suggest without borrowing money, which is something I never do.'

'I would naturally expect to pay a higher rent.'

'Indeed,' said Sandrine, 'but that is not the point. We are discussing capital, not income.'

That particular distinction was lost on me, as it had been for my entire life. 'In that case, would you permit me to make the alterations myself?'

'Well, that is a different matter, Feliks. I should be perfectly content if you wanted to do that. Naturally, I should wish to approve the precise changes you make. Apart from that, I have no objections.'

'Thank you,' I said. 'And the rent?'

Sandrine Lefèvre reflected for a moment. 'That could remain unaltered for five years.'

'Could it perhaps be reduced?'

'I do not think so, Monsieur Zhukovski. Having you here all the year will increase my expenses considerably. So I would say that, in reality, you're already getting a reduction.'

'I see. And what if I decided to leave in a year or two's time?'

'I am not sure I understand you. I thought the point of this was that you wanted to remain in the apartment.'

'I do. But circumstances can always change.'

'Most unusual for that thought to occur to you, Feliks.'

'Or to you, Sandrine.'

'It hadn't occurred to me.'

'I thought I should mention the possibility.' Although I had no intention of moving elsewhere, it seemed, since so many things had already altered in a short space of time, that it might be prudent to anticipate further changes.

'If you put it like that,' said Sandrine, 'anything is possible. I do not think it useful to speculate on any circumstance that could conceivably arise, or to provide for them all. If you would like to make these changes, I approve in principle and the rent will remain the same for five years. I think we should leave it at that.'

This was clearly the end of the negotiation. I did not know whether I had obtained a good deal. I suppose I should have sat down beforehand and worked it out, but I was not sure how one did that. At any rate, I would be able to make the changes I wanted and have a fixed rent for five years. I was satisfied with that conclusion, whether it was a good deal or not. We had finished the excellent veal escalope in cream and mustard sauce that the *traîteur* had kindly prepared for me, and I cleared the plates away and returned with a substantial cheese-board.

'You are spoiling me,' she said. 'Anyone would think you were trying to wheedle something out of me, Feliks.'

'I should think the chances of anyone wheedling anything out of you were remote, Sandrine.'

'I should certainly hope so.' I think we were both relieved that the business discussions had been resolved without acrimony.

'I shall look forward to a new apartment.'

'I hope at least you'll get rid of these dreadful books while you're about it.'

'Yes, perhaps I should. I expect I could get something for them.'

'Really? I cannot imagine anyone giving them house space, let alone paying good money for them.'

'There is always a market for books, Sandrine.'

'I can't think why. Books make me ill.'

There did not seem any future in this conversation. We had already exhausted the obvious topics and I wondered what we would talk about for the remainder of the evening. I decided I would tell Sandrine about my recent voyages. The hotel manager in Warsaw had been correct. I did feel the need to talk about these things and I had not done so yet. I am not sure I would normally have selected Sandrine Lefèvre as my confidante, but she was there and by the time we had finished the meal and were ensconced in armchairs, and I had broached the second bottle of Chénas, it did not seem an impossible thing to do. I told her everything, from my visit to Woody in Columbus, to my trip to Warsaw and the discovery of Mama's letter. The only things I did not mention were my connections to René Dufour, and the things in Mama's letter which were the most private and of which I felt most ashamed. I must have spoken for nearly an hour. Most of the time I felt calm and unemotional. But, when it came to talking about some of the things that had

284

happened to Mama, there was a slight catch in my voice and I felt close to tears. They did not come, though.

I had no idea how Sandrine would react to the story. Normally, I would have expected some barbed remark about communism, but I hoped she would now think that inappropriate. She had proved a most attentive listener, concentrating on every word I spoke, sympathy evident in her eyes.

'Your poor mother,' she said; 'your poor, poor mother.'

'I know.'

She sighed deeply. 'All this war. All this trouble. All these evil people.'

'Yes.'

'I despair of it.'

'Yes. I do too.'

'Still,' she said, 'at least you have discovered your family. And at least you know that your family loved you.' I noticed a certain regret in her tone, a bitterness almost, as there had also been when she mentioned the word family back in January.

'Your family did not love you?'

Sandrine snorted. 'Oh, one or two of them did. But not the others.'

'Why was that?' It was an intrusive question, but Sandrine seemed to be inviting it.

'I am from Normandy,' she said. Since that statement had no apparent connection to my question, I sensed this remark was the prelude to another story. I wondered whether she had told it before. 'You are a casualty of one war, Feliks,

285

but I am a casualty of two.' Then she stopped. I waited for a moment.

'How was that?' I asked.

'I was born in 1916. I never saw my father. He died before I was born. He was killed at Verdun.'

'I am sorry,' I said. So that made two of us who had never met our fathers.

'They say he was a charming man. If he'd lived, perhaps the rest of it would not have happened. He was in business in Normandy, in the town where we lived. My grandfather started the business and my father worked with him until the war came.' She paused again and I waited for her to continue.

'It cannot have been easy for my mother, but it was all right. We had enough money. That part of it was all right. I had a perfectly normal childhood except that I did not have a father. I suppose even that was normal. It was normal in France at that time. When I was 22, I fell in love. Laurent was 25, I think. He was local, came from a farming family nearby. He was a nice man and I loved him very much. We were engaged to be married.' There was another pause.

'He was killed too. In the first months of the next war. Few enough Frenchmen were killed in that war. Maybe that was a good thing; maybe not. I don't know. But he was one of them.' Sandrine stopped again.

'Would you rather not talk about this?' I asked.

'No, it's all right. You have told me your story and I will tell you mine. It's not easy, though.' I allowed her to collect her thoughts.

'Our town was occupied by the Germans for most of the war. They had a small garrison there. We avoided them, of course, and tried to get on with our lives. One day, in 1943 it was, I was coming home late from my work. It was dark and there was no one on the street. I was on the edge of town. I met two German soldiers on patrol. That was not unusual. But on this occasion they each grabbed me by the arm and dragged me off. When I screamed, one of them took out a handkerchief and stuffed it in my mouth. They took me to a barn nearby, pushed me down on the hay and . . . well, you can guess what they did. One after the other. Then they left me there. They straightened their uniforms, walked out and resumed their patrol as if nothing had happened.'

'What did you do?'

'What could I do? I lay there for a while and then I went home.'

'Did you tell anyone?'

'No. Not even my mother. Not even the priest at confession. I had never been with a man before. I felt completely ashamed.'

'But you had done nothing to be ashamed of.'

'I know. I kept telling myself that, but it did no good. I still felt ashamed. That is why I could not tell anyone. I wish I had. I wish I'd found the courage to tell everyone, to make a formal complaint about it to the commanding officer. I expect it would have changed what happened afterwards.' Sandrine went silent again and took a deep breath as she continued.

'A little while later, I discovered I was

pregnant. Can you imagine that? A good Catholic girl from a good French family pregnant because she had been raped by two German soldiers.' She sighed. 'What could I do? I could not keep the baby. I did not want the baby. It did not feel as if it was my baby, although of course it was. I could not suddenly tell everyone what had happened. They would wonder why I had not said anything at the time. I would have brought disgrace on myself, on my family. No, I could not possibly have the baby.

'There was a woman in the town. She was a baker's wife. I knew her slightly. She was said to be able to help in circumstances like this. I had heard people making crude comments about it. 'No one better at getting buns out of the oven.' Things like that. I went to see her. I told her what had happened, exactly what had happened, and she helped me. She disposed of the baby and that was that, for the time being. I tried to live a normal life, as far as possible. And then came the Liberation.

'It should have been such a wonderful moment. It was what we had been waiting for since five years. But it was awful. I don't know if you know what small town life is like, Feliks. It seems so cosy on the surface, but underneath are thousands of little resentments and jealousies, slights never forgotten, scores waiting to be settled from one generation to the next. And always the gossip. Yatter, yatter, yatter. Well, the yattering had to be muted while the Germans were in town, but it poured out the moment they left. And so much had happened. It is not easy living under enemy occupation and trying to keep your principles, always assuming you had any to start with. Of course, some people from the town had done well out of the war, made a lot of money from it. And of course some of the girls did go with German soldiers, perfectly willingly. In fact they flaunted it, some of them, if you can believe it. So there were a lot of scores to be settled when the Liberation came, a lot of muck to be raked out from the stables.

'And somehow I got caught up in that. I do not know exactly how. I don't know if the baker's wife did not believe my story and said something to someone. I don't know if someone had observed me creeping in or out of her back door. I have no idea. But word went round the town that I had been guilty of *la collaboration horizontale*. People I had known all my life spat at me in the street. I tried to defend myself, of course, but it was too late. No one would believe me. The only person who believed me was my mother. No one else did. I had other family in the town: uncles, cousins. They didn't stand up for me. They ostracised me completely. Can you believe it? My own family.

'A few days after the Liberation, three young men came to find me. They dragged me to a barber's shop near the town square. There were about a dozen other women there, all accused of the same crime. How many of them were guilty, I cannot say. We were forced to have our heads shaved. All our hair was cut off. We were completely bald.' Sandrine paused again. I do not think she was aware of my presence at that point. Her eyes were in some distant place as she stroked her long mane of chestnut hair again and again.

'Yes, they shaved us completely. Then they hung placards round our neck saying what we had done, what we were alleged to have done. 'German whore', mine said. Then we were pushed out into the town square. Hundreds of people were there, all come to show what they thought of us. We had to pass down this enfilade, running the gauntlet of their hatred, while they hemmed us in and shouted abuse and spat at us and hammered us with their fists. It was terrifying. It was mob rule. We were lucky not to be lynched. That happened in other towns. There was no justice. There was no attempt to establish the facts. There was no defence. Guilt was assumed. But they were the guilty ones. Guilty for what they did to us. Guilty for what they had done, or hadn't done, for the previous five years. And we received the full force of their guilt. It was hideous.

'My mother was not a well woman and that finished her. When she tried to defend me, she was insulted. She wasn't treated as I was treated, but people made their feelings plain. Her own relatives refused to have anything to do with her. Shops that had received her custom for years refused to serve her. She was not strong enough to survive the pain and humiliation. She, who had given her husband to France, was destroyed by France. She died two months later. Hardly anyone came to the funeral. A few of us rattled around in the huge church. I couldn't stay in the town. I had no desire to see it again. My home had disowned me and I disowned it. I received a modest inheritance. I came to Paris as soon as my hair had grown back a little.' She stroked it again. 'I bought this house. Property was not expensive in Paris after the war. And here I am.

'And that is why, Feliks, whatever you think and whatever you say, I shall be voting for Monsieur Le Pen at the next election as I always have in the past. I have seen mob justice at first hand. I know what it is like when law and order break down. I vote for people who also understand that and whom I can rely upon to make sure that such a thing never happens again. Someone who is strong and who is not ashamed to say what he thinks.'

I did not have it in me at that moment to point out that this was precisely why Germans had voted for Hitler in the 1930s. All I could see was an endless spiral of warped emotions, recycling themselves constantly into new forms of disaster.

'Yes, I see,' I said.

'Good. I hoped you would.'

'Have you told this story to anyone else?' I asked.

'Never. And I've probably only told you because you told me your story, and also because you are a foreigner. We still cannot talk about these things here. We never will. When my generation dies, all this will die with us. We will never speak about it to each other. No one wants to admit that these things happened.'

'Did you . . . did you ever meet anyone else?'

'No, not really. I don't know if I wanted to.

Not after that. Love had seemed pure when I was young. If Laurent had not been killed, if I had married him, perhaps it would have remained pure. But now? No. What has happened has happened. There's nothing to be done about it. What about you, Feliks? Have you ever met anyone?'

'No,' I said, 'no, not really.'

'Well, there we are then,' said Sandrine. 'And now I must go. It is way past my bedtime and I seem to have drunk a lot of wine. And of course I have a long journey home.' She smiled bravely. We both got up and she kissed me warmly on both cheeks. 'That was a delicious dinner, dear Feliks. Thank you so much. It is nice to meet one's neighbours eventually, isn't it?'

'It is indeed,' I said.

'Yes. And I hope that you will allow me to entertain you some time soon.'

'It would be a pleasure.'

I sank back into the armchair when she had gone and poured the remainder of the wine. I thought about what Sandrine had said. I did not know why it had taken me until my age in life to have this sort of conversation with anyone. I wondered why I was still a foreigner to her, despite having been a naturalised Frenchman for more than 40 years. There were aspects of Sandrine's story that confused me. I could understand why Mama should have felt guilty for sleeping with a German soldier, but why should Sandrine feel guilty for being raped? The more I had discovered in recent weeks, the more complex life had become. Everything had become blurred at the edges. Nothing was simple any more. Nothing was certain any more. And once there had been certainties.

More than anything, I realised I was not alone. All my life I had felt that I, uniquely in the world, had needed to carry the emotional burden of the past, and that this made me special and deserving of a special sympathy, which I never received. But I was not special. A vast number of other people had carried comparable burdens, many of them worse than mine. A far worse thing had happened to Sandrine than had happened to me. One could say that a far worse thing had happened to Woody, although to look at him you would not know it. And as for Mama . . .

It was not universal, of course. Millions of Europeans did not lose close relatives in either war, did not have their lives dislocated and their futures blighted by the vicissitudes of a vicious century. They were the ones, perhaps, who had lived normal lives, who had married and raised families, who had counted their blessings. But that still left the others: those who walked, with eyes averted, down the boulevards of Europe, whose lives had been damaged, who apologised for Stalin or voted for Le Pen or goodness knows what else, who were not healed. And there were hundreds of thousands of those. In fact, millions of them.

13

'If we come here any more often,' said René, 'they'll have to start putting 'Reserved' signs on our seats.'

We were back in Le Comptoir du Faubourg in the Rue d'Anjou. It had been my idea and I was regretting it already. I had telephoned René and suggested we meet there for a drink. I wanted to tell him what had happened in Warsaw. But I was out of sorts when the evening came: fractious and tetchy, spoiling for an argument. And it was not the first time I had felt like that recently. The pleasure of being back in Paris had worn off. The sense of liberation from Mama's letter had dissipated. At times I still felt elated. At others, I felt thoroughly bad-tempered. It was René's ill fortune to encounter me in the latter mood.

'I thought you liked it,' I said.

'I do like it.'

'It is not much, is it?' I said. 'Still, I suppose it is neutral territory.'

'Is that important?'

'It is when you are conducting negotiations.'

'And what do these negotiations concern?'

'Politics,' I said. 'The 20th century and what it was about. The past 50 years.'

'I feel humbled,' said René. 'I had no idea I'd been selected to take part in such a grand negotiation. I'm not sure I have the competence for it.'

'You have a point of view.'

'Well, of course I have a point of view. We all have a point of view. It's impossible not to have a point of view.'

'And I have a different point of view.'

'Yes, I know that, Feliks. Where is this leading?'

'Perhaps there could be some form of settlement. Perhaps there is some common ground between us.'

'I expect there is, Feliks. But there won't be much of it unless you've shifted your position remarkably. Have you?'

'To some extent, perhaps. And what about you, René? Have you never shifted your position?'

'Not particularly. Nothing much has happened to make me change my mind.'

'So I am the one who needs to change. Is that what you are saying? I am the only one who needs to compromise in these negotiations?'

'Please yourself,' said René. 'You're the one who has conceived the idea of negotiations, not me. I don't know why you've suddenly become so spiky again, Feliks. As far as I'm concerned, I have my opinion and you have yours and that's fine. But if you want me to play along with your pretence, I would observe that, in any negotiations, it is customary for the defeated party to make the concessions.'

'That is the sort of remark I would expect from the enemy.'

'I'm not the enemy, Feliks. Why don't you stop this and tell me what happened in Warsaw?'

I told him in great detail and, when I had finished, René was silent for a while. 'I am so sorry,' he said. 'That is a truly shocking story. I am also sorry I denied you the opportunity to hear it at first hand.'

'That is all right,' I said. 'I forgive you.' That might have been a lie. I was not sure that I had forgiven him.

'Would I be right in thinking,' asked René, 'that what you have learned is making you reassess your position?'

'Possibly,' I said. 'I feel confused about the subject. And I keep coming back to the thought that it does not matter any more. I am left with two contradictory thoughts. The first is that, since everything has changed, the matter is irrelevant. The second is, how can it be irrelevant when it has defined my life and who I am?'

'Perhaps that would seem less important to you if you could find a future that you wanted.'

'I am not interested in the future.'

'That's an unusual thing for a communist to say.'

'A leftist,' I corrected.

'It is still an unusual thing for a leftist to say.'

I ignored the remark. 'Then there is the further contradiction between everything I have believed and the story of what happened to Mama. I keep thinking about that phrase she used: the breaking of eggs. I feel that was aimed especially at me, which is of course absurd. Yet that is precisely what I did believe: that sacrifices were needed to create the perfect society. I still do believe that. When I phrase it in that way, it

296

sounds like a noble ideal. As soon as you use different words to describe it, like the breaking of eggs, it already sounds rather less noble. And by the time the eggs have acquired the faces of your mother, of your aunt and uncle, of your cousin and your father, it sounds positively disgusting.'

'I think,' said René, 'that all of us are inclined to believe that sacrifices are necessary when we do not personally have to make them. It's when one sees history sharpening its knife at the altar that perceptions can change. That is not unusual. Communism isn't the only cause for which sacrifices were made, or for which people have felt that sacrifices were necessary. What seems to be troubling you is not so much that sacrifices were made, but that you now suspect they were monumental sacrifices in the wrong cause. Is that what you feel?'

'Certainly not,' I said. 'I absolutely do not feel it was the wrong cause.'

'That is where we part company then, Feliks.'

'I will tell you a funny story,' I said. 'As you know, I resigned from the Communist Party in 1968. Everyone always assumes, as Oberman did, that it was because of what happened in Czechoslovakia. But that was not the reason. I resigned from the Communist Party because I thought it had betrayed me. Because it had apparently promised to put me in touch with Mama and had then reneged on the promise. I expect you will find that ironic.'

René burst out laughing. 'Isn't life ridiculous?'

'Yes. I leave the Communist Party because you deceive me.'

'You were only in it in the first place because of another deception, if you ask me.'

'Thank you, René. I do not ask you. But I agree that there seems to have been a great deal of deception, one way or the other. And not a great deal of truth.'

'Truth is a highly subjective commodity, I find,' said René.

'That is an absurd statement. That is the one thing it is not. If there is one thing that distinguishes the human race it is the capacity for rational thought. For my part, I study the facts in a particular situation. I analyse them according to logic. I reach objective conclusions from them. That is how I arrive at the truth. The absolute truth.'

'Bollocks.'

'I beg your pardon?'

'Well it is. It's complete bollocks.'

'Would you care to explain why?'

'Feliks, it is a myth that we come to rational conclusions. The best we can do is to give ourselves reasons for what we feel. The whole world is based on emotion. The process of logic is to give us a justification for it.'

'I have never heard such a ridiculous notion in my life,' I said. 'To listen to you, no one would think the age of reason had ever dawned.'

'It hasn't,' said René. 'The age of post-rationalisation has. The symptoms are similar, but they are different things. When I was in the security services, I amused myself at meetings by observing how people justified their points of view. The men went into a long and detailed analysis before tabulating a list of arguments to support their proposed course of action. The women were content to go with their feelings. They usually put forward a single argument.'

'And who won the debates?'

'The men, of course. There were more of them, admittedly. But it didn't mean they were right. In fact, they frequently weren't.'

'They must have had poor intellects, then,' I said. 'Which does not surprise me, as I would not expect to find much intelligence in such a reactionary organisation.'

'Thank you,' said René. 'I bow to your superior mind, this paradigm of rational thought that can trash a hotel room in Warsaw in the name of reason.'

'Those were exceptional circumstances.'

'They were extreme circumstances. I'm not sure I would call them exceptional. Other people have received news like yours without reacting as you did. But I dare say they are more in touch with their feelings than you are. Even you must have read stories of people who suffered in similar ways to your mother. I doubt you have left a trail of wrecked hotel rooms across Europe. But when you discovered what had happened to your own flesh and blood, you exploded. Plainly that experience is changing your attitudes, and so it should. Now you sit here trying to tell me this has nothing to do with your emotions. Don't be ridiculous, Feliks, and don't patronise me.'

I ignored this juvenile outburst. 'So you would admit, would you,' I resumed, 'that these opinions of yours about politics and communism and fascism and patriotism and the rest of it are the product of your emotions?'

'Absolutely.'

'No wonder they are so archaic. But I suppose you would say, would you, that they are superior to mine, which are based on careful study and objective reason?'

'Oh, Feliks, I don't know whether you are wilfully misunderstanding me or just playing intellectual games again. I am saying that your opinions are formed in exactly the same way as mine. And I'm not saying that either of them is superior, merely that they are both different because we are different people, who have had different experiences, which have created different emotions.'

'And what would you say yours are, René?'

'To answer that, you would need to go to Die and walk the fields where I grew up and see the land my family farmed, and go up to the Vercors and imagine what it would have been like for a young man to fight a guerrilla war against the Nazis from there, and to meet my family and to have known Dominique. And, if you could understand all that, you would probably understand almost everything there is to know about me.'

'So what about me, then?' I was not sure that I wanted to hear René's answer to the question.

'Feliks, I think that is for you to work out, don't you? I will be your friend; God knows why. I'll be your negotiator, if it amuses you. I'll be your missing persons bureau, if you insist. But I'm buggered if I'll be your therapist.'

'That reminds me,' I said, 'did you manage to find out anything about Kristin Bauer?'

René delved in his pocket and produced a scrap of paper. 'I thought you'd never ask,' he said.

I studied the address on the piece of paper. 'So she is still in Berlin?'

'It would appear so.'

'Are you confident in the information?'

'Yes, pretty much so. We found a Kristin Bauer who worked at a Stasi bar in Lichtenberg in the early '60s and still lives nearby. It's probably your friend. You have to hand it to the Stasi. They knew how to be thorough. Billions of pieces of information about millions of people, neatly cross-referenced and pigeonholed. And almost all of it done without computers.'

He stood up and prepared to leave. It was not late, but I think he had tired of the conversation.

'Woody and Wanda are coming over at Christmas,' I said.

'Good. I shall look forward to that.'

'I hope we shall meet again before then.'

'I am sure we shall. The negotiations do not appear to have been concluded.' He gave me a wave and walked out of the door.

I stayed at the bar and had several more beers while I tried to work out what was happening to me. It had not turned out to be the conversation I had expected, or had wanted. I had hoped to clarify my political position: to use René as a sounding board to define where I now stood. Not only had that failed to happen, but the man who was meant to clarify things for me had in fact confused them. He had undermined my process. He had attempted to demolish the entire efficacy of reason. It may have been an interesting conversation, but there was no intrinsic merit in sitting in a bar and listening to a litany of emotional rubbish. I could now see why, although I might like Dufour, I would never agree with him. The man was a thoroughgoing reactionary.

Naturally I have made a study of history. As far as I am concerned, the French Revolution was the first act of modern politics. The Revolution not only swept away kings and feudalism, courtiers and *bourgeoisie*, bishops and priests, it asserted the supremacy of reason over the ludicrous superstitions of the medieval world. Robespierre had even renamed Notre Dame Cathedral the Temple of Reason. What a gesture! It may have been the case that the Revolution was accompanied by the regrettable Terror, but it facilitated almost everything important that came afterwards. It made human progress possible. René Dufour had been a servant of the French state, an heir to that great tradition. Yet he had now revealed himself to be a sympathist of the *ancien régime*, a recidivist who wished to dispute the supremacy of reason and restore the dark potency of unreason, of emotion, of superstition, of medieval hocus-pocus and the rest of it.

I had spent my life fighting these primitive attitudes. I had reached my conclusions after a thorough and objective study of the relevant facts. I was prepared to acknowledge that some of my conclusions might have been misguided, which was more than he was prepared to do. I was sufficiently open-minded to lay my views open for inspection, to allow for them to be corrected according to a more experienced understanding of the process of reason. I was not prepared to be told that the process itself was false. Just because René Dufour was in thrall to his emotions did not mean that I was. Him refusing to be my psychotherapist indeed! What arrogance! His views might have derived from a warped psychology. Mine did not.

14

For several weeks I remained in Paris. I obtained brochures and catalogues for my new bathroom and kitchen, visited furniture shops and even the flea market at the Porte de Clignancourt. There was a great deal to plan. I suppose I did not do it hurriedly, but I am a methodical man and I like to do things carefully.

But I was also delaying a decision, and that was whether I should go to Berlin and attempt to visit Kristin Bauer. All through those weeks, the piece of paper that Dufour had given me sat on my desk. I looked at it daily, several times a day. It was a piece of information and it was an invitation. I did not know whether I should accept or decline.

I first met Kristin Bauer in 1958. It was, I think, my third visit to the Russian zone of the city since I started the *Guide*. I had discovered a bar that I liked on my first visit, around the corner from the Stasi headquarters in Normannenstrasse, as a matter of fact. That evening, in 1958, I was in the bar, drinking my beer and having a rather vexatious conversation with an earnest fellow communist, very likely a Stasi official himself, I should think. He asked me what I did and why I was there and I told him.

'So you are a capitalist,' he had said.

'I beg your pardon!' I retorted. 'I am no such thing.'

'No? You have your own business in the West. You sell something. You make a profit from it. What do you think you are?'

'I do not make much profit from it,' I said.

'So. An unsuccessful capitalist, then?'

'I am not trying to make much money from it. Just to live. I am trying to explain to people in the West what you have achieved.'

'So you admire our achievements?'

'Very much so.'

'Then why are you choosing to exploit them for your own self-interest?'

'I am not exploiting them.'

'You are making money for yourself from what our people have done.'

'I am making money from people in the West. What there is of it. And besides that, the people who buy my book come here and put more of their money into your economy.'

'So you are exploiting your own people then, are you not?'

Needless to say, I was unenamoured of this conversation. He may have been a good communist, but I can recognise a crashing bore when I see one. He showed every sign of wanting to continue this dismissive and illogical debate indefinitely. I asked if he would excuse me, as I needed to make some arrangements with the girl behind the bar. I had noticed her when I came in and, I must admit, I did not need this excuse to talk to her. She was new there. At least she had not been there on the two previous occasions that I had visited the bar. Her name was Kristin Bauer. I suppose she can only have been about

305

21 at the time. Something like that. I was, what, 28. She was blonde, a little overweight perhaps. Not a great beauty, but with a sparkle and vivacity in her eyes that made her something much more than plain. Made her very attractive to me, in fact.

So I went up to the bar and started talking to her and she seemed to like that and I certainly liked it. I mean, she needed to interrupt our conversation to serve other people of course, and she did not need to return to me again afterwards. But she did. I started talking about politics, naturally, but she said that was boring and could we please talk about something else. In fact I think she has remained the only person I have known with whom I have never discussed politics. For some strange reason, this was rather refreshing. I do not remember now what we did discuss, but we chatted away happily enough. I was in the city for about a week on that occasion, I think, and every night I went back to the bar and every night we talked.

Strangely, I did not suggest that she might like to come back to my hotel when the bar closed, or I to her apartment. I do not know why. Normally I would do that if I liked a girl. She might say yes, or she might say no, but normally I would ask. I would not want it to be thought that I habitually spent my time propositioning barmaids across eastern Europe, but it happened sometimes and it did not happen now. I must say that these other encounters were not especially satisfying. I suppose they may have been gratifying at the time, but they never meant much to me. Kristin did. And I flirted with her, and she with me.

I went back to Berlin in 1959 and again in 1960, although only for a few days on each occasion, as far as I remember. I would spend every night in the same bar, and there was Kristin, and we would spend the evenings talking to each other. It may seem an absurd thing to say of someone I only saw briefly once a year, but she became a really close friend. Still I did not suggest that we should sleep together. I do not know why not. It was a curious omission. Perhaps I was scared it might become a relationship. Perhaps I feared it would change things, make her like all the others. I do not know.

I had last seen Kristin in March 1961. Berlin was my first port of call in the season. I had not needed to visit again so soon; I had been there in September only. There were other places I would normally have visited first. But I had spent much of the previous five months in Paris thinking about Kristin, which was unusual in itself. I had decided the time had come to discover for certain what her feelings were for me. And I wanted to make love to her and I did not know whether she would want that, and I needed to discover that also. So I went to Berlin in March.

She was a little surprised to see me, I remember. I had probably said I would return the following autumn. The bar was nearly empty that evening, so we had plenty of opportunity to talk without interruption. At closing time I asked if she would come back to my hotel with me and she said yes. I could clearly remember making love to Kristin. In fact, for once the phrase had been apposite: making love. Perhaps it was the only time for me that it was making love, not just copulation, some instant carnal gratification. I remembered what it felt like. It felt like home. Kristin had been tender. I had not been used to tenderness in my life. Mama had been tender to me. But I could not think that anyone else had been. Except Kristin.

She had not needed to be at work until noon the next day, and I had no appointments, nor any need to be in Berlin at all at that moment, except to see her. So we had lain in bed together for most of the morning, talking about all sorts of things, plans for the future. Kristin wanted to leave East Berlin. She was not political, but she did not like what was happening in the GDR, did not like living there, and was making her plans to leave. I remonstrated with her, of course, and asked how — if the best people left — it would be possible to build a successful communist state. She replied that if the best people wanted to leave perhaps there was something fundamentally wrong with a communist state. When I attempted to argue with her, she put her fingers in her ears and went 'la, la, la, la, la, la, la, la, la' until I stopped. Somehow I forgave her for that, which I would not have done with anyone else. In fact, I think I laughed. Anyway, Kristin was determined to leave the East. She had relatives in West Berlin and was making plans to join them.

Until that moment, I had developed this crazy

idea that I would ask Kristin to marry me. That was one of the thoughts that had possessed me in Paris, that I had reflected on over the winter. Now, after our night together, I felt this was absolutely what I wanted to do. But, after she had announced her plans, I thought perhaps this was not the right moment to suggest it. In retrospect, of course, it was the perfect moment. At the time there seemed to be no hurry. It would be better to wait until she had moved. There was no necessity to make a commitment at that moment. So I did not ask. There was one of those moments, a pause in the conversation, a time when angels are said to pass through the room. Both of us seemed aware of the words that might be spoken to fill the void, but the words went unspoken and the moment passed. Instead, I said I would come back to see her in her new home in the autumn, and she was pleased with that. Then, I said, she would be able to come and visit me in Paris and she was excited by that because she had never been to Paris. We had made love again in the decadent indolence of mid-morning. Then Kristin got up and washed and dressed, kissed me gently goodbye as she stroked my penis, promised to leave her new address for me at the bar, and left for work. It was the last time I saw her.

Five months later, the Wall went up. I was in Moscow at the time, as it happens. I remember that, unusually for me, my first thought when I heard the news was for Kristin and not for the politics. I wondered whether she had been able to carry out her plans before the Wall was built. I hoped she had. This was illogical because, intellectually speaking, I had not approved of her plans in the first place. But I did hope that. Selfishly, I thought it would not change anything much for me either way. Whether she was in the East or the West made no difference: I had equal access to both. If we did decide to marry, I did not know if it would cause complications for an East German citizen to receive permission to come to Paris, but I had not known that before the Wall. Besides which, the issue was not relevant. There was no reason why Kristin and I should not live together in Berlin. It would be perfectly possible to make the minor adjustments in my life that would enable this to happen.

So when I returned to Berlin in early October, to the newly divided city, I was looking forward to the prospect. When I entered the bar, I would find either a letter for me with a new address or I would find Kristin still there in person. But I found neither. I was told that she had left in June. No one knew where she had gone. There was no forwarding address. I insisted that she must have left a note for me. In fact, I requested that they make a thorough search of the drawers and cupboards, so confident was I in my belief. But there was nothing. I had never known her address in the East, nor any information that would enable me to locate her. There was nothing I could do. I felt devastated. Two days later, dejectedly and with extreme reluctance, I returned to Paris. Needless to say, I went back to the bar every year, every time I was in Berlin, for many years to come. But she was never there, and there was never any news. In the end, I became known in that bar as 'the man who is looking for Kristin'.

I spent so much time thinking about what could have happened. I was in a bad state about it for a while, almost obsessive one might say. The only certain information was that Kristin had left the bar in June. It was immaterial whether she had left to go to the West, or for another job in the East. Either way, I should have expected her to leave a note for me. There were only two possibilities: either she had left a note and it had not reached me, or she had not left a note. I did not want to consider the second possibility, but I was obliged to. My feelings rebelled against the notion that, after the night and the morning we had spent, Kristin had decided she wanted me to have no part in her life. I could not possibly see how she would have decided that.

But I did not like the first possibility either. The fact is that things did change when the Wall went up. Until then, it was normal for people to move from one part of the city to the other. Of course, many people had relatives in other sectors. It would have been natural for Kristin to have left a note with an address in the West and for the note to have been passed on to me without a problem. But the Wall polarised the city in a new way. Increasingly it became a question of them and us. If Kristin had managed to move to the West before the Wall went up, I could see that other people might be envious of that, however unreasonably, and might not wish me to receive any note she had left. I could also see that other people might now regard it as an act of treachery and, especially in a bar so heavily frequented by Stasi personnel, might regard it as their duty to ensure that Kristin's new address never reached me.

I could not resolve this issue and, after a while, it was pointless to consider it further. There was nothing I could do. For whatever reason, I had lost contact with Kristin. I had to get on with my life without her. As is the way, I eventually convinced myself it had not been important, just a silly notion that would never have amounted to anything, and in time it ceased to matter. Until Woody, with his habitual acuity, had reminded me not only that it once had mattered, but that it still did. The other unfortunate thing was that I never knew what part the creation of the Berlin Wall had played in events. Of course, when Woody had raised that question, I had hotly denied it. But, according to one interpretation, the Wall had been the decisive event that had separated me from Kristin. According to the other interpretation, it was irrelevant. Perhaps that is why I always had an ambivalent attitude to the Wall. I could never decide whether it was a justifiable political act or not. When it came down, I think it was the only event in the collapse of communism in eastern Europe that gave me some degree of pleasure.

All these thoughts came back to me as I sat in Paris, surrounded by brochures for kitchens and swatches of home furnishings, gnawed by inaction, trying to decide whether a visit to

Berlin would be a pointless revisitation of the past or a positive exploration of the possibilities of a resumption. The facts suggested the former. In so far as I had reached a conclusion on the matter, I had concluded that, if Kristin had moved to the West, she had probably left me a note and it had never reached me, whereas if she had stayed in the East, she had probably never written the note. Now that Dufour had produced an address for her in the East, the second alternative became the more likely. In which case, for whatever improbable reason, Kristin had decided to sever contact with me. But I did not know any of this. She might have moved back to the east of the city, where she came from, after the Wall came down. Even if she had lived in the West for 30 years, there might still have been a Stasi file on her for Dufour to discover. Everything remained speculative.

In the end, I made a half-decision. I decided I would go to Berlin. I did not decide whether I would try to see Kristin. I wanted to see Berlin again anyway. I had always loved the city. And, as I have explained, I had not been there since the Wall came down. So I would go on a jaunt to Berlin and, while I was there, I would decide what if anything I would do with the address that Dufour had given me.

It was mid-June when I made the journey. It was a strange feeling, another strange feeling in a year of strange feelings. On most previous occasions, I had approached Berlin from the east, like Marshal Zhukov in 1945, not from the west like Colonel Howley. To me, Berlin was the western outpost of one empire, not the eastern outpost of the other. It did not need to be that way. I had the necessary permits and could have passed through the Wall at one of the checkpoints, but I did not. In fact, I had never visited West Berlin since the Wall went up; I had not been to West Germany at all. To me, Berlin meant East Berlin. So it felt strange to be approaching a united city and to be approaching it from the west.

I had no desire to stay in the west of the city. I wanted to go back to the east, to the places that I knew. I had booked a hotel in advance: the same hotel in Fanningerstrasse where I always stayed. The hotel where I had made love to Kristin, in fact. I arrived there in the early evening. All the rooms had been refurbished since my previous visit two years earlier and the whole appearance of the hotel was noticeably smarter. I made a mental note that I should upgrade it in the next edition of the *Guide* before remembering that there was a *Guide* no longer, or none that I would recognise or could contribute towards. I showered and then rested on the bed for a while, wondering if it was the same room in which I had lain with Kristin, unable now to remember. Wondering if I would try to visit her; unable still to decide.

In the evening, again from habit, I walked round the corner to where the bar had been, where Kristin's bar had been. It was still there. Or rather, I should say, *a* bar was still there, but not *the* bar. It had changed. It had become a theme bar and, I suppose because of where it

314

was and the visitors the area attracted, the theme was the Stasi. The walls were covered with files and reports. Binoculars, old tape recorders and filing cabinets were artfully staged. The ceiling was covered with a painting of hundreds of pairs of eyes, looking at you from a variety of angles. I found it most disconcerting, and in fact distasteful. I mean, I accept that the Stasi acted excessively. But they had a necessary job to do and, if they did it a trifle overzealously, that was surely a fault on the right side. To see their work insulted, trivialised, reduced to this superficial pastiche, was nauseating. Another solid fact of my world had been liquefied. Another point of the utmost seriousness had become some sort of postmodernist joke. I might as well have been at the Wild West Extravaganza in Columbus for all the connection this bar now had with reality. It was vile to think that this was the place where I had met Kristin, had talked to her, had come to know her, had propositioned her. I left immediately and spent the evening elsewhere.

The next day I still did not know what to do, but thought I should at least reacquaint myself with the city and see what had changed, however distressing that might be. I walked all the way up Frankfurter Allee until it became Karl Marx Allee, and that now had a curious, antiquated ring to it. I passed the vast Stalinist apartment blocks, built in the early '50s for important communists, where I had once envisaged living with Kristin. I turned left at Alexanderplatz and walked up Karl Liebknecht Street and Unter den Linden until I reached the Brandenburg Gate.

And there I stood for a while, as I had so many times before, but this time staring in disbelief at the broad swathe of derelict land where formerly the Wall had been. I just stared at the gap. I could not believe the Wall was not there. Then I walked the few hundred yards across it and looked back at the eastern side of the city from the western perspective, the view I had never seen. I could not believe that either. So I walked back to the eastern side, and then to the western again. Back and forth. Back and forth. I do not know how many times I did that: dozens of times, I should think. I spent almost the entire morning walking backwards and forwards across the same stretch of land, aware only of what was not there.

Whatever my ambivalence about the Wall, I had accepted it as a definite fact, a defining fact. The Wall was a challenge. You could be on one side of it or you could be on the other, but you could not be on both. The Wall was a separation. For a city built on sand, it was the line drawn in the sand. It sliced through the city, separating one side from the other. It sliced through the human mind, separating one side from the other. It sliced through all thoughts of what political life could be, should be and would be, separating one side from the other. It imposed order. It defied the fragmentary chaos of perishable ideas and demanded an absolute certainty. It despised relativism. Truth; lies. Hope; fear. The future; the past. The Wall defined them all. And now it had gone, hurled stone by stone by ungrateful hooligans from its cemented moorings into an uncertain future. And so those lines had become blurred again. The truth ran into lies. The future dissolved into the past. The colours of hope ran into a muddied pool and fluxed with the colours of fear. Order commingled with chaos.

And I did not know what I thought of it in its absence. I did not know whether this had been the edifice that had supported my life or that, by separating me from Kristin, had denied it. Whichever it was, there had been a parallel dismantling of my own life and I did not know whether that was a good thing or a bad thing either. There was a souvenir shop selling chunks of the Wall marked with a green official stamp. I had no idea whether they were genuine. I bought one.

In the afternoon, I walked the length of the Wall, of the ex-Wall. Well, not quite the length of it, but a great deal of it. Not all the demolition work had been completed. There were still stretches where the masonry was intact. No doubt they would be dismantled later and broken up by profiteers to provide more souvenirs for visitors to the theme park of my past. I held my rock in my hand, pressing it, feeling its jagged edges bite into my palm and fingers. It hurt. There was a little blood when I returned to the hotel. I washed it off. Then I returned to the bar, to the Stasi theme bar. I do not know why I did that. It was illogical. If there was one place in Berlin I did not want to be, it was in that bar. Nevertheless I went. It was better the second time, actually. Perhaps I had got used to the idea of it. I did not attempt to talk to anyone. I sat in the corner on my own, feeling a little maudlin in fact, drinking several beers, eating a sausage, recalling earlier conversations in the bar a long time before, enumerating the changes since then, how unimaginable they had been, wondering what the future would hold.

Something must have happened in the night because by the morning my mind was clear and I knew exactly what I would do. I was downstairs waiting outside the breakfast room before it had even opened. I left the hotel shortly after 8. The address that Dufour had given me was not far away, at 18a Bietzkestrasse. I made for it urgently. It was not an exciting neighbourhood. Mostly it consisted of small blocks of flats, utilitarian, functional, unsympathetic. Built in the '50s, I would say. I walked down Lincolnstrasse. It was bad enough to have a brother named after one American President without finding that Kristin lived near a street named for another. I found Bietzkestrasse. I did not hesitate. There were no second thoughts. I marched straight up to what I hoped was still Kristin Bauer's front door and knocked on it. It was opened almost immediately.

Kristin gasped audibly and put her hand to her mouth.

'Feliks!' she said; 'what on earth are you doing here?'

Age had treated her kindly. That is to say, she looked like an older version of the Kristin I had last seen at 24. The blonde hair had become a little mousier, slightly more lank. She had put on

318

a little more weight, but not too much. There was still a glimmer of the old sparkle in the eyes. She was not a great beauty; she never had been. But she was still attractive to me, and immensely desirable. She had aged in the way one might have expected, that an identikit artist might have anticipated, that I might have hoped she would. As, I think, had I. We had both recognised each other without hesitation, which must have meant something.

I did not know what to say. Or what to do. I mean, what do you say or do with someone whom you last saw stroking your penis 30 years earlier? I wanted to hug her, to kiss her warmly. But that seemed an impossibly intimate and presumptuous thing to do. However, to have shaken her hand would have been ridiculously formal. So I did nothing. Just stood there, feeling rather awkward.

'I was passing,' I said. 'I thought I would look you up.'

Kristin stared at me, contemplating the vast inadequacy of my answer, its utter implausibility. She looked shaken, not sure how to react to this unannounced reapparition. She turned away from me and picked up her handbag from a table.

'I have to go out now,' she said with a slight sigh. 'I need to be at work by 9. Why don't you come back later?'

'Are you sure you want me to?'

'Yes. Come back later. Come back at 6 this evening.'

We walked down the stairs together in silence.

At the bottom, she turned one way and I turned the other.

'I will see you this evening,' I said.

'Yes. At 6.'

My feeling was one of huge relief. At long last, I had found Kristin again. Found her, seen her, talked to her. And she had invited me to come back. At the very least we could now have a proper conversation and perhaps I could find out what had happened 30 years earlier. In those brief few moments, I had learned something else too. I realised that I had not deceived myself with what I had always felt, that there was something special about my feelings for Kristin, that perhaps also they were reciprocated. Although we had hardly said anything, I had not felt I was meeting a stranger. In some peculiar way, it felt like 30 minutes rather than 30 years since we had seen each other. 30 minutes in which rather a lot had happened. So, although I now had nine hours to kill until I could return, it seemed like no time at all. I was not fretful about the prospect, nor was I impatient at the wait. I felt entirely natural, as I still did when I knocked at her door on the dot of 6 o'clock.

Kristin opened it a little more slowly this time. She had changed out of her work clothes and had put on some makeup. I felt flattered by the attention. She rested her hand on my shoulder and kissed me lightly on each cheek. It was not an expansive gesture, but neither was it cold. Tentative, I should say. Tentative and provisional.

'Now, Feliks,' she said; 'let's start again, shall we?'

She led me into a simple sitting room. It was a small room, clean and tidy, a little threadbare: the room of someone who did not have a great deal of money, but who managed. Also the room of someone who lived on her own, I thought. But I did not know this.

'I got you some beer, Feliks. Would you like one?'

'Yes please,' I said. She fetched me the beer and made a cup of coffee for herself.

'It is good to see you, Kristin,' I said.

'Well, it's good to see you too, Feliks. Now I've had a little time to get used to the idea. Christ Almighty, did you have to do it this way? You might have given me some warning. It came as quite a shock, you know.'

'I am sorry.'

'You might have rung first.'

'I did not have your number.' That was another inadequate answer. I could probably have found her number. The idea had not occurred to me.

'Well, you could have written, or dropped a note through my door or something.' Her tone was not unkind, but she wanted me to know that I had been insensitive.

'I did not know this was the correct address,' I said. I could not think why I pursued this line of argument, defending the indefensible.

'Dear old Feliks,' said Kristin. 'You always did have an answer for everything. Not always the right answer, mind, but always an answer. Still, I think I heard you say sorry a moment ago.'

'I did, yes. I am very sorry.'

'Well, that seems to be a major step forward in your life.' Kristin smiled at me and I smiled back. I did not normally like it when people made fun of me, but with Kristin I did not mind. 'In fact,' she continued, 'life these days seems to be full of communists saying they are sorry.'

'I think you will find,' I said, 'that this is a somewhat simplistic explanation for what . . . '

'Oh, do shut up, Feliks. We can talk about that later, if we must. I don't suppose that is why you came. I hope it isn't, anyway. I want to know what's happened to you these last 30 years.'

'Not a great deal, as a matter of fact,' I said. 'I have continued with my life. I continued with the *Guide* until recently. I have spent the years travelling in eastern Europe, revising it, as I did before. I continue to live in Paris. Earlier this year, I managed to sell the *Guide*. So now I suppose I am retired.'

'That's good,' said Kristin. 'Who did you sell it to?'

'To an American firm,' I said. 'Bergelson & King. They are based in New York.'

'You sold your guide to an American firm?'

'Yes.'

'God, that's funny. That is hilarious. Now I know the world has changed.'

'So people keep telling me,' I said. 'I was surprised I could still walk down Karl Marx Allee. I should have thought it would be Ronald Reagan Allee by now.'

'That's due to happen next year.'

'You are joking, I hope.'

'Yes, Feliks. I'm joking. At least, as far as I know I am.'

'And what about you, Kristin?' I asked. 'How have things been with you? Life seems to have been kind to you.'

'Has it? How would you know?'

'You look well.'

'Looks can be deceptive.'

'Has life not been kind to you?'

Kristin gazed around the room and I followed her gaze. 'Up and down,' she said. 'Like everyone else's. It's been all right, I suppose. It's been all right most of the time. It could have been worse.'

'And your work?'

'Oh, I just have a cleaning job. It's part-time, but it is something. There is not a lot of work here at the moment.'

'Was it always like that?'

Kristin laughed. 'That was a very restrained question, Feliks. Indeed, I would almost call it tactful. No, it was not always like that. In that respect things have got more difficult. In most other respects they've got a great deal better. Since you ask.'

'I am pleased,' I said.

'Tell me about other things,' said Kristin. 'Are you married?'

'No,' I said.

'Never?'

'No, never.'

'A girlfriend? Some chic Left Bank barmaid to talk politics with you?'

I smiled. 'Not even that,' I said. 'More is the pity. What about you?'

'Likewise,' said Kristin. 'Although I was married. I was married in 1963. It lasted for about 12 years, but then it finished.'

'I am sorry.'

'Don't be. I minded at the time, but I do not mind now.'

'Did the two of you have children?'

'No,' said Kristin. 'We did not.'

There was a silence. The preliminary information had been exchanged. It was important, but not essential. I had not said anything about what had happened to me in recent months, about Mama, about Woody, about Dufour. What Kristin had not said, I did not know. And of course neither of us had said anything about what had happened 30 years earlier, or what might have happened, or what had not happened. I still did not know whether she had gone to West Berlin and had come back, or whether she had never gone. That was part of the same question and I did not like to broach it so soon. The next step was not a step at all. It was a plunge. I think Kristin knew this. I think that was why she stayed silent. She was not normally at a loss for words. She could have said something, but she chose not to. I could see her point. I had burst into her life again in this melodramatic fashion. She had accepted the intrusion, but it was up to me to explain why I had come, and she would choose how to respond, whether to respond. The problem was that I did not know myself exactly why I had come. I had taken an impromptu decision to knock on her door. I may have agonised over it for weeks, but the agony had concerned the question of whether I should knock on her door, not of what would happen afterwards if I did. I could have left at that moment. I could have finished my beer and left. It would have been unsatisfactory for both of us, but I could have done it. I did not know whether that was what she wanted or not. Perhaps that was what her silence meant. But it was not what I wanted to do, so I did not do it.

'I was wondering,' I said, 'whether I might be permitted to take you out for dinner?'

Kristin smiled. 'Goodness,' she said; 'it's been a long time since any man asked me that. Thank you. I would like to do that.'

'Where would you like to go?'

'Oh, I don't know,' said Kristin. 'The Harlekin or the Bamberger Reiter, perhaps. Or maybe to Meyer's.'

'Ah,' I said. The Harlekin and Bamberger Reiter were two of the smartest and most expensive restaurants in Berlin. I had not heard of Meyer's. It was new probably, and perhaps more expensive still. 'Well of course, Kristin, I should be delighted to take you to any of those places. Which would you prefer?'

'I think I rather fancy Meyer's tonight.'

'Then we shall go there. Will I need to make a reservation?'

'No, Feliks; I shouldn't think that will be necessary.'

'Am I smart enough? Should I change?'

'You are just fine.'

'Then let me call a taxi.'

'That would be a little extravagant, Feliks. It will only take two minutes to walk.'

I was perplexed, I must admit. I could not believe there would be a fine restaurant in this neighbourhood, but it would have been insulting to have said so. We left the apartment, walked a short distance and stopped outside an ordinary little bar with a few tables set up for eating in the corner.

'Meyer's,' said Kristin. 'Shall we go in?'

'You are very unkind to me,' I said.

'Nonsense,' said Kristin.. 'I've given you the satisfaction of letting me know that you would have taken me to the Harlekin or the Bamberger Reiter. Which,' she said with a wide smile, 'I appreciate enormously.'

'So you should,' I said.

We sat facing each other across a small wooden table covered with a white paper cloth and I ordered some pasta for both of us and a bottle of red wine. Kristin chinked her glass against mine when they were both filled.

'To the future,' she said.

'Whatever that might be.'

'Different from the past anyway,' she said.

'It is already,' I said. 'Do you know, I went back to the bar last night. The bar where you worked. Where we met. Have you seen it recently?'

'Yes. Isn't it wonderful?'

'Wonderful? I must say that was not the word that occurred to me. To be honest, I did not know whether to laugh or to cry.'

'Oh,' said Kristin, 'I think it's always better to

laugh, don't you? Now one has the choice, that is.'

'Perhaps.'

'Tell me,' said Kristin; 'did you ever find your mother?'

'What?'

'Did you find her?'

'What made you ask that?'

'I just wondered. You talked about her all the time, you know. Her and politics. But I didn't like to hear you talk politics.'

'Did I?'

'Yes, constantly.'

'I have no recollection of that.' I was astonished. I had no recollection of it whatsoever. But it must have been true, or why else would Kristin have said it. 'Well, no, I never did find Mama. But I did find out what happened to her. Very recently, as it happens. In fact, only a few weeks ago.'

For the fourth time in a month, I found myself recounting the story of Mama's letter. I told it differently this time. With Tomasz and Sandrine Lefèvre and René Dufour I had omitted some things. Also, I had concentrated more on the facts, not on the emotions. Now I told Kristin everything. The entire story without omissions. About Dufour and how I was unwittingly recruited as a French agent. About Woody too, because somehow that seemed to belong to the same story. About what I did in the hotel bathroom in Warsaw. The whole lot. I do not know how long it took. Ages. I think we were on the third bottle of wine when I finished. Kristin did not say much, but she was not silent. She concentrated on my story, asking occasional questions, seeking amplifications and clarifications. I must admit that I was very emotional about it. Really, it all came out. In the end, I had to borrow Kristin's handkerchief. Mine was soaking wet by then. I have no idea what the waiter would have made of it. Or the other diners. No, there were no other diners.

'I always told you politics were crap,' said Kristin when I had finished, and for possibly the first time in my life I was inclined to agree with her.

'And what about you, Kristin?' I asked. 'Did you move to the West?'

'Do you think I would be here now if I had?'

'You were always talking about it. You were planning to go soon after we last saw each other.'

'Yes I was. But I didn't.'

'Why not?'

Kristin smiled, but it was not a happy smile. More rueful, I would say. 'Oh, life changed,' she said. 'The way it does. And then the Wall went up, so in the end I had no choice.' She smiled again, more bleakly still. I may not be the most sensitive of men, but I could tell that a huge amount was being left unsaid. I wanted to know what it was, but Kristin changed the subject before I could ask.

'Where are you staying, Feliks?'

'Oh,' I said, 'in a little hotel off the Frankfurter Allee. Actually . . . actually, it is the . . . '

' . . . the Adler?'

'Yes.'

328

Kristin laughed. 'Feliks, I didn't have you down as a sentimentalist.'

'Neither did I,' I said. 'Will you come back there with me now?'

'Feliks Zhukovski, you should be ashamed of yourself. I don't know. You take a girl out on a first date to some cheap restaurant, ply her with bad wine and then expect her to sleep with you.'

'It used to work,' I said.

'Lots of things used to work,' said Kristin. 'Feliks, I am flattered to be asked, but not tonight, no. However, you may give my love to the Adler and its bedsprings.'

'I should think they have changed by now.'

'I should certainly hope so. Boing. Boing. Boing.'

'It was not that bad,' I said.

'No, it wasn't that bad. Anyway, I'm not going to invite you back to my apartment either, Feliks. But it has been nice to see you.'

'It has been nice to see you too, Kristin. Perhaps we could see each other again.'

'That would be nice.'

'Perhaps you would like to come to Paris.'

'I would love to. I've never been to Paris.'

'That is what you said 30 years ago.'

I do not know why it was that remark that did it, that loosened everything. They were ordinary words. A simple statement of fact, really. I did not say them for any particular reason. I did not know they would be the key that would unlock the door. But suddenly Kristin started to cry. She did not say anything, but great tears rolled down her cheeks and she began to sob. She took both my hands in hers, intertwining her fingers in mine. She brought them up to her face, using them to wipe the tears from her eyes, then brought them back down to the table, kneading them with her own, massaging her tears into my skin, giving me an intravenous drip of her sorrow.

'I am so sorry, Kristin,' I said. 'I did not mean to upset you.'

'Thirty years ago,' she said. 'It was March 1961 when we last met, wasn't it?'

'Yes,' I said.

'And I was moving to the west of the city in June.'

'Yes.'

'I had relatives there. Cousins. One of them was taking up a position in Düsseldorf. A room would become available for me then. It was all arranged. But I couldn't go until June.'

'What happened?'

'I found I was pregnant.'

'I thought you said you did not have children.'

'You asked me if I had children with Dieter, with my husband. Which I did not. Anyway, in 1961 I found I was pregnant.'

'I did not know you were seeing anyone else.'

'I wasn't seeing anyone else. I was seeing you. Occasionally.'

'What are you saying, Kristin?'

'What do you think I'm saying? I'm telling you that I was pregnant with our daughter, Feliks.'

'Our daughter?'

'Yes.'

'You are sure?'

'Yes.' This time I took Kristin's hands in mine and rubbed them gently. I did not know what to say. 'Anyhow, I decided to have the baby. And stupidly I decided to delay my plans for moving until after the baby was born. I did not want to move into a new part of the city at that time, with new doctors and hospitals and everything. My parents lived nearby. I needed their support. My cousin said it was no problem; he would keep the room available for me. I thought I would go later. I did not know that would become impossible. How could I? No one did. One day the Wall went up. Fmmphhh. Like that. On 12th August you could cross into the western sectors; on 13th August you could not. There was no warning. It happened overnight. Then I was trapped.'

I could not say anything for a while. I was overwhelmed by the enormity of the information I had been given. I did not lack for questions, merely for the nerve to ask them. I was not sure I would want to know the answers. Kristin had decided to have our baby without me. We sat there, rubbing each other's hands. She was looking at me. I think I was mostly looking at the table.

'Kristin,' I said, 'when we last met, you promised me you would leave a note for me at the bar to tell me where you were. Why did you not do that?'

'Feliks, I've just told you that you have a daughter. And the first question you can think to ask me is why I did not leave you a note. Does that not tell you something? Does that not possibly even answer your question?'

I was extremely hurt by the remark and it must have shown because Kristin continued almost immediately. 'I am sorry, Feliks. That was unkind. And not entirely true either. But you're an infuriating man sometimes. And it has not always been easy.'

'Your daughter,' I said. 'Our daughter. How is she?'

'That's better. She is well. She is OK.'

'What is her name?'

'Angelika.'

'Where is she?'

'In the city.'

'Can I see her?'

'I don't know.'

'Well, why not? Why should I not see her?'

'Feliks, I might get angry with you in a moment. You have waltzed up to my doorstep after 30 years without warning. You have stirred up a lot of things that were only settled with great difficulty. You are in no position to start making demands on me, or on Angelika.'

'Kristin, does it not occur to you that I might be angry with you too? I would have waltzed up to your doorstep, as you put it, 30 years ago, if you had only told me where the doorstep was. I am only stirring things up because you chose to bury them. You deliberately withheld information from me that I had a right to know. Information that would have changed my life and might have changed yours as well. Do not blame me for your mistakes.'

'I have spent most of the day,' said Kristin,

'trying to decide whether I would even tell you about Angelika. In fact, I had decided I wouldn't, or not for the moment anyway. Now it has all come out and just look at us. I knew I should never have said anything.'

'Well you have,' I said. 'Can I see her or not?'

'That is not for me to say, Feliks. Angelika is a grown woman. She's 29, for goodness' sake. It's up to her to decide whether she wants to see you.'

'Will you ask her?'

'Yes, Feliks, I will.'

'When?'

'I will ask her tomorrow morning. I am not working tomorrow. Now, can we go please? It is late. I am tired and it has been an upsetting day.'

We walked back to Kristin's apartment in silence. We did not kiss each other goodnight.

'Shall I call round tomorrow?' I asked.

'If you like.'

'What time?'

'About mid-morning, Feliks. I should have been able to talk to Angelika by then.'

'I will see you at 11 then.'

15

I was not able to sleep that night. I think maybe I dozed off at about 5, but that was all. There were so many thoughts in my head, questions unanswered, recriminations directed at Kristin and at myself. All my emotions were fermenting.

So I was a father. I had a daughter. It was all very well Kristin saying I had unsettled her life, but what did she think she had done to mine? I suppose we all like to think we make a difference to the world: that our footprint remains upon it when we die. A vain hope, no doubt, but a common one. What footprint would I leave? Once I had dared to hope that the *Guide* would be my legacy. Now it was being mangled by some American publisher and would not survive my life, let alone my death, in any form I would recognise. Once I had dared to hope that I would have made some small contribution to the eventual success of the communist cause. Now, apart from the fact that I was starting to doubt the value of such a legacy, it had been rendered impossible by the apparent dissolution of communism. My efforts would be bequeathed to the ashes of history, not to its flame.

But I had a daughter. Now there was Angelika. Something and someone that was mine, who but for me would not exist, who would hopefully survive me. So suddenly it did seem that I would have a legacy after all.

There was so much that I wanted to know about Angelika. How did I imagine her? How would I imagine her? As a younger, prettier version of Kristin, a beautiful blonde German woman. I thought of what I would want to do for her. I should want to shower her with affection and with gifts, undoubtedly. I did not know how well I would be able to do this. The affection, I mean. I am not normally a demonstrative man. I could see that yet more changes would be required of me, more difficult changes.

But I was running ahead of myself. Suppose she did not want to see me. That was absurd. What child would not wish to meet its father? But Kristin had suggested there was some doubt about it. These were the darker thoughts of the night. I could not put my finger on the problem. When I had asked Kristin how Angelika was, she had said 'she's OK' or something like that. I did not find this a convincing answer. In fact, it perhaps suggested the opposite: that Angelika was not OK. It suggested there might be problems. I tried to think what those problems might be. Another pointless exercise, but I did it anyway. I thought there could be health problems, some illness or other, that prevented her from leading a normal life. Or perhaps she had marriage problems. Or a difficulty with money. That would not be surprising. There were many possibilities.

I wondered whether Kristin had told Angelika that I was her father. Maybe this was the difficulty about whether I would be able to see her. Perhaps Kristin had even told her that

Dieter was her father. I mean, she said she had married Dieter in 1963, two years or less after Angelika's birth, so that was not impossible. If so, what would Kristin do now? Tell Angelika the truth; tell Angelika she had lied; tell Angelika she had grown up believing her father was someone else? Would Kristin be able to do that? Or would she tell me the next day that no, she was sorry, but Angelika did not want to see me? And would I be forced to accept it, and never to know whether it was true or not?

And if Kristin had told Angelika the truth from the beginning, which particular truth would she have told? As soon as I asked myself the question, I was reminded of my last conversation with René Dufour in Le Comptoir du Faubourg. According to my own argument, there was only one version of the truth. In which case, why had I framed the question to myself in this way? It was Dufour who had said the truth was subjective, derived from emotional perspective, not a rational process. I had derided the notion. In fact, it had made me angry. Suppose he was right. What emotions of Kristin's would have coloured the truth she told to Angelika? Well, she had not maintained contact with me for a start. She had not directly answered my question on the subject, but she had more or less confirmed that she had deliberately not left an address for me at the bar. Why not? Was she angry with me? Did she blame me for denying her the opportunity to start a new life in the West? Was that it? Had Angelika grown up with her mother's resentment at being forced to remain in East Berlin? But why, rationally speaking, should that be a source of resentment?

I thought about Kristin a lot too. It had been so nice to see her. I did remain very fond of her. And I thought she was still fond of me too. She had teased me a lot, which I did not like but which seemed a good sign, a sign of affection. There had been some anger, of course; a little bitterness. But I had not felt that it was deep rooted on either side. It must have been a shock for Kristin to see me. That was stupid of me. I could perfectly well have telephoned, or left a note, as she had said. I should have done. Why had that not occurred to me? Why had I been so wrapped up in my own decision or indecision that, in truth, it had never once crossed my mind to consider Kristin's feelings in the matter? Perhaps I had subconsciously wanted to deny her the opportunity to say she would not see me. She had been very good about it. I know I am a difficult man. I had known 30 years earlier that I had been lucky to find such a good-natured woman who appeared to like me. And what if I had proposed to her at that angel moment, as I had intended to before caution and the advantages of delay intervened? That would have changed everything for both of us. For all three of us.

At least she still wanted to come to Paris. That was good. I wanted her to come so very much myself. I wanted to erase the last 30 years and to start again. I hoped she would still feel the same way the next day. I hoped I would.

I did not wake until 9:30 and I still felt tired,

not surprisingly. I had this fantastic sense of expectation, and also this feeling of depression. It was weird. The breakfast room in the hotel was closed already, so I stopped for two strong black coffees on the way to Kristin's apartment. I arrived exactly at 11.

Kristin smiled as she opened the door. We still did not embrace each other, but I sensed that everything would be all right. She made another cup of coffee for the both of us and sat me down.

'How did you sleep, Feliks?'

'Not well,' I said.

'Me neither,' said Kristin.

'There is so much to think about.'

'For both of us.'

'Yes. For both of us.'

'Well, Feliks, I've talked to Angelika and the good news is that she will see you today. I have arranged for us to go round in an hour or two. I was not sure she would want to, but she will. Please don't expect too much, Feliks. To be honest, I think it's pure curiosity. I don't want to upset you, but I don't think she's much bothered either way.'

'So that is the bad news,' I said.

'That is part of the bad news,' said Kristin. 'The rest is what I will now tell you. That is why we are not going round for a little while. I want to tell you more about Angelika and the life we have led. It will upset you, Feliks, but you had better be prepared. You won't like much of this. In fact, you won't like any of it. But you've made your choice and you'll have to deal with the consequences. If you still want to, that is.'

338

'Go on then,' I said.

Kristin took a deep breath. 'When I decided I would have Angelika,' she said, 'I decided that, to start with at least, I would bring her up on my own. That was all part of why I never left you a note. We can discuss that if you want to, Feliks, but let's do it some other time. Let's concentrate on Angelika for the moment. For whatever reason, right or wrong, I'm not sure I know, I decided to bring Angelika up on my own. It was not easy. My parents were nearby and they helped, but it was never easy. About a year after Angelika was born, I met Dieter. He was not the great love of my life, I suppose, but he was kind and good to me then, and he was sweet with Angelika and didn't seem to mind her, and anyway we got married soon afterwards. It didn't work out. In fact, it started not working out shortly after we were married. I can't say exactly why. It just didn't. It might have helped had we had our own children, but that never happened. Possibly Dieter started resenting Angelika. I don't know. If he did, I can't say I blame him. Angelika was a difficult child. She's always been difficult. She's difficult now, as you'll discover. Anyway, Dieter and I stayed together for about 12 years and then we split up. Since then I've been on my own.

'I did try to bring Angelika up the right way. I was always truthful with her. I told her who her father was, Feliks, in case you were wondering. Not immediately, of course, but when she was about eight or so. I never tried to pretend that Dieter was her father. I told her who you were, what your name was, what you did. I told her about the Wall going up. I told her you didn't even know she had been born, but that if you did you would be sure to love her very much. I didn't like the idea of her growing up thinking she was not wanted. I encouraged her to be independent, to think for herself, not to believe everything she was told, but not to be stupid about it, to be practical, not to get herself into trouble. Not easy when the Stasi were encouraging young children to inform on their parents.

'You know I hate politics, Feliks, but I will talk about it now because it's part of the story. You'll probably disagree, but I don't want to debate it with you. This was an evil regime that we lived under. Not just a bad regime, not just an incompetent regime, but an evil one. All right, there were some good things about it. You were more or less guaranteed a job. The state looked after you when you were sick or old. That sort of thing. Not to be sneezed at, I know, but my goodness those things came at a price.

'We were prisoners in our own country, governed by pretend Germans taking orders from all too real Russians. We couldn't go anywhere. We couldn't do anything. There was no freedom of any sort. You couldn't believe a single word you read in the newspapers, or heard on the TV or the radio. Not a single thing. Every word of it was propaganda, most of it flattering us so we would believe the rest of it. You couldn't say what you thought. You wouldn't dream of saying it to strangers. It would be risky saying it

340

to your own family. There were spies everywhere. A quarter of a million of them. Reading what you wrote, listening to what you said, reporting everything, writing it down, making files of it. We had got rid of the Nazis and now we had this.

'I don't remember all the things I said to you, Feliks. Maybe I told you about my childhood. I don't know. I was born in 1937, so I grew up under the Nazis and during the war. My father belonged to the Nazi Party. He fought willingly for Hitler. Not everyone did, but he did. I mean, it was not like he was a member of the Gestapo or the SS or anything. He was just a regular German guy who thought Hitler was doing all the right things and had all the right answers. I don't think he ever had any crisis of conscience about it. I don't even think that eventually discovering what had happened to the Jews changed anything. I'm not sure he truly believed that the Holocaust had happened. It didn't make him feel he had been wrong. He certainly didn't feel it was just for Germany to have lost the war. Not at all. Yet he was the most wonderful father. He was kind. He was gentle. He was loving. He was all the things to his own family that he denied to other families. And he was unaware of any contradiction. Totally. The two things had no connection for him.

'I don't know what it is with men. I have tried to think about it, but it's no use. I do not see how private behaviour can be in such conflict with political beliefs and for men to be unaware of it. And you're as bad yourself, Feliks, unless

341

your opinions have changed, which I doubt. Anyway, as far as I am concerned, the Nazis peddled one set of lies and the communists peddled another and the behaviour of both of them was truly atrocious. I will tell you one of the communist lies. They liked to pretend that we Germans who lived in the East had no connection with Hitler, that we were innocent of guilt. They told us that all the Nazis came from West Germany and that they returned there after the war to set up another fascist state. That's what we were told. If you don't believe me, go to Dresden. You will find a bridge across the Elbe with a plaque on it commemorating the liberation of the East German people from their Nazi oppressors by their brothers the Russians. Not even you could believe something that ridiculous, Feliks. We were the bloody Nazis.

'When the Wall fell, when the criminals were chased out, when it was all over, they started opening the files. They haven't finished yet and they'll probably never finish; there are so many of them. Amongst other things, they found a list of 85,939 Germans, complete names and addresses, who would be arrested and incarcerated the moment there was a major crisis. That's on top of the thousands of political prisoners who were already in jail. I could go on. What is the point? If you have not understood the reality by now, if you have not understood what I've told you, if you have not understood what your mother has told you, you will never understand anything. If you think these things were minor inconveniences, some little trivialities in the great cause of life, you are deluding yourself. They were life. And if you think that murder and torture and slavery and lies and control are a necessary price to pay for some magnificent ideal, you are no better than my father, no better than any of these other men with charming smiles and split personalities. Sad to say, you are no better than your daughter either.

'Angelika was always a wild child. She had a vicious temper to her even when she was young, a rage burning inside her. It's still there now. It didn't help with Dieter leaving when she was 13. She went her own way after that. There was nothing I could do to stop it. Angelika loathed communism. Well, that was all right in one way because I loathed communism too. But there was a destructiveness to her, an embracing of violence, that was not all right. She never talked about what she did, or what she believed. To be honest, I didn't know she believed in anything. I thought she was pretty much a nihilist. That would have been understandable. But I was always afraid she would get into trouble. I have no doubt she would have been on the list of 85,939 names.

'About eight years ago, when she was in her early 20s, Angelika took up with a hard young man called Lukas Krause. He is a nasty piece of work, I can tell you. He was a fascist, a neo-Nazi. Still is. So I could now see what had been going on, where this was leading. Angelika had become a fascist. Anyway, they got married. They have two children — a boy and a girl — so you are not only a father, Feliks, but a grandfather too. They

343

live on this slum estate a little way east of here. Really, it is awful. Quite disgusting. When the GDR collapsed two years ago, Lukas came out into the open politically. I suppose he thought it had become safer, which shows how much he understands. He lost his job last year. No doubt that hardened him even more. Last November, he was convicted of desecrating graves in a Jewish cemetery. He's in prison for several years. There were a group of them. They were all caught. Angelika was amongst them. She only escaped jail because of the children.

'Feliks, I seem to remember you telling me once that you were partly Jewish.'

'Yes I am,' I said. 'My mother's father was a Jew. I am quarter-Jewish.'

'I haven't told Angelika that. It's none of my business, but I think it might be better if you did not tell her either, not yet anyway.'

'Can she not face the truth?'

'I should have thought it was perfectly obvious that she cannot face the truth, Feliks. You will have to make your own mind up about these things, if Angelika gives you the chance. I could have washed my hands of her years ago. God knows, part of me wanted to. But I chose not to. She's my daughter, after all. She knows what I think, but we don't argue about it any more. We are perfectly civil to each other. I can't say that everything is all right between us, because of course it isn't, but it sort of works and that is the best I can hope for at the moment. And I still hope that one day she may change. And I certainly think that her children should grow up knowing at least one adult who does not share these evil opinions. And I also hope that, while she is thankfully removed from Lukas's influence for a while, she might start to think about things a little differently. Not that there's the slightest sign of that happening at the moment.'

'All things considered, Kristin,' I said, 'it does not sound as though you chose the most appropriate name for our daughter.'

'All things considered, Feliks,' said Kristin, 'it doesn't sound as though your mother chose the most appropriate name for you. Now, do you want to see her or not?'

'Yes,' I said. 'I would like to. But I do not think it will be easy for me.'

'No it won't,' said Kristin. 'And it won't be easy for Angelika either. Please remember that. I don't want to give you advice, but I do most strongly suggest that you keep right away from politics. Don't even go near the subject.'

'That is absurd,' I said. 'It is clearly the subject on which we most definitely need to have a conversation, so I can correct her errors. Especially now that you have given up on it.'

'Feliks, I do not propose to be lectured by you on the parenting of Angelika. If you think you can do a better job, fine. Get on with it. See how easy you find it. I do not seem to be able to get a simple idea into your obtuse head. The problem with Angelika, and with everyone else like her, is that they are incapable of seeing other people first and foremost as fellow human beings. And the trouble is, Feliks, that's your problem too. It always was. That was why I would never talk to you about politics. That's why I never talk to Angelika about politics now. I try to concentrate on the little things, the human things, to keep the little human things going. It's not much, but it works. If you go in there determined to treat her as a fascist and allowing her to treat you as a communist, it will be a disaster. If you go in there as her father and treat her as your daughter, you have a chance. Not much of a chance, I admit, but some chance.'

'Well, we will see about that,' I said.

Kristin sighed in considerable exasperation and I felt pretty exasperated myself. She was a lovely woman, and I was sure she had done her best with Angelika, but if you ask me mothers can be too soft with children. The sterner hand of the father is sometimes needed. It had been Kristin's decision to bring Angelika up without me and now it fell to me to rectify the situation that had resulted. I could see that this would be difficult, unpleasant even. I did not need any lectures from Kristin on that score. But that was not my fault. If Kristin thought I should accept having a neo-Nazi for a daughter and politely talk about the weather or something, she was much mistaken. No, I would gently but firmly point out to my daughter the error of her opinions, the evil of her opinions, the historical falseness of her opinions, and give her time to reflect on them before our next meeting.

Angelika lived a few kilometres to the east of Kristin, on the Marchwitzastrasse estate in the suburb of Marzahn. It was a fine day and we decided to walk. We did not talk much. All that

346

could be said for the time being had already been said. No doubt there would be plenty to talk about later. We arranged that I would return to Kristin's apartment at 6 that evening.

Kristin had not exaggerated when she said that Angelika lived on a slum estate. I mean, it was filthy. Apparently it had not always been like this, but things had deteriorated after 1989. The walls were covered with graffiti saying the most disgusting things. They had been painted over by the authorities, but fresh slogans had been superimposed. The staircase stank of urine. There was rubbish everywhere. It was unbearable to think of my daughter living in a place like this. We walked up to the third floor and Kristin stopped in front of a black door reinforced with a variety of steel plates. Loud music came from within. I could not remember what they called that type of music. Hard metal or something. Kristin knocked loudly on the door and eventually the music stopped.

The woman who answered the door was fat, substantially overweight. She had long hair, unevenly streaked with bleach, with several inches of dark roots showing. It did not look as if it had been washed in weeks. She was wearing a pair of ill-fitting blue jeans, sandals and a battledress top which suggested two very large breasts. This could not be my daughter. There was no way this could possibly be my daughter.

'Hello, darling,' said Kristin; 'I've brought your dad. Feliks, this is Angelika. I'll leave you both to it.'

So I stood there looking at Angelika, and

Angelika stood there looking at me and neither of us said anything immediately. I was beginning to think it was a terrible mistake to have come, to have come to Berlin at all.

'Well,' said Angelika, 'I suppose you'd better come in.'

I stepped into the apartment, which was in much the same condition as the rest of the estate. There was a single living room with kitchen. Dirty dishes were piled all over the place. Clothes and newspapers were strewn everywhere. There were several ashtrays overflowing with ash and dead butts. How could anyone live like this? Had she no pride? How could you possibly bring up young children in a place like this? The children, my grandchildren, were not there. I did not know where they were. Perhaps they were at school. Kristin had not told me how old they were. Perhaps they had been dumped on neighbours. Perhaps they were roaming the streets already. Who could tell? Anything seemed possible.

'Coffee?'

'No, thank you,' I said. Goodness knows what germs I might catch if I accepted a coffee.

'Sit down if you want to.'

'Thank you,' I said. I cleared away some of the clothes and newspapers and perched on the edge of an armchair. Angelika did the same.

'Yes?' she said.

'I do not know what to say. As I expect your mother told you, I did not know I had a daughter until yesterday. So naturally I wanted to meet you and to say hello.'

348

'OK,' said Angelika. 'Well, we've done that. What else do you want to talk about?'

'I do not know what else,' I said. 'Perhaps we could just have a chat.'

'What about?'

'Whatever you like.'

'I don't care.'

'Well, have you lived here long?'

'Five years.'

'Do you like it?'

Angelika shrugged her shoulders. 'What do you think?' she said.

'Well, I can see it is a poor neighbourhood.'

'It's a crap neighbourhood.'

'Is there perhaps a possibility of your moving?'

'Two kids; no money; no work. What would you say?'

'It must be difficult with your husband in prison.'

'That too.'

'Are you able to cope on your own?'

'I manage. We've got friends.'

I tried hard not to think about the friends. I did not want to think about the rest of Angelika's life. As a matter of fact, I still could not believe I was talking to my own daughter. It was clear that any form of conversation would be difficult, so I thought I might as well get to the point.

'Your mother told me about the offence for which your husband was convicted,' I said, 'and about your involvement in it. I was most upset.'

'Five minutes,' said Angelika.

'I beg your pardon?'

'Five fucking minutes.'

'I do not understand.'

'Mum said you'd be talking politics to me inside five minutes and you are.'

'Did she also tell you that I am partly Jewish?'

'No. So what?'

'So you are partly Jewish too.'

'So?'

'Does that not make any difference to you?'

'No. Why should it?'

'It is part of who you are.'

'I know who I am.'

'No, you do not know who you are, Angelika. I am telling you who you are. And when you and your husband were desecrating those graves, they could just as well have been the graves of your own family.'

'Oh, for fuck's sake leave off. Until this morning I didn't even know I had a family, or not your family anyway. Now you're trying to tell me that something I did months ago I shouldn't have done because of something I didn't know about when I did it.'

'You should not have done it anyway.'

'It's my life and I'll do what I fucking like. I won't be told by someone I've never seen in 30 years.'

'That was not my fault.'

'I don't care whose fault it was. I don't know anything about you apart from the fact you screwed my mother once and here I am. Do you think that gives you rights over me or something? You say you want to see me. You say you want to talk to me. You're not seeing me. You're not talking to me. You're just criticising my opinions.

And if that's all you're going to do, you can fuck right out of here and not come back for another 30 years.'

'Is that what you want?'

'I couldn't give a shit either way.'

This was useless. I mean, there was no point in it whatsoever. I stood up and walked towards the door.

'Look at me.'

I turned around to look at my daughter.

'Look at me.'

'I am looking.'

'Here is a person. Here is a human being. Talk to me if you want to, but talk to me properly. You are my father. I am your daughter. If that's not enough for you, sod off. I'm not some fucking freak that has somehow managed to survive your social experiments. I'm not criticising your opinions. I'm not asking how you've managed to spend your whole life as a fucking communist . . . '

'Leftist,' I corrected.

Angelika snorted. 'I'm not asking why you've spent your whole life walking around Europe with your eyes fucking closed, seeing only what you want to see, hearing only what you want to hear, writing only what it suits you to write. Mum gave me a copy of your book. She found it in a bookshop last year. I suppose she thought it would help me to understand you. Let me get it. Let me read something to you.' She rummaged around in a drawer and produced an edition of the *Guide*.

'Now,' she said; 'where is it? Oh yes, here we

351

are. 'The German Democratic Republic has experienced a continuing economic miracle since 1945 and is now universally recognised as one of the most advanced states in the world.' ' It was the same passage that Mark Bergelson had quoted back at me. 'Do you really believe that crap? Take a look around you. Do you think this shithole belonged to one of the most advanced states in the world? If you do, you're the only fucking idiot who does.'

I was still standing up and Angelika was seated, staring at me with blazing eyes, demanding a response I was unwilling to give.

'I do not know,' I said.

'Oh, you know all right,' said Angelika. 'You just don't want to admit it. It upsets your precious theories. You don't mind criticising everyone else for what they believe, but you can't take it yourself, can you?'

'It is not that simple,' I said.

'It is if you live here.'

'There are many places like this in other countries,' I said; 'in capitalist countries.'

'I wouldn't know about that,' said Angelika. 'Until recently, I wasn't allowed out of this place.'

'Well, it is true.'

'And that makes it all right, does it?'

'It is regrettable.'

'That's all you can say, is it? 'It's regrettable.' Everything in this fucking country was regrettable for the people who lived here. Always the fault of everyone except the people who were actually fucking you up. Do you know why I keep your book? Are you flattered that I keep it? Don't be. It's here for just one reason and that is to remind me, however much I've screwed my life up, that I'm not as big an arsehole as my father.'

I was standing with my back to the door, looking at Angelika as she said this. I had hoped to love my daughter, to be loved by her. I had not expected to be hated. I must admit that tears came into my eyes.

'The truth hurts, does it?' It was a harsh question, but actually the harshness had left her voice.

'Everything hurts at the moment,' I said.

'Well, now you know how I feel.'

I came back into the centre of the room. 'And have you screwed up your life?' I asked.

Angelika cast her eyes around the detritus of her room. 'Well, something has,' she said. 'I don't know if it's me or not.' Now she seemed to be on the verge of tears.

I took her by the hand and raised her gently to her feet. I put my arms around her and gave her a hug. We stayed that way for several minutes. Angelika broke away, but still stood close to me, looking at me. Then she laughed.

'You're a funny man,' she said.

'I know. I cannot help it. I would like to see you again, if that is possible. Would you like that?'

'I don't know,' said Angelika. 'What would we do? Have more arguments? What's the point?'

'We could have conversations,' I said. 'Perhaps they would not need to be arguments.'

'Perhaps.'

'We could go to Poland,' I said. 'I could show you where my family came from. Where we lived.' I do not know why I said that. It was on the spur of the moment. Perhaps I thought that if I showed Angelika the remains of the Łódź ghetto it might change something.

'Why the fuck should I want to do that?'

'I thought perhaps you might. It is up to you.'

'I don't know what I want at the moment,' said Angelika. 'I need to think about things.'

'Yes,' I said. 'And will you also perhaps think about what I have said to you?'

'There you go again,' said Angelika, but she was smiling this time. 'Asking me if I'll think about what you've said to me. I don't suppose there's any chance that you might think about what I've said to you?'

'I will try,' I said. 'Yes, I will try.'

16

I left Angelika's apartment in the early afternoon. I had arranged to meet Kristin in the evening. I could have gone sooner, but I did not want to. I needed to relieve this constant assault on my life, this bombardment of my emotions. Every experience of this insane year had given me the sensation of something trying to lift me up bodily and put me down in a different place. I did not want to be lifted up. I did not want to be placed elsewhere. So I dug my toes and heels into the ground and held on fast to the railings and bars of familiarity. Yet the more I did so, the more I kept making these compromises — with others, with myself even — as if I were a co-conspirator in the attempted movement.

I found myself catching a bus towards the centre of the city. I found myself going back to the Brandenburg Gate. I found myself pacing again those metres of formerly determinate ground, now bare and impressionable.

I recalled the night when the Wall came down: the television images of young Germans, toxic with joy, pulling down in one night what had been built in one night. Twenty-eight years of security begun and ended in lightning. I remembered the cranes that came afterwards, the metal ball of destruction squaring up to the concrete of construction. It was no match. It never was. When I was young and I too wanted to tear down walls, there was a constant refrain from the old guard: it is all very well destroying things, they said, but what will you replace them with? Now I asked myself the same question. How had I answered it as a young man? By saying that only the wholesale obliteration of the past could create the freedom to construct a new future. I never listened to older people in my youth, and younger people did not listen to me now. And nobody ever listens to each other or ever will.

I had not listened to Angelika. Angelika had not listened to me. Our wall came down through weakness. My weakness in allowing myself to be hurt by the taunts of a fascist. Her weakness in allowing a pinch of vulnerability to sneak beneath her defences and make her momentarily confess the wretchedness of her life. Two moments of weakness resulting in, what, a moment of strength? How could strength come about in such a way? How could that be the way you built strength? You built strength by constructing walls, not by demolishing them. Surely that is what you did.

I found a patch of unattended ground and sat on it. I remembered reading about a French bishop living in the 17th century, who continued to insist that the sun revolved around the earth long after Galileo had proved the opposite and everyone else had reluctantly accepted the fact. Père Bossuet, his name was. He had always been a hero of mine. It was unlikely that I should have had a prelate as a hero, but I did. I found the tenacity of his belief admirable. I thought about

Père Bossuet again. The fact was that, although he might have been heroic, he had also been wrong. The problem was that I still admired him. Why should I wish to admire someone who was wrong?

I thought about the piece of rock from the Wall that I had bought the previous day; the one that had caused my hand to bleed, so tightly had I held it. Why had I bought it? It was as if it were some sort of holy relic, to be placed on a shrine and venerated. It did not matter that it might be a fake. It symbolised something. Père Bossuet could have gone on a pilgrimage and been sold a piece of wood and told it was a fragment of the true Cross. What I had done was no different. I had even simulated my own stigmata to prove the divinity of the artefact. A piece of stone. A piece of wood. Fragments of truth. Articles of faith. Faith threatened by Copernicus and Galileo. Faith threatened by Ronald Reagan, by Mikhail Gorbachev, by whomever. Faith that needed to be asserted. Faith that needed to be argued unto everything. Even unto the denial of truth. Faith that was indivisible and supreme, impermeable to reason. Faith that would be powered by a relic of uncertain provenance. A piece of wood. A piece of stone.

My choices were clear to me. I could have Kristin in my life, if I wanted her. I did not know that for certain, I suppose, but this is what I felt was available to me. There was a condition attached, and it was the same condition that Kristin had attached 30 years previously: no politics. Possibly I could have Angelika in my life too. Much the same terms would attach. I did not think I had decided either of these matters, yet somehow I had invited one of them to Paris and the other to Poland. It was in these ways that I was conspiring with a new future against myself.

When leaders fell out of favour in communist countries, it was necessary for them to appear in public and admit to having made grave errors. The errors always had to be grave, as I recall. This was the word used to describe them. I had approved of this process. It showed there were rules, a way in which things should be done, that you could not willy-nilly impose improvisations of your own. I liked those rules. Principles needed to be set out clearly, with no deviation. I liked the lines that the rules created. I liked the boxes you could make from the lines, the compartments you could form. I liked the barriers and partitions that sprang from them, the bulwarks and groynes of clarity. To me these things symbolised order. They laid life out in a logical way. They prevented error. They precluded chaos. I did not like chaos. I wanted to know where I stood.

Now, improbably, I found myself wondering what would happen if I took a sledgehammer to the walls in my life, pulverised them with a ball and chain as those young Germans had done two years earlier. If I levelled myself also to the bare ground on which I was sitting. Where would I begin again? What new construction would I place upon the plot? For, unless I wished to remain like Père Bossuet in joyous denial and celebration of his ignorance, I too was forced to admit errors, grave errors. Except that my mistake was not to have deviated from the true path, but to have denied that others had.

It was pointless to hope the year had not changed me. It had. I kept having revisionist thoughts and then pretending I had not. I was defending things in which I no longer believed out of habit, out of the lack of an alternative to argue. The problem was that, while I no longer wholly believed these things, I did not wholly disbelieve them either. Galileo had appeared in the unlikely shapes of Mama, of Woody, of Kristin, of Angelika, and had proved that the sun did not revolve around the earth, but not yet that the earth did revolve around the sun. I still hoped that it might not.

Where had it started? With the belief that people should not be oppressed by the powerful, the rich and the privileged. With the belief that there was dignity in labour and that labour should be rewarded fairly, materially, with assistance in need, with a reflected dignity. With the belief that war was waged for power, for money, for control, and that it was always the poor who were slaughtered, always the poor who suffered afterwards and always the poor who were sacrificed the next time. With the belief that all people were equal and should be treated equally. With the belief in the common humanity of mankind.

What was I now supposed to do? Put these assorted beliefs into a bin-liner and throw them into a landfill site, to be covered with ordure, levelled over and populated with green asymmetrical trees, so no one would know they had been there? Was I to take the best part of me and excise it from myself, leaving the sutured wound to heal with time and for new skin to grow over? How could I deny or conceal or dispose of any of these beliefs? None of them had ceased to be true, or to be necessary. The abuses of humanity were no fewer than they had ever been. Yet neither could I deny that the ideology that had been founded to terminate them had not only perpetuated them, but had often intensified them. I could no longer pretend that the cause of humanity had been served by communism, but I could see nothing else that had served it, or that now would. For Kristin, in her kind and personal world, humanity meant not talking to our daughter about her odious beliefs. I could not see how this served humanity either.

I grew up in an age of mass movements. Perhaps we are all influenced too much by the times in which we are raised. All I could see were agglomerations and amassments and it was a question only of which one to choose, and you chose the one that most opposed the ones you did not wish to choose. In the 1930s and '40s, men with hatred in their souls were offering the mass delusion of fascism. Men with money in their souls were offering the temptation of mass production and consumption. Men with what I mistook for love in their souls, with what in many cases I mistook for souls at all, were offering the mass hope of communism. It had seemed an easy choice to make. It had seemed the only correct choice. I do not think it occurred to me that perhaps none of the choices was correct. Ironically, I had ended up living in France: perhaps the one country that had always declined to make that choice, that had flirted with all three alternatives, that still did flirt with them, but had made the eccentric choice to reject all blandishments, to mistrust all mass movements, to live life on an individual scale. Perhaps that was what I needed to do also.

I had invited Kristin to visit me in Paris, but that was not all I wanted. I wanted to live with Kristin, to share my life with her. It was what I had wanted 30 years earlier and it was what I still wanted. I had no idea how that might be possible. I had no idea whether I could manage to live happily with another person. But, having concluded there were so many other things I did not know, there did not seem to be any sense in worrying about it.

I walked to a bar on the east side of the former Wall and bought myself a bottle of beer. I walked to a bar on the west side of the former Wall and bought myself a bottle of beer. I carried both bottles to where I had been sitting and drank them. Then I belched and told myself I was a prat.

I had arranged to see Kristin at 6 and it was nearly that already, but I was in no hurry. If I was to share my life with Kristin, an hour or so would be of no consequence. If I was not, it would be of no consequence either. I had always been a punctual man, arriving precisely at the time demanded of me. I was not certain how one went about the business of embracing chaos, but perhaps predictability needed to be the first casualty of the process. I ambled off in the general direction of Kristin's apartment, stopping at two more bars on the way to refresh myself with a beer. It felt liberating, this idea of being late and deliberately making myself later still.

'Oh there you are,' said Kristin when I eventually arrived on her doorstep.

'Yes, here I am,' I said.

'I thought you'd got cold feet and decided not to come.'

'One does not get cold feet in the middle of June,' I said.

'God, Feliks, was that a joke?' said Kristin as she handed me a beer. 'You seem very frisky. Are you sure you're all right?'

'I am perfectly all right. I have been thinking.'

'I didn't know those two things went together.'

'I did not know you were opposed to thinking also, Kristin. Thinking and politics.'

'They are all right in moderation,' said Kristin. 'But you don't do things moderately.'

'Certainly not,' I said. 'Have you talked to Angelika?'

'Yes. I rang her a couple of hours ago.'

'And?'

'And she is as well as can be expected in the circumstances.' Kristin gave me a little grin as she said this.

'What did she say?'

'She said it was all right.'

'All right?'

'Yes. I should take that as a compliment if I were you, Feliks. I would say that is at the top end of what could have been expected.'

'You have low expectations, then.'

'No, I have realistic expectations.'

'Did she tell you what we talked about?'

'A bit. She estimated that it took you 3 minutes and 48 seconds to start talking about politics.'

'Yes, I was a little slow, I must admit. So I expect you are feeling rather smug. It must be so gratifying to be right all the time.'

'I'm not right all the time. She told me that you had a blazing argument and made each other cry, and then that you hugged her. Is that what happened?'

'Yes,' I said. 'That is what happened.'

'She also said you would never have hugged her if you hadn't had the argument. Is that true, would you think?'

'Probably,' I said.

'So, you see, I can also be wrong.'

'There was no possible way for me not to talk about politics.'

'Nor for her, perhaps. I should think she was spoiling for the fight.'

'We both were,' I said.

'You're very much alike, you know.'

'Thank you,' I said. 'I do not believe I have been compared to a neo-Nazi before.'

'I suppose I thought that because I cannot bear to talk to you about politics, and because I cannot bear to talk to Angelika about politics, then you should not talk to each other about politics. But that was completely wrong. It's the one thing you can both talk about, or shout about. It's the one thing that brings you both alive. And of course,' said Kristin, 'it helps that you both have such similar views.'

I snorted derisively. 'Now you are being ridiculous,' I said.

'Not at all. I mean it. You both have this stupid idea that everything will be perfect one day, once there has been a little more violence to help it on its way. Angelika didn't get that from me, I can assure you.'

'I am currently rethinking my opinions,' I said.

'That sounds dangerous,' said Kristin. 'You'll be admitting grave errors next.'

'I already am,' I said. 'To myself, anyway.'

'Well that's a start,' said Kristin. 'What errors are you proposing to admit?'

'Paying attention to other people's mouths,' I said, 'rather than to my own eyes and ears. Anyway, you do not want to hear me talk about politics. I am sick of hearing myself talk about it, actually. Can I take you out to dinner? I thought we might go to the Harlekin or the Bamberger Reiter.'

'Meyer's not good enough for you?'

'As you prefer, Kristin.'

'I think I've had enough excitement for one week, Feliks. Why don't we eat here? I've bought us a couple of chops if you'd like that.'

'That would be nice,' I said.

'And you might like to go out and buy us a bottle of wine.'

'I shall go out and buy us two bottles of wine. Or three perhaps.'

'No, Feliks, I think two will be more than enough.'

'I am not used to all this moderation.'

'Well you had better start.'

So I walked out to a shop on the corner. I had hoped they might stock champagne, but there was no champagne and I returned with two bottles of ordinary red wine. Kristin was cooking the chops, and I opened one of the bottles and poured us both a glass and stood in the small kitchen, talking to her. I supposed this was how millions of people all over the world spent their evenings, when they were not arguing with each other. It seemed so prosaic: relaxed and unremarkable. The remarkable thing was that I had never done it. I wondered whether I could become used to doing it, or whether it would become boring after a while. Any form of domesticity had been alien to my life, as had any notion of going to bed with someone and waking up with them and not necessarily making love to them in between. I did not think I had slept with a woman without making love to her. It occurred to me that I had done things in my life that other people could not have done, and had done them easily and without problem. And the things that other people did all the time, the simple basic things of life, the things that were second nature to the whole world — falling in love, sustaining a relationship, getting married, raising a family — I had never attempted. I did not know whether that was because they were too easy to bother with, or for me too difficult, or whether it was one of those things that had happened that way for no particular reason and had become a habit of life, as certain other things had become habits of thought.

Kristin finished her cooking and produced two plates, each with a pork chop piled high with potato and cabbage. She put a candle on the table and lit it.

'There,' she said; 'isn't this better than the Harlekin?'

'Much better.'

'What did you make of Angelika?'

'I thought she was unhappy,' I said.

'Yes,' said Kristin; 'I think she is. The trouble is that recognising you're in a bad place and getting out of it are two different things.'

'She needs to move,' I said. 'That place is filthy. It is disgusting.'

'I know, but she can't.'

'I am not trying to be political,' I said; 'I am making a factual point. The idea of communism was that it should help people in situations like that.'

'But it didn't. And actually it can't unless you're prepared to help yourself.'

'Does Angelika love Lukas?'

'She worships him. I don't know that I would call it love.'

'How can you worship a man like that?'

'Because he offers certainty. I suppose that is the one thing Angelika never had, any more than you did when you were young. I think she likes having someone who will tell her what is right

366

and what is wrong, and exactly how things should be and what the answer is to everything.'

'He tells her the opposite.'

'It comes to the same thing. It still appears to be certainty.'

'I told her that she was partly Jewish. It did not seem to have the slightest effect on her.'

'No, I don't expect it did. For people like Angelika, this is not one human being smashing the grave of another. It is one idea destroying another.'

'I do not know how people can think that way,' I said.

'Well you should,' said Kristin. 'You've been doing it all your life.'

'So why did you want to know me?'

'Because I never felt it was you. You may have felt it was, but to me it felt like something extraneous. That was why I never wanted to talk to you about it. It wasn't just that it was boring, or that I disagreed with you; it was like talking to someone else, or in fact like talking to an automaton, one of those government spokesmen I saw on TV every night repeating lie after lie as if no one would notice. When I made you talk about other things, you were different. You could be amusing. You could be interesting. You could be sensitive.'

'Really?'

'Yes, really.'

'So perhaps there is hope for Angelika too.'

'There's hope for all of us, but it doesn't mean any of us will get there.'

'I am hoping I will see her again soon. I have

invited her to come to Poland.'

'Yes. She told me. What made you do that?'

'I do not know. It just occurred to me. I suppose I have been thinking more about family lately, what with finding Woody, and Mama's letter, and now Angelika. I want her to know where she comes from. Perhaps I hope it will make a difference to her. She did not seem too keen on the idea.'

'You can't tell with Angelika,' said Kristin. 'She's all over the place at the moment, especially with Lukas inside. She's quite liable to go from one extreme to another. I don't think she's an ideological fascist, the way Lukas is. I think she's just very angry; angry and confused. I wouldn't put it past her to change her mind and decide she does want to see Poland. But that's not to say she will. Most people are interested in their history, whatever they may say, but they relate to it as it suits them. I can't change the fact that my father was a Nazi, but I can ignore it. Angelika can't change the fact that you are a Pole, or a Jew, or a communist, but she can ignore it. And, to be honest, I'm not against that. If you ask me, we pay too much attention to the past, and each precise nuance of where we came from and what our families did. It gets in the way.'

'That is what Woody thinks.'

'He's right.'

'Yes, perhaps he is. It is always better to think about the future.'

'No,' said Kristin; 'it's always better to think about the present. It's all there ever is.'

'Kristin,' I said, 'why did you not leave a note for me 30 years ago?'

'Well, I will tell you as best I can, Feliks, but it will not be easy.'

'We do not have to talk about it.'

'No, it's not that. I don't mind talking about it. But when people are asked questions like that, it's as if there ought to be one simple answer. There isn't a simple answer. There isn't one answer. There were so many thoughts in my head, all leading in different directions. In the end, I came to a decision and that was it. But it doesn't mean that on a different day I mightn't have made a different decision.'

'Was it to do with my politics?'

'No, Feliks, it wasn't to do with your bloody politics. I know you think everything is to do with politics, but really it wasn't. If I could love my father, I dare say I could have managed to love you.'

'Well what then?'

'Feliks, you have to look at it from my point of view. I was in that bar for pretty much 365 nights a year. You were there for, what, two or three of them. You were not an important part of my life. Now, whether I wanted you to be, or hoped you might be, was another matter, but you weren't. I know you were all over me when you came, wanting to monopolise me all evening, and that was flattering, but I didn't know if I meant anything much to you. I mean, it was hardly a relationship, not what I would call a relationship. For all I knew, you would be doing the same thing in a bar in Warsaw the following week.'

'I adored you,' I said.

'Well, you never told me. I had no idea what you felt about me. You could just have enjoyed flirting with me when you were bored. There were plenty of others who did that.'

'And did you sleep with them too?'

'No, Feliks, I did not. Well, I think I may have done with one or two, but no more. If you want to know, I wondered why it took so long for you to ask. It was all part of thinking that perhaps you didn't like me that much. And then you did ask me, and I was so pleased, and we did have a wonderful night together, didn't we?'

'Yes,' I said. 'We did.'

'You were very tender, you know. It surprised me how tender you were.'

'Was I?'

'Yes, very. I thought how hurt you must be to come across so cold and then be so tender. That is how I have thought of you.'

'So why did you not leave a note?'

'There was a moment the next morning, a pause while we were lying in bed. I expect you've forgotten about it. I know it sounds crazy, but at that moment I suddenly had this idea that you were going to ask me to marry you.'

'I was,' I said.

Kristin looked at me sorrowfully. 'Well, why didn't you?' she said.

'Because you had said you were about to move to the West, because I thought there was plenty of time, because I thought we could get to know each other better and I would ask you later.'

'Silly old Feliks,' she said; 'always thinking of

the future. You should have listened to the present.'

'I am sorry,' I replied.

'It was not just that,' said Kristin. 'You never said anything to me about your feelings. You never said you loved me. You never even said you liked me. You never telephoned me the rest of the year, or wrote me a letter, not so much as a postcard. What was I supposed to think?'

'I am sorry,' I said. 'I did not realise.'

'We need to be told,' said Kristin gently. 'I couldn't guess what you were feeling. And if we're not told, we usually fear the worst. When I found out I was pregnant, I couldn't get in touch with you. You never gave me your address or phone number. In any case, you would have been travelling. All I could do was wait until you came back to the bar, assuming you did. I didn't know how you would react to the news. I didn't know if it would please you or horrify you. I was feeling vulnerable, I suppose, very alone. It did not seem wise for me to hang all my hopes on your return. I couldn't bear the thought that you might reject me and our baby. I did not want to run that risk. I don't know. I didn't feel this way all the time. Some days I felt this way; others I felt the opposite. But mostly this was how I felt. So, in the end, I decided not to continue at the bar, not to leave you a note, not to run the risk of seeing you again, not to run the risk of rejection.

'I also decided not to go to the West for the time being. It was a bad decision, but I could not know that. Then the Wall went up. I said I was trapped, that there was no way out. But there was a way out, and it was a lot easier than the route those poor bastards took who tried to climb over the wire, or to tunnel underneath, or to jump from trains, or to swim the canals. My way out was you. I thought I would tell you, and make you marry me, and make you take me to Paris. I don't know if that would have been allowed, but I expect it would. You knew the right people.'

'I wish you had done that,' I said.

'How could I? What would that have made me? Rightly or wrongly, I had decided what I would do before the Wall went up. If I wasn't going to see you for the right reasons, I didn't want to see you for the wrong ones.'

'It would not have been wrong if you wanted me,' I said.

'I did want you. But I didn't know whether you wanted me. It felt almost like blackmail to do it that way. Even if you had said yes, I didn't want to live with someone who did not want me, who had done it to be kind, or because he felt he had to. So I left things the way they were.'

I felt incredibly depressed. I could not believe something so important could be decided in ways that were so tenuous. I mean, what had happened was entirely arbitrary. It could equally well have happened the other way. I thought of Mama deciding not to take the train with us to Basle. I thought of René deciding not to give me Mama's address, or to tell Woody where I was, or where she was. I thought of Kristin deciding to delay her move to West Berlin, deciding not to leave me a note. I thought of myself deciding not to ask Kristin to marry me. All borderline decisions that might as well have been resolved by the toss of a coin. I beat my fists on the table in frustration.

'There's nothing to be done about it,' said Kristin.

'No, but it makes me angry,' I said. 'Why did I not ask you that morning? Why did I not say it?'

'You can't even think like that, Feliks. The moment you begin, you have to unpick the tapestry of everybody's lives. Millions of people make bad decisions every day; decisions based on imperfect knowledge, imperfect understanding. It can't be helped. It wasn't stupid for you to think there would be more time. It wasn't stupid for me to think the same thing later. It was just wrong. At least we are alive, we are here, we have found each other. Millions of other people have been denied that. We are the lucky ones, really.'

I thought of Mama again and I knew she was right. 'So what now, Kristin? What happens next?'

'What would you like to happen, Feliks?'

'I do not think that is for me to say,' I said.

'That's what you thought last time, and look where it got us. I think it is absolutely for you to say. Not,' said Kristin, 'that I need necessarily agree with it.'

'Would you still like to come to Paris?'

'Yes I would. Very much.'

'How long for?'

'I think that is for the host to suggest.'

'How about for ever?'

'Oh, Feliks, what a suggestion. It is very nice

to feel that such a thing could happen. Thank you. But I also feel it is a little soon for us to decide about that right now.'

'I thought we were meant to be living for the present.'

'We are. And at present it feels too soon to make that decision.'

'But it is not impossible?'

'No, Feliks, it's not impossible. And I think it is a lovely idea. In principle.'

'And what would make it a lovely idea in practice?'

'Feliks, let me gently tell you one or two things. You are over 60 and you have lived life on your own. You are not used to taking other people into account. You are not used to being with someone, seeing them as they actually are every day. This is not a criticism; it's the way things have been for you. You are not unkind; you do not impose yourself forcefully upon others, but you are used to doing things your way. Other people have now come into your life, or come back into your life, and I think that is exciting for you and I'm so pleased for you it has happened, and pleased for myself too. But I don't see that you can yet know exactly what you want, or how you will feel about it as time goes by, so I don't see how I can feel certain about it either.

'And perhaps I'm not that different myself. I don't know. It's been over ten years since Angelika left. I've lived on my own for all this time. Maybe I will not find it easy to adjust either.'

'I think I have changed,' I said.

'I think changes have happened to you,' said Kristin. 'But that is not the same thing. Let's see what happens. I don't think either of us should feel pressurised in any way. Let's take it moment by moment.'

'I like this moment,' I said.

'So do I,' said Kristin. 'Which reminds me: what are your sleeping arrangements for tonight?'

'Is that an invitation?'

'It does rather sound like one.'

'I would be delighted to accept,' I said, 'if you think that the springs would stand it. Mind you, I do not know if the springs have anything to fear. I am not sure I am up to it any more.'

'It doesn't matter,' said Kristin. 'I just want to hold you.'

17

It is midnight on 31st December 1991 and everywhere there is the sound of bells, harbingers of the new year. Not the methodical, metronomic, buttoned-up bells of Basle, but the ramshackle, rumbustious, anarchic bells of Paris. How good they sound. I have thrown open the windows of my apartment on the Avenue Secrétan to admit their glory to my presence, as they peal in arpeggios and cadenzas across the breadth of the city. Never has it felt so wonderful to be here; never so impossible the thought of living anywhere else, now or ever.

There is an added poignancy to the bells tonight. Tonight they are both the angelus for my future and the tocsin for my past. The counterpoints of life have never seemed more vivid to me. I stand at a still point of time, momentarily balanced by the competing weights of past and future, in harmony with both of them. By tomorrow the balance will have changed and I shall have embraced the future with the naïve enthusiasm, the undirected energy, of a teenager. This may be the last serious moment of history I shall witness. These bells are the death knell of the Soviet Union. As of this moment, this precise moment, the Soviet Union ceases to exist. The edifice constructed upon it has collapsed already. *Requiescat in pace.*

And if you want to know what I think about it, what my emotions are as I raise a glass of wine to my bells, I am still not sure. I feel I am attending simultaneously a funeral and a baptism. I have thought constantly about these things in the last six months, but my thoughts have not progressed beyond the day I met Angelika, the day I slept with Kristin again, the day I sat on the waste ground where the Wall had been and reached some form of settlement with myself. I think that is as close as I shall get to a final view on the matter. It is not conclusive. But in a year when almost every established certainty in my life has been demolished, there can now be no certainties. I am not sure why I moored my boat at such a deceptive quay.

I am sick of politics. I am sick of a world in which everything one does is an act of politics. Where your country of birth is a political act, where your race or religion, or the lack of one, is a political act. Where the books you read, the music you listen to, the person you fuck are all political acts. I lost my family to political acts. Unknowingly, I compromised my integrity for political acts. My daughter's life is a political act, or a political reaction. I am sick of it. The old struggle between communism and capitalism, once so important to me, now seems irrelevant and distasteful. It is not a question of whether I was right or wrong. I was wrong to believe it mattered so much, more than anything else. More than people, I suppose. Yet, as I jettison this baggage, it still feels that I am walking away from the better part of myself. And I do not wish to do that either.

The stations of my youth had grand departure boards, with gilded destinations cascading down them in an avalanche of letters. But none of the trains arrived. Perhaps there is now something to be said for travelling hopefully, for riding on a train with no announced destination. Perhaps it is time to pay more attention to the journey than to the terminus.

Some former comrades embrace the changes, zealots in a new cause. Others sit in bars, the bars I once frequented and that I visit no longer. They will sing the old songs. They will hymn Stalin and regret the passing of his empire. They will dream of a new Stalin who will arise like a phoenix from the ashes of the East, just as their counterparts in Germany, and perhaps my daughter, will dream of a new Hitler. Let them eat their omelettes.

I have wondered so much about what I should have known, and when I should have known it. I suppose the one true point of comparison should have been Germany. For both halves of the country, 1945 was year zero. But if two lines on a graph start at the same point, even if their gradients are very different, it will take many years for the discrepancy to become apparent. And if you do not wish to believe the discrepancy, the recognition can be delayed further. And if you do not even visit the other half of the country, you can pretend that no discrepancy exists. And if you would like to believe, as Kristin accused, that living in a

378

outsized prisoner-of-war camp amounted to no more than a trivial inconvenience, you can believe anything you want. Mama said there was no limit to what anyone might do in certain circumstances. There is also no limit to what anyone may believe.

I remain a leftist. This little conceit of mine has turned out to be the truth after all. It is what I am. With the same ideals and hopes that I had as a young man, untrammelled by cynicism, undiminished by time, but no longer deceived by the illusion of certainty, the illusion of purity. It does not deter me that at present, and perhaps never again, will I find a cause to which I may attach my colours. I will troop them in private, in the quiet hopeful corners of my mind, and that will be enough. One day there will be a new movement, a new steed to which these hopes may be harnessed. New leaders will issue a call to the colours, and I shall rally to it, in spirit if not in body. And if those hopes are dashed also on the rocks of human frailty, of megalomania and murderousness, we shall try again. Like Mama, I cannot imagine a life without hope.

Now the bells are quiet. Occasional fireworks punctuate the night sky, fizzling out to earth. I should return to bed soon, to the bed I share with Kristin.

After we had parted company in Berlin in June, it did not take long for Kristin to make her visit to Paris: as long as it took me to complete the redecoration of the apartment so as to be ready to receive her. It was peculiar. I had undertaken the redecoration, I thought, for different reasons. Now it turned out that I had in fact undertaken it for this reason, a reason I did not know about. By the time I had finished, it felt like a new apartment, fit to welcome a new visitor, and a changed inhabitant.

Kristin stayed for three weeks and they were such wonderful weeks. They felt so natural. I think she was pleased to be with me. Certainly she was pleased to be in Paris. I found it hard to comprehend, but actually — at the age of 53 — this was the first time that Kristin had been outside eastern Germany, unless you counted visits to the west of Berlin. I found this impossible to understand. I was so used to being in other countries, to travelling all the time, to making the comparisons, or failing to make them. I could not conceive of someone who had never done this. Or, as Kristin reminded me, been allowed to do it. So Kristin saw Paris with fresh eyes, and in a way the world with fresh eyes, and was caught up in its wonder and caught me up with her. I felt so proud of Paris. It was shocking, but I did not know the city so well myself. Now I found myself in this unexpected role of tourist guide and I think I learned as many new things about Paris as Kristin did. And the things she found most wonderful were the things she had never known, and the things I had taken for granted, and I told myself never to take anything for granted again.

It felt so comfortable to be with Kristin, to be with a woman who felt like home. I had once heard living with another person described as living alone in half as much space. But it did not seem that way. On the contrary, it seemed like having double the space. I found it a miracle that she had come back into my life, and no less a miracle that somehow I had managed to encompass the changes that had enabled it. I did not know that at my age it was still possible to make changes like these. At some point we started talking about the future. It did not feel like a great decision for either of us. Not one of those huge issues you wrestle with grimly in the small hours of the night, when no answer seems the right one. It did not feel like a decision at all. We wanted to be with each other. We both wanted to be in Paris. So it remained only for Kristin to return to Berlin, to pack up her things, to say unregretful farewells, and then to return. We did not discuss whether it would be for ever, but I think we both assumed it probably would. We did not mention marriage, because there was no need.

The time that Kristin had to spend back in Berlin gave me the time to take Angelika to Poland. Kristin had been correct: Angelika was not consistent in her attitudes. For a while she maintained her refusal, and then she suddenly changed her mind. I have no idea why. Kristin had wanted to come too, and I had said we could do it together another time, but that now I wanted to go with Angelika alone. I think she understood. She understands most things. More than me, certainly. And we both agreed that if there was ever likely to be a time to wean Angelika off her evil beliefs, to give her a different perspective on life, it was now, while

Lukas was in prison and she was feeling vulnerable. So Kristin looked after the grandchildren, Lorenz and Gitta. Very nice they were too, six and four years old and — as far as I could tell — remarkably uncorrupted by everything that surrounded them. Young enough to start again, if that could be made to happen; young enough to be capable of any possibility in life.

Angelika and I spent a week together in Poland. It is difficult to say how it went, but I think it was perhaps as successful as it could have been. I made a compromise with myself about the politics. Kristin had begged me the first time not to talk to Angelika about politics. I had ignored her and I think that I had been right to do so. There was no denying that this boil existed between us and it had needed to be lanced. But now that it had been lanced, now that respective positions had been established and acknowledged, there seemed no immediate point in scratching at the scab. So I decided there would be no overt mention of politics on this trip, on my side anyway. I would show Angelika the landmarks of our family: the places where we had lived and that had borne witness to our small part in the commotions of the 20th century.

But of course I was aware that, in doing this, I would silently be conducting a political argument. Because everything that had happened, the disruptions and dislocations to our lives, had been caused by politics. To stand in a verdant park in the Łódź ghetto and to say 'this is where I was born', and to explain how I had come to leave the house, and why it was no longer there, were all acts and accusations of politics. But it would be politics in a different way, and history in a different way, and I hoped it would have more resonance for that reason. For I had also grown tired of arguments and assertions. I had spent my life standing up and arguing my truths. In fact, that is what I had thought truths were: things you saw and that other people did not, perceptions that needed to be imparted with force to others, argued to their death, defended against all comers, taking no prisoners. I still believed in truths like this, but because the certainty that had underlain them had evaporated, they now seemed less like truths and more like opinions. Or subjective truths, if you like, as René had argued. At any rate, I now separated these things — truths, perceptions, opinions, whatever you want to call them — from any notion of objective truth. Because I had come to see that there were such things as objective truths, which brooked no argument and were different. These truths had no need of mouthpieces or spokespersons. They became neither more true nor less true whether they were broadcast by loudhailers or whispered in corners. They spoke their own truth. They could still be denied, of course, and they often were, but that did not diminish them. The truths I had learned in Mama's letter, from other things that had happened to me this year, belonged to this category. I hoped that if I let these truths speak to Angelika in the way they had spoken to me, they might have some effect. In this way,

383

diplomacy became war conducted by other means.

We went first to Warsaw. I had wanted to return to the hotel where I had purged myself of so much that was wrong with me, as I saw it now. Also the hotel where I had unwittingly betrayed what I thought I believed, but had in fact betrayed something I had turned out not to believe. But I was not brave enough to go back. We stayed elsewhere. I found a few moments to return, to see Tomasz and to thank him for what he had done. I did at least manage to do that. I also told Angelika what had happened to me in the hotel, on both occasions. I told her everything about my life, in fact. I could see no reason for concealment.

We went to the depressing block where Mama had spent her final years. I took her to see Zofia Wisniewska and we stayed there a long time. Angelika asked many questions, while I acted as her interpreter. They did not seem to point in any direction. I think she had become engaged with this unseen part of her history, but I had no sense that she had changed her opinions. We toured the old town of Warsaw, rebuilt completely out of the rubble of 1944, a convincing facsimile of itself. I thought again about theme parks. I do not know why I have this obsession with theme parks. And I still could not decide, any more than I could in Verdun, whether I was visiting a reconstructed monument to reality, or an ersatz replica of it. It seemed that nothing was authentic without the dimension of time. We paced streets that Mama might have run to take news to the printing presses, past rebuilt houses where she might have lived. The streets were not the same, but her absent footsteps haunted them still.

We went to Łódź, of course. I took Angelika to the lake that marked the place where I was born, where we had lived. I described life there as I remembered it. I told her about the leaving of it. I told her what had happened afterwards. I placed no interpretation on these events, argued no cause from them: merely let the truth speak for itself. I had already told Angelika how I had come to know so many of these things, about Mama's letter, and it was in Łódź that she asked to see it. I had brought it with me. I had hoped she might ask, but I had not wanted to foist it on her. I read it to her, translating from the Polish into German. She made no comment, gave me no clue as to how she had reacted. But the next morning she asked if I still remembered the fields where the family had picnicked, the lake where Mordechaj and I had pretended to fish, the place where they had died. I was not sure that I did remember, but I hired a taxi for the day and we tried many different routes out of Łódź and spent fruitless hours on the quest, until suddenly there it was. There was the spot. Exactly as I remembered it; exactly as it had lain in the memory for all these years.

And it was August again. And farmers were harvesting the fields, as they had in 1939. And the small lake was still there, overhung by boughs, half strangled with weeds. The lake in which the bodies of Mordechaj and Aunt Lilia had floated to the surface 52 summers earlier. It was too much for me. I was completely overcome. And I did not mind that Angelika could see me like that; in fact, I was glad about it. And she came and sat beside me in the field, on the stubble sprung from new seed sown in bloodied soil, and put her arm around me and gently kissed my cheek.

We visited Piatek too. Angelika wanted to do that and I did also, uncertain as to whether I had ever been there. We asked around to see if anyone had recollection of a Zhukovski family, or a Zhuravski family, but no one did. Too much time, too much dislocation. But somewhere in that town was the site of the *shetl* that my grandfather had left for an unimaginable liaison with the Gentile world, and the site of the house where he and my grandmother had lived, where my grandmother had died, tended by Mama, an oasis of calm in the cacophony of war. And still I did not know what effect this had on my daughter. She spoke with questions, but not with comments, and I did not seek them.

I could not see the point. Either these truths would speak to her or they would not. They might speak to her in five years' time, or in 50, or they might be speaking now. But I felt that at some point they would speak to her. And I felt that Angelika was expecting to be asked for her reactions, expecting to be harangued again, and that the more I did not do that, the greater the chance that the truth would speak sooner rather than later. So I kept quiet, content to know my daughter, content that I would be allowed to continue to know her. She was aware of course that her mother was coming to live with me in Paris. With Lukas in prison, I felt no need to hurry things. I felt that a period of time was needed for Angelika to absorb what she had learned, as I had needed time to absorb things; a period of time without Kristin on her doorstep to lend support; a period of time alone in that stinking apartment to contemplate what she wanted for herself, for Lorenz and for Gitta.

So I invited Angelika and the grandchildren to come and stay with us for Christmas, and then Kristin and I and Kristin's belongings made our way to Paris.

It was to be a busy Christmas, a crowded Christmas. There were long conversations with Woody, planning his and Wanda's visit. In the end they arrived on 14th December, on Kristin's birthday in fact, flying into strange territory on a reassuringly American airliner. Kristin and I went to Charles de Gaulle airport to meet them. Again there was plenty of hugging and this time it felt natural. This time it felt like a family reunion.

There was not room for them to stay in the apartment. There would not be room for Angelika and the grandchildren to stay there either, but somehow they would have to be accommodated. I booked a room for Woody and Wanda in an American hotel. At least, I assume it is an American hotel: it is impossible to know about such things these days. Maybe it is now a Russian hotel. Or Malaysian. I do not know. It was an international hotel, anyway. It was not especially close to the apartment. In fact, there are no international hotels close to the apartment, which is a good reason to live here. I hoped it would feel familiar to them, be comfortable for them, and it was. I have this theory that Americans do not like to be anywhere that does not remind them of home, which I must say is a curious attitude for a country that is trying to run the world, but there we are. Anyway, they liked the hotel and they loved being in Paris.

I discussed the visit exhaustively with René. In fact I saw a great deal of René during the autumn. When Kristin moved to Paris at the end of August, she said she wanted to meet my friends. I explained that my friendships were in a state of transition. If she wished to meet my old friends, I said I could direct her to the bars where they drank, but I would not be accompanying her. I pointed out that, when couples got together, it was customary for the woman to oblige the man to dispense with his old friends, but that I had already saved her the trouble. She laughed and said, in that case, I had better introduce her to my new friends. So she met René, and Mike Martins, and of course she could hardly fail to have met Sandrine Lefèvre.

I had been a little worried at the prospect of this last encounter. In fact, I did not know whether the terms of my lease precluded a second occupant of the apartment. I could not find the lease. I expect it had got lost in the grand clear-out. In the event, it was not a problem. Kristin and Sandrine hit it off immediately. The only difficulty was that Sandrine spoke little German, and Kristin rather antiquated French. However, since it would be necessary for Kristin to speak French well, Sandrine kindly offered to be her teacher. I think she was delighted to have something new to do in her life. Sandrine did not request a higher rent for Kristin's presence. I was not sure she would be entitled to it, but I expected she would ask. Instead, she waved a finger at me in what was almost a coquettish manner and told me what a shrewd businessman I was to have negotiated a rent freeze for five years before slyly insinuating Kristin into the apartment. I wanted to tell her it was a coincidence but, since no one had called me a shrewd businessman before or perhaps would again, I decided it was preferable to accept the compliment.

Kristin liked René too. It was difficult not to like René. I had tried on two occasions and had failed abysmally. He became a frequent visitor to the apartment. Pleasant though it was to see René with Kristin, I missed the evenings when the two of us would sit in the bar and drink beer and argue. I did not suggest it because I thought Kristin would object. One day I did mention it, and Kristin told me not to be silly, and that of course René and I should drink together and, besides, if she was to live in Paris it would obviously be obligatory for her to take a lover and how was she supposed to do that if I hung around her all the time. I replied that, since I lived in Paris, I naturally had a mistress already and how could I possibly see her if I could not invent a drink with an old friend to provide me with an alibi. You see, I am getting better at these things.

So René and I would sit and talk in our bar, and there we made the plans for Woody's visit. It was a tripartite visit, I suppose. In part it was a holiday, a sightseeing trip, a chance for Wanda to see Europe. And in part it was a family visit, a journey to see me, a reciprocation for the visit I had made to Ohio. I had told Woody about Kristin, and about Angelika and the grandchildren, so he knew he would be meeting them too, getting to know his own extended family. He had not seemed especially surprised; maybe little in life surprised Woody any longer. To him, this was another adventure, as it was also starting to seem for me.

But in addition to this, there was also the other element, the element of a reunion, of a remembrance. And this was the part that was to do with René and not to do with me, from which in fact I felt excluded. René was very good about it. He did not attempt to hijack the visit, as he might have done. He enquired how it might be convenient to fit these things into the schedule. There were still several of them left alive from the old days, from the Resistance, scattered across France, living in retirement. René knew where they were. Of course he did. René knew everything. It would not be feasible to visit them all, of course, but most of them would be able to visit Paris and would be certain to do so if they knew that Woody was there, if there was to be a celebration. And then there was the question of a visit to the Vercors, which we had touched on earlier, which Woody was adamant he would make, which René was unsure whether he should. René and I arranged these things between us. And then there were Woody and Wanda at the airport and we were hugging each other.

It was on the third day of the visit that we drove south. Woody and Wanda came to the apartment after breakfast and René arrived in mid-morning. It was the first time they had seen each other in 47 years. I shall not easily forget the meeting: the warmth of it, the depth of it. They say that blood is thicker than water, but it occurs to me that there are two types of blood. There is the blood of family and the blood of warfare, and I would not care to say which is the thicker.

We set off on the journey, all five of us, in René's battered old Peugeot. It was a venerable machine, a proper car. So old, said René, that I might have built it myself at Sochaux. I was not that old, I said, and besides I had been far too busy going on strike to have built any cars. René thought that was just as well. He and Woody chatted away to each other in the front seat. There was not a great deal of conversation between the rest of us, more a succession of unrelated remarks. Kristin was still impressed by her new freedom and greeted everything with a wondrous eye. Wanda commented only on things that she found different from America, which gave her a great deal on which to comment.

'Oh my,' she said, as we were cut up for the

umpteenth time by some aggressive Citroën or Renault, 'that would never happen in Columbus.' It seemed to me there was a great deal that never happened in Columbus. Life, for example. There I go again. I must remember that I am supposed not to be anti-American now. (It is rather unkind, but since this journey Kristin and I have been saying 'that would never happen in Columbus' to each other whenever we encounter anything especially banal.)

René had reserved rooms for us at a hotel in Lyons. That was some distance from the Vercors, but he had a reason for it. We arrived at about seven in the evening and had dinner shortly afterwards. It was a distracted affair. Woody and René had their minds on other things, itching to talk properly to each other once the non-combatants were out of the way. Wanda remained an enigma, as ever. I should like to be able to say it was on this trip that I began to know Wanda, but I did not. She remained a closed book to me, pleasant on a superficial level, but inaccessible on every other. Kristin found her the same. At the end of the visit, I had hoped she would enlighten me about Wanda, but she could not, and I could not enlighten her. Perhaps Woody was the only one who could unlock that door, or perhaps he could not either and perhaps they both wanted it that way. Who can say?

So it was a distracted meal, and Kristin and I needed to make most of the conversation. We retired early. At the end of breakfast the next morning, René announced plans for the day.

'Woody,' he said; 'the two of us should be leaving shortly.'

'Oh,' said Woody, 'aren't we all going?'

'No,' said René, 'just the two of us.'

'My,' said Wanda, 'you mean the rest of us have come all this way for nothing?'

'Not at all,' I said. 'I for one have no desire to go for a drive in the country. We are in Lyons, for goodness' sake, one of the gastronomic centres of Europe. I have booked lunch for us at Paul Bocuse. I can assure you we have much the better deal.'

'We certainly have,' said Kristin, who had been well briefed in advance.

'Oh well, in that case,' said Wanda, 'I guess it's fine. Are you sure you'll be all right, honey?'

'I'll be fine,' said Woody.

So they went their way and we went ours and there is nothing I can say about the day at first hand. Woody was silent afterwards, silent on the trip back to Paris. We had a few moments on our own in later days and I raised the subject with him, but he did not want to talk about it. He did not brush the subject away, as I might have done. He simply did not wish to discuss it.

We decided to detour back to Paris via Basle. That was a decidedly strange experience: neither Woody nor I had been there since the war. Woody found the house where Aunt Maria and Uncle Ernst had lived without difficulty, in a quarter on the east bank of the Rhine. We saw the small windows and the large shrubs outside and knew the house must still be as gloomy and depressing as it had always been. I wondered what had happened to them both. I said that I had come to feel sorry for Aunt Maria.

'I don't,' said Woody. 'She got what she deserved, if you ask me. That's what came of marrying a German.'

'Careful,' I said.

'Feliks, I don't mean now. Stop being so sensitive.'

We drove to the city centre and walked up to the Münsterplatz. The five of us stood on the balcony at the back of the cathedral, looking out over the Rhine, threading its way through our pasts. A few kilometres away on the left, on the west bank, lay France. A few kilometres away on the right, on the east bank and to the hills beyond, lay Germany. We stood in Switzerland, studiedly neutral, non-committal Switzerland, and watched the traffic moving freely between the three countries, where armed guards and barbed wire and checkpoints had been the last time we were here. Still there were the bells.

'Perhaps Switzerland won the war,' said Woody.

'Switzerland wins every war,' said René.

We drove back into France and René deliberately took me past the Peugeot factory at Sochaux. Surprisingly, I managed to locate the back street in Montbéliard where I had made the drop in 1968. I had told Woody about that by then. He had told Wanda, but Wanda showed no signs of having understood the information, and seemed to think I had been some hero. Well, I suppose in a way I had been. Oh, I do not know. This is too complicated. Perhaps she has the right idea after all. Let it pass over your head. If you have one.

Yesterday I saw René and he told me more about the day he had spent with Woody on the Vercors. Yes, it had been very emotional. No, René still did not think it had been a good idea to have gone. It was necessary, he said, to be selective about the past. Things happened to all of us that should not happen, that we wished had not happened. We had to put these things behind us, not to pretend they had not happened, but not to dwell on them either, and to make a new life and meet new people and get on with it. There were fault lines, he said, in the cloths that each of us had woven, places where the warp and the weft of life had become disjointed. If you revisited those places, there was always the danger that everything you had subsequently woven would unravel. That had been his fear for the day.

I pointed out that this, in fact, was exactly what I had done with my own life over the course of the year. I had returned to the fault lines of my past and most of the subsequent fabric had unravelled. I might not have done that deliberately, or have appreciated it at the time, but now I was glad it had happened.

'The difference,' said René, 'is that you have a new direction in which to take your life. If there were mistakes, they were remediable. It's different for Woody. There is no way on earth to change what happened to Yvette and there never has been.'

'And you think he still loves her?'

395

'I'm sure he still loves her. I know how much he loved her at the time.'

'But these things fade,' I said.

'Not necessarily,' said René. 'They fade if things don't work, if a relationship ends, if you can convince yourself it would have been hopeless. They also fade if things do work. Or rather, they change and, all right, you lose that wonderful first flush of passion, but you gain so many other things. But, when neither of those things happen, it's different. Woody only knew perfection with Yvette. The time for change and compromise had not arrived. It was pure and undiluted love. And so, I suspect, it has remained: frozen for all time in a state of perfection that could never have been sustained, an impossible standard against which all other loves will be tested and will fail.'

'Like Wanda?'

'Like Wanda. Oh, I don't mean that Woody doesn't love Wanda. I'm sure he does. But it will be a different love. I don't just mean now. I mean when he met her, when they married. It will have been different.'

'What did you both do that day?'

'What we set out to do. We went to the places we had shared, the farmhouses where we had sheltered, the scenes of incidents, that sort of thing.'

'You went to Treffort?'

'Yes, we went to Treffort: We visited Yvette's grave. There were no flowers to pick, and Woody didn't want shop flowers, so he picked branches and berries and laid them on her grave.'

'Did he say anything?'

'He didn't need to. I knew what he was thinking. He was wondering what would have happened if Yvette had lived. What sort of life they would have had together. What children they would have had. And then he would have felt disgusted with himself, for cheapening the wife he did marry, for demeaning the children he did have. But he would not have been able to help himself. That is what he would have felt: love, regret, bitterness, guilt, all mixed up together.'

'Do you think that Wanda understands this?'

'Who knows?' said René. 'I've no idea whether Wanda even knows about Yvette.'

'What happened after we got back to Paris?' I asked. I had not seen Woody for three days after that. It had been the time for the reunion with old comrades.

'He was fine,' said René. 'In fact, he was the life and soul of the party. So he put it behind him then. But it will sneak up on him one day and catch him off his guard. It was best left undisturbed. It's a terrible thing to have known perfection and to have lost it before you discovered it could never have been perfect.'

'Yes,' I said.

★ ★ ★

While Woody was off with René playing old soldiers, while Wanda was with him, playing the old soldier's wife he should not have had, Kristin and I were making plans for the arrival

397

of Angelika and Lorenz and Gitta. We had debated the sleeping arrangements and concluded that they had to be in the apartment with us. Fortunately, it transpired that the sofa I had recently bought folded down into some sort of bed arrangement, so that gave Angelika somewhere to sleep, and we put the little ones into our own bed in the evening and then carried them through on to a mattress next to Angelika when we went to bed.

They arrived a couple of days before Christmas and I must say it was a happy occasion. Angelika is different away from home. I had noticed the same thing in Poland. I do not say her opinions have changed. As far as I know they have not. We still do not discuss them. I mean that her demeanour is different. I think she feels more insecure when she is in other places. This makes her more polite, more accommodating. Of course, I do not wish my daughter to feel insecure. In fact, I welcome the idea that she should be assertive. It is just that I do not like the things she asserts.

Late on Christmas Eve, as we all returned from supper at a local bistro, we encountered Sandrine on the landing wearing an outfit grander yet than the one with which she had honoured me when she came to dine.

'Good evening, Sandrine,' I said. 'You are looking very smart tonight.'

'Well naturally,' she said; 'I am off to midnight Mass at Notre Dame.'

'I did not know you went in for that sort of thing,' I said.

'Only occasionally,' said Sandrine.

Suddenly there was a quiet presence at my shoulder and a small voice that said 'can I come too?'. It was Angelika. I stared at her in disbelief. Before I had a chance to say anything, Sandrine had said 'of course you can come — and why don't you bring the children with you?' So the four of them set off into the night towards an improbable destination.

'Well,' I said when they had gone; 'I am astounded.'

'So am I,' said Kristin.

'I did not know you were Catholic.'

'I'm not.'

'That is even more extraordinary,' I said. 'I cannot say I am happy about it. Especially indoctrinating young children in this way.'

'What would you prefer,' said Kristin; 'the Hitler Youth?'

'Certainly not,' I said. 'I cannot imagine what people like that would grow up into.'

'Into people like me,' said Kristin.

'You were a member of the Hitler Youth?'

'Actually, no,' said Kristin. 'I was too young, fortunately. But I easily could have been. I'm sure my father would have been delighted to recruit me.'

'It does not bear thinking about.'

'As far as I'm concerned, it is a step in the right direction for Angelika.'

'As far as I am concerned, it is a different step in the same direction,' I said. 'I must admit it is ironic. Just when I finally renounce certainty, I find I have a daughter who wishes to sample every known form of it.'

'Someone has to carry on the family tradition,' said Kristin. 'Anyway, I wouldn't be too exercised about it if I were you. I should think it is pure curiosity.'

'That is what you said when you told me she would see me. And look where that has led us.'

'Are you complaining?'

'No,' I said, 'I am not complaining. I am not complaining about anything. And I suppose I would prefer to have a daughter who believes in God to one who believes in Adolf Hitler, if I am forced to make the choice.'

'That must have been a tough decision,' said Kristin. 'What about Joseph Stalin?'

'Yes, all right,' I said. 'Him too. Thank you for bringing it up.'

The next day, Christmas Day, Kristin and I had planned a grand dinner in honour of our various guests. It was not something I would dare to have attempted on my own, but she did not seem fazed by the idea of cooking for ten. A delicious meal it was too, I must say. There were the five of us, including Lorenz and Gitta, who were allowed up late for the second night running in honour of the occasion. Then of course there were Woody and Wanda. And we invited René and Sandrine. Finally, I decided to ask Mike Martins to make up numbers.

'Are you sure that is a good idea?' Kristin asked.

'Why not?' I said. 'A nice eligible young man

for Angelika. Why on earth not?'

'I can think of two reasons why not,' said Kristin.

'Which are?'

'That Mike is a liberal East Coast American and you're proposing to couple him with our daughter who, as far as we know, is still a neo-Nazi.'

'Mike is fanatical about everything European,' I said, 'so we will be broadening his experience. We are all mad here anyway, and the sooner he discovers that the better. In any case, I am not trying to couple them.'

'That's probably just as well,' said Kristin, 'because the second reason is that I should think Mike Martins is almost certainly gay.'

'Oh for goodness' sake, Kristin,' I said; 'how do you manage to work that one out?'

'I just think he is.'

'I do not know,' I said. 'Mike Martins a homosexual? Surely not. I like the man.'

'Feliks, darling, it has nothing to do with whether you like him or not. Why shouldn't you like him? I thought I was moving in with a communist. I didn't realise the communist was already doubling up as a reactionary.'

'Perhaps I should learn to be more adaptable,' I said. 'Maybe I should introduce Mike to Lukas when he gets out of jail. That would achieve the same effect.'

'God knows how you lot ever thought of yourselves as progressives,' said Kristin.

Christmas Day was quiet for us. Kristin busied herself with the cooking. The children slept in after their late night. Woody and Wanda were absent for much of the day. I had gone to considerable trouble to locate a Baptist church in Paris and had eventually found some such establishment in a remote suburb, to their evident gratitude. I must say I find this ridiculous. The Christian Church is as fissiparous as the Communist Party. It has admittedly not yet murdered as many people, but not for want of trying over the centuries. I think I am going off ideologues of all sorts.

We gave each other presents in a subdued fashion. There were toys for the children. No toy soldiers, I am pleased to say, so I had no need to refuse permission for the Waffen SS to manoeuvre on my sitting room floor. Kristin thought that Angelika would like some new clothes, so we had bought those for her. I had thought the same thing for Kristin and gave her a large cheque for her to choose what she wanted. I do not think I would be much good at choosing clothes for other people. Actually, I am not much good at choosing them for myself. I told her that, left to my own devices, I would probably have chosen an endless array of sexy bras and knickers and she said, good, I could do that the next time. Kristin gave me, of all things, a framed picture of Józef Piłsudski that she found in some flea market. She is very resourceful like that. I still do not know what I feel about Piłsudski. It goes without saying that I would have detested him at the time, but now I am not so sure. I have put the picture by our bed.

So the day passed and the evening arrived, and with it our guests. I was a little anxious, I think. I am not used to entertaining. Also, I was concerned about the communication. Everyone spoke bits of other people's languages, bits of French, bits of German, bits of English. I think I was the only one to speak all of them fluently. I could foresee a tower of Babel during the evening, but in the event it was not as bad as I feared. Somehow we managed. Nevertheless, it was an odd assortment of people around that table. After the meal was over, the children were put to bed and the rest of us settled down with a bottle of Armagnac.

'You've done this apartment very nicely, Feliks,' said Sandrine.

'Thank you,' I said. 'I am pleased you approve.'

'Certainly better than those dreary books.'

'Feliks always liked books,' said Woody. 'Had his head in one all the time.'

'That accounts for a lot,' said Sandrine.

'What have you done with them?' asked René.

'They are in storage,' I said.

'Storage?' said Sandrine. 'You mean you're paying someone to keep that rubbish for you?'

'That is right,' I said. 'You never know when they might come in useful. I expect I will require them for my next business venture.'

'You never told me about that,' said Kristin.

'Well, I might as well get on the bandwagon like everyone else,' I said. 'I thought I would open a theme park to communism.'

'Oh my,' said Wanda; 'how exciting. We have

lots of theme parks in Ohio.'

'I think Feliks is joking, honey,' said Woody.

'Life was a great deal easier when Feliks never joked,' said Kristin.

'But more boring, surely,' said Mike. 'Actually, I think a theme park to communism is a great idea.'

'Someone will do it,' I said. 'I bet you within ten years there will be one somewhere in Europe. And we will all pay a lot of money to watch an artist's impression of our lives.'

'I hope it will be more entertaining than the original,' said Kristin.

'Personally, I did find the original quite entertaining,' said René. 'As well as providing me with useful employment.'

'Hardly useful,' I said.

'René was in the security forces,' said Woody. 'In fact, so darned secure that he didn't even tell me that he knew where my mother and brother lived.'

'I've already apologised for that,' said René.

'It's all right,' said Woody. 'I could have had a heart condition. Learning that my brother was a communist spy might have finished me off.'

'I always knew it,' said Sandrine. 'The moment you came here, I knew you were a spy. And as for the day when that policeman came round to search your apartment, well!'

'When was that?' I asked.

'Years ago,' said Sandrine. 'I can't remember. In the '60s probably. A handsome young officer he was too.'

'Thank you,' said René. Sandrine blushed.

'You searched my apartment?' I said.

'Of course,' said René. 'And very boring it was too. All those books and old copies of *L'Humanité.*'

'What's *L'Humanité?*' asked Woody.

'It's a communist newspaper,' said René.

'I do not buy it any more,' I said.

'No,' said Sandrine; 'he buys *Libération* now.'

'Much more appropriate,' said Kristin.

'Mark my words,' said Sandrine; 'when a man changes his newspaper after 36 years, it signifies a great deal.'

'I think you can tell a lot about people by the newspaper they read,' said Mike.

'I don't read a newspaper,' said René. 'I don't believe a word in any of them.'

'A case in point then, Mike,' I said.

'We read the *Columbus Dispatch*,' said Wanda.

'And what is the perspective of that newspaper?' I asked.

'That Columbus, Ohio, is a pretty darned good place,' said Mike.

'Hardly a world view,' I said.

'It is if you live in Columbus,' said Woody.

So that is the sort of conversation we were having: mostly banter, with the occasional nugget of interesting information. Such as that René had once searched my apartment. It did not surprise me. I had long assumed that someone would have done. I doubt he had any legal authority to do so. Equally, I doubt whether it would have made any difference if he had been found out. The French state had a retrospective justification for everything.

The change in the conversation was dramatic and, as far as I know, entirely accidental. It was occasioned by Angelika. I suppose it could have been provocative, but I expect it was just thoughtless. It was winter of course and everyone was wearing warm clothes. But it was not a cold night and the heating was on and Angelika must have been feeling hot. I paid no particular attention as she started peeling off her cardigan. Until the conversation abruptly stopped as all eyes turned to look at her.

On Angelika's bare arm was a swastika tattoo.

No one spoke for a moment. They just stared. Angelika continued eating her food as if nothing had happened. It was Sandrine who broke the silence.

'What is that, my child?'

Angelika shrugged her shoulders.

'I should like to tell you a story,' said Sandrine. 'Please will you listen to it most carefully.'

Sandrine recounted the story of her rape. I do not mean that, in some vague way, she mentioned that she had been raped by Nazi soldiers. I mean that she recited the entire story in detail. I was astonished. I had been fairly astonished when she had told me such an intimate story, but now she was broadcasting it to a room full of virtual strangers. Except that she was only incidentally doing that. Her eyes were focused on Angelika. I think she was oblivious to everyone else in the room.

It was certainly dramatic, and there was an

added piquancy because, in the few days she had been with us, Angelika had formed a close bond with Sandrine. They had spent a lot of time talking together. Sandrine had fussed after the children and had tended them if Angelika wanted to go out. Certainly, Angelika talked to Sandrine more easily than to Kristin or myself. It was because of Sandrine that Angelika had conceived the idea of attending midnight Mass. I had wondered whether they had discussed politics. As far as I was concerned, if Sandrine supported Monsieur Le Pen, her politics were little better than my daughter's. An overt fascist and a crypto-fascist. Take your pick. But now the crypto-fascist was taking fascism apart, and doing it far more effectively than I would have done.

I suppose it had to do with the raw power of personal experience. If I had done it, I would have talked of philosophies and beliefs, of impersonal things. I was the unblinking eye who could see everything and reach dispassionate intellectual conclusions. The others saw with eyes of lightning, spoke in tongues of thunder and drew life from the furnace. I had always despised that approach. It was so subjective. But that had been Mama's approach also and, since reading her letter, I had found it hard to deny the validity of experience or, I suppose, the subjectivity of the truth.

Angelika looked straight back into Sandrine's eyes. She did not recoil from the gaze. This was a private communication, conducted in semi-public. When Sandrine had finished, she loosened the bands from her hair and gently shook her chestnut mane. She reached over to Angelika, stroked her hair, and placed her cardigan around her shoulders again.

'You are young,' said Sandrine, 'and you have excuses. But please sometimes listen to the past. Do not place your faith in monsters. Ask your father. He can tell you.'

'Is that what you would like to say?' Angelika asked me.

'I do not know,' I said. 'I am not sure I am in a position to say anything.'

Of course, there was a great deal that I wanted to say, but for once I could not find a way of saying it, or at least a way that would not rebound equally on me. I was appalled at Angelika's tattoo, and deeply ashamed. But, had tattoos been fashionable when I was young, might I have worn a tattoo of a hammer and sickle? Well, yes, I might have done. And, had I now been sitting at a dinner table with Mama, and with my father, would they have been repelled by it in the same way that the rest of us were repelled by Angelika's, and for much the same reasons? Well, yes, of course they would. And would they have been justified in their feelings? Yes, that too.

I wanted to say things also to Sandrine, but again could not. I wanted to ask her why, if she felt that faith should not be placed in monsters, she continued to place hers in Monsieur Le Pen. But that would have invited more questions as to where my faith had been placed over the years, and why, so that was another conversation that I

408

did not wish to have.

I wanted also to say to Sandrine that her rape had nothing to do with fascism. Sandrine was raped because that is how soldiers behave in occupied countries. It is how they have behaved for thousands of years. It is how the Red Army behaved when they liberated Poland and Germany, abominably so, and that is something else I have disregarded over the years.

But to have commenced that debate would have led to a discussion on the distinction between the actions of individual human beings and the ideal in the name of which they were enacted. I was in no position to have that discussion. For my entire life, I had failed to acknowledge any distinction between people and their ideas. As I had always said, people were their ideas; that is all they were. Look where that belief had taken me.

As Mark Bergelson had said (and he said so many things that now seem pertinent to me), my childhood was destroyed by fascism. Communism opposed fascism, so I supported it. Communism was embodied by the Soviet Union, so I supported that. The Soviet Union was ruled by Joseph Stalin, so I supported him. Somewhere I think there must have been a fault in the logic.

I think I did need certainty when I was a young man. I think that was exactly what I needed. It was what my life had always lacked. Possibly I needed to believe anything, or anyone, that bolstered my certainty. And also to reject anyone, or anything, that threatened it. But I seem to be grown up now. Perhaps I should need certainty no longer. I still believe that communism was a noble ideal, however much it was perverted by Stalin. I am prepared to equate Hitler and Stalin, but I will never equate fascism and communism. However, perhaps I should stop talking about the ideology altogether. Personal experiences matter. Millions of personal experiences matter. Mine matter. And Angelika's. If it has taken a swastika tattoo for me to be able to see that, perhaps I should not reproach Angelika for it, but be grateful.

After that dramatic interlude, the conversation remained on sober subjects as we picked over the bones of a fractured past and an uncertain future. Mike wanted to know how much each of us felt European. Well, of course, all of us felt European to some extent, but that was subsidiary to other feelings. René and Sandrine declared themselves to be firmly French. Kristin and Angelika were equally sure they were German. Woody and Wanda were surprised to be asked the question.

'And what about you, Feliks?' asked Mike.

'It is peculiar,' I said. 'That is where this whole ridiculous year started. Ridiculous and wonderful, that is. It started with you, Sandrine, saying how good it was to be at home when one was ill, and with me wondering where on earth home was.'

'Where did you think it was?' asked Sandrine.

'I did not know. In the end, I think I concluded that for me home had always been an idea, not any specific place.'

'And where is it now?' asked Kristin.

'With you,' I said. 'Wherever that may be. In fact, if you want to know, I think I am the only proper European round this table. The rest of you are all nationalists of one sort or another. I would like to propose a toast to internationalism.'

'I,' said René, 'would like to propose a toast to mark the conclusion of negotiations at the end of the Second World War. Finally.'

'I will drink to that,' I said. 'In fact, frankly I will drink to anything right now.'

'And I,' said Kristin, 'would like to propose a toast to your mother, Feliks. And to your father too. And to everyone who has made it possible for us to be together here tonight.'

★ ★ ★

This particular group may never again meet around the same table. The same assembly of historical scars may never again parade for surgical inspection. We have dispersed in the last few days. Woody and Wanda have returned to Columbus, Ohio, centre of the known universe, immunised once more against the contents of those paper parcels, biscuit tins, sandwich boxes and ditty bags with their fragments of old European quarrels, for the time being at any rate. Woody and I have talked about many things over the fortnight, but never at any length about Mama's letter. While her fate had been a matter of speculation, there had seemed so much to discuss. But now it was all known, all settled, suddenly there was nothing to be said about it. You could say the same about communism too.

Angelika, Lorenz and Gitta have returned to Berlin, hopefully with something to think about in Angelika's case. She is no longer swearing at me, but — despite our visit to Poland — I have no sense that anything fundamental has yet changed. Mike has flown to Boston for a short holiday and to see his family. For some reason, René has taken Sandrine for a New Year jaunt in the venerable Peugeot to visit his son in Nantes. They have scattered, unconstrained by boundaries, unimpeded by armies, unhindered by ideologies, into some other homeland of their hearts.

It has felt empty in the apartment. And today was so beautiful, full sun in a cloudless sky, warm if you kept out of the wind, that Kristin and I decided to hire a car and Kristin drove us out into the glorious countryside for the day. We sat on the side of an escarpment, wrapped up well but still able to picnic. Charcuterie and cheeses, fruit and wine, were spread around us. I thought of pieces of bread, an apple core, a half-drunk bottle of water.

'Happy?' asked Kristin.

'Yes,' I said. 'Very.'

'Then why so sad?'

'Guilt, I suppose,' I said.

'What have you got to feel guilty about?'

'Happiness,' I said. 'It has been such an extraordinary year. I could not believe I would have such an incredible year. I have got you. I have got Angelika. I have found Woody. I have sold my business. It is amazing.'

'Then what's the problem?'

'Mama,' I said. 'Finding out what happened to Mama. Discovering so much about other people's misery. And my own stupidity, I suppose.'

'You mustn't make it your misery.'

'No. I will not. But it does not seem right. You think, if you are going to have a great year, that is what it will be: a great year. But to have such a year and to find out these awful things and still to feel fantastic . . . well, it does not feel right.'

'That's life,' said Kristin. 'Take it.'

We had an early supper in Auxerre this evening and then Kristin drove us back to Paris. And now it is the early hours of a new year, a year that has commenced without the presence of the Soviet Union, and I am still trying to make sense of the whole thing.

I have lived in a time of changes. Yet, sitting on the escarpment this afternoon, the very notion of change seemed absurd. I could count on the fingers of one hand the things I could not have seen had I been seated there a hundred years before: the telegraph poles, the polythene tunnels for hothousing produce, a tarmac road, the water-sprinklers in the fields. Not much to show for a century of commotions.

Then there was me, I suppose. I would not have been there. I would have been in some village in rural Poland. I would not have been in the French countryside with a German lover. Especially not that.

I think there are two types of history. There is

413

the history of great events, the march of scientific progress, the clash of ideologies, wars and disasters. Then there is history as it is lived by millions of people, across Europe, across the world. The history of births and mewling infants, of innocent childhood and surly adolescence, of loss of innocence, of love and its slow evaporation, of toil and wages, of marriage and family, of death. And none of the grand events, however stupendous, destroys the chronicle of individual lives for those that survive them. All that remains is the changing and changeless cycle of time.

The history of great events is radical and revolutionary. It rips jagged lines through the fabric of our seamless world. And then the history of little things reasserts itself. Rhythms and cycles of life resume, conservative and cautious, the history of mothers and of the continuum, the seamstress at her wheel, diligently stitching the jagged tears, making the fabric whole again.

Perhaps there is a third history also, the real history: the croupier of time that takes these two other histories, that rolls them together like two dice in a cup and watches with neutral insouciance as the tides of great events wash capriciously on the vessels of individual lives. And which of us feels lucky today? *Faîtes vos jeux.*

Somewhere in this concatenation of events great and small exists the shape of all our lives.

There is a knock from the bedroom door. Kristin is standing there, naked. The windows

414

are still open and light is beaming out into the street.

'Kristin,' I say; 'what are you thinking of?'

'I am thinking of you,' she says. 'Why don't you come to bed?'

Other titles published by
The House of Ulverscroft:

THIS PERFECT WORLD

Suzanne Bugler

Laura Hamley is the woman who has everything: a loving and successful husband, two beautiful children, an expensive home and a set of equally fortunate friends. But Laura's perfect world is suddenly threatened when she receives an unwelcome phone call from Mrs Partridge, mother of Heddy — the girl Laura and her friends bullied mercilessly at school. Heddy has been hospitalized following a mental breakdown, and Mrs Partridge wants Laura's help to get her released. As Laura reluctantly gets drawn back into the past, she is forced to face the terrible consequences of her cruelty. But, even as her secrets are revealed so too is another even more devastating truth, and the perfect world Laura has so carefully constructed for herself begins to fall apart.

THE PLEASURE SEEKERS

Tishani Doshi

It all started in August 1968 when Babo, left the Patel family in Madras to fly to England and further his education . . . Living in London, he'd fallen head over heels with a cream-skinned Welsh girl, Sian Jones. A mixed-up love in a topsy-turvy world — now two families will never be the same again. Meet the Patel-Joneses: Babo, Sian, Mayuri and Bean, in their little house next door to the Punjab Women's Association. As the twentieth century creaks along this 'hybrid' family navigate uncharted waters: the hustle and bustle of Babo's relatives, the faraway phone-line crackle of Sian's; the perils of first love, lost innocence and old age, and the big question — what do you do with the space your loved ones leave behind?

GIRL IN TRANSLATION

Jean Kwok

Kimberly Chang has her world turned upside-down when she moves to New York with her mother from their home in Hong Kong. But their new life doesn't quite live up to their expectations — living in a vermin-ridden apartment in Brooklyn, the pair have only an intermittently working oven to keep them warm. They have nothing but debt and neither of them speak a word of English. While her mother works to earn two cents a garment at a sweatshop, intellectually gifted eleven-year-old Kim faces a new and trying challenge: school. Exiled by language, estranged in a new culture and weighed down by staggering poverty, Kim must learn to translate not just her language but who she is, as she straddles these two very different worlds.

THE YEAR OF FOG

Michelle Richmond

On a beach in San Francisco, Abby Mason looks away from her six-year-old stepdaughter for a moment. By the time she looks back, Emma has disappeared . . . Devastated by guilt, Abby refuses to believe that Emma is dead. But as the days drag into weeks and the police lose interest, Emma's father wants to start moving on with his life. Unable to forgive Abby, he withdraws from their relationship. It is left to Abby to keep hoping and to follow the evidence no matter where it might lead . . .

THE SONGWRITER

Beatrice Colin

New York, 1916. While war rages in Europe, vaudeville performers sing the newest songs by night and young women march for the vote during the day. Monroe Simonov, a song-plugger, is in love with a Ziegfeld Follies dancer who's left him for California. Inez Kennedy, a department store fashion model, needs to find a wealthy husband before she must return to the Midwest. Anna Denisova, a political exile, waits for the overthrow of the Tsar. Then America joins the war, jazz sweeps the city's dance floors, the old order is swept away by newly minted millionaires and the nation is gripped by the Red Scare. The world is rapidly changing, but Monroe, Inez and Anna are still subject to the tyranny of the heart . . .

NOT MY DAUGHTER

Barbara Delinsky

A pregnancy pact between three teenage girls stuns their parents, shocks the town and electrifies the media. Susan Tate, one of these mothers, has struggled to do everything right. A single mother herself, she is the headmistress of the girls' high school. Soon fingers start pointing, criticising her as a role model. She is seen as unworthy of the responsibility of young students, and as a lax mother. Battling with the implications of her daughter's pregnancy, Susan knows that her job, her reputation and her dreams are all at risk. The emotional ties between mothers and daughters are stretched to breaking point. Can they all fight back against the rising tide of scandal and find their own way?